HER CHOICE

To Alison Cook
with respect +
admiration !

Anne Sloan

a novel

ANNE SLOAN

STEPHEN F. AUSTIN STATE UNIVERSITY PRESS

For more information:
Stephen F. Austin State University Press
P.O. Box 13007 SFA Station
Nacogdoches, Texas 75962
sfapress@sfasu.edu
www.sfasu.edu/sfapress

Managing Editor: Kimberly Verhines
Editorial Assistant: Meredith Janning
Cover Design: Lisa Cari
www.tamupress.com

ISBN: 978-1-62288-927-3
FIRST EDITION

To Phillis Lemley Lapthisophon, my friend, my colleague and my mentor

To Peter with whom all things are possible

And to my parents who found their way into this book.

PROLOGUE

"GOOD EVENING, MR. JONES. Welcome back to the Mayflower."

Jesse Jones waved at the doorman as he motioned his assistant Bob Thompson to get the room key and request more chairs for the parlor table.

Once in their suite, Thompson stepped to the window looking down on Connecticut Avenue.

"Look at the automobiles in the street. They're lined up for two blocks, ploughing through all this snow. No wonder people call this the 'Park Avenue of Washington.'"

Jones ignored his chatter. Only one thing was on his mind: How to get the Democratic Convention to pick Houston. Whatever it cost would be worth it. How much money would they want to bring it to south of the Mason Dixon line? A couple hundred, at least.

"Has Franklin checked in?"

"Yes, sir, the entire membership of the Democratic Party's National Committee is here. Mayflower's a big hotel, but the Rice has just as many rooms."

"You're right, but the rooms aren't as large."

"Bob, it's time to put my plan to work. I intend for this national convention to be held in Houston." Jones took a deep breath and watched his employee's jaw drop.

A knock on the door ended their conversation. The bellhop carried in chairs, no sooner in place, than the subcommittee members from Detroit and San Francisco file into the room.

Jones listened to Detroit offer $125,000 to host the convention and then excused himself to go to his bedroom.

He returned carrying his personal check for $200,000, which he laid on the table. Snickering in the room as the California delegate triumphantly slammed a check for $250,000 on top of his. The room fell silent. Jesse's jaw tightened and took out his watch. "Gentlemen, it's time to go downstairs."

The ballroom was a madhouse. Committee members milled around him as he tried to think through what had just occurred. The size of the check determines where the convention would be held. What else can he offer to bring them south? He knew no convention had been held there since the Civil War.

Groups of delegates boomed for their cities. No delegates boomed for Houston. He asked to speak last.

When it was his turn, Chairman Clem Shaver called for attention. "Delegates, next is our Finance Director who needs no introduction. Jesse Jones of Houston."

A handsome man, fifty-four years old, over six feet tall, with graying hair, he rose to his feet as the roomful of delegates applauded and yelled, "Hear, hear." Very much aware this display reflected their gratitude for his having kept the Democratic Party solvent for fifteen years, he smiled cynically knowing he was about to put their feelings to a test.

He did not read a speech, later insisting he spoke from his heart. "On behalf of the Mayor and City Council and all the people of Houston, I respectfully extend a most cordial invitation to the Democratic National Committee to hold its 1928 convention in Houston, Texas."

The hall went silent. He looked around and continued, "We have the 1,000-plus-room Rice Hotel as well as twelve other hotels. We have a beach resort and thirty-four beautiful parks." He paused and conveyed his most audacious offer, "Houston's hospitality is a blank check to be filled in for whatever the committee desires."

Cheering broke out upon hearing this incredible promise.

The Californian, who nervously rubbed his chin, asked, "How many people will your convention hall seat?"

"Five thousand but if you give us the convention, I'll build one to seat 25,000."

"What about the weather? Aren't Texas summers hot as you-know-what?" the Detroit spokesman asked.

"Houston's temperature in June is very comfortable. Ranges from the eighties to the low nineties."

The delegates roared with laughter, but by the fifth ballot, Houston had won with fifty-four votes.

The following day, Jones answered reporters who asked how he contrived to win the convention for his hometown.

"No log-rolling, no trading, and no pre-campaign whatsoever. I didn't solicit any votes. The delegates just want to come to Houston."

It was time for him to telephone Oscar to tell him what he had done. Mayor Holcombe listened to his news and asked, "What will Houston's obligation be?"

"$200,000 and an auditorium built in six months to seat 25,000 people."

Her Choice

John Knott, *The Dallas Morning News*, © 1928

CHAPTER ONE

Sunday, January 15, 1928
The Gargoyle is still goggle-eyed over the legerdemain of the miraculous Mr. Jones
at Washington the other day. A few deft paces with a blank check and Presto!
The Democratic Convention pops out of the hat, as pretty as any pink-eyed rabbit.

January 1928

"WILLIE MAE FISHER" PHILLIS GASPED AS SHE woke up. "Holy smokes. Is this what I'm facing?" Two days ago, when her co-worker Miss Fisher dropped dead, she was assigned to write the dear lady's obituary. *Will mine be just like it?*

> *Phillis Flanagan, Fort Worth Star-Telegram reporter for fifty years, author of*
> *thousands of local obituaries, was buried today at Eternal Stone Cemetery. Family*
> *and friends are invited to gather at 4 p.m. in the First Methodist Church parlor.*

Slapping together a sugar and butter sandwich, she poured her first cup of coffee and sat down to read the Sunday *Dallas Morning News* draped over the dinette table. Mehitabel sidled over and curled around her feet, "I'm not an old maid. I just refuse to marry, right, Mehitabel?"

Page one with John Knott's cartoon nearly gave her a lap full of coffee. Her favorite cartoonist dumbfounded her again. Today's offering, titled "Her Choice" depicted John Knott's stock character, "Old Man Texas," wearing his trusty Stetson as he galloped toward Houston. She frowned, *Of all places.*

Their only meeting had occured when the popular Pulitzer-Prize-winning journalist had accepted an honorary degree from Baylor University at Phillis's commencement ceremony. Elbowing her way through the crowd, she boldly addressed him. "My name's Phillis Flanagan. I'm looking for a job as a journalist."

"Oh, really?" With a snort, he shook his head in disbelief. Then he winked and gave her an avuncular pat on the shoulder. Did he think her a brazen intruder or an addlepated dunce? She never figured out which.

Knott's cartoon exploded with contradictions. A barefoot, démodé gal representing the Democratic Party swept off her feet by a man whose horse is heading to Houston and outrunning the opposition cities' automobiles. Two unlikely partners galloping toward a city few people in America could place on a map. *What the heck was going on?*

A small article on page three supplied the answer. "Houston businessman, Jesse Jones, has convinced the Democratic party to hold its June convention in Houston." Phillis dropped the paper, her eyes circling the peeling rose-patterned walls of her apartment. How far was Houston? Re-examining the cartoon, she nodded her head and chuckled. Newspapers provide waste-can liners, not road maps for the future. But, to Phillis, this road sign stuck in the dirt was an invitation to change her life.

Scissoring out the cartoon, she set it aside to paste into the blue notebook she took from her bureau drawer. From high school on, Phillis had recorded everything she considered important in what became her diaries.

Responding to a yowl from Mehitabel, she announced, "Cat, I've got a hunch Houston 's gonna be my brass ring." With a grin, Phillis wrote,

1/15/28. Amon Carter must finance my trip to Houston. If not, I will do <u>anything</u> to get there. Mother will call me a daredevil, but who cares?

CHAPTER TWO

It is quaintly interesting that when the WBAP dynamo broke down in midst of a program, Mr. Carter mounted to the roof and broadcast a speech with no other facilities than those vocal organs the good Lord had given him, and that coils were burned out in receiving sets five hundred miles away.

Menu Legend, Ritz Hotel, New York City, 1928

GETTING AN APPOINTMENT WITH AMON Carter took Phillis over a month. She finally cajoled Miss Deakins, his personal secretary, to set up a fifteen-minute meeting at eleven o'clock to discuss her request to cover the upcoming political convention. "Don't be surprised if the appointment doesn't happen," Miss Deakins had warned. "Mr. Carter's a busy man."

Butterflies in her stomach, Phillis exited the trolley at 400 West Seventh Street at eight o'clock that morning alongside a handful of female employees who piled into the newspaper's four-story headquarters. As the elevator descended to her office, Phillis marveled at riding to the basement instead of pounding the cracked concrete stairs like the ones at the school in Killeen where she wasted two years trying to teach English and history to thirty unwashed, illiterate fourth graders. A bearable stint only because in her free time, she hunched over a rackety typewriter in the dingy office of the *Killeen Morning News* and pounded out stories for the kindly editor, Franklin Barnes. Her stories slamming the Ku Klux Klan prohibition provided her only chance, so far, to write front-page news, but Barnes' approval was all she needed to fuel her journalism aspirations.

At ten-thirty, aware of Amon Carter's reputation for punctuality, Phillis rushed back to the elevator and glanced around the room where her colleagues shuffled papers. Hopefully, she would soon leave them behind in this gray basement.

Her co-workers loved the comforts of working at the "finest newspaper plant in the Southwest." Yes, the comfy sofas in the library room were nice and having a separate restroom for female workers was remarkable, but she saw a lot more wrong at the *Star-Telegram* than right. For one thing, Amon Carter was no newspaperman, and he was also a bigot, with no concern for social ills who expected his reporters to write "clean," lively news. His only interest seemed to be promoting himself and the city of Fort Worth.

No chance for women to advance working for the *Star*, but she knew most Texas newspaper owners were no different. Women employees composed recipes for Mama's Best Cornbread or Molasses Fudge or wrote about white dead folks who had eaten them. And little else.

"Hi, there, Miss Phillis."

"Good morning, Buzzy," Phillis said, "Third floor, please."

"An appointment with the big man, himself?" Buzzy Jenkins asked as he closed the elevator doors.

"Yes."

In the mirror's reflection Buzzy watched Phillis pinch her nose. "Yeah, Mr. Amon's already rode up." He gave her a sympathetic grin then started the elevator. "You've heard of 'Evenin' in Paris'?" he asked.

She hoped she wasn't going to puke.

Buzzy laughed, "We call his foo foo juice, 'A Night in Fort Worth.'"

The elevator jerked to a stop, and Phillis rushed out as soon as the doors opened.

She nodded "hello" to Miss Deakins, who was on the telephone and took a seat on the wooden bench in the waiting room, crossing her legs at the ankles and folding her hands in her lap. She straightened her maroon tie and smoothed her knee-length, navy skirt.

The fellows who were passing in and out of Carter's anteroom gave her only the briefest of glances. Her friend Ethel teased her, "A little lipstick doesn't make you a jazz baby!" Phillis's pinned-up hair and skirts that covreed her knees fit the image she settled on after college believing this to be a smarter image than the one favored by the empty-headed flappers who were everywhere. Serious, not frivolous, would be her ticket to the top.

Trying not to squirm, she drummed her fingers on the wooden bench as she listened to his secretary's coolly assured responses. "No, Mr. Carter is sorry he's unavailable for lunch with Governor Moody next Wednesday." "No, Mr. Carter can't come to New York City for the opening of your new restaurant." "Please deliver the order for Mr. Carter's monogrammed pajamas to 400 West Seventh Street, Fort Worth, Texas, Attention Katrine Deakins."

Phillis kept reminding herself, *Don't try to show him how smart I am. Don't be cheeky.* Only a few weeks ago, Carter knocked one of her colleagues to the ground at a political rally because she questioned the candidate's wife too aggressively. According to a witness, the reporter picked herself up and remained at the event, taking notes. Phillis applauded her aplomb but doubted she could have shown such control over her emotions. *That's the problem, women are helpless to protest an employer's actions.*

Two years ago, when she told Franklin Barnes she had landed a job at the *Star-Telegram*, he looked up at her through his green eyeshade, pointed her to a chair and launched into a juicy account of the newspaper's screwy history.

"I was there when it all began. Amon Carter was a crackerjack ad salesman." Barnes began, "but the *Star* was going broke. The paper was a corpse. Carter suggested the owners buy their competitor, the *Telegram*. His bosses held their sides laughing, knowing they couldn't even meet the next payroll. When he offered to pawn his own jewelry to raise the $2,500 they needed for a down payment, they wised up and accepted his offer."

Barnes chuckled, "The first edition of the *Star-Telegram* rolled off the presses on January 1, 1909, not even twenty years ago."

"Gosh darn," Barnes bragged, "if that rag isn't Texas's largest newspaper now." Proudly, leaning back until he almost tipped his chair over, he continued, "Circulation of over a hundred thousand. Has more readers than the high-and-mighty *Dallas Morning News*. I watched him do it. You wanna know how?"

Phillis nodded, her eyes widening.

He smiled, "Every politician and newspaper man in the state ignored the 'nothingness' of West Texas. Ungodly weather. No people. No telephones to speak of. Only a few ranchers with running water and electricity. Amon Carter gave those beaten-down cowpokes and farmers who lived west of Fort Worth a lifeline, a connection to the rest of the world. The *Star-Telegram's* circulation soared in the seventy-odd Texas counties Carter calls 'my backyard,' and it hasn't quit soaring yet. His so-called "kingdom" stretches from Fort

Worth to the Pacific Ocean."

Phillis jerked back to the present as Carter bellowed, "Gawddam, gawddam, gawddam. Don't get in a dander. I'll think of something." Amon Carter entered his office like Caesar entering Rome, three lackeys trailing behind him.

Phillis sat up straight. *He's the most powerful man in my world.* The room where she sat suddenly felt like a furnace.

As Miss Deakins showed her into his office, Carter tore off his suit coat and dropped it on the floor, motioning her sit. His fingers circled inside the stiff collar of his purple-and-white striped shirt. He patted his crooked red bow tie.

She blurted out with a louder voice than she intended, "Mr. Carter, my name is Phillis Flanagan. For two years, I've been a journalist, I mean reporter, for the *Star-Telegram's* obituary and women's department. The Democratic National Convention will be at Houston in June. I want to report on this for our readers."

Carter scowled. Sighing heavily, he asked, "You mean you want to go there? You ever been to Houston?"

"No, sir, I understand they're making huge plans."

"You have a notion you could cover this event for my newspaper?" His incredulity was obvious.

Before she could answer, he snickered, "You follow politics?"

"Yes, sir, "I studied politics at Baylor, but my real aim is the chance to report on the events planned for the wives of the great men who will be in Houston." The bald-faced lie rolled off her tongue. "Did you know Alice Roosevelt Longworth will be there?"

"Don't know that grandstander needs any more press," he growled.

That's certainly the pot calling the kettle black, Phillis thought to herself.

"You look old enough to be a lady reporter. Good thing you're not one of those short-haired flappers, Miss, uh, Miss…." Slapping the side of his head in frustration, he continued, "You're from Fort Worth?"

She nodded, not about to tell him she spent most of her life in Dallas.

"I don't suppose you've been to New York City?"

"No, but I know New Yorkers are coming. I'm ready to report what they think about Texas."

Carter waved his right hand dismissively to shush her. The phone outside his office had rung three times during their five-minute conversation. His mind was wandering.

"All right, all right," he barked. "I give up. Somebody's got to write this sheep-headed nonsense. How much do I pay you?"

"Twenty-four dollars a week, sir."

"Okay, but you've got to get to Houston on your own. I won't buy any train tickets or pay for room and board. You better make sure your gawddam stories are peppy and cheerful. My paper doesn't print articles that nag people to change their views about anything."

He began to turn away, then bellowed, "Oh, and none of those 'sob sister' stories, get it?"

She bit her tongue to keep from screaming, "Shut your mouth."

Carter muttered, "They don't know it yet, but one of the fancy New Yorkers traveling in his private train car will stop in Fort Worth for an unscheduled visit before he gets to Houston."

With a grin, he rubbed his hands together, "I have a hijacking planned that'll put me in the driver's seat when I arrive at Mr. Jones's convention."

Remembering Phillis's presence, Carter pulled a face. "You do know I'll be right there in Houston with you the whole time. Some say I got eyes in the back of my head. So, no sleeping on the job, sister," shaking his finger at her.

"Who's your editor?"

"Miss Jefferson."

"Deakins," he hollered, "send a memo to Jefferson. This gal's covering the convention's social events for a week."

He stood up issuing a final threat: "I better not see you where you're not supposed to be."

Waving Phillis toward the door, he brushed aside her attempt to shake his hand and crossed the room, yelling, "Bring me those AP clippings and get Ross Sterling on the line."

Phillis pasted a smile on her face as she edged past him and mouthed "thank you" to Miss Deakins.

Not waiting for the elevator, she hustled down the stairs and ran outside. Ignoring the lunch crowd, she hooted at the third floor of the *Star-Telegram* Building and shook her fist, "Mr. Amon Carter, you aren't the only one who has private plans for this convention."

2/21/28. I did it. I got my assignment to go to Houston for the DNC. By lying to Amon Carter. I will find a news story. No writing about tea parties anymore. He may fire me, but that is okay by me.

CHAPTER THREE

The eyes of the nation are now turned toward Houston, and the convention will lead to a finer understanding between North and South. It will help wonderfully to enlighten people of the whole nation as to the great possibilities here.

National Democratic Convention
Official Souvenir Program

Saturday, June 16, 1928

RUSHING DOWN THE PLATFORM OF TRACK 9, Phillis slowed her pace and took a deep breath, mingling with other passengers boarding the *Sam Houston Zephyr* for Houston. Mothers swarmed alongside her, clutching their screaming children while holding onto lunch baskets, sun hats, and valises. It was the first week of summer vacation and the youngsters' highjinks were understandable. Phillis envied their ability to whoop it up, reining in her desire to do the same now that she was finally on her way south.

Car 16 was filled with rows of men's heads barely visible above a sea of newspapers. No women in sight. Four rows back, she found an empty aisle seat and lifted her new typewriter in its case to the overhead rack, then removed her cloche and placed it on top. Taking off her gloves, she turned around and saw the newspaper across from her lowering.

A carefully groomed young man with pomaded hair gave her a bored looked and returned to his paper.

"Hello to you, too," Phillis said under her breath. His brown tweed suit told her he had never traveled south in the month of June, while his *New York Times* suggested he was one of the Yankees coming to Houston for the convention.

She sat down, trying to ignore the snoring of her seatmate, a bald-headed Humpty-Dumpty sort of fellow already asleep though the train had not left the station as she leaned in front of him to look out the open train window.

A burly porter stood beside his empty pushcart chatting with a red cap as he fanned himself with a folded newspaper while the conductor bellowed, "All Aboard." Holding on to her floppy straw hat, a woman dashed down the platform, stopping abruptly next to Phillis's car.

When she appeared in the open doorway, a jolt of electricity passed through the car. Murmurs circulated as all eyes fastened on the sweet young thing posed in the entrance. Scarcely five-feet tall, no more than ninety pounds, she wore a short blue gauzy dress and patent leather high-heeled shoes. A head full of yellow curls framed her Kewpie-doll face with softly rouged cheeks, and a bow-shaped mouth. She languidly fanned herself with her hat, while her blue eyes circled the car.

The passengers let out an appreciative "Ah," and the man Phillis assumed to be a New Yorker whispered, "Lorelei."

She giggled at his reference to the heroine in *Gentlemen Prefer Blondes* and called out, "Daisy?"

"Phillis," the woman answered in a breathy voice, advancing down the aisle as the train began moving. Realizing the seat next to Phillis was occupied, she again surveyed the car filled with male passengers and smiled invitingly. Several men rose, beckoning her to come their way.

"Talk to you later," Daisy said, patting her shoulder on the way to a seat several rows back.

The man in the brown suit extended his hand to Phillis, "I'm Reginald Bludworth with *Manhattan Grandstand* traveling from New York to Houston for the Democratic National Convention," he said, now eager to make her acquaintance. "Obviously, you know this bewitching woman. Is she in moving pictures?"

"Phillis Flanagan with the *Fort Worth Star-Telegram*, heading to Houston for the same reason," she replied, ignoring his question as she reached to shake his hand.

He clasped her fingers then turned her hand over, staring at her palm. "Where's the ink?" he asked.

"I'm careful with my carbon copies?" she retorted.

"Just kidding. I saw you carrying a typewriter case. Female journalists aren't so rare anymore. I know several coming from New York to cover the convention."

With a shift back to his subject, he asked, "So, how do you know Daisy?"

"We were freshmen in high school together," Phillis replied. "I have no idea if she's in pictures, but I imagine she's still an heiress, unless the Spanish count her father married her to made away with her money before he ran his car off a cliff."

"Oh, my God!" Bludworth said, sitting up straighter. "How splendid!"

"'Splendid' she's a widow? 'Or splendid' she's got money?" Phillis asked. Bludworth laughed unabashedly. "Both," he said. Looking earnestly at Phillis, he pleaded, "I must meet her. Will you introduce me?"

"Yes," she replied. "But only if you hand over your *New York Times.*"

"Here, take it," he said. "Tell me, is she a natural blonde?"

Phillis ignored his lewd question. "*Manhattan Grandstand.* You're the editor if I remember the masthead correctly. And you want to know if she dyes her hair? You aren't the first journalist hornswoggled by a chorus girl. Let's see," she said, starting to count on her fingers, "There's Mencken, Damon Runyon, and...." She smiled at him pityingly "She's the stock character in popular fiction, isn't she?"

"Of course," he said, "Say, let's wait a little before you introduce me to this chorus girl. I don't want to seem too obvious."

"That's as silly as your arriving in Houston in June wearing a brown tweed suit," Phillis said. "Will you wear it all week?"

"Heck, no. I'll get a Palm Beach linen suit as soon as I hit town," Bludworth said. "I've burned up since we crossed the Texas state line."

"I'm afraid the hottest weather's yet to come," Phillis warned.

He frowned. "Holding this year's convention anywhere besides Denver or San Francisco is a mistake but, even so," he said, brightening, "I'm looking forward to seeing the 'Great State of Texas.' And I plan on going to the shore."

"The 'shore'?" Phillis asked, confused. "Galveston beach? Yes, I'm looking forward to visiting there as well."

"Quite a few New Yorkers are coming by ship and staying in Galveston instead of Houston."

Phillis raised her eyebrows, and he responded. "It's only a four-day trip with a fifteen-hour stopover in Havana to buy real booze. No phony rotgut hooch. They'll dock at the Port of Galveston well rested and well stocked though I've heard every newsstand, café, and barbershop on Seawall Boulevard sells bootleg whiskey."

"Have you heard of the Galvez Hotel?" he asked, seriously. "My magazine just gave it a rave review. Our esteemed mayor Jimmy Walker and his family will stay there all four days."

"It's supposed to be the best on the island. I believe a special train runs from Galveston to Houston."

"Yes, every hour on the hour. Picks you up in downtown Galveston and lets you out close to the convention center. Personally," Bludworth confided, "I'm not going to the convention sessions."

"You're not?" Her jaw dropped.

"Why should I? They're so boring. Al Smith's nomination is a shoo-in. The convention only makes Tammany Hall's candidate official. For most of us the event is just an excuse to come to Texas. We want to know all about these cowboys and Indians."

Phillis was amused by his reference to the wild-west aura that branded Texas.

"Everything I've read indicates Houston's rolling out the red carpet for you," she replied. "Locals say Jesse Jones dealt himself a Royal Flush to persuade the Democrats to hold this convention in Houston. He's a booster for Houston. Like Amon Carter boosts Fort Worth."

"Oh, no! Not another Texas blowhard." Bludworth groaned and Phillis groaned with him.

"Wait. Carter's your boss, isn't he?"

"Yes, I've worked for him for two years," Phillis said, suppressing a sigh.

"You know he comes to New York City, keeps a suite at the Ritz. A sure enough cowboy."

Phillis rolled her eyes and nodded, "He only plays at being a cowboy."

"I once read his newspaper. Don't envy anyone who has to write 'down' to his standards."

Before she could reply, Bludworth apologized. "Sorry, hope I didn't hurt your feelings. Some New Yorkers love his brand of humor. In fact, I think they're expecting a whole state full of Amon Carters to entertain them all four days."

"He's a character, all right," she laughed, declining to admit his criticism of Amon Carter mirrored her own.

"A Fort Worther like yourself probably has a ten-gallon hat." Bludworth teased. "When Amon Carter's in town, he gives 'em away like candy. His parties and ribald jokes splash into our newspapers. The menus of society cafes have printed quotes from him."

Phillis shook her head, tucking away this information, then, remembering the one promise she had made to Carter, which she could keep, she asked, "By my calculations you have traveled inside Texas for about five-hundred miles. What's your impression so far?"

"Lots of green countryside and thirty-foot oil derricks. Why does every town we stop in have more derricks than people?" Not waiting for her to answer, he continued, "Houston's the smallest city to ever host a convention."

"Population's nearly 200,000. We'll see some crowds there, at least downtown."

"Wonderful. I'm ready to be wined and dined. I've heard the hotel rooms are equipped with permanent corkscrews."

Wrinkling her nose, she commented, "I doubt that since Jesse Jones is a dry Democrat."

"Oh yeah. I'm staying at the Lamar Hotel. I think he owns it."

"He not only owns it; he and his wife live in the penthouse."

"Swell! I'm sure I'll meet him. I've already met a front-page reporter and her dazzling sidekick who left me breathless."

She dismissed his wisecrack with a hand wave, "Maybe so," she said, wondering how far Reginal Bludworth's credentials would take him.

"In fact," he said, picking up her newspaper, "I'm going to read your *Dallas Morning News* and find out more about Texas."

"You just do that, Yank," she quipped instead of focusing on the words from the *New York Times* she demanded as payment for information about Daisy, all she could think of was her first day at Miss Smitherman's Select School for Young Women. The short, curly-haired twelve-year-old in navy wool bloomers and a white middy blouse standing next to her, Daisy, was the tallest and skinniest girl in the new freshman class. The two girls' indignation at being enrolled in the private day school instead of the local junior high with all of their friends created an unlikely friendship. They became inseparable, especially since Daisy's servant-filled home offered little adult supervision. Her father, Waylon Leatherbury, a wealthy meat packer whose empire stretched from Dallas to Chicago, and her mother, Delorez Marquez, an aloof woman with a penchant for séances, relegated the rearing of their only child to the help. This escape from her own homelife with her dictatorial stepfather and her mother who obeyed his every request, suited Phillis perfectly.

She gladly let her new friend copy her homework and giggled when Daisy shocked their teachers by wearing face powder and lipstick, and they eagerly smoked their first cigarette in Daisy's bathroom. Fascinated by this poor-little-rich-girl life, Phillis loved it all.

Their friendship ended abruptly when Daisy persuaded her to recreate a Ku Klux Klan parade she had witnessed the month before. On a starless Dallas night, the two girls donned white KKK robes they found hidden in Mr. Leatherbury's upstairs closet and waved a large black flashlight across the night sky as they trailed down Mockingbird Lane singing the Klan's hymn, "Onward Christian Soldiers." Terrified Highland Park neighbors called the police. Phillis was expelled from Miss Smitherman's and was forbidden to see Daisy Leatherbury again.

Before her marriage to Horace Wilkerson, her mother might have been sympathetic, but not this woman who had begun retreating to her room with headaches most of the time. The son Wilkerson brought to the marriage was all that made their family life tolerable for Phillis. Her stepfather's criticism of Junior as well as her drew the two together and provided the only love in this sterile household. Fiercely, she defended her brother, and as he grew older, he served as a buffer for her as well.

Dallas gossip provided all she knew of Daisy's life since then. Until thirty minutes ago she had not laid eyes on her since Miss Smitherman's. But even later when she could have, Phillis had felt no desire to rekindle their friendship. She admitted to herself, this unexpected appearance spurred her interest in the unpredictable young woman. Mouthing the words louder than she intended, she acknowledged, "That girl's a story waiting to be written."

"Who's a story?" Reginald asked.

Phillis gritted her teeth, having forgotten her nosy neighbor across the aisle. Pointing to an article, she asked, "You know anything about the White Ribboners coming to Houston? What if they stop your shoo-in candidate?"

"You're talking about the teetotalers? The Women's Christian Temperance Union," Bludworth replied, looking up from his newspaper. "They know nothing about politics. Isn't the South happy about hosting the convention? They should be. You haven't had one here since the Civil War."

"For sure Houston is. They know the 25,000 visitors will fill the city's coffers. The rest of the southern states don't get anything. The Southern Baptists think Tammany Hall and Al Smith are too cozy and too wet."

Bludworth dismissed her pronouncements with a wave of his hand and resumed reading.

She shook her head. *This religious group that considered New York City a reincarnation of Sodom and Gomorrah might balk at voting for a wet Gotham City Roman Catholic. Smith needed all the South's votes, even the "wet" ones to win.*

"I know what women reporters are paid," Bludworth's voice broke into her thoughts. "You didn't buy that outfit with your salary. Are you a Texas heiress like Daisy?"

"Good God Almighty" she exclaimed, wishing for a clever response to his rudeness.

Bludworth, hearing her expletive, laughed. "Sorry," he said, "your gray suit is lovely. Please excuse me. I'm a little clumsy with people outside my circle. You said you'd never been to New York. You'll find out many of us are like this."

"Well, Texans aren't," Phillis huffed. "You're apt to offend some of the locals."

"Wouldn't want to do that," he laughed again, then changed the subject.

"Say, I read they're holding a rodeo at Rice Institute with cowboys and cowgirls from all over the state."

"Yes," Phillis said. "Even Will Rogers will be here. Not sure if it's for the rodeo or the convention."

"He covers all the conventions whether he attends them or not," Bludworth said.

"What?"

"If he misses a convention," Bludworth explained, "he just writes some made-up dialogue with the candidate. He's a champion ad-libber, an Oklahoma hick with a gift for gab. And funnier than anyone. 'There are men running for government who shouldn't be allowed to play with matches' or 'The trouble with practical jokes is that very often they get elected.'"

Phillis laughed, "I like him. No sham or bluffing about him. I think he calls it 'straight shooting.' I wonder what he'll say about Al Smith. The *Houston Chronicle* said Rogers is coming in an airplane."

"I've met Rogers, he's nuts about airplanes. Personally, I don't share his love of this fad. Never gone up in an airplane and doubt I ever will.."

"I've not flown yet but I'm dying to go up," she replied. "Surely you know flying's no longer a barnstorming lark. Lindbergh's flights and Amelia Earhart's? It's here to stay just like the automobile," Phillis asserted. "Women have been pilots since the Great War," she commented, straining to look out her window at the sky. "I would love to be level with the clouds. It beats a six-hour train trip from Fort Worth to Houston."

"Miss Flanagan, you're a bigger risk taker than I would have guessed. Anyone who goes up in one of those flimsy wooden planes is either very brave or very foolhardy. Which is it?"

"Maybe I just like calculated risks," she replied.

"Is that what you call your trip to Houston?" he asked. "Or is it just a chance to spread your wings? What kind of news stories do you write? I don't see you as a 'sob sister' type."

"Thank you," Phillis replied trying to frame an answer that wouldn't be a total falsehood. "When I reported for the *Morning News* in Killeen, I wrote articles about Prohibition and the KKK. In Houston, I hope to write about the candidates, men and women."

"Candidates? How odd," Bludworth said. "Like maybe a woman for president?" He laughed. "That won't happen in our lifetime. Women just got the vote. It's too soon."

"We shall see, shan't we," she bristled and glared at him before hiding behind the newspaper. *You will never know how risky this trip is for me. I've staked everything on Houston.* Mailing her few possessions to her mother in Dallas and turning in her apartment keys, Phillis said goodbye to Fort Worth. She hoped forever.

A scrawny kid, swaying from side to side, made his way down the aisle calling "Candy, Crackerjacks, chewing gum. Only a nickel. Get your treats before they are gone." She beckoned the butch vendor as she grabbed her pocketbook for a coin. "A box of Crackerjacks, please."

Bludworth bought peanuts.

After the boy passed, Phillis settled back to her paper, read several articles, and scanned others while contentedly munching her snack. Outside the train window, the north Texas prairies had become farmland with steamy black soil and rows of bright green cotton plants. Creosote telephone poles connected by swooping black wires appeared alongside the tracks. Blurred black and white dairy cows and the clickety-clack of the train's wheels generated a sleep-inducing rhythm. She yawned, but not wanting to doze off in front of

Reginald, she shook herself began reading the *Times.*

After a while, Bludworth leaned over and began kibitzing everything she was trying to read, as well as making snide remarks about the Dallas newspaper. For a snooty New Yorker, Phillis thought, he had turned quite chummy. She half-listened to his patter until he mentioned his college roommate from Dallas who would be joining him in Houston.

"Bradley Nicholson, but I call him 'B. J.' He used to live in Dallas, did you know him? He writes for the *Nation.* Has a great apartment in the Village. His editor's a woman," Reginald announced, raising his eyebrows, and looking up at the train car's ceiling as if he expected it to fall in.

"You guys went to Princeton." Phillis stated.

"How did you know? What do you think about women editors?"

"I knew Bradley Nicholson at Highland Park High," she said, trying to sound casual. "Haven't seen him since he left for college, but someone told me he's working as a journalist in New York. And yes, women editors easily function in our man's world if they're given a chance."

"That's him!" Bludworth exclaimed. "We'll have to get together in Houston."

Before Phillis could respond, the butch vendor returned, calling out his wares.

"How about some more Crackerjacks?" Bludworth asked. "My treat. And now that we're friends, please call me 'Reggie.'"

"No more Crackerjacks, thank you. I must excuse myself." Jumping to her feet, she swayed down the aisle, finally reaching the toilet. She groaned, examined her flushed cheeks reflected in the lavatory mirror, and wet her handkerchief with the water trickling from the faucet. She slapped her face and closed her eyes, trying to think of how to end this nightmare. First Daisy, now Bradley. Two monstrous reminders of times best forgotten. During their senior year, she and Bradley had co-edited the *Highland Park Bagpipe*. Though battling over copyediting, they always saw eye to eye on politics. It was no surprise they became sweethearts, but their families' vastly different economic status separated them. When she left for Baylor, he took off for the east coast. Lame efforts at correspondence soon ended.

A sharp rap on the restroom door startled her, and she realized this was a second coincidence. First, Daisy, now Bradley's college roommate, both here on the same train.

Phillis returned to her seat only to hear Reggie announce, "B. J. will flip when I tell him I met you," Reggie chortled.

"Why so?"

"Something he said once after escorting a Cliffie to the Princeton-Yale game. She was his regular date, but they never were close. When I asked why, he replied, 'Roslind reminds me of a feisty girl I used to know. Independent as all get out.'" Reggie frowned, "but, her name wasn't Phillis."

She waited as he groped for the name she knew only too well.

"Scottie, now I remember. Aren't you Scottie?" He pointed his finger at her fiery cheeks and started laughing.

Phillis sighed, but gave him a look that dared him to use this nickname Bradley had given her in high school.

"You two are still speaking, aren't you?"

"I imagine so." Phillis smiled stiffly, wondering how she could say this since they had had no contact for seven years.

"Where will you be staying?" he asked, taking a notebook and pencil from his coat pocket. "Houston's short of hotel rooms. Everyone's complaining."

"I'm lodging in Houston Heights," she said. "Supposedly fifteen minutes from downtown by trolley. With my mother's friend. Don't know if she has a telephone."

"Call us at the Lamar Hotel when you get settled. I can hardly wait to see you and B. J. together."

Thankfully, the conductor boomed, "Next Stop, Houston."

More than ready to get off this train, Phillis rose from her seat as soon as the wheels stopped and turned, almost bumping into Daisy, who was smiling happily. Four men were on the aisle floor, looking for the handkerchief she had dropped. A short, black-haired man with a mustache bowed and handed it over. Daisy air waved him a kiss.

Turning to Phillis, she said, "I have a suite at the Plaza Hotel. Want to join me?"

Noticing Reggie standing nearby, waiting for an introduction, Phillis obliged him, "Daisy Leatherbury, may I present Reginald Bludworth? He is a journalist coming to Houston for the convention."

"Miss Leatherbury, how do you do?" Reggie gushed. "I am pleased to make your acquaintance because, frankly, I took you for Anita Loos' heroine when you first boarded. You're what I imagined she would be. Surely, you've come to perform here at some event."

"How did you know I am a dancer?" Daisy batted her eyes, giggling. "I'm amazed you spotted my talent so quickly. Can I call you 'Reggie'?"

Turning to Phillis, she said, "I'm sure I will just love getting to know your friend."

Phillis smiled politely, lifted down her hat and typewriter case and followed behind Reginald, now oblivious to anyone but Daisy, whom he was escorting off the train as if shielding her from a jungle full of tigers.

Houston's mammoth Union Station was jammed with red caps pushing carts of luggage and passengers trying to find their rides. Voices from every direction called, "Yellow Cab."

Outside, the sidewalk, hot enough to fry an egg, was filled with men standing around wiping their brows and a score of women, all of whom furiously waved fans as they waited in the taxicab line.

A jolly-looking fellow, wearing a plaid shirt and work pants held up by red suspenders, stood and doffed his Panama hat. Phillis let out a belly laugh as she saw he had been sitting on a canvas cushion atop a fifty-pound block of ice.

He handed her one of the cardboard fans and said, "Welcome to Houston, the Gateway to the South."

CHAPTER FOUR

What first struck me in Houston was the absolute, the miraculous flatness of its site. A suburb is known as Houston Heights, because it was a good eight feet higher than the center of the city.

Albert L Guerard
Rice Institute Professor, 1913
Literary Houston
David Theiss, editor

PHILLIS JOINED THE QUEUE WAITING FOR BRIGHT yellow taxis. Surprised at how quickly the line moved, she soon climbed into a cab's back seat and watched excitedly as the driver entered the line of cars on Texas Avenue.

"Welcome to Houston, miss. My name's Sonny Buggs. We're sure glad you're here." He tipped his cap, providing Phillis a peek at his baldhead and cauliflower ears.

All Houstonians must have been charged with welcoming the visitors. She settled herself on the worn leather seat and looked out the window, ready to begin what her mother called "her foolhardy adventure."

"Miss, look both ways when we stop here at Main Street and Texas Avenue. There's the Rice all decorated just like for a parade."

The ground floor of the hotel where all the journalists would be staying was adorned with fan-shaped stars and stripes banner hanging from the iron canopy that surrounded the ground floor of the hotel. Both sides of the street were awash in American flags and state flags. Yards and yards of red, white, and blue bunting hung from the top-floor windows of every building. Nothing like Fort Worth's Main Street.

"You from up north?"

"Yeah, North Texas," Phillis replied. "I'm a reporter for the *Fort Worth Star-Telegram* here to write about the convention. Where's the new hall?"

"Just a minute. We're coming to it," Sonny Buggs turned left onto Bagby Street and pointed to a huge white building on their right encircled by chicken-wire fencing.

"There it is, Sam Houston Hall," he announced. "Ain't it grand? You can see it from blocks away. It officially opens June 24. That's when the fencing comes down."

"Holy cow! I had no idea it was this big!"

Phillis's amazement must have pleased the driver, who chuckled, "Yes, ma'am. Look at all these folks walking around outside. They're Houstonians gawking just like you."

He waved out the window at a workman pushing a cart loaded with chairs.

"Mr. Jones and the big operators in charge chose this spot at the edge of downtown," he explained. "Don't see any tall buildings around, do you? Of course, no one says much about the forty houses they got rid of to clear this land. My friend, Dan Bellamy, lost the house he'd lived in for fifty years. But the convention hall's worth it."

"It looks like it's made out of wood." Phillis commented.

"East Texas yellow pine. The *Chronicle* says 80,000 square feet. Largest building on earth under one roof but, of course," Buggs said wryly, "that's Jesse Jones's newspaper."

"Well, regardless, it's a fine building," Phillis said. "I know Houston's proud."

"Took 'em only sixty-four days," Buggs responded. "Everyone in Houston breathed a sigh of relief when they finished it in time, but I bet you a nickel the paint's not yet dry on that green and gold trim."

Mr. Buggs kept up his commentary as he steered the automobile over a large bridge that spanned a sluggish, brownish stream of water.

"We're crossing Buffalo Bayou. Look back and see how the hall stops right at the edge of the water. This'll let the Gulf breezes circulate at night, so it won't be so hot."

She heard Houston was called the "City of Bayous," but this was her first glimpse of one. If they all looked like this, even the Chamber of Commerce could not call them scenic.

"I know, I know," Mr. Buggs said. "You think it looks like a mudhole. But Houston's good at making monkeys out of its critics. Back in 1914 we turned this little ditch into the Port of Houston. Believe me, we're always ahead when it comes to ideas."

She believed him but right now her concern was the heat. Soggy stockings, a soggy slip. God awful heat.

"Is it always this hot?" she asked.

"Well, miss, it's just past noon. You've come south almost three-hundred miles," he replied, laughing. "You're as bad as all them Yankees I been carrying around. Did you think it was gonna be cooler?"

Phillis sighed while Mr. Buggs turned left onto Washington Avenue. *How long until the sun sets? Surely it will be cooler then.*

Buggs' voice faded as she drummed her fingers on the worn leather seat, tired of his jabbering. She was only staying in Houston Heights because hotel rooms downtown were filled when she got the nod from her boss to come for the convention. Tent accommodations in two Houston parks were offered by the city but camping out and sharing a bath with twenty or thirty strangers sounded dreadful. That left private homes.

When her mother reminded her that Maymie Banion's latest letter said she was lodging a few visitors for the convention, Phillis contacted her immediately. For six dollars a week, she would enjoy a private room, a shared bath, and at least one meal a day. Perfect for her budget.

Phillis had met her mother's friend seventeen years ago when she came for dinner. The handsome, well-dressed woman had entered their Dallas apartment, clutching a magenta-flowered carpetbag, which Phillis, dancing on her tippy toes, just knew was full of treats.

But when Miss Banion opened the carpetbag after dinner, instead of chocolates or little buttery cakes, out fell a pile of satin and lace corsets. Her mother and Miss Banion laughed at her disappointment and began pawing at the frilly, pastel garments. Holding up a pink, lace-trimmed corset, her mother exclaimed, "This one's so much better than last year's."

"I told you I'm getting improved models," Maymie said. "You're the first to see my new line, Lena Belle."

"There was a dress I copied from *Vogue* just last month that needed a corset like this," Phillis's mother said, pulling on the whalebone stiffening with delight. "You'll sell a bunch of these, Maymie. I bet Corsicana's La Mode already ordered every model."

"Yes, Corsicana was fine, but the Monarch Hotel wasn't," she answered, rolling her eyes as she recounted her recent visit.

"'No vacancies!' the night clerk said when I arrived. To me! One of his regular customers. 'Sorry, Miss Banion. The Dallas Odd Fellows Club's statewide meeting. We're setting up cots in the hallway to sleep all of them.'"

"Well," Miss Banion snorted indignantly. "I told that whippersnapper he'd have to set up a cot for me because I couldn't sleep in the street."

Phillis's mother gasped, "I never heard of such."

"He got a piece of my mind," Miss Banion said, efficiently whipping a handkerchief from her sleeve cuff and patting her cheeks.

"He told me not to 'puff up.' 'If you were a man, I could put you up.' But 'I'm not a man,' I told him. 'I'm a woman working same as a man does. I expect to be treated with just as much consideration.'" She paused again and asked Phillis to get her a glass of water.

"Well, he gave me a big smile like he needed to show off his perfect teeth, and offered to let me have his housekeeper's room, shoving her in the attic with the maids."

She took a sip of water and leaned over to Phillis's mother, whispering, "Let me tell you, Lena Belle, that was a close call. I thought I was going to have to sleep on a cold, hard bench in the train station."

Sitting up and taking another sip, she rolled her eyes again and said, "Have to admit, I've done that more than once."

Her mother smiled broadly as she fingered her garnet beads, nodding her head. Phillis suspected she envied her friend's lifestyle. Eight-year-old Phillis adored Miss Banion's spunk and determination. Her battle to succeed in a man's world began working its way into her own hopes and dreams.

The very next year, Maymie Banion wrote saying she had married Rudolph Shuddemagen, the owner of the corset company, but vowed she would never be a stay-at-home wife. By this time, Lena Belle had also married her boss, which drew the two women closer even though her mother had abandoned her own career.

When Miss Maymie, as Phillis now was old enough to call her, moved to Houston, she wrote "Tell your husband to stop carrying corsets in his dress store. They are dead, out of style; only stout matrons who live in one-horse towns buy them. I made my husband sell his factory and we've switched to real estate."

Her mother nodded as she read the letter to Phillis, "Wouldn't you know Miss Maymie would be ahead of the game?"

The next letter informed them, "We're moving to a subdivision called Houston Heights where bungalow construction is running wild. We are selling Crain Ready-Cut homes as fast as the company can ship them to us. Rudy and I are equal partners, but I outsell him every month."

Letters from Houston continued until Maymie wrote, "Dear Lena Belle, I lost my Rudolph two weeks ago. He couldn't leave the beer and sausage alone. Not to speak of the wiener schnitzel. I knew German food would be the death of him. I buried him properly but went to court and changed my name back to Banion, a better-sounding name for a business. I was not going to order gold decals with a name like

'Shuddemagen' for the sign at my new office. I've sold our real estate business and formed the

Maymie Banion Insurance Agency. So, please, address my letters thusly."

Miss Maymie had not changed her ways. Another life, another bold adventure. She always seemed to land upright. Her mother's continued close contact with her friend made Phillis wonder if she still envied Miss Banion despite her own luxurious life. It seemed as if her mother's marriage had trapped her into a cage of her own making. No longer using her extraordinary dressmaking skills, Lena Wilkerson wore expensive garments chosen by her husband and sat playing solitaire while servants cleaned her house. Yes, though she would die before admitting it, perhaps, her mother kept up their correspondence because Maymie was a successful businesswoman who had never bowed to any man.

A loud clanging bell startled her, as Mr. Buggs turned right onto Heights Boulevard, passing a trolley traveling in the opposite direction. A few blocks later they crossed a trestle bridge with another stream of brownish, slow-moving water below.

"Is this the same bayou we crossed in town?" she asked.

"No, no, that was the big one." he replied. "This is White Oak Bayou. It feeds into Buffalo Bayou."

"Tell me about the trolley that just passed us," Phillis asked. "Does it go downtown?"

"Absolutely," Mr. Buggs replied. "Costs a nickel and takes fifteen minutes. No one has any complaints about our trolleys."

"That's a relief." Phillis knew she would be as dependent on the trolleys here as she had been in Fort Worth.

Sonny Buggs's taxicab clattered north on Heights Boulevard, and Phillis looked at her wristwatch and frowned, "How much longer until we reach Harvard Street?"

"Maybe fifteen minutes. Look around you. The Boulevard runs north to south," Mr. Buggs explained. "Numbered streets run east to west. You can't get lost here even if you don't know where you are," he said, laughing at his own joke, "Whenever Carter or Cooley ride in my cab, I always thank 'em for laying out the streets so sensibly."

Another clanging bell signaled the approach of a second trolley headed for downtown.

"Is that new-looking building with the white trim a church?" Phillis asked.

"Heights Church of Christ," Mr. Buggs replied. "We've got more churches in Houston Heights than anywhere in this city. Two Baptist churches, if you can believe it. Heights' folks have got lots of religion. We're so religious, we voted to be dry in 1912. When the City of Houston annexed us, we insisted on staying dry. No wets in the Heights, and now there's none in the whole country. Isn't that a joke?" Mr. Buggs cackled.

Phillis noticed the air seemed slightly cooler. "Mr. Buggs," she said, "it doesn't seem as hot now. Is that because of all these trees and this grassy park in the middle of this street?"

He laughed, "Miss, you're twenty-three feet above downtown Houston. That's why it's called the 'Heights.'"

Phillis found it hard to imagine that would make a difference but was grateful for the respite.

Tall, narrow, old-fashioned houses lined the Boulevard next to modern stucco bungalows similar to the house where she grew up. Tiny wooden cottages with white picket fences sat beside stately Victorian mansions on oversized lots surrounded by elaborate iron fences.

Buggs pointed to a massive, three-story brown home on the right. "There's the Cooley house, first house built on the Boulevard," he said. "You'll only be a couple of blocks away."

He took a right turn and stopped at the end of the block. "Are you just here for the convention, or are you going to make this your home?"

Not waiting for her answer, he said, proudly. "If you're planning to stay in Houston, I'll give you some free advice. The Heights beats any other neighborhood and it's a dang sight better than any city in north Texas."

Phillis laughed and shrugged her shoulders. "Thank you, Mr. Buggs. You are as good at promoting Houston Heights as Amon Carter is the city of Fort Worth. Don't know what I'll do after this convention. My future's up in the air."

"Never been farther north than College Station myself," he said.

Walking to the taxicab's trunk, he pointed to an imposing home topped with steeple like towers. "This is it. 1750 Harvard Street."

Phillis could hardly believe her eyes. Surely this large home with its soaring tower and gables was not Maymie Banion's. It looked like a birthday cake.

She opened her pocketbook and asked Mr. Buggs what she owed for the ride. Handing him the coins, she stepped out of the cab. "Thank you for your kind welcome to Houston."

He took the money and grabbed her valise, following her up the walk to the steep wooden stairs that led to the front door. "Thank you, Mr. Buggs," she said.

A closer look indicated the house needed a new coat of paint, but airy white lace curtains floated from every window and the empty porch swing rocked gently. It looked comfortable and homey. Sort of like a grandmother's house.

Phillis climbed the stairway and reached for the screened door as it flew open in her face and banged against the wall of the house. She stepped back to avoid colliding with a young man who barreled past her as he slammed on his straw boater. Halfway down the stairs, he turned and shouted, "Are you the lady reporter from Fort Worth?"

When she nodded, he smiled and saluted before continuing to the sidewalk. As an explanation, she supposed, for his haste, he yelled up at her, "Gotta go see a man about a dog," then loped toward a shiny blue roadster, slid in, started up the engine, and waved goodbye.

Which was more amusing? His snappy red-and-white-striped blazer and snug white trousers or his pressing need to find a bootlegger. Standing on the porch, she chuckled as his car roared up the street, then picked up her valise and turned to enter the house.

It smells moldy, Phillis thought, closing the door behind her. The dark wood walls shut out the light. When her eyes adjusted to the dim interior, she saw a hefty, stone-faced woman wearing a black day dress and large white apron.

"My name is Phillis Flanagan. Will you please tell Miss Banion I'm here?"

"I'm Mrs. Della Hinkle, the housekeeper," the woman replied in a guttural voice. Her faded blue eyes blinked open and shut spookily behind her wire-framed spectacles.

"Miss Banion's at her office."

After looking her up and down, Mrs. Hinkle said, "You must be the new boarder."

Phillis pushed a straggling lock of hair back under her hat, glanced at her wrinkled skirt, and sighed loudly.

"Yes, I am," she replied. "I would appreciate having a glass of cold water before I go to my room."

"Follow me," Della Hinkle said marching down the hall to a dark wood-paneled kitchen lit only by a small rectangular window over a zinc counter. Nothing was up to date, including the wooden icebox. No electric motor humming. The whole kitchen spoke to an earlier period. Its bare pine floor, the coal bucket sitting next to the large white enamel stove indicated Maymie Banion did not spend her money on the kitchen.

The woman set a pitcher of lemonade on a table covered with a faded red turkey cloth. Was the lemonade to be a treat instead of the water she had requested? No matter. Phillis sat down and drank a few sips of the lukewarm sugary beverage then stood and waited to be shown to her room.

"Is this all you brought?" Mrs. Hinkle asked, pointing at Phillis's valise.

"Yes, ma'am," Phillis said. She picked it up with her left hand then bent over to retrieve her typewriter case.

Her typewriter case!

In all the commotion of arriving at the house, nearly colliding with the jellybean kid, and encountering this apron-clad witch, she had lost it.

"Is something amiss?" the housekeeper asked. "You look like you just swallowed a pickle," laughing at Phillis's panic-stricken face.

"Oh, Mrs. Hinkle," Phillis screamed, "My typewriter must be in the taxi. "How can I get it back." Her eyes circled the green kitchen walls.

"What a shame no one taught you to keep ahold of your things when you travel. Especially if this thing's important to you," Mrs. Hinkle admonished, shaking her head. "You're hardly a schoolgirl anymore. Do you still live with your family?"

"No, I assure you I'm on my own."

"Maybe this is the problem. How long since you left home?"

Phillis's first inclination was to throw the glass of lemonade in the housekeeper's face. Instead, she dropped her valise, rushed back down the hall, and stepped into the bright sunshine.

The housekeeper followed her. "You're leaving already?" she asked.

Phillis ignored her question, inspecting the front porch to see if the typewriter case was there. She ran back down the front stairs even more quickly than the young man earlier. There was no typewriter case on the sidewalk or amidst the flowerbed filled with green spires and orange day lilies.

It was gone.

No canary-colored taxi idled on the street. Mr. Buggs had long since pulled away.

Phillis wished like crazy she had paid more attention to his drivel when he told her he lived in Houston Heights. Why didn't she ask him if his house was nearby?

Maybe she could telephone him. Reluctantly, Phillis asked the housekeeper, "Is there a telephone here?"

Mrs. Hinkle led her back inside the house and pointed to an instrument that luckily had an automatic dialing device at its base. Phillis sat down and opened the directory sitting on the table. She started to dial the first listing for "Buggs," then remembered to ask, "May I make a call?"

"As long as it's local," came the cold reply. "No boarders can make long-distance calls. Better not try to fool Miss Maymie."

Phillis dialed the first number. No answer. The second number produced a busy signal.

"Is Ashland a street in Houston Heights?" she asked Mrs. Hinkle.

The housekeeper nodded and watched as Phillis dialed 4-4-7-5.

When a woman answered, Phillis blurted, "Is Mr. Sonny Buggs there? My name is Phillis Flanagan. I left my typewriter case in his taxi."

"Sonny's my nephew," the woman answered. "He drives a cab every day. He's got no phone, but he uses mine. What's your number?"

As Phillis gave the woman the phone number written on the pad pushed in front of her by the housekeeper.

"Okay," the woman said. "Now what was it you left in his automobile?"

"My typewriter," Phillis answered. "I arrived on the afternoon train from Fort Worth. Please ask him to call me as soon as possible."

"A typewriter, you say? Now, who would have thought anyone could carry one of those things on a train?" Phillis heard crackling cellophane and munching, "Can't say for sure but Sonny might be home tonight at ten. Don't fret, dear. I'm sure it's safe. Last summer, my next-door neighbor, Sadie Wilson, left her new picnic basket in his cab and he returned it to her the very next day."

The woman's twittery comparison of her typewriter with a picnic basket gave Phillis small comfort. "Did you write down 4-1-2-9? You did? Thank you.

I will wait for his call."

Phillis placed the receiver back on the hook and turned to Mrs. Hinkle. "May I go to my room now?"

"I'm just waiting on you, miss," the woman responded curtly.

Upstairs, Phillis was shown to a corner room with a spool bed and a dreadfully old-fashioned coverlet hand-painted with blue birds. A matching scarf covered the dresser top.

Mrs. Hinkle announced, "This is the largest bedroom in the house. Over there's a wardrobe for your clothes."

"It's perfect. Thank you."

"Don't thank me," the woman said coldly. "I wouldn't have given it to you."

Phillis was stunned by her response.

"Girl, this is a double bed, wide enough for two adults," Mrs. Hinkle continued resentfully. "Miss Maymie should have gotten twice what she's charging you. The pitiful letter your mother sent begging her to help you, softened her head." The housekeeper clenched her fists. "I hear her car in the driveway."

Mrs. Hinkle left the room and clomped down the stairs.

At the window, Phillis pushed aside the lace curtain and watched Maymie Banion alight from a handsome maroon Packard sedan. Mrs. Hinkle appeared in the backyard, the words "typewriter" and "lost" drifting up as Mrs. Hinkle pointed to her room. Then the two women clasped arms and walked back toward the house.

Phillis ran from the room and down the stairs, two at a time, landing on the first floor as Miss Banion set a leather satchel on a console in the hallway, reminding her of the magical carpet bag the woman brought to dinner the night they first met.

"Ah, here's Lena Belle's grown-up daughter. Step out into the light where I can look at you."

As Phillis approached Miss Maymie with a broad smile, the older woman gave her a once over and frowned. "I see your sweet mother's eyes, but you're even taller than I remembered. Long legs and long skinny feet."

Her height and 10 1/2 quad shoe size had been a source of embarrassment since ninth grade, though at this moment neither mattered a whit. With a sinking feeling, Phillis realized the welcome she expected was not going to happen.

In a rush of words, Miss Maymie continued, "Good to see you after all this time, but we're chasing around like chickens with our heads cut off, trying to get ready for this big event. Tell you about that later. Mrs. Hinkle told me about your typewriter. We must see about getting it back. Will the cab driver know what it is? I saw one of those cases recently and thought at first it was a hatbox. They call them 'portables,' don't they? Lord, I'm grateful I don't have to tote one around."

The penetrating gray eyes Phillis remembered raked her over as the woman kept adding to her discomfort. *And I thought Mrs. Hinkle was rude.*

Miss Banion continued, eyebrows raised, "I know how expensive these machines are. I bought one for my secretary." Patting her on the shoulder, she asked, "Honey, are you sure this reporting business is what you want to do? I was shocked when your mother told me your salary. Imagine, spending four years on a college degree with so little to show. And for what? Writing about dead white men? Accounts of boring tea parties that are just lollygagging events. Aren't you bored to death?"

The more Maymie Banion talked, the worse it got. With a satisfied smile, the housekeeper stood close by nodding agreement as if she were part of their conversations. How humiliating.

"In case you don't know, your mother is worried sick, and she says your stepfather pokes fun at your "career" all the time. I pay the typist in my office the same as your weekly salary," Her sonorous voice echoed down the hall, "And I certainly don't expect her to buy her own typewriter."

Phillis bristled as she framed a comeback, but the words caught in her throat when she saw the pity in Miss Maymie's eyes.

Shaking her head, Miss Maymie said, "I don't know what the answer is, Phillis. Maybe you could write a 'sob sister' story. With all these people coming to town, there's likely to be tons of drama."

The phrase "sob sister," the hated insult used by those who labeled women reporters as big-hearted but soft-minded, was a bucket of ice water.

Phillis answered, "I didn't choose newspapering to get rich. I know what the salaries are. Journalism may make no sense to you, and sometimes the ugly real news doesn't make sense to me either. But sometimes things happen that take your breath away. I came here for a chance to hear stories and meet people I can write about."

Maymie Banion and Mrs. Hinkley both frowned as Phillis folded her arms across her chest and stared them down. The lengthening silence and the ladies' dumbstruck faces convinced Phillis this conversation needed to end. "I believe I shall take a walk."

"What in Sam Hill has gotten into her?" Mrs. Hinkle demanded. "That's the second time this afternoon she's stormed out of this house."

Ignoring the housekeeper, Miss Maymie walked to the front window. She did not 'storm,'" she whispered. Watching Phillis marching down the street, she clapped her hands and said, "In order to be a woman, you have to have fire."

CHAPTER FIVE

The history of Houston Heights reads like a fairy story in which a magician has waved his magic wand and wonders have sprung into existence.

Mrs. W.G. Love (Lillian)
Wife of Houston Heights first mayor
"The Key to the City" 1908

PHILLIS STRUCK OUT WALKING WEST ON Eighteenth Avenue toward the Boulevard. She needed food and a comfort room with not a clue how to find either. In less than four hours since her arrival, she had lost her typewriter and probably, her promised room. Would Maymie Banion kick her out? If not, could she survive two weeks in this creepy old house? It was a Saturday afternoon, and she had few options. Surely some of the businesses Mr. Buggs spoke of were open. Dear Lord, it was hotter than she ever expected it to be. The boiling sunshine beat down on her back and the blistering concrete sidewalk came through her shoes.

Ahead, the esplanade offered no real footpath, but she welcomed the shade of giant pine trees, the tallest she had ever seen. Who would have imagined a bower like this so near the heartbeat of one of Texas' largest cities. Slippery brown pine needles crunched under her feet until the Boulevard abruptly ended.

Across the street, a handsome, two-story, buff-brick building spanned the width of the boulevard as well as the esplanade. "Alexander Hamilton Junior High School" according to concrete letters at the top of the building. Phillis looked down Twentieth Avenue. Bungalows lined the street both ways. Where could she find a café? Oh yes, the taxicab driver told her Nineteenth Street was Main Street in the Heights. Reversing her steps, Phillis headed back and could see a promising row of automobiles parked in front of a long low of storefronts down the block.

In front of her was a one-story, white stucco building with a cross at the peak of its front gable across which said, "St. Andrew's." A church might provide a comfort station. They were bound to have a restroom if it was only open.

After knocking politely on the side door, she increased her pressure and was rewarded by a faint "halloo." A slight man opened the door and asked, "May I help you?" Phillis ducked her head. She had hoped for a female.

"Sir, I've come from Fort Worth on the afternoon train and find myself needing a comfort room. Do you have a facility I can use?" She did not recall ever being so embarrassed in her entire life.

"Of course, Miss," the man replied kindly. "Come in."

"Thank you," said Phillis as he stepped aside and pointed, "The ladies' room is just ahead."

Passing through the church vestibule, she entered a small bathroom off the hall. Hastily, she used the toilet and checked her image in the mirror hanging over the lavatory. Horrified by her hot, sweaty appearance, she wet her handkerchief with cold water from the faucet, wiped her face and pushed her hair back up under her hat. When she opened the door, the gentleman stood waiting patiently.

"Are you okay?" he asked in a lilting voice that turned his question into a song. "You look all played out."

Phillis was charmed by his English accent, the silky bow which softened the stiff white shirt collar and his cherubic face framed by wavy dark hair. Either a poet or a performer she decided while noticing the cardboard folder he carried overflowed with sheet music.

"Are you a singer?"

"Yes, my name is Fred Dexter, the choirmaster at Christ Episcopal Church downtown. This is my home church. I do many jobs here. He pointed to the papers he carried and smiled, "Music for the choir to sing tomorrow at the eleven-o'clock service." He looked at her curiously. "May I ask how is it you happened to be walking down Nineteenth Street? We don't see many strangers in the Heights."

"I've come from Fort Worth to report on the Democratic Convention for my newspaper. Do you know Miss Maymie Banion?" When his face lit up, she continued, "I'm lodging at 1750 Harvard, but right now, I need to buy some hosiery."

Pointing to the irritating hole in her right stocking, she cocked her head and shrugged her shoulders. Mr. Dexter quickly responded, "Kaplan's Ben-Hur, just up the street. You can find anything you need. And please consider joining us for Morning Prayer at 11:00 tomorrow morning.

Thanking him for his assistance and his invitation, she walked back into the afternoon heat in a somewhat improved frame of mind. Yale Street provided no shade as she made her way, betting herself that Mr. Dexter was watching to make certain she found her way to the store. Except her purse was upstairs in her room at the boarding house. Luckily, she found forty-five cents in her jacket pocket. Enough to buy a meal and a drink but no stockings.

The large white building marked Kaplan's Ben-Hur was not as important to her as the "Yale Street Drugs and Lunch Counter" sign across the street. Making a beeline for the green and white wooden store, she pulled open the screened door greeted by a young woman wearing a short- sleeved white uniform. Phillis slid onto a stool at the counter and studied the chalkboard menu. When the waitress asked, "What'll it be?" Phillis ordered a fried-egg sandwich and asked for a glass of water.

"Sure thing," the waitress replied. "Here's your water. I'll fix the sandwich right away." Phillis watched as she broke an egg onto a sizzling black griddle. "My name's Juanita. Are you one of the convention visitors? I sure hope so since I told my boss we needed to keep this grill on extra hours for these strangers coming to town. They're gonna be hungry."

Phillis nodded vigorously and fiddled with the saltshaker, her own stomach growling.

"Mrs. Dupuis argued they would all be downtown," Juanita continued, "but I knew better. There's not enough room for all of them there."

Phillis laughed, "You guessed right. I'm staying here and I'll bet I am not the only one."

Juanita popped some sliced bread into an electric toaster. "Across the street," she said, "Kaplan's is selling cots for eight dollars. They call it their 'Convention Special.'"

Phillis nodded and wished she had explored the idea of camping in Memorial Park more thoroughly before agreeing to stay with Miss Maymie.

"I saw Sam Houston Hall today when I came into town from Fort Worth," she told Juanita. "It's a monster."

"It's the biggest thing I ever saw," Juanita grinned. "Can't wait to see inside once they take down the fence. It'll have to be after the convention. We were asked not to take up space there while the visitors are here. Even if you have a ticket."

She placed a steaming plate in front of Phillis. "Here you go, one fried-egg sandwich," she said and pointed to a jar filled with forks and a stack of paper napkins.

Phillis took a bite of the sandwich as soon as the plate hit the counter. "Juanita," she asked, "tell me about the button you're wearing."

"Ain't it a beaut!"? Juanita said. "It's my Me-Too button. I'm keeping it forever. My boss bought it for me. She's a member of the Woman's National Democratic Club here in Houston. They're the ladies who thought of this. Didn't think they were helping enough so they designed these buttons. Sold twenty-five thousand in less than a month." She took Phillis's glass and refilled it from the spigot.

"How did they sell them so quickly?" Phillis finished her sandwich and slipped her notepad and pencil from her pocket.

"They got a city map and marked off the downtown sections," Juanita replied. "Began selling buttons to everyone they could find on the street and inside buildings and stores. Started when it was cold weather, not hot like it is today. For three days, Mrs. Dupuis and her friends walked from floor to floor inside the office buildings selling their Me-Too buttons. They called themselves 'the women's button brigade.'"

Phillis scribbled in her notebook.

"It turned out everyone in the state wanted a button," Juanita boasted. "Well, maybe not everyone, but Governor Moody organized a club up in Austin to sell the buttons for the Houston women. Each button costs a dollar. I'm surprised they got that much for this itty-bitty button. But it was a good cause."

"Is your boss here?" Phillis asked.

"She's taken her son to the zoo to see the new house for chimpanzees," Juanita replied. "Mrs. Dupuis and her husband own this drugstore together but to me, she's really the brains. He only compounds the prescriptions and fills the orders. I'm sorry you can't meet her." Juanita offered. "Now, she's hired an architect to draw up plans for a new building. It's going to be at the other end of the block. It'll be a brick building, much nicer than this."

Juanita smiled. "She's terrific. Never had a woman boss before her. I like it. Things like giving me this button. That's the stuff she thinks of."

"What a great story!" Phillis said. "Thank you for sharing it. My name's Phillis Flanagan and I'm a reporter for the *Star-Telegram* in Fort Worth. Have you ever heard of my newspaper?"

Juanita shook her head.

"That's okay," Phillis said. "Houston's three-hundred miles from there. I'm here to write about convention visitors' reactions to the big event."

"You want everyone's ideas about the convention? Or just the big shots?" Not waiting for Phillis to answer, Juanita asked, "Could you put *me* in the paper? All I mostly do with a newspaper is put it by the griddle and drain bacon onto it. I don't read much. But" she said "I can sure tell you what everybody in Houston Heights thinks about this event. My customers have talked about it for five months. Arguing about candidates and guessing what happens next. You know it's really about wet and dry and the Heights mainly has dry's. You'd know that if you've been in our neighborhood for ten minutes. No speakeasies here, hidden or unhidden."

As Phillis laughed, Juanita said, "It's no laughing matter, let me tell you. I have to be careful what I say when the women come in. Most likely, they're WCTU teetotalers. I bet there's more than a thousand of them in the Heights. They hate Al Smith and they're positive he takes orders from the Pope."

Phillis paused, her pencil in mid-air, a puzzled look on her face. "Do you believe that?"

"Nobody with a lick of sense would think that," Juanita said indignantly.

"Imagine someone across the ocean telling the President of the United States what to do. That'll never happen, but I keep quiet and make sure I don't spill what I am thinking."

She took Phillis's plate away and wiped the counter.

"How will they react at the convention when Smith is nominated?" Phillis asked her.

"Don't think it will happen. The women are in love with Governor Moody. All I heard for two months was 'Dan's the Man' or 'Moody for President' every single day. He's young and good looking, but they especially love him 'cause he's dry."

Juanita stopped wiping down the counter. "Folks don't talk about him much anymore. I can't figure out what happened," she said.

"Maybe he decided he didn't want the office," Phillis suggested, remembering what she had read in the newspapers.

"Oh, I hadn't thought about that," Juanita said, putting her forefinger to her temple. "Someone turning down the chance to be president." She grinned. "I'll bet no woman would turn down the chance. I'd like to see a woman be president. Isn't it about time? We got the vote. Let's do something with it."

The waitress's political views confounded Phillis who could not connect her self-proclaimed disinterest in newspapers with her progressive views. One would think she read the *New York Times* daily. "I would love to talk with you again about the residents' reactions to the convention. Here's my telephone number."

Juanita nodded seriously and tucked the slip of paper into her uniform pocket.

"Thanks for your help," Phillis said, looking at her bill. "If my editor prints the article about the Me-Too buttons, I'll bring you a copy."

Handing Juanita twenty cents, Phillis told her to keep the change and returned to 1750 Harvard Street with her first interview, wondering if she could stretch it to make an article. The door stuck as she pulled on it, and for a sinking moment she thought it had been locked out. Jerking it harder, she slipped in but the shadowy front hall provided no welcome. Plates tinkled as she walked by the kitchen breaking the silence of the deathly still interior. Phillis again regretted her choice of lodging.

6/16/28. I am here. Maymie Banion's not the person I remembered. Her house is old and dingy. The housekeeper must chew nails for breakfast. I blew my stack right after I arrived. Don't want to be asked to leave. Must learn to keep my mouth shut if this battle axe lets me stay. Is Houston going to be as thrilling as I hoped? So far, nothing is working out. I will write my first story even if I have to use a pencil. I must go to sleep, but I'm wide-awake and ready for it all to begin.

CHAPTER SIX

Solid Living is the least expensive kind. The true definition of solid-living is to be found in Houston Heights, a model home community, nestling in a virgin forest which clothes a sloping landscape.

Oscar Martin Carter, 1914
Founder of Houston Heights
Sunday, June 17, 1928

EVERY AVAILABLE CHURCH BELL WAS ANNOUNCING the arrival of this Sunday morning in the Heights. With a stretch, Phillis luxuriated in her lovely new bedroom with its lace-filled windows filtering the morning sunshine. She lay in bed and groaned, realizing soon she would face the indomitable Miss Banion and learn her fate, and within minutes, a sharp rap on her door fulfilled these expectations. "Yes, who is it?"

"It's me. Maymie Banion."

Phillis jumped out of bed. What could she say? Would she be asked to leave? Opening the door, her landlady stood there in a pink chenille robe, her long hair braided into a pigtail.

"Do you want me to pack up and get out?" Phillis asked.

"Of course not, silly girl. Come downstairs and thank Mr. Buggs for bringing back your typewriter. Do you have a robe to cover yourself up?"

Phillis whooped and wanted to give somebody a hug, but not anyone in this house.

Throwing on her wrapper, she hustled down the stairs close behind Miss Maymie. Mr. Buggs stood in the hall, holding her typewriter and grinning like the proverbial canary-eating cat.

"You're a welcome sight, Mr. Buggs. Did your aunt tell you I telephoned?"

"Yes, she told me to get your case back to you as soon as possible. She said you sounded like you were gonna bust out crying." He held out the typewriter case, saying, "So, here it is, miss."

Miss Maymie walked to the hall table and came back with a quarter, which she handed him. "Thank you," she said and then turned to Phillis. "This is what makes the Heights a great place to live. Good neighbors like the Buggs family. We appreciate Mr. Buggs' kindness, don't we, dear?"

Phillis hoped the kindly taxi driver could see her gratitude as she took her case from him and set it on the floor. Pumping his hand, she said, "Thank you, sir, I'm so relieved. Have a great day. I'm going to consider the advice you gave me."

After he left, when Miss Maymie asked her what advice Mr. Buggs had offered, Phillis replied. "Nothing really to my thinking. I wish I'd thought to bring money downstairs to tip him."

"That's okay." Miss Maymie said. "You'll learn someday. You're luckier than you know to have gotten this expensive machine back. All these strangers in town, no telling what all's going to go missing." Hands on her hips, Miss Banion asked, "Are you hungry for breakfast? Go see Josie in the kitchen. She will get out the Post Toasties for you. Eat fast. We're going to church in forty-five minutes."

Phillis swallowed her surprise at this news and headed for the kitchen. As she sank onto a kitchen chair, she introduced herself to the diminutive woman standing at the sink. She wore a colorful cotton turban and a starched white apron that crackled as she whipped a rag back and forth over the counter.

"Oh, I knowed you was comin' long time since," Josie said. "Your mama's Miss Maymie's friend, right? My name's Josie." Without asking, she poured a large white mug full of steaming coffee. "You drink coffee, don't you?"

Phillis nodded appreciatively as Josie set the mug down in front of her. "Cream's in that pitcher and sugar's in the bowl. Miss Banion said to feed you cereal 'cause you got to get dressed snappy for church."

As Phillis doctored her coffee liberally with cream and sugar, Josie said, "Old Hinkle's mad as a wet hen since she found out she had to give you the best room upstairs."

Glad for at least a partial explanation for Mrs. Hinkle's contrariness, Phillis asked, "Why am I going to church?"

"That's what Heights' folks do, on Sundays. Don't go thinking Miss Maymie's a Bible thumper. For her this is business. Grace Methodist is the church you'll be going in two shakes of a lamb's tail."

"And what lamb might that be?" Phillis asked.

"Ha, that's funny," Josie said. "Just a way of sayin' things. Anyway, here's a bowl and some cereal. I'd fix you bacon but no time for that. Miss Maymie's usually out the door by five of nine, so you best be standing there ready to go."

Phillis rolled her eyes as she poured cereal and milk into the bowl. "Tell me more about Mrs. Hinkle. She really got my goat."

"I'm the boss of my kitchen. She don't give me no trouble. Pretty much goes after everyone else, except Miss Olivia. She's the nurse."

"I met Olivia briefly yesterday evening," Phillis said. "Why doesn't Mrs. Hinkle go after her?"

"Mrs. Hinkle feels sorry for her because nursing is such hard work," Josie replied. "She don't know Olivia Jones like I do."

"Oh?" Phillis set about shoveling the cereal into her mouth as quickly as possible, deciding not to ask any more though she still wondered why Miss Banion tolerated Hinkle's rudeness.

Gulping down her coffee, Phillis asked, "Will we have Sunday dinner at noon?"

"No," the cook replied. "Miss Banion has a meeting today. It's about those nametags. They call 'em 'badges.' No tellin' what time she gets home. We won't eat till she does. My husband, Charlie, is out there in the backyard wringin' the chickens' necks. We got three big fat hens. Hear 'em squawking? Got to get them girls plucked and cleaned up. I'll pop 'em in the skillet soon as Miss Banion gets home. So, dinner'll probably be at five this evenin'."

"Thanks for the breakfast. I'm glad to meet you," Phillis grinned as she rose and ran upstairs to dress for church.

According to her wristwatch, she arrived downstairs, ready to leave right at eight-forty-five. Dressed in a simple navy twill skirt and a long-sleeved pink blouse, she had slid on her last decent pair of hose and exchanged her brown walking shoes for her navy pumps. Maymie walked in as she was adjusting her hat and nodded her approval.

Starting the Packard, Maymie explained. "Going to church on Sundays is what every Heights resident does and since an insurance saleswoman has to have lots of contacts, I just fit the two things together. Contacts won't drop into my lap the way they drop into a man's. Watch me after the service. You might learn something."

Phillis looked out the window, biting her lip to keep from laughing. She watched as Miss Maymie turned left onto the Boulevard asked, "Do you have a Me-Too button?"

"Of course." Miss Maymie said, pointing to her lapel before realizing that there was no pin. "I must have left it on the blue jacket I wore yesterday. I walked the streets downtown selling them. Contacted my clients and the tenants in my building. Last I counted, I sold one hundred buttons. I even bought one of the Me-Too cookie tins."

Turning to Phillis, she asked, "How'd you hear about 'em?"

Phillis mumbled, "Yale Street Drugs."

"Who've you been talking to? Mildred Dupuis? She's a sharp businesswoman. I respect women who get out and do things. A licensed pharmacist, and a successful business. That Heights Woman's Club down the street wouldn't be able to function without her. Let's put it this way, she's a very generous member."

"I didn't get to meet her," she said as Miss Maymie braked the Packard at the curb on Thirteenth Avenue beside a large redbrick church with imposing square towers flanking an elevated covered porch.

Alighting from the car, she stopped Phillis and pointed down to the curb imbedded with a series of iron rings. "You're old enough to remember tying carriage reins up to a hitching rail like that, aren't you?"

Phillis nodded and said, "Glad we don't need those anymore." Maymie guided her to the wide concrete front stairs where an usher stood handing out church bulletins. "Good morning, Miss Banion."

They were no sooner seated than the choir marched in singing "What a Friend We Have in Jesus." Phillis studied the bulletin, which differed little from the one at Highland Park Methodist where she used to go with her mother and stepfather. Sunday after Sunday, she endured the boring genteel service listening to dull sermons containing no political references but thankfully no threats of hellfire and brimstone.

This minister, who, Miss Maymie whispered, was Brother Hastings, began with the usual preacher joke.

"These times in Houston remind me of a man riding a train in one of those parlor cars. He fell asleep and snored with gusto, annoying everyone sitting around him. An old woman shook him awake. 'What's the matter?' the snorer asked. 'Your snoring is bothering everyone in this car,' the woman replied. 'How do you know I'm snoring?' 'Why, we can't help hearing it,' she answered. 'Well, don't believe all you hear,' replied the stranger and went to sleep again."

After the laughter subsided, Brother Hastings looked down at his notes, then out at the congregation, "This man gave his fellow passengers good advice and I'm advising you to heed his words. Fellow Christians don't believe all you hear. We're hearing a lot of people say the upcoming convention will choose Alfred Smith as their presidential candidate. Don't believe it. One thousand men and women have already met to form a third party. They're an undaunted squadron who're going up against a mighty hostile force. We will not be dominated by Tammany Hall and the wet forces."

The congregation responded with vigorous "amens." Phillis was shocked this minister talked about politics. Maymie was right, she could learn something here.

Brother Hastings continued, "The South is warning the wets, 'We won't be used for window dressing. We're not going to sail under the flag of a ship manned by blackguards.'"

Another chorus of "amens."

"What good is a dry platform with a wet candidate? It's worthless, isn't it? Does anyone believe Al Smith is going to enforce our sacred Eighteenth Amendment?"

As the congregated shouted, "No," Phillis sat dismayed by Brother Hastings' sermon and the congregation's approval.

"We must vote together," he said. "The women, thank God, the women can now vote. They will be the salvation of our country. There are seventy-thousand WCTU members who will not vote for a ticket chosen by Tammany Hall."

Brother Hastings' face glowed either from religious conviction or the stifling heat in the sanctuary. "I have neighbors who are Roman Catholics, members of All Saints church five blocks from here. They are fine people and I'm sure Mr. Smith is a fine person. We don't care if he holds the Pope of Rome up as his God. We are against him because he is wet."

Brother Hastings paused and surveyed his congregation. Phillis always wondered if ministers weren't actually checking to make sure everyone was awake. "So, I say to you today, let's go forth with resolve and fervor to spread our word. Let's use our banners, our marches and our prayer vigils, which will be held right across the street from Sam Houston Hall, regardless of the awful heat, the rain showers, and the thousands of visitors. Our work will be worthy of His name. Amen."

A loud chorus of answering "amens" worried Phillis.

The pianist played an introductory chord for the choir that stood and sang all five verses of "A Mighty Fortress Is My God."

"Get up, girl," Miss Maymie said, handing her a hymnal. As she sang, Phillis looked around at the congregation, appalled by their sentiments regarding Al Smith. Her visit to this church full of Heights Methodists confirmed what the Yale Street Grill's waitress had said.

It was slow work leaving the church since Miss Maymie stopped and introduced Phillis to everyone whom she considered important as they made their way to the parish hall for a mandatory cup of lukewarm coffee. Whispering gossipy tidbits to Phillis, Maymie smiled cordially, glad-handing everyone who passed their way.

"The lady in the purple hat has two insurance policies with me," she informed Phillis greeting her client graciously. "The man on your right, wearing a beige linen suit, is tight as Dick's hat band. He has no insurance policy at all and won't leave ten cents to his heirs when he dies." "How are you, Mr. Adamson? Did you enjoy Brother Hastings' sermon?" Miss Maymie said with a smile then nudged Phillis, "I'm positive he's a tippler. Did you notice his nose?" "My goodness, do you hear that high-pitched voice? That's Evelyn Perkins, the old maid who teaches fifth grade at Harvard Elementary. Heaven knows why she bought a life insurance policy, not that I'm knocking it."

Once she finished her greetings, Miss Maymie steered Phillis out the door and back to the car. As they whizzed up the Boulevard and turned into her driveway, Miss Maymie asked Phillis, "Do you get it? You now see why churchgoing is important. These parishioners are my clients and seeing them every Sunday cements our business relationship."

Phillis inquired, "What about St. Andrew's Episcopal Church on Yale Street? I met a man named Fred Dexter there yesterday. He invited me to their service."

"Well, that's a fine congregation," Miss Maymie said, "Just one problem for me. Old Man Cooley holds up one corner of that church. If any member needs insurance, they're going to buy it from him. Besides, their service begins at eleven. That's too late. You'd waste half the day before you got outta there. I'm sticking with the Methodists."

Miss Maymie laughed heartily as she joked, "You'd have gotten a wet sermon at St. Andrew's. Everyone knows about Whiskeypalians. If you see four Episcopalians together, there's always a *fifth*. Not that I mind a drink or two in my home. For socializing. Most of the time I'm a dry. The Methodist service starts at nine," she continued, "which means you're done and ready for other work by ten-fifteen. I generally spend the rest of my day downtown, going over paperwork and planning the coming week. Today, I'm going meet with the badge committee before welcoming special guests for an early supper at five. Plan to be there."

With that, Miss Maymie pulled the key from the ignition switch and got out of the car. Smiling broadly, she linked arms with Phillis as they walked to the house. Despite her landlady's lecture, she decided St. Andrew's and Mr. Dexter's kindly invitation sounded much better than Grace. That is, if she decided she needed a church.

For the life of her, Phillis could not figure Maymie Banion out. She never spoke of yesterday's argument but certainly voiced no apology for accusing Phillis of wasting her time by aspiring to write news stories. This morning she dragged Phillis to church for a lesson on what she considered the rules of business. Since her objection to journalism seemed to hinge on the low salary, Phillis suspected money was the only God worshipped by Maymie Banion. She shuddered to think of Maymie as being of Horace Wilkerson's ilk.

Climbing the stairs to her room, Phillis realized Brother Hastings' sermon would provide her with inspiration for an article on the dry's' viewpoint and their plan of action. First, she would write her Me-Too article.

She removed her typewriter from its case and set it on the library table. Patting its fire engine red metal, she settled down to reproduce her conversation with Juanita at the Yale Street drugstore. Using the title, "Houston Women's Triumphant 'Me Too' Buttons," Phillis began to describe their efforts to support the upcoming convention. She hoped this would be a woman's piece satisfying Amon Carter's requirements. So what if it described Phillis's fried-egg sandwich instead of a square of tomato aspic.

As she finished, a soft tap interrupted her typing. She opened the door, and Olivia Jones stood framed by a shaft of light from the windows above. No nurse's uniform. Instead, the strikingly beautiful young woman wore a simple white voile frock and some delicate floral scent.

As Phillis started to say "hello," Olivia put her finger to her lips and entered Phillis's room, quietly closing the door behind her. "Finally finding time to write," she said, noticing the typewriter and notepad. "Am I bothering you?"

Phillis waved her hand dismissively. "Almost through with my first article. Wish me luck sending it on the telegraph machine tomorrow."

"I came to apologize for Mrs. Hinkle," Olivia blurted out.

"That's okay. Josie told me this morning that you are her 'favored person.' You apparently found the key to her heart."

Phillis offered Olivia her chair as she perched on the bed.

"Not really." Olivia replied. "I just know her history. This used to be Mrs. Hinkle's home. When her husband died, all he left were debts. Miss Maymie bought the mortgage and hired the desperate woman as her housekeeper. Hinkle's still sore she's not lady of the house."

"That explains a lot. Thanks for filling me in." Phillis rolled her eyes trying to work up some sympathy for the widow's sad plight. "May I ask you something personal?"

Olivia nodded, looking surprised.

"Why are you in nursing school?" Phillis blurted out. "With your looks and that silky voice of yours. I'm thinking Hollywood. The new 'talkies' would fight for you, and I'll bet the cameras would love you."

Olivia's eyes widened. "How did you know?"

"Know what?"

"How did you know I want to be in the theater? "Emptying smelly bedpans, nasty old nurses, and arrogant doctors. Everything about the field of medicine is dreadful."

Phillis asked. "Isn't your father a doctor?"

"Yes. And that's the root of the problem. As a child, all I could think of was following in his footsteps."

"But you saw yourself as a doctor, never a nurse," she interrupted her with a smile.

Olivia nodded. "Not many female doctors. Still, I did imagine working beside my father. Isn't that crazy? How did you guess?" Phillis shrugged.

Wringing her hands, the young woman continued, "Anyway, Father wouldn't hear of it. Instead, he enrolled me in the nursing school here at Baptist Sanitarium and Hospital. Louisiana schools are not so good, according to him. As he put me on the bus for Houston, he said, 'Olivia, the subject is closed. You'll make a fine nurse. How could you ever have thought you were smart enough to be a doctor?'"

"It's because you are his daughter instead of his son." Phillis shook her head. "The old and the new. The classic battle we're still fighting. You and I are right in the middle of this change. We argued if they let us vote, we could be better wives and mothers. That wasn't the goal at all. It was all a big lie." Phillis rubbed her finger over the quilt coverlet and thought of her lie to Amon Carter. "What we really wanted was the power to control our own lives."

Olivia smile, "I heard your conversation with Miss Banion yesterday. I couldn't believe she was so ugly. I was glad you stood up to her."

"She disgusts me. I've admired her for so many years, but now I learn all she thinks about is money. You should have seen her at church today." Phillis rolled her eyes.

"Okay, but let me tell you, money's important. A woman has got to have her own money to do what she wants." Olivia took a deep breath, "I'm putting as much as I can aside," she said. "Soon as I have enough for a train ticket and some living expenses, I'm headed north."

"North?"

Olivia explained, "Not west. My dream is New York City. It's a better place for me."

"New York City," Phillis repeated. "That's funny. It's my goal too. Every journalist in America wants to live there. You won't regret not trying for medical school?"

"I worshipped my father," Olivia responded. "I was probably just trying to get his attention. These months at the hospital opened my eyes. I'm not cut out for medicine."

"I hope you aren't leaving right away."

"No, it'll take me at least six months. I'm going to ask for overtime so I can fill my piggy bank."

Olivia heard Josie's dinner bell and stood up. "Time for Sunday dinner," she smiled. "Let's go see who's on Miss Maymie's guest list this week."

Phillis felt a closeness to Olivia. She was another woman with dreams. "Let's talk again," she whispered to Olivia as they entered the dining room.

Voices fell silent as all eyes focused on the two young women whose looks were so different. Olivia, slight of stature, with dark hair and eyes, was a graceful nymph. Though, Phillis, tall and thin, ginger-haired and flashing brown eyes was not a "looker." Like Olivia, she possessed "presence."

As they slid into the empty chairs, two of Miss Maymie's male guests rose. Phillis noticed that the man to her left remained seated, busily writing on a pocket-sized notepad.

"These are my two boarders, Olivia Jones and Phillis Flanagan," Maymie Banion announced to her guests, and then clamped her hand on the shoulder of the white-haired man sitting on her right.

The portly older gentleman dressed in crisp white linen smiled and looked
around the table. "I'm Clayton Mansfield," he said with a gravelly Texas drawl. "I'm honored to be here and happy to meet you both."

Maymie explained, "Judge Mansfield is my gentleman caller."

Phillis stifled a giggle. No one else batted an eye.

Miss Maymie turned to her left. "This is Teddy," she said as Phillis recognized the youth who rushed past her on the porch as she arrived yesterday. Although he didn't look old enough to shave, much less drink alcohol, Phillis assumed that the two bootleg liquor bottles sitting in the middle of the table were his contribution.

Sitting to Teddy's left was a young woman with sleek bobbed hair and a carefully painted face wearing a shimmering red dress that matched her Clara Bow lips. Teddy caught Phillis's eye and pointed to his dinner partner. "Estelle," he announced. She fluttered her eyelashes as a greeting and waved her cocktail.

Miss Banion introduced the man on Phillis's left, whose notebook protruded from his jacket breast pocket. "Please welcome my friend, Stanley Staples, a reporter for the *Houston Press*. Maybe he'll help you, Phillis," she pointedly remarked. "Sort of show you the ropes. He's a respected journalist who has his own column. Everyone in Houston reads him."

Phillis snorted at the title, "respected journalist" considering Miss Banion's comments yesterday. Perhaps Mr. Staples was invited as another peace offering from her landlady or was his presence proof that she only objected to female journalists. More than likely, it was the latter, but also, she was sure Mr. Staples was not working for $12.00 a week.

He wore an ill-fitting brown suit that showed its age and a loosened tie with food spots. A good haircut would help. Giving Phillis only the briefest of glances, he turned his attention to Olivia. Phillis doubted she would ever get any help from him.

Sitting at the foot of the table opposite Miss Maymie was the indomitable housekeeper, Della Hinkle, who had exchanged her long black day dress for a similarly styled navy-blue bombazine that was probably as old as Phillis. Its long sleeves and high neck made Phillis itch. How could this woman breathe?

Pinned under Mrs. Hinkle's chin was a large white cameo brooch set in a gold bezel with the stern image of a Roman general in raised relief. On her right hand she wore a handsome garnet ring, the center stone encircled by seed pearls. Her hair was still drawn back in a severe bun, but her cheeks and mouth were suspiciously pink, and her face heavily dusted with powder.

Miss Maymie rang the dinner bell and Josie marched in carrying a turkey-sized platter of fried chicken. Rather than serving the guests, she placed the dish in the center of the table and turned back to the kitchen, immediately reappearing with two oversized serving bowls, which she placed on both sides of the platter.

Miss Maymie explained, "We eat family style here since this is officially a boarding house, folks, so help yourselves."

The guests did so, and the room quieted as the diners went to work on Josie's chicken and vegetables. Looking around the table approvingly, Miss Maymie beamed and called out, "Josie, come in and take a bow."

The cook reappeared and smiled as she surveyed the happy faces.

Suddenly emitting a whoop, she ran for the kitchen and rushed back with a basket of biscuits. "I 'bout forgot the bread," she confessed, putting a hand to her mouth. Miss Maymie waved indulgently as she reached for a biscuit and took another for the judge's plate before passing the basket to her guests.

Teddy circled the table filling the diners' glasses with their alcoholic preference, except for Mrs. Hinkle who held her hand on top of her glass as she turned to Phillis and asked, "Miss Flanagan, your Dallas County sheriff arrested over eleven-hundred bootleggers last year?" Her voice booming to ensure everyone present heard this information. Phillis froze for a moment before continuing to sip her bourbon as she tried to think of a response.

Clayton Mansfield inquired mildly, "Mrs. Hinkle, you are obviously one of the dry's."

"I certainly am, Judge Mansfield. Happily, I can report thirty-one dry organizations will be headquartered at the Rice Hotel for the upcoming convention." She proudly eyed the other diners to see their response. Her face fell at their bored expressions.

Determined to work up some interest, she continued, "Yessiree, we'll do our best to make sure this wet Yankee doesn't become the Democratic candidate for president. I'm proud to say our Governor Moody is leading us against this New York Papist. I only wish Mr. Moody had allowed his name to be presented as a nominee for president."

"Ah, yes. I understand he's now called the redheaded 'Dry Moses,'" Judge Mansfield replied as he ran a finger around the edge of his glass and shook his head. "Americans never wanted Prohibition."

Before Mrs. Hinkle could object to his statement, Teddy's flapper girlfriend broke in. "My mother's one of the dry's," she cooed. "She would have a fit if she saw me now with this Pink Lady my sweetie mixed for me. It's all too silly.

Judge Mansfield barked, "Young lady, it's much worse than silly. When the WCTU and the Anti-Saloon League terrorized the U.S. Congress, the result was our government's most recent mistake." He took a sip of his drink then held up his glass. "Here's to the Eighteenth Amendment, the answer to every criminal's prayers. We outlawed the legal business of selling alcohol and lined the bootleggers' pockets."

Estelle giggled and added. "Nobody likes being told what to do, especially by do-gooders." She eyed Della Hinkle. "Even Irving Berlin says so. His new song, 'You Can't Make Your Shimmy Shake on Tea' has us all dancing." She patted Teddy's sleeve and circled her finger in the air.

Mrs. Hinkle retorted, "I have something to say to you, Miss." She glared at the young flapper. "I'll be voting dry till the cows came home and that's that. Since I have no interest in dancing with bob-haired flappers, drinking tea will suit me just fine."

"Jeez Louise," Phillis heard Stanley Staples mutter under his breath, "Better listen to her, people. Thousands of Democrats are coming to Houston to choose a candidate the South won't vote for."

He raised his glass of Scotch, "A toast to Al Smith, a Roman Catholic, an avowed wet, and a Tammany Hall flunky." Looking each person at the table in the eye, he continued, "He'll win the nomination, but I predict Texas will go Republican for the first time in more than sixty years. And so will the other southern states."

"Mr. Staples, that's presumptuous and premature," Phillis spoke firmly. "You don't think Smith can carry enough states to win the presidency?"

He shook his head.

"What about Prohibition?" she asked.

"We're in for four more years of the dry's, if not longer," Staples said. "You don't have to believe me. You can read Will Rogers. His column appears in six hundred newspapers. Only one paper carries mine. He claims the Eighteenth Amendment divided our country into three groups: 'wets, dry's, and hypocrites.'" He looked around the table again, singling out Mrs. Hinkle. "To the dry's," he toasted, "or, as Rogers says, 'We wish they would get so perfect, the Lord would call them away from this earth up into heaven. Otherwise, we're stuck with this so-called 'Noble Experiment.'"

Hinkle, missing Stanley's sarcasm, smiled broadly and called to Josie, "Please serve the strawberry ice cream now."

Miss Maymie nodded agreement, saying, "Yes, and let's please change the subject."

Judge Mansfield gave her a smile and said, "Okey dokey, sweetheart. Let's switch to Will Horwitz. He's always good for some fun. Y'all know what he's done now?" he asked.

When no one answered, he said, "He's shipped in fifty donkeys for the convention. Brought them by Southern Pacific rail car from west Texas. Every state delegation is getting one with a note telling them this will be their transportation to Sam Houston Hall."

Teddy piped up, "Yeah, and they might get a kick out of it too."

Even Mrs. Hinkle laughed for the first time this evening.

Maymie Banion looked around the table and suggested, "Shall we retire to the front parlor for a little entertainment."

As Phillis moved along with the others, Stanley Staples stopped in the hallway to pluck his disreputable-looking brown fedora from row of hooks. With a tip of his hat, he said, "Thanks for the great chow. You'll for sure keep me and your gentleman caller coming back for more."

"Shaking the Blues Away" burbled from the Sears Silvertone Record Player as Staples put his hand on Phillis's arm and whispered, "Let's slip out onto the porch and have a cigarette."

Phillis was flabbergasted. The man hardly spoke to her all evening.

Once they were settled on the porch swing, Stanley grinned and said, "I got you here under false pretenses. My father died from smoking. I don't touch coffin nails. Feel free to light up. I'm the only reporter I know who doesn't."

Phillis laughed out loud. "I have chronic asthma," she confessed. "I'm happy to have a conversation without listening to Della Hinkle's views. She's awful."

Their eyes met as they laughed together, enjoying the joke while rocking gently in the dim light. Phillis wondered if this acerbic journalist knew the romantic implications of a couple sitting together on a front porch swing. She certainly was not going to bring it up, preferring instead the symphony of sounds — crickets, cicadas, and the jazzy notes from the Victrola floated in the air.

"Judging from the bourbon you were swigging in there, you must be one of the few southern women rooting for Al Smith," Staples finally said. "Your WCTU members are working hard to defeat him."

"Wait a minute," she snapped, irritated he had broken her mood. "WCTU is not even five percent of the nation's twenty-million registered women voters. Look it up, Mr. Staples. I despise the WCTU, mainly because of their unholy alliance with the KKK. I would never join their organization even if I were a teetotaler. Contrary to your prediction, I strongly believe Al Smith will win the nomination and become our next president."

He grinned roguishly and asked, "Care to put any money on that?"

When Phillis laughed and shook her head, "No?" Staples said, "Shucks, I hate to take filthy lucre from a lady. But, maybe in this case."

Turning to look at him, she said, "Mrs. Hinkle made me so angry tonight I had to sit on my hands to keep from calling her down."

"I know Della," Staples said, looking back at her, "and she's the biggest hypocrite of all."

"What?" Phillis exclaimed. "You have grounds for that accusation?"

"Lean close to her sometime when she's been in her room for a while," Stanley winked. "Come on now, Miss Flanagan. Have you ever known a dry German?"

"Why did you come to Houston for the convention?" he asked abruptly. "Is Fort Worth that boring?"

"I told you. I'm on assignment for the *Star-Telegram*," she replied. "Amon Carter sent me here."

"He's paid for you to come for the convention?"

Phillis replied stiffly, "I did not say he paid for my train fare. He's paying my salary."

"Okay. He's letting you join the press corps as his representative?"

"Well, not exactly. I'm supposed to write articles for women."

"Oh. No news stories. Just the usual female stuff, luncheons and tea parties."

"Well, yes," she said before taking a chance and telling him the truth. "Call me crazy, but I know I will write human-interest stories, if not news stories, that will find their way into print. I heard one yesterday at the Yale Street drugstore."

He eyed her incredulously. "From what I've heard about your boss," Staples said, "you have a better chance of being struck by lightning, unless it is, pardon the expression, a sob sister story." He laughed as Phillis bristled at this insult.

"I'm not exactly following his orders," she said. "You might call it taking a few liberties."

"That's called playing with fire, Miss Flanagan," Staples growled. "Are you really going to cross that man? You know he's going to be here. How are you gonna stay out of his way?"

"My stories will be so good he'll want to publish them," Phillis retorted.

Suddenly remembering the paper still rolled into her typewriter platen, she looked at Staples and smiled. "I've enjoyed meeting you this evening, Mr. Staples. Can I count on you to throw some bones my way? I would be awfully grateful."

"Sure, kid," Staples answered, realizing their conversation was over. "See you around."

As they rose from the swing, he joked, "Don't take any wooden nickels."

Phillis watched him walk off into the night. *He does have a very nice smile. His face crinkles when he laughs and his eyes light up. They're the color of sherry.* She passed the dancers still going full swing as she climbed the stairs to her room.

STANLEY FOUND HIMSELF WHISTLING "Fascinating Rhythm" as he ambled down Eighteenth Avenue reflecting on this woman he'd met. Phillis Flanagan. A contradiction. Too much bite to be what most men would call a "sweetheart." Too smart to be a flapper. Doggone it, he meant to tease her about why she did not have bobbed hair.

Her outsmarting Amon Carter was foolishness, and he didn't, for a second, believe she'd ever written a news story, although he suspected she was good enough to do it. Stanley wasn't a man who wasted his time helping dames who were 'wanna-be' reporters. Still, he hoped she could get at least one story published.

As he climbed the stairs to his garage apartment, he thought, "She's a summer breeze. She's different. She's fun."

CHAPTER SEVEN

I believe we have been on the front pages of a thousand newspapers a day since we got the convention. We can not imagine, we can not conceive, the benefits in advertising we have obtained from securing this convention.

Jesse H. Jones
Houston Chronicle
June 10, 1928

Monday, June 18, 1928

PHILLIS OPENED ONE EYE WHEN SHE HEARD Charlie's truck. This was the advantage or disadvantage, she supposed, of having the room closest to the driveway. Though not quite awake, she knew the significance of this day. It was Monday, her first real workday in Houston. If she were still in Fort Worth, she would already be headed for the *Star-Telegram* offices. Not today. No regular office hours meant she got to plan her own day. How was that going to work?

The Rice Hotel telegraph office would be her first stop this morning. After she wired her article to Fort Worth, she needed to read all three local papers to decide her approach to Prohibition.

Nothing about her job over the last two years had prepared her for this. Grinding out obits and covering women's teas provided little training for writing about this convention.

Saturday's conversation with the waitress wearing a Me-Too button at the Yale Street drugstore was a lucky break. Phillis, generally, did not believe in luck. Her mother always said "luck" was a very good word if you put a "p" in front of it.

Dressing hurriedly in the navy skirt and pink blouse she had worn to church yesterday, Phillis tugged a brush through her hair, put on her tan cloche and powdered her nose. She straightened her room, made her bed, and placed her article in a white envelope. According to Miss Maymie, breakfast was served until nine a.m. When she arrived in the kitchen, she was delighted to smell coffee and see Josie and Olivia.

"You look a whole lot more awake than I do," Phillis told Olivia, noting the nurse's crisp white uniform, and smoothly arranged hair.

"Good morning, Josie," she greeted the cook as she slid into a chair at the kitchen table. "Have you seen Mrs. Hinkle or Miss Maymie this morning?"

"Oh, yessum," Josie said. "They both been here and left. Miss Banion rumbled out of here in her Packard and Charlie's carrying Mrs. Hinkle to the farmer's market in the truck."

"Great," Phillis said. "We can visit. What did y'all think about last night's dinner?"

"The usual Banion style of entertaining," Olivia replied as she methodically buttered a piece of toast. "Josie, your fried chicken was terrific."

"Aside from that," she told Phillis, "it was the same old political talk. Teddy and Estelle's lovey-dovey relationship amused me. He brings a different girl here every week. This one was a real Dumb Dora, even for Teddy. So," she concluded, taking a bite of her toast, "I found the rest of the dinner quite boring. I have no interest in politics. Seldom bother to vote."

"Why?"

"Seems like a whole lot of red-faced men screaming and yelling about farmers and teapots and Tammany tigers, and women trying to bully men into paying attention to them," Olivia replied.

Phillis laughed, "Okay, okay. I get your point even if I don't agree with it. Politics fascinate me. So, let's change the subject. Tell me about Teddy. He's Miss Banion's nephew, isn't he?"

"He calls her 'Aunt Maymie,'" Olivia said, "but sometimes he calls her 'Mom.' It's some sort of secret why she took him in. He has lots of privileges for a nephew. I remember when she bought him that Ford last fall."

Phillis nodded her agreement. "Miss Maymie boasted about enrolling him in the new junior college after telling me my attending college had been a waste of my time." She reached for the cream pitcher.

"Obviously, she meant a waste of time just for women. Teddy told me last night at dinner that he breezed through last semester, confessing that three of his professors were students at Rice Institute." She laughed, remembering the conversation. "He wants to major in engineering because he likes to work on his fliver."

"Girls. Girls," Josie piped up. "Don't be so hard on him. Charlie says he's just slow tasseling out."

"Well, he's gonna be a page at the convention," Olivia said, explaining to Phillis. "He does make a good errand boy. Always picks up the bootleg stuff for Miss Banion."

"Who's an errand boy? You talking about me, Olivia?"

Teddy surprised all three women who did a double take when they saw him dressed in a suit and tie at eight o'clock in the morning.

"Whatcha got for breakfast this morning, Josie?" he asked the cook, joining the two women at the kitchen table. "I don't smell any bacon or eggs and you know I don't like cold cereal. Have you got any cinnamon buns?"

"No, Mr. Teddy," huffed Josie. "And you know I cook a hot breakfast only on Tuesday and Thursday. Your aunt's rule. Don't be telling me I have to fix a special breakfast for you."

"Sorry. Sorry, Josie," Teddy apologized. "Never mind. I'll eat downtown."

"What are you up so early for?" Olivia asked him with a smile. "It's not noon yet."

"That's not nice," Teddy blushed. "I've got convention business to attend to. This morning there's a nine-o'clock meeting for ushers and pages and I will be there on time." With that, he stood up, "Sorry not to stay and visit with you ladies. Gotta go." And he left the kitchen as quickly as he came.

The women laughed. Olivia and Phillis resumed eating while Josie refilled their coffee cups and said, "Miss Maymie's sure gonna be pleased when I tell her he's up early this mornin'."

Thanking Josie for breakfast, both women left to go their separate ways.

BY 8:45 A.M. THE DARK GREEN STREETCAR was crammed with passengers. The conductor let her board and Phillis grabbed the leather strap, expecting to stand. Surprisingly, an older woman whose marcel waves would have made any Hollywood star proud moved her satchel to the floor and motioned Phillis to the empty seat beside her. Introducing herself as Mrs. Rumsfeld, she pointed to Phillis's hat. "My dear, you're certainly brave to wear that wool cloche. You'd best look for a cool straw one. I cannot imagine what you Yankees are thinking coming all this way south at the end of June and expecting the cool balmy weather you enjoy up north. You'll be shelling out plenty of coins for new clothing by the time the convention begins."

"Yes, ma'am, I'm sure you're right. What sort of hats do you favor?" she asked, looking pointedly at the woman's bare head.

"I have a soft straw cloche in my bag. I needed to let my waves dry before I put it on," the woman patted her curls.

Phillis was not about to wear her lovely new straw hat to town every day and her cloche was the only other one she had.

"Where should I go to replace my inappropriate wardrobe?"

"Well, Foley Brothers, of course, unless you have money to burn." Her tone of voice indicated that she doubted Phillis fell into this category.

"Thanks for that advice, Mrs. Rumsfeld," Phillis said politely before changing the subject. "Do you subscribe to the morning newspaper?"

Observing Mrs. Rumsfeld's startled expression, Phillis quickly explained, "My name is Phillis Flanagan. I'm here from Fort Worth to cover the convention for the *Star-Telegram.*"

She looked around the car for a different seat. Next time I'll remain standing, she decided.

"Well, who would have thought it?" said Mrs. Rumsfeld, with a big smile on her face. "Here I am sitting by a fellow reporter. I'm Gladys Rumsfeld, dear," she said, "social editor of the *Post-Dispatch* newspaper. Did you say you write for Amon Carter's paper?"

"Yes," replied Phillis, obviously caught off guard, "I seldom write society news."

"How do you stand working for him," Mrs. Rumsfeld exclaimed. "I've heard stories about the awful things he does. My editor's the sweetest man I know. He lets me write anything I want about social goings on, as long as I spell everyone's name correctly."

"Don't you get tired of writing about clothes and food and table decorations?"

"Of course not, dear, I love every detail. I've taught myself about ladies' wardrobes, about their hats and gloves, how to tell one fabric from another. Didn't I spot your felt hat right off?" she asked with a smile. "And I keep a notebook of 'who's who' in Houston because if I forget to list any of the *Mesdames* who are at a party, my name is mud. Titles are also important. For instance, no social editor accidentally calls Florence Sterling 'Mrs.' if she wants to stay on the payroll. I bet it's the same in Fort Worth."

She gave Phillis a sideways glance. "Now that I think about it, isn't it sort of a cow town? Dallas is the place. Best parties, richest people."

"It's lucky my boss isn't on this trolley," she said. "To him 'Dallas' is a dirty word. He takes a sack lunch if he's going 'over there' because their restaurants don't serve enough steak and potatoes. Fort Worth is definitely a cow town. After his visit to the two cities, Damon Runyon wrote, 'in Dallas, the women wear high heels; in Fort Worth, the men do.'" Phillis looked down and tucked her low-heeled brown oxfords out of sight before Gladys glimpsed their shabbiness.

Mrs. Rumsfeld laughed, "Is Damon Runyon someone I should know?"

Phillis lifted her eyebrows and continued, "I can write human-interest stories if they slam Dallas. I got an article published about a bunch of Dallas bootleggers who were jailed when they tried to sell their booze to a sheriff. By the way, I'm riding downtown to the *Post-Dispatch* to find Bess Scott. You probably know her."

"Of course, I do," Mrs. Rumsfeld replied. "She writes for the *Press* now. And, please, call me 'Gladys.' How do you know Bess?"

"Thank you, Gladys," Phillis said politely before confessing, "Bess is a fellow Baylor alum. Ahead of me by a few years. I never met her."

"My desk used to be right next to hers," Gladys said. "When you see her, say 'hello' for me and ask her to tell you about her friend Clark Gable."

"Clark Gable? How in the world does she know him?"

"She tells the story best," Gladys grinned and dismissed the subject with a wave of her hand.

WHEN PHILLIS ARRIVED AT THE RICE, the line for using the telegraph was twenty feet long. Every visiting journalist was waiting to send in his copy. As she stood waiting impatiently, the nicest bellhop Phillis ever met approached her and whispered, "The Lamar Hotel has the shortest line, Miss." He grinned and saluted her when she handed him a nickel.

It was only five blocks to the Lamar Hotel, but the minute she entered the doors, it hit her. The Lamar Hotel! Bradley Nicholson and Reginald Bludworth were staying here.

To heck with it. Might as well let it happen. Can't hide from them for the next twelve days. Keeping out of Amon Carter's sight is hard enough." Yet when she heard Bradley's familiar voice call her name, her stomach dropped to her toes.

Wheeling around, she pasted on her brightest smile. "My, my," she said. "It's the famous New York journalist, Bradley Nicholson?" She extended her hand.

Brad brushed her hand aside, grabbed Phillis around the waist, and pulled her towards him. "You're a sight for sore eyes, Scottie," he exclaimed, hugging her, "and, my, don't you look swell!"

Letting her go, he called out, "Reggie, come here and see who I found."

Remembering how quickly she had dressed only an hour ago, Phillis knew exactly how she looked, and "swell" was not the adjective she would have used.

Phillis greeted her train buddy with more enthusiasm than she felt. "Hello, Reggie."

As he shook her extended hand, Phillis said, "Hurry up and tell me how you like Houston. I'm dying to know."

"The weather's hell, to be quite frank," he replied. "But, we're treated like royalty. Brad agrees with me, don't you, that we've never met such nice folks."

Brad nodded as the two young men began steering Phillis toward the hotel's café. "Even the mounted policemen, decked out in brand-new uniforms, act like they're getting a huge kick out of their job," Reggie enthused. "Nothing like our New York cops."

"Let's all have a cup of coffee," Brad suggested. "Maybe even some ham and eggs?"

A hostess greeted the trio as Reggie asked Phillis if she had been to this new coffee shop that Jesse Jones, the hotel's owner, had just opened for the convention visitors.

"Sorry, Reggie," she replied as she turned back toward the lobby. "I'm working, remember? I only came to this hotel to send an article to my editor in Fort Worth. Where's the telegraph office located?"

"I thought you came to see us," Reggie frowned, ignoring the hostess. "If it's only the telegraph office you want, I think it's over there in the corner." He pointed to the back of the lobby. "Really not sure since we haven't used it. After you take care of your business, come back and join us for breakfast, or at least a cup of java."

Phillis hesitated, trying to come up with a plausible excuse to refuse him before remembering these two guys were contacts. They could introduce her to some of the East-Coast notables.

"Will do," she agreed brightly. "First things first." As she turned away, Brad familiarly patted her shoulder before following Reggie and the hostess into the hotel's coffee shop.

As the Rice Hotel's bellhop promised, there was no line at this hotel's telegraph office, and when Phillis came back to the coffee shop, she found Brad and Reggie digging into a stack of pancakes swimming in syrup and butter. A waitress hurried over as she joined their table and took her order for coffee and toast. "Do you want it medium or well toasted, miss?" she asked Phillis. "We have a wonderful new electric toaster. It's the best one in town."

Phillis smiled and said "medium." As she placed her napkin in her lap, she realized that both guys were wolfing down pancakes, napkins tucked under their chins and elbows on the table. Their side of the table was a sticky mess. Were these New York table manners? Where was Emily Post?

"What syrup have you slathered on your pancakes that you can't get enough of?" Phillis asked, breaking her toast into dainty pieces and buttering only one bite at a time.

"The waitress called it cane syrup. Comes from sugar cane," Brad replied, wiping his mouth.

"Doesn't taste a thing like our maple syrup," agreed Reggie between bites. "If I could find a gal that could cook like this, I'd already be married."

Phillis laughed. "The syrup's probably from Louisiana," she explained. "I guess it hasn't traveled north of the Mason-Dixon." Nibbling her bread, she asked them, "You found any stories yet?"

"No. We're busy having fun," Reggie replied. "Houston is dressed to the nines with bells and whistles on every corner. Last night we went to a speakeasy called 'End of Main.'"

Brad frowned, shaking his finger at Reggie. "We stayed out a little past our bedtime," then added, drily, "One or two fascinating distractions."

Reggie happily elaborated, "Yeah, a girl dressed in red and blue sequins and not much else. We bought her drinks all night while she waited to perform. By the time she finally got on stage, we were in no condition to appreciate her dancing." He watched gleefully as Brad's face reddened. "As much as you drank, it's no wonder you kept yelling, 'Hot Dog.'" Reggie laughed, drawing the attention of guests sitting at three other tables. "Phillis, you should have seen your sweetheart, tossing 'em back."

"Doesn't sound like fun to me," Phillis replied sarcastically. "As long as you didn't get sick or go blind, it was a successful speakeasy evening."

"Have you been to the Rice Roof?" Brad asked, realizing it was time to change the subject.

Phillis raised her eyebrows, "Don't tell me there's a speakeasy in the Rice Hotel?"

Brad chuckled. "Not officially," he said. "Houston's elite keeps their liquor stored at the Rice Hotel. It's high-class, not like the joint we visited last night." He leaned over toward her. "What do you say, sweetheart?" he asked. "Let's go."

"Tonight?" she asked, ignoring the endearment. "So sorry. I'll have to take a raincheck."

"That's exactly where the three of us must go tonight," Reggie said, refusing to accept her answer. "You and Brad need to get reacquainted. We have no time for rainchecks. I insist."

"I'll introduce you to Allen Peden if you come," Brad coaxed.

"Who's he?" Phillis inquired sarcastically. "Another friend from New York?"

"Editor and owner of the *Houston Gargoyle* magazine," Brad replied seriously. "This town's answer to Harold Ross's *New Yorker*. He was my classmate at Princeton. Heck of a nice guy. You'll like him."

Phillis remembered Peden's publication laying on Maymie Banion's parlor table. It did indeed resemble Ross's *New Yorker*. She had wondered at the time if Houstonians were as addicted to their weekly as New Yorkers were to theirs.

"Okay," she agreed. *Allen Peden better be a good contact if I waste an evening with these two lounge lizards.* "What time do I need to arrive at the Rice Hotel? I'm not going to one of those parties that doesn't begin until midnight."

"We'll see you at eight on the roof of the Rice," Brad said, holding her hand much too long for Phillis's comfort.

PHILLIS FOUND HER WAY TO THE *Houston Press* office. Both Bess Scott and Stanley Staples were out. Why hadn't Stanley mentioned Bess last night, she wondered.

A stumpy little man dressed in a checked suit suggested, "Check Billy McKinnon's café about noon. You might catch both there."

Hustling back to the trolley, Phillis, by this time drowning in perspiration, jerked her hat off as she rode back to Texas Avenue. The cafe was nothing but a sliver wedged in between a department store and the Milby Hotel, McKinnon's was the café every Houston reporter favored.

The first thing she heard when she entered was, "Hey, Carrot Head! Come on over."

Stanley Staples was standing up, beckoning to her. This was hardly the welcome she expected.

"My hair is not orange," Phillis said, glaring at him as he pulled out a chair and motioned her to join him and an attractive woman.

"I like you better without your hat. It hides your curls," Staples said as she sat down. She gave him a hard look. *I barely know this man. I cannot believe he has the cheek to make references to my hair.*

He turned to his companion. "Here's an important journalist you need to meet. Bess, meet Phillis Flanagan. Phillis — Bess Scott."

Stanley beamed at both women as he sat down, tilted his chair back, and put his hands in his pockets.

"I'm glad to meet you, Phillis," Bess Scott said sincerely. "Welcome to Houston where female reporters, including visiting members of the press, are a close-knit family regardless of who signs our paychecks."

Scott's kind words helped Phillis calm down. "I followed behind you at Baylor, Miss Scott. I was class of '24."

"Great college. Proud I went there. And, please, call me 'Bess.'"

As a waitress approached to take Phillis's order, Stanley's chair hit the floor with a bang. "Can't believe I'm sitting here having lunch with two college girls. Only thing I graduated from was the school of hard knocks. Whole bunch more of you educated females coming for the convention or so I've read. Wonder how many women covered the 1924 convention at Madison Square Garden?"

"Don't know," Bess replied as she looked at Phillis who shook her head after telling the waitress she wanted a ham sandwich.

"I think Ruth Finney's coming from Washington, D.C. She's a front-page reporter. Got her break in Sacramento when forty-seven miners were trapped underground."

Stanley broke in. "Those articles should have won her a Pulitzer. She wasn't even nominated."

"I agree," said Bess, "but this freed her to write only news stories. She swears it only takes one scoop. If you are ready." Turning to Phillis, she added. "She's having a lifetime of adventure."

The waitress brought Phillis her sandwich. It sat untouched as she hung on Bess Scott's words. "Finney's writing for the *Christian Science Monitor* during her stay in Houston, along with Mary Roberts Rinehart who says she will be looking for ideas. Rinehart's written thirty novels, Broadway plays, short stories and lots of articles for magazines."

"I wonder what she'll think of Houston?" Phillis asked. "I've read some of her mystery novels," she said. "The Miss Pinkerton's. I'd love to see one of her plays on Broadway. Heck," she told Bess, laughing, "I wish I could see any play on Broadway. I've never been north of Dallas."

Bess replied. "She's quite a pessimist about women in politics.

According to her, both the Democrats and Republicans only give us the dirty work. Despite all the women coming for this convention, she insists politics is still the men's game."

"I keep hearing that. Do you agree with her?"

"Of course," Bess said. "Nothing's gonna change till we have a woman in the White House. Who knows how close that is?"

Phillis slowly shook her head and grimaced as Stanley laughed out loud. "What's so funny," Phillis asked.

"Oh, just the thought of interviewing a 'Madam President.'"

"Well, get ready, buster, because that's what's coming," Bess replied. She leaned toward Phillis, "I was told, Finney and Rinehart are staying at the new Warwick Hotel waiting for their friend Alice Roosevelt Longworth to arrive."

"That's an interesting threesome," Stanley commented, trying to snag the women's attention. "A reporter told me Mrs. Longworth comes to all of the conventions just to try out different golf courses. She's mad about the sport. Are you gals going to compete with us men in everything?"

Phillis glared at him and returned to Finney's promise. "Only one scoop?" she asked Bess. "I've been at the *Star* for two years and my only successes are three news stories buried on the back page."

"At least you've learned patience," Stanley teased. "A lot of you quit and go back to school teaching."

"I'll never do that," Phillis asserted, exchanging a knowing look with Bess. "Will women get any of the big stories?"

"Who knows?" Stanley said unsympathetically. "Never thought *The Emporia's* William Allen White, H. L. Mencken and Damon Runyon would be hanging out in Houston. Doesn't get any ritzier than that."

Stanley tilted back in his chair again. "Most of the guys are already here," he added, his eyes twinkling, "on the links."

"Playing golf?" Phillis looked incredulous.

"The two-week break between conventions wasn't long enough for a trip back to their homes, so they just came down to Houston early, 'looking for action.'" Stanley cocked his head, "Playing golf at the Houston Country Club or catching some sun in Galveston."

Bess complained, "Local editors are gushing about all the celebrity reporters they'll be publishing once the convention begins. You'll enjoy rubbing elbows with these legends, Stanley, since you have your own column. The rest of us, like Phillis and I, will be fighting for space."

"It's only for two weeks, Bess," Stanley said, sitting up. "In the meantime," he grinned, looking at both women, "Andy Anderson, the best darned sportswriter in Houston, gave me three tickets for the Buffs' game against the Fort Worth Panthers. Interested?" he asked. "How about it?"

"When is it?" Bess asked.

"Tomorrow afternoon," Stanley replied.

"No. I'm slated to cover a luncheon for the dry women," she replied then turned to Phillis. "It's scary how organized they are," Bess said. "They're determined to upset Al Smith's applecart."

Stanley turned to Phillis, "What about you?" he asked.

"Fort Worth Panthers" was all he needed to say. That was her stepbrother's team. She would be able to see Junior play.

"I would like that very much," she said. "What time tomorrow?"

"Three o'clock or thereabouts."

"Does the streetcar go there?"

Stanley nodded, then suggested. "Why don't you see if Teddy wants the other ticket?"

"I'll call you back this afternoon if I can find him," she said. "He's like a loose cannon."

"It'll be a good game," Stanley said. "Not sure Teddy's been to the new stadium. We can meet tomorrow at the trolley stop."

Stanley turned to Bess. "Sorry you can't make the game." Then, he brightened, "Hey, Bess, I bet Phillis hasn't seen the hall yet."

"Only a glimpse when I arrived on Saturday. The taxicab driver pointed it out as he sped by."

"Bess, why don't we walk her over right now?" Stanley asked, pushing his chair back and standing up. "Let's show her Houston's jubilee clothes. I'm telling you, Red, Sam Houston Hall's surrounded by more flapping, noisy flags than I've ever seen. Houston's never been so draped and drowned in decorations since the soldiers came home from the Great War."

He ignored Phillis's frown as he called for the check while she hastily wrapped her uneaten sandwich in a paper napkin. Phillis was learning when Stanley made a suggestion, he considered it a done deal.

They strolled west on Texas Avenue, stopping as Bess or Stanley pointed out landmarks. A group of young boys swarmed around them, passing out circulars. Stanley crumpled his and warned the women to do the same. "Ye Gods and little fishes," he swore, "these are ads for the WCTU. You don't want what they're peddling."

A freckle-faced kid ignored him. "Please, miss," he cried, looking at Phillis. "When we get all these handed out, the boss will give us strawberry ice cream."

Phillis laughed and tucked the pamphlet into her pocketbook.

In the next block, a tall thin man played a white concertina while singing Al Smith's trademark song, "Sidewalks of New York." Marching behind him to the beat of his music, a group of flappers clutched white plastic donkey-head wooden canes, giving passersby big smiles as they strutted along the sidewalk.

When Stanley reached Bagby Street, he guided them across to the hall. Goose prickles went down Phillis's spine as her jaw dropped. Stanley saw it and chuckled.

Jesse Jones's 64-day wonder took up two blocks. It seemed much larger than it had when she drove by in the back seat of Sonny Buggs's taxi. Despite the wire fencing, the white wooden building, dressed up with green and gold paint, looked like new money glistening in the afternoon sunshine.

Stanley bragged, "We're ready for the big show. Truth to tell, I'm actually a little excited."

For Phillis, this hall looked like an invitation. Her dream of a lifetime was happening in this city full of dreamers. Jesse Jones had created the perfect auditorium to house his event. How could this not be a winner for everyone? She took leave of her new friends who returned to their office as she headed for home. As the trolley traveled up the Boulevard, Phillis noticed a long funeral cortege of mounted policemen passing by on the west side of the street.

"I wonder who died?" she thought.

CHAPTER EIGHT

Bands were playing "I'll See you in My Dreams" on the Rice Roof.

Marie Phelps McAshan
On the Corner of Main and Texas
A Houston Legacy, 1985

ENTERING THE FRONT HALL THAT AFTERNOON, Phillis heard a great clatter of what sounded like metal objects hitting the floor followed by a vehement, "Damnation." With hands on hips, Maymie Banion stood in the dining room looking down at a floor filled with shiny brass-colored medals attached to red and white ribbons.

"Oh, look at this mess. I had them organized into separate job titles. Now they're just a mishmash. It'll take forever to put them back in order."

To her surprise, Phillis could not help sympathizing. "I can fix this in a jiffy."

Soon, the dining room table was lined with neat rows of badges. Badges for delegates, alternates, legislators, even badges for pages and ushers.

"Bless you. I can't believe we're done. I'm going to find a flat box to store them in. Don't want to have this problem again. I can't thank you enough."

Before she could stop herself, Phillis blurted out, "Do you have a dress I can wear to the Rice Roof tonight? All I brought is the dress I had on at dinner last night."

"Wow! That's the swankiest dance spot in Houston. I heard they've got a ten-piece band."

"According to whom? *The Houston Gargoyle*?"

"Don't knock that magazine. I put an ad in there every week."

"I know. I saw the issue on that table in the parlor."

"Maybe we can pin a velvet flower on the waist of your dress. I don't remember what color it is."

"Light blue."

"My heliotrope would be too dark."

Her eyes lit up. "Wait, Fiona Watterton, that's the answer. Last year, she stayed in your room. She was an art teacher. Thought she was a real artist." Maymie laughed. "Hung pieces of paper all around with watercolor streaks on them. Even downstairs in my front parlor," pointing to the room. "Sometimes, she smeared a canvass with stuff out of tubes. Smelled awful. She was about as talented as a catfish."

Maymie started up the stairs, "Let's find the dress."

"What dress?" Phillis asked, her heart skipping a beat.

"She stayed about six months then crept out one night, and no one ever saw her again. Disappeared into thin air, along with the rent she owed me. All she left was an evening gown hanging in the bedroom's armoire."

"She left you without paying her rent? Whatever she left wouldn't be nice enough to wear tonight, would it?"

"You're dead wrong. Fiona always dressed to the nines. She looked like an Everitt-Buelow model whenever she left this house. Wore all the money she made on her back."

Maymie rummaged in the hall closet, pulled out a lavender dress, and held it against Phillis's body. "Look, it's gonna be a perfect fit. I knew you were her size."

Phillis gasped. The dress was poetry.

"This pays you back for helping me with my badges. Besides, I will love seeing you in this dress. When I call her, your mother will want to know who your date is."

"You and my mother spend money talking about me long distance on the telephone?" Phillis's mouth fell open. "That's interesting. Tell her Brad Nicholson is here covering the convention for his New York publisher. We met by accident. She and my stepfather will be thrilled. The Nicholson's are old Highland Park money. Mother might even revise her criticism of my trip to Houston."

"Hmn, I'll tell you what she says. What time is he picking you up?"

Phillis shook her head. "I'm meeting him at the hotel."

"Why he doesn't send a taxicab to pick you up if he's so well-heeled," Maymie sniffed disapprovingly. "You certainly can't ride the trolley in this dress." She held up her finger. "I know. Charlie will deliver you downtown in my car."

"Oh golly, that's awfully nice. Thanks for everything."

Phillis dressed with a care she seldom practiced. The dress hanging on the closet hook inspired her. Her heavy, shoulder-length mop of auburn hair was her biggest problem. Couldn't be hid under a hat. She was going to need a lot of time to pin it up.

A rap on her door caused Phillis to drop her hairpins. "Darn it. Who's there?"

"It's me. Olivia."

"Thank God. You can help pin up my hair. Look at this mess."

Olivia laughed. "Oh, how fun. This is easy. Where're your hair pins?" She retrieved them from the floor and began brushing Phillis's hair. "You just have too much of it. No thoughts of bobbing?"

"Yes, of course, I've thought of it, but some bobs look better than others. My neck's too long and skinny. I'm scared how I'd look and besides I don't have the money to keep it bobbed. My idea is to stand apart from the shorthaired, short-skirted flappers. I want to look more serious, sort of intellectual."

Olivia laughed and gasped, "You've succeeded."

"Frankly, women reporters sometimes come across as pushy or brassy. I'm planning to impress people with my words. Not a fancy hairdo or fancy dresses."

"Okay, okay. There now, the chignon will stay put but it needs something else."

Olivia examined the dress on the hanger carefully. "Is this what you're wearing? My God, where did it come from? Not from your suitcase, I'll bet."

They both laughed as Phillis answered, "Miss Maymie, my new fairy godmother, said a former boarder left it here for the rent she owed."

"Don't care how much I owed; I wouldn't have left without this. It's a dreamy dress. Perfect for your coloring. Wait. Don't move whatever you do. I'll be right back."

Phillis ignored her and slipped into the dress.

Olivia rushed back in, stopping when she saw Phillis twirling in front of the mirror. "You look terrific. Let me just add a few things."

She held up a wide piece of silk ribbon close to the color of the dress and circled Phillis's head, tying the ends together.

"A bandeau!" Phillis grinned. "They show those in magazines, but I've never worn one."

"Just a few more additions," Olivia said, pulling Phillis over to the mirror. She applied a darker shade of lipstick and expertly highlighted Phillis's cheeks with more color.

"There now. You'll knock 'em dead."

A honking horn in the driveway signaled Charlie waiting in the Packard.

Phillis floated down the stairs, waving a kiss to Maymie and Josie who clapped as Olivia looked on.

Downtown, Brad stood at the curb, visiting with a bellman. When Phillis arrived, she tried to hide her delight at his astonished expression. A five-foot-seven woman is not normally described as delicate, but Brad helped her from the car as if she were a hothouse lily. He tucked her hand under his arm and led her to the elevator, clearing a path through the hotel guests congregating in the Rice Hotel lobby.

The crowded elevator stopped at the top floor. Stepping out, Phillis was unaccountably happy she had accepted Brad's invitation to come dancing this evening.

Before her was an impressive ballroom three hundred feet above the sidewalk. The Rice Roof's French doors lined the walls, thrown open, to allow the Gulf breeze to circulate."Peck's Bad Boys is supposed to be the best band in town," Brad informed her as the heavy-set blonde soloist belted out a bluesy rendition of "What'll I Do?"

When Phillis arrived at their table, she asked herself the same question. There sat Reginald with Daisy, a pair of cozy lovebirds. He jumped to his feet and gave Phillis a hug, as Brad whispered in her ear, "Better watch him. He thinks he's the Sheik of Arabi."

Daisy fluttered her blue eyes and winked impishly at Brad. She finally acknowledged Phillis by asking, "Wherever did you get a dress that gorgeous?"

Phillis stifled a groan as she questioned her sanity in coming here. Her motive seemed less and less rational.

When the band swung into "I'll See You in My Dreams," Brad looked at Phillis and pointed to the dance floor. She panicked. Her mouth filled with a weird sour taste and her ankles felt like jelly. It was too much like being back at Highland Park High, same guy, and same emotions welling up inside her. Feelings she no longer welcomed. It was not an experience she cared to repeat.

Brad leaned into her cheek and whispered, "You're still in my dreams, Miss Independent."

Phillis pulled away and gave him a hard look, "You're kidding, right? It's been too long between dances for you to have kept me on your mind."

"All I can say is, you're hard to forget. We had good times together. We were a good team."

"Brad, I'm still at the starting gate while you've made it big. I'm happy for you. A little jealous, I admit, but glad for your success."

She stopped talking and concentrated on his swooping dance moves. "I can see being on the East Coast polished your skills on the dance floor."

"And I'm noticing you're not out of practice," he replied.

Phillis steered the conversation away from old memories. "What's the deal with Daisy? She's in a snit. Reggie looks like he's mad about her. Why aren't they dancing?"

"I would imagine their infatuation with each other will last the length of his visit to Houston. No dancing since Reggie turned his ankle on the golf course yesterday. He's limping badly."

"Too bad." Phillis judged Brad's attraction to her would cease about the same time. *Do I care? Coming here tonight is risky. I need to watch myself.*

When they returned to their seats, Reginald was ordering another Pink Lady for Daisy and a Manhattan for a new guest. Sitting in Brad's chair was a gentleman who was born to wear a tuxedo. Brad clapped him on the back and grinned broadly as he stood up and shook hands. Pulling Phillis forward, he said, "Meet Allen Peden, editor and owner of the *Gargoyle*, Houston's newest weekly."

"Delighted to make your acquaintance, Miss Flanagan. Brad says you hail from Fort Worth. Not a city I've visited. Only been to Dallas."

Phillis smiled and thought there was no surprise there.

"I assume you're here for the convention like your friends. And you are a journalist as well?"

She nodded as Brad pulled up a chair for Peden.

"From what I know of Brad, you're most likely a Democrat and in love with politics. What about women's issues? Have you written about them? Whom have you met since you arrived?"

"Good questions, Mr. Peden. No interviews yet, but I have my eyes out for the celebrities coming. Surely I'll snag an interview with at least one."

"Too late to grab a seat at the Women's Breakfast next Wednesday. That's supposedly the high point for the ladies. It's oversold as it is. Maybe the dinner for women writers at the ROCC? You could cover it for your newspaper. You want a ticket?"

"Silly question. Of course, I'd love one. What is ROCC?"

"A little club in my neighborhood. You'll have to take a taxi. Don't think a trolley runs out to River Oaks at night. Trust me, it'll be worth it. Brad says Maymie Banion is your hostess. I'll have two tickets sent over to her office."

Phillis, trying not to stammer, shook his hand and said, "Thank you for your generosity, Mr. Peden. I'm sure Maymie will be delighted as well."

"Who knows, perhaps I can use some of your stuff. Ruth West is my assistant editor. I would like to introduce her. Maybe lunch?"

He rose to leave. "I can always reach you through Miss Banion, right?"

And off he went, hopping over to a group sitting at what Brad identified as the "Movers and Shakers" table. "Those are the Hogg brothers, you remember their father Governor Hogg, and Ross Sterling. He owns the *Houston Post*. Peden says Houston's just like Dallas, a small coterie of old money."

"How do you know all this?" Phillis asked.

"Connections, my dear, Princeton connections."

When the band struck up "It Had to Be You," Brad held out his hand and they walked to the dance floor. Behind her, Phillis heard Daisy whine, "This is the most boring place. That fellow that just left, whatever his name was, didn't even notice me." She pointed to her empty glass. "What a stick in the mud you guys are, she said, shoving his shoulder. "Reginald, go over and ask the band to play at least one Charleston. Something besides slowpoke stuff. This band is putting me to sleep."

She watched Reggie hail a waiter who bent to hear him and must have conveyed Daisy's request. The conductor seamlessly shifted into a lively version of "Ain't She Sweet" and Daisy nearly ran the other dancers down in her haste to get on the floor. Dancing solo presented no problem for her, and every eye in the place focused on her swinging legs.

"She's so much fun to watch," Reginald exclaimed when they returned to the table. Clapping to the music, "He whispered in Phillis's ear, I think I'm in love."

Peck kept his musicians playing one jazz number after another, closing with "Toot, Toot, Tootsie," after which his band took a much-deserved break. Phillis and Brad clasped hands and sang the words to the popular tune as they strolled outside to enjoy the night air.

"I hear this is the coolest place in Houston," Phillis said as she faced the breeze and smiled.

"Yeah, someone bragged you can see the lights of Galveston from the Rice Roof. Must have been a Chamber of Commerce official or maybe Mr. Houston. Maymie says that's what they call Mr. Jones. But, he doesn't just operate here. He's one of the largest real-estate operators in America. Owns four buildings in New York City, all of which he built. One of them is forty-four stories high."

"Yeah, he definitely has a big stack of chips. I saw a photograph of him in a brochure," Brad said. "He looked genial but very intense. What do you suppose drives him?"

"I don't know," Phillis replied, yawning. "His hotels are packed to the gills and the Democratic National Committee is renting office space in one of his buildings. He says he loves to plan and work and build. Some call his actions to get this convention held in Houston self-serving. But this wasn't a solo effort. From what I've read, the whole town worked together to make it jell."

"Yeah, he definitely had some help," Brad said, then asked, "Where's the 'White Way'? Is that the glow coming from over there?"

"In the *Press*, I read it's on Rusk Street. You can kind of see the light from here. All the blocks from Main to Bagby are electrified with six hundred candlepower. Eight lights have been installed on every block to help the delegates get to and from the convention hall after the night sessions."

"They're really going all out. Reggie's writing an article about the Hospitality House," Brad said. "It's an entire city block with a canvas roof and open sides. Benches, ice water, fans, and it's free for anyone to use. Certainly a boon for the visitors. No one back East has ever heard of such a thing. The amenities Houston's providing are unprecedented."

Phillis yawned again and apologized. "Not used to these late hours. Sorry."

They walked back inside to their table. "You guys going to close the place down?" Brad asked. Reggie nodded, pointing to his fresh drink.

When they reached the street, Brad insisted on hiring a taxicab, and he and Phillis rode back to Houston Heights through the darkness in companionable silence.

"It was a lovely evening, Brad. Thank you for inviting me," Phillis said as he helped her out of the cab. "Meeting Allen Peden was the icing on the cake."

He kissed her on the cheek then waited while she climbed the steps. Turning, she waved goodbye and let herself into the house.

In her room, she carefully hung up the lavender dress, knowing she would wrestle with the feelings Brad had revived this evening. It was hard for her to admit, but she had enjoyed wearing the swell dress, enjoyed the attention of a handsome fellow and loved the Rice Roof.

CHAPTER NINE

'Batter Up!' New Buffalo Stadium is one of the finest and most complete minor league stadiums in the country. Many new innovations are to be found for the comfort and convenience of the baseball fan. Features ordinarily found only in major league parks are incorporated in Buffalo Stadium.

Houston Chronicle
April 10, 1928

Tuesday, June 19, 1928

THE NOON DAY SUN HAD SCORCHED THE sidewalks, and Teddy griped about the heat as he and Phillis waited for Stanley at the streetcar stop on the Boulevard. When he hadn't appeared, they waved on the approaching southbound car. Phillis checked her wristwatch, but without tickets there was no point in their riding to the stadium. Finally, they saw him loping down Eighteenth Avenue.

"Sorry, I'm late," Stanley said, out of breath. "My landlady's dog dug under the fence. I chased him for two blocks and he's back home now."

With rolled-up shirtsleeves, sweat streaming down his face, and a battered straw bowler under his arm, Stanley Staples was no woman's idea of the perfect escort, even to a ball game. Phillis smiled as she compared him to Bradley and last night's evening at the Rice. The two men were night and day.

"Sure is hot," Stanley said as they handed their passes to the conductor. The crowded car lacked adjacent seats, so Stanley sat next to a man who waved him over, and Phillis squeezed onto the edge of a seat occupied by a large woman wearing an overly decorated Sunday-Go-To-Meetin' hat. Teddy, naturally, found a cute flapper to sit beside.

Phillis's seatmate carried a bag stuffed full. A thermos jug, red-checkered napkins, and from the heavenly smell, a box of recently fried chicken. Strapped onto the bag was a cookie tin with the Me-Too insignia stamped on the lid.

"You know, we could've stayed home," the woman announced in one of those voices that reaches everyone at the back of an auditorium.

"Really?" Phillis asked.

The woman ignored her. "I could've heard the game on KPRC instead of sitting in the blistering sun at Buff Stadium. With my living room windows open and the fan going, I tell you, I hardly notice the heat. I had to come to this game 'cause we gotta show 'em loyalty. They deserve it 'cause they're Houston's team."

She turned to Phillis and said, "My name is Teenie Mae Newsom. You see the games regular, miss?"

Phillis shook her head.

Mopping her face with one of the napkins she pulled from her bag, Teenie Mae snickered as she eyed Phillis from the corner of her eye. "You wondering about my name? Can't help it. I've put on a few pounds since my mama called me that."

Phillis's face reddened, embarrassed the woman had noticed her reaction. "I'm Phillis Flanagan, just arrived from Fort Worth to report on the convention. I've got a few nicknames myself. Some refer to me as 'beanpole,' but the worst is 'Olive Oyl.' Then there's my hair. Redheads," Phillis rolled her eyes.

Teenie's eyes looked her up and down and cocked her head to one side, "Catch all those curls up into a bun and get yourself a flapper dress. Yeah, you got the skinny elbows and long feet. "Olive Oyl." She nodded sympathetically.

Sputtering, Phillis admitted, "All my nicknames fit me to a tee." *Gadsooks, I've got to shift this conversation to a different subject?*

"It's my first Buffs' game. My stepbrother's a rookie for the Fort Worth Cats. He's already got a nickname. His teammates call him 'Rube.'" *There I go with another nickname.*

"So, he's a farm boy?" Teenie asked.

"Far from it. He grew up in Dallas's snooty Highland Park. Looks like a kid who came to town on a pumpkin truck."

They laughed together and she offered Phillis a cookie from her tin. "Did you notice my Me-Too cookie tin? You been in town long enough to know about the Me-Too campaign?"

Phillis leaned forward so her seatmate could see her button. "I learned about it my first day here. I'm impressed the women here came up with this idea. Your loyalty to the Buffs sounds like sort of the same stuff." She grinned at Teenie and said, "But, have to admit, I'm gonna root for Rube and the opposition."

The glary sun and the three-o'clock game time was like someone's idea of punishment. Phillis felt sorry for the unsuspecting convention visitors who would be arriving next week. How would someone who hailed from the east coast, handle the heat?

"Go ahead, root for the Cats. I'll bet our Buffs beat 'em," Teenie predicted as she and Phillis shook hands, and everybody scrambled to transfer to the Leeland trolley.

In less than fifteen minutes, they arrived at the Ball Park stop where the whole car emptied of passengers who walked together across the parking lot toward the stadium. Surprisingly, five or six cars were parked there. Phillis couldn't imagine anyone driving out here since the trolley deposited its passengers right at the ball field.

Whistling, "It Ain't Gonna Rain No More," Staples jovially slammed on his straw boater and linked arms with Phillis and Teddy.

Phillis laughed and asked, "Does it ever rain in Houston?"

Teddy spoke up. "Lots of showers, that's what we mostly have in the summer. No torrential downpours until late August. It never spoils the whole day. Are you worried, Phil?" He laughed out loud, "Afraid it might ruin your new hat?"

"I gave seventy-five cents for this hat, but I wouldn't mind a shower if it cooled things off, patting the crown of her wide-brimmed straw hat. "Forgot to ask the saleslady if it was waterproof."

Teddy guffawed. "She'd probably have said 'yes' just to make the sale. No such thing as a waterproof straw hat."

At the end of the parking lot, Stanley pointed to the palatial stadium encircled by a four-foot-wide strip of grass struggling to survive. "The park's opening game was in April."

Handing their tickets to the attendant, they entered through the turnstiles, stepping onto the concrete floor. Stanley said, "No more wooden baseball parks for Houston."

A kid stood beside a stack of red canvas cushions taller than he was. Stanley said, "Phillis, if you have a nickel to spare, you better rent a seat. Sometimes fans get angry about an umpire's call and everyone throws cushions at each other. Might need to defend yourself."

"You're kidding me," Phillis replied. After looking at his face, she fished a nickel from her pocketbook and grabbed one from the stack.

Stanley led them to the bleacher seats. Pointing to the dazzling emerald field, he explained, "That's new mown Bermuda grass, just waiting for the game."

He swung his arm around the stadium, "Holds 13,397 fans. The St. Louis Cardinals forked over four hundred thousand, plus the land.

Can you believe it? They say they'll buy lights next year so the Buffs can play at night. A baseball game held in the dark of night. Wouldn't that be something?"

The announcer spoke into the microphone requesting they stand for the national anthem to be played by the Texas Dental College brass band. At 3:15, Phillis applauded with the rest of the fans, welcoming the Houston Buffaloes onto the field.

Stanley cupped his hands and spoke to her, "Hear that clapping? That's what happens when you're number one in the league. Guess what? The St.

Louis Cardinals are number one in their league, too. We're just their farm team and they're housing us in this swell stadium."

He reached over and removed Phillis's hat. "There, that's better. Cooler for you. Okay?"

She smiled at him and nodded.

"Uh oh, Phillis look at the front row behind the Cats dugout. Is that who I think it is?"

She nodded. Amon Carter sat in shirt-sleeves, wearing his ten-gallon hat and smoking a cigar.

"Maybe I better put my hat back on. There's probably some afternoon tea I'm supposed to be covering for the *Star*."

"I wouldn't worry. He can't pick you out from where we're sitting."

"I hope not. Look at him, surrounded by his entourage of admirers. He loves the Cats. Broadcasts their games on his radio station."

"Not surprised he came. This is a big game for both teams. Buffs are betting we'll take the title. We're the favorite. Sportscasters brag on us though they admit it'll be tough. We haven't won a pennant since 1914. That's a long dry spell."

Dressed in spanking white uniforms trimmed in red, the team began throwing balls to each other, spinning their arms and doing squats. "There's the third baseman, number 10, Stan 'Punk' Baker. Fans love him. He's an ex-Aggie and hits the ball real regular."

The Fort Worth Panthers came onto the field in fine fettle despite being the underdog. Phillis had eyes for only one player, grinning widely when she spotted him. Her stepbrother's six-foot, barrel-chested frame stood out among the other players. The Cats stretched their limbs and she grinned when she saw a team member throw his arm over Junior's shoulder and another pat his back.

Phillis said, "Stanley, see the tall guy over on the right side near the visitors' dugout?"

"Number 12? The bare-headed one whose hat just fell off?"

"Yes. That's Rube Wilkerson, my stepbrother."

An inveterate eavesdropper, Teddy asked, "Why didn't you tell us you had a brother on the Cats' team?"

"I didn't know if he was playing today. It's his first season. When he signed up with them instead of going to college, it caused a terrible row. He didn't care. He just wanted to play ball."

At that moment, the announcer yelled as if he had heard her, "Play ball!" and the pitcher walked up to the mound. The Buffs took their spots on the field while the Cats returned to their dugout. The beginning pitcher, George "Grandpa" Woods, was identified as a Houston boy so he got a big hand.

"Why's he called 'Grandpa?'" Phillis asked Stanley. "He doesn't look old to me."

"I don't know. He's a Rice Institute grad so he's older than the ones who didn't go to college. Already tried the majors. No luck."

Phillis thought of Junior and his refusal to "waste" four years at Southern Methodist University. What will happen when he is too old to play? Maybe he will take over Horace's dress shop. She could not imagine Junior running a ladies ready-to-wear store, much less married. Of course, she could not see herself with a wedding band either.

"Woods isn't doing so good," she heard Teddy complain. "Pancho needs to take him out."

"Calm down, Teddy. It's only the first inning," Stanley laughed.

"Who's Pancho?" Phillis asked.

"He's the new manager of the team," Teddy answered. "Frank 'Pancho' Snyder. From San Antonio originally. He's also the catcher. Big guy, six-feet, three-inches tall. Looks like a mean sucker to me."

"Is he? Mean?" Phillis asked. "Is that why he got that nickname?"

"'Pancho' is Spanish for Frank. But the moniker can also mean 'cool'.

"Is he?"

"Is he mean or cool? He keeps these guys in check, especially the young ones, though most of them aren't in rompers. They've already been around the block once or twice."

"Did you just see 'Rabbit' Powell catch that ball?" Teddy asked.

"I don't suppose anyone knows why he's called 'Rabbit'?" Phillis asked.

Stanley teased her, "He can run like hell. Try watching the game."

"Nicknames interest me." Phillis insisted. "You yell nicknames at me whether I like them or not. Nicknames add dash to baseball.

Do football players have nicknames?"

"So, can you learn to like my nicknames for you?" Stanley asked with a grin. "You know they just mean I like you."

Phillis snorted and clammed up for a few minutes.

"I repeat, let's watch the game. That's what we came for, isn't it?" He looked at Teddy who nodded. Phillis's concentration improved when Junior came to bat in the third inning and slammed a ball over the fence.

The announcer cried, "That's one run for the Cats. Would you look at Rube Wilkerson swing that lumber? Fans, he's a young ball player from Dallas, making his first appearance at our grand Buffalo Stadium."

Phillis could not restrain from clapping and yelling, "Woo Hoo!"

A loud chorus of boos erupted around them. A gruff-voiced fan asked, "Who let you in, lady? Go home or sit somewhere else."

"Nuts to you," another voice yelled.

"Sorry, sorry," she responded. Stanley and Teddy turned their backs to her.

Stonewalled, she switched to thinking about Junior, the one member of the family who made her feel loved. When she got into trouble for neglecting to do her chores, he would plead, "Don't hurt Phillis, she's my big sister." She towered over him for years, but once he started growing, he never stopped. It was fun to have to look up to talk with him now.

Despite Horace Wilkerson's warnings, he had elected to play ball, knowing he might never be welcomed back home. She doubted his father had softened. Her mother, though she had a soft spot for her stepson that made Phillis happy, never went against her husband's decisions and had likely never attended a baseball game in her life. She and Junior were both out on a limb, so to speak.

"Folks, it's the top of the sixth and slugger Watty Watkins leads off."

"This one's probably a shortening of his last name," Phillis suggested. Stanley nodded, never taking his eye off the batter's box.

"It looks like the Cats are beating us, doesn't it?" Phillis tried to sound dejected.

"Not a clue. She doesn't have a clue," Teddy snickered. "The score is only one to nothing."

"Okay, so we've got three more innings?"

"I'm learning. So, no questions about names, no predictions, no rooting for the opposing team. I got it. And eight more innings to go?" She looked at her wristwatch and sighed.

They ignored her and kept watching. The fan sitting next to her leaned over and said, "Lady, if you'll just shut your trap, we'll all be happier."

She glared at him and icily replied, "Thanks." She was struggling to understand the popularity of baseball. Why was this America's favorite game? An hour dragged by before the seventh inning stretch brought some relief. Stanley and Teddy pulled her to her feet and they swayed as they sang "Take me Out to the Ballgame," along with the other fans. Stanley treated them to hot dogs, and Phillis bought them some popcorn from the vendor carrying it up and down the aisles. Mustard splashed on her blouse as she bit into the dog, but no one seemed to notice. When Stanley threw his hat up in the air and deftly caught it on its way down, Teddy gave a whoop and pounded him on the back. With the resumption of the game, the three of them linked their little piggies together for luck. Maybe the seventh inning was the magic of the game.

Phillis made it to the eighth inning. "Hear that man up in the grandstand yelling? Who's he saying needs to be taken out of the game?"

"Can't you see the pitcher's struggling?" Teddy asked. "The Cats are leading three to nothing. Pancho's got to do something."

Junior had homered in the seventh inning with one man on base, adding two runs to the run he had brought in earlier. So far, he had scored all of Fort Worth's runs. Her smile stretched from ear to ear as she thought of the headlines to come, "Fort Worth Cat's Babe Ruth." She offhandedly studied her scorecard and tapped her foot.

"Take 'Grandpa' out! Get him a wheelchair." An obnoxious fan sitting nearly at the top of the bleachers yelled so loud it made Phillis look up to see if he had a megaphone.

What if that was Junior pitching? She would hate for someone to yell ugly remarks about him in front of everyone sitting in the stadium. Twisting to look up at the seat where the voice was coming from, she rose off the bleacher and hollered, "Mister, you're rude. Let the manager make the decisions. Okay?"

Teddy fell backwards out of his seat laughing. Stanley grabbed her arm and pulled her down.

The offensive fan roared back at her, "Who let you out of the kitchen?" The next thing she knew a red cushion landed squarely on Stanley's back. "Bottle it, sister. Next one I throw is gonna be for you. You got it coming."

When Phillis turned to give the man a piece of her mind, Stanley clamped her arms and held her in place. "Shush," he whispered. "You've already said enough. Cause a ruckus and your boss will spot you for sure. Just sit here and watch the game like a lady."

A cup of ice-water in her face would not have felt worse. 'Like a lady' was the most offensive thing he could have said. She wanted to smack him, along with her pillow-throwing adversary. *Damn him anyway.*

All her life, she thumbed her nose at society's expectations. Stanley's sarcasm successfully shut her down, but she seethed as he sat beside her. He was nothing but a blockhead who had just ruined their outing.

After Snyder pulled 'Grandpa' Woods out and put 'Tex' Carleton in, the Cat's offense lost its steam. Two late grand slams brought in four runs for Houston. Junior, with his three runs for the Cats, had come close to beating the Buffs single-handedly. No doubt about it, her stepbrother was a budding star. His height and strength made him a power to be reckoned with. She kept her eye on Amon and watched him stand and storm out of the stadium as the announcer declared the Buffs winners.

"I'm going over to say hello to Junior," Philllis told Stanley and Teddy. "I'll meet you fellows at the entrance."

Stepping lightly on the spongy green carpet grass, she crossed the field, avoiding the chalk lines and bases. One of the Cat's conferring with an umpire looked up and she yelled, "Is Junior Wilkerson still here?"

He thumbed her toward the dugout where Junior was buttoning his jacket and talking with a teammate. "I gave away that run and that's what lost the game for us," he groaned, hanging his head.

"Rube, the ball went right up against the fence. I don't see how anyone could've caught it."

When Phillis called, "Junior," he looked up and cracked a big smile, reaching out his long arms to pat her on the shoulders. "How did you get here, Sis?" His gloom disappeared as he hugged her close. "If I'd known you were out there watching, I swear I would have caught that fly."

Stepping back, he said, "Remember, I've dropped 'Junior.' It's 'Rube' now. Meet Scooter. He's our shortstop. The one who gave me my nickname. He said I looked like a big old country boy, didn't you?"

As Scooter nodded, Rube said, "This is Phillis, my big sister. Can't you see the resemblance? We're both redheads." Junior loved to make people think they were related by blood instead of marriage.

"You're sure she's not your little sister?" Scooter laughed. "You're a head taller."

Phillis gazed at her stepbrother fondly and wondered if Scooter realized how on the mark his nickname was. "Rube" went to the very core of Junior's personality, open and unsophisticated. He had stuck out like a sore thumb when he entered Highland Park High, saying the place made him break out in hives. To her, Rube fit him as well as his baseball glove. Scooter's affection for Junior warmed Phillis's heart.

"How's it going, sis? You like Houston? I thought it was fine when I got here. After losing this game, I'm down on the whole place. They whipped us."

She looked up at his face. "You're happy, aren't you? How's being on the road? Do you do anything besides live out of grips and hotel rooms?"

"Nope, but playing ball makes every day okay. How about you? You still writing those stories?"

"Yes," Phillis replied. "I'm making my typewriter talk. Houston's ready for the convention and I can hardly wait. It's a boom town. Sort of an uptown version of Fort Worth. Same spirit and civic pride. Not snooty and boring like Dallas. I love it."

A deep voice yelled, "Hey, Rube, you riding this bus, or staying here?"

Junior gave Phillis another hug, grabbed his mitt, and walked backwards toward the bus so he could keep her in view. Waving goodbye, he hollered, "See you next time. The Cats play the Buffs again in July. I hope you're still here." He hopped on board just as the bus took off down the road.

After Phillis found Stanley and Teddy, they walked out of the stadium with the thinning crowd.

Stanley rubbed his chin. "You should be proud of your brother, Phillis," he said, sincerely. "I'll bet he's making at least a hundred-and-fifty-dollars a month. That's nothing to sneeze at, especially for a youngster. How old did you say he is?"

Phillis held up ten and seven fingers and turned back to look at the stadium.

She had no interest in engaging with Stanley Staples. His "like a lady" remark still rankled with her.

"You mean he's getting paid that much just for playing baseball?" Teddy asked. "Maybe I should drop out of college and become an athlete."

"Kid, you don't know nothin' from nothin' if you think what Phillis's brother does is easy," Stanley said sharply, giving Teddy a withering look. "You better stay close to home where you've got someone who babies you."

Phillis winced at this jab.

"That's not fair," Teddy whined. "I help Aunt Maymie all the time. She's not out that much."

"Not much? Only food, board, tuition, books, clothes, spending money, and a car and gasoline," Stanley laughed sarcastically. "You're how old? Nineteen? I picked a thousand bales of cotton, milked cows, and swept the floors at the hardware store in Corsicana before I was twelve. Been on my own since I was fifteen. You're so soft you remind me of cotton candy."

Teddy threw his hands across his head as if warding off blows. His face crumpled like he was about to cry.

But Stanley kept pounding, "What are your future plans, buddy boy? Get a job so we'll know what kind of work you've been out of."

The attack shocked Phillis. "Jeez, Stanley what's up with you? You're bent on insulting both of us."

Teddy gave her the answer or at least a clue. "Stanley, lay off me. I'm sorry about the trouble I made for you at your newspaper. I didn't mean to."

"I'll accept your apology because of my respect for your aunt," Stanley said quietly. "But don't do it again."

Their angry exchange was a sour end to the evening.

THE TRIO WAS QUIET ON THE TROLLEY ride home. She did not care if it was unwise to have battled that heckler. *I wish I had called that guy's bluff. After two- and one-half hours of sitting through this baseball game, I would have enjoyed a battle. Baseball is like watching paint dry.*

As the trolley turned onto the Boulevard, Stanley whispered in her ear, "I know you're sore. Sorry I was so hard on the kid."

Phillis narrowed her eyes and threw him a long look before shrugging her shoulders nonchalantly.

The porch light was on at 1750 Harvard Street. Teddy seemed his normal, jaunty self as he thanked them for taking him to the game, jumped into his Ford and sped off who knows where.

"Good night, Phillis," Stanley said it, but did not tarry, walking off down the street without looking back. No whistling tune filled the night air.

Depressed by the way the day ended, Phillis opened the front door. Before her foot hit the first step to go upstairs, Miss Maymie's voice called from the kitchen.

"Is that you, Phillis?"

Phillis dreaded a conversation with Miss Maymie right now. She needed to make sense out of Stanley's feud before she discussed it with Teddy or her. A mysterious relationship she had never understood.

Stopping at the kitchen doorway, she said, "I'm bushed. That afternoon heat really takes it out of you. I'm ready for bed."

"Come and sit down for a minute," Maymie said. "I'll fix you a glass of lemonade. Josie put aside a plate of dinner for you, if you're hungry."

As she pointed to the stove, Maymie said, "I need to ask you something."

Phillis dragged herself over to the kitchen table where Maymie, of all things, was sitting in Josie's rocker, snapping beans into a large enameled bowl cradled in her lap. Phillis was astounded to see her doing anything in her kitchen other than eating or directing Josie. Maymie went to the icebox to get a pictcher of lemonade. When she set it down in front of Phillis, she saw Maymie's anxious face.

"Thank you," Phillis looked up questioningly.

"How was the game?" Maymie said, returning to the rocker. "How were Stanley and Teddy?" She pulled the bowl into her lap and for several moments the only sound was the snap, snap of the beans.

"Fine." She set her glass down on the table and eyed Miss Maymie expectantly. She couldn't know about the showdown. Unless she had caused it. "Except for Stanley's attack on Teddy."

"Attack!" Maymie exclaimed. "What do you mean?"

"I don't know, Miss Maymie," she frowned. "Why don't you tell me?"

"Oh, rats. I guess my idea didn't work out." Maymie snapped a long green bean decisively, and her voice faltered as she continued, "I asked Stanley to build a fire under Teddy. My poor boy has never had a man to guide him. Goodness knows, my late husband called him 'my stray.' I hoped Stanley could give him a push."

"He gave him a push all right," Phillis said shortly. "He pushed him right down into the dirt."

"Oh, no. Was Teddy hurt?"

"Only his feelings. He seemed his usual cheery self when we got home. Took off in the Ford."

"All I wanted was for Stanley to steer him in the right direction." Maymie stopped and wiped her eyes with her sleeve. "He's the person in this world I love the most." Tears welled up in her eyes again. "I've not done right by him."

Horrified, Phillis watched the stalwart Maymie Banion break down. Her sobs filled the room.

"I bet you never thought of me as a crybaby," Maymie said, pulling a handkerchief from her sleeve.

"Teddy's almost reached manhood," Phillis said, "He's terribly immature, but he's not a bad person."

"Not yet. That's what worries me. I don't know what he is deep down. He's been given free rein." Miss Maymie started to cry again, her tears dropping on the forgotten bowl full of beans she unconsciously clutched.

"Oh, God, he's gotten in with the wrong group, but how do you crack the whip on a nineteen-year-old? Do I owe him an explanation? Is it better I go to my grave without telling him the truth?" She rushed on, hardly taking a breath. "Still grieving. My bad memories just won't go away. Forgive me, for sharing this with you."

With this ominous beginning, Phillis realized how little she really knew about her landlady.

In a calmer voice Miss Maymie said, "You need to know about my boy. You need to know why he's mine."

"I had a twin sister named Ginny. We were born on a hardscrabble, forty-acre farm in north Texas at the tail end of five children. Three died in the Civil War. After it was over, the only thing country people like us had for comfort was religion. Luckily, we were Missionary Baptists. Ginny and I learned to read because we had a Bible, unlike most of the other children we knew." Maymie smiled and pushed her spectacles up on her nose.

"Your mother grew up on a farm in Waxahachie, and she didn't have such a great time of it either. We have that in common, among other things. My childhood was picking cotton and wearing flour-sack dresses. Plenty to eat, but not much schooling. After the age of seventeen, you married. Ginny and I weren't interested in that. We had big plans for our future. Much like you, Phillis. And that's something else I've been thinking of."

She reached over and put her hand on top of Phillis's. "We had no choices. No college in our neck of the woods even if we'd had the money. So, Ginny and I got a job in town cleaning rooms at a hotel. After we sent money home, our sixty-hour week netted us a total of twenty-four dollars a month. Lo and behold, a business school opened, and we used our savings for tuition, continuing to work at the hotel for our room and board."

Maymie put the bowl up on the counter and began pacing across the kitchen. "Though we weren't identical twins, we were both bonny young women, if I do say so. The first time we differed about the slightest thing was on our studies. I loved the bookkeeping part while Ginny preferred the stenography course.

"When Newell Hancock, a wealthy investor from St. Louis, checked into the hotel, he began paying me a lot of attention. I tell you, my head was turned. Before long, I decided I'd found the love of my life. Mr. Hancock was tall and handsome, a real charmer."

Maymie stopped pacing and wiped her eyes again with her handkerchief. "When I accused Ginny of being jealous, she said she was just worried she might lose me. I was so in love with Newie, I gave her little thought."

"All was glorious," Miss Maymie said, sitting back down at the table and looking at Phillis, "until I woke up one morning and found Ginny's bed empty. On the bureau sat a large envelope addressed to me. When I opened it, I got the shock of my life. In her beautiful handwriting, my sweet sister wrote:

> *Dear Maymie,*
>
> *Don't be mad at me. I know you will be surprised. Newell and I are on our way to Kansas City where we will be married today. I did not mean to hurt you. You will always be the best friend a sister could have.*
>
> *Love, Ginny.*

Maymie Banion dropped her chin to her chest. She looked at Phillis and clutched the air with a fist. "My world fell apart. It's been twenty years, but I feel the pain of her words like a fresh knife wound. I will love Newell until the day I die."

She crossed her heart and straightened her shoulders as she grabbed her bowl and resumed snapping the beans. "I managed to pull myself together, got my diploma at the business college and went to Fort Worth where I became a saleswoman. No way was I going to bang on a typewriter for the rest of my life. Soon I was a traveling saleswoman, which got me out on the road doing something with my life."

Smiling at Phillis, she said, "I was selling corsets when I got a telegram notifying me that Newell and Ginny were killed in a train wreck just outside St. Louis. I did not attend the funeral. A few weeks later, I received a copy of their Last Will and Testament from an attorney. They had appointed me guardian of their five-year-old son. My sorrow over losing my only sister and the man I loved was compounded by the news that I now had a nephew to take care of."

Maymie laughed. "Me, an unmarried woman, free as a bird. I had never heard from Ginny or Newell after they eloped. I asked myself, why did I owe them anything? I knew nothing about raising . . . ."

She paused, then finished her thought, "a kid who wasn't mine. Phillis, once I thought about it, I realized Teddy was the child of my heart because he was all I had left of his father. I could use my undying love for Newell to raise his only child."

Maymie heaved a great sigh and rose. "I've told Teddy who his parents are, I've never told him of my love for his father."

She set the bowl full of beans on the counter, untied her apron, and laid it over the back of the chair. "I've spoiled Teddy rotten. He is sweet and kind, but he's lazy. Cares nothing for school."

Eying Phillis, she confessed, "Yesterday, I asked Stanley to talk to him. I wish I'd asked you to do it instead."

Phillis gasped, "No, not me. I can't help Teddy. But Stanley can. He could be a steady influence on Teddy. Tonight, he was mad about something Teddy's done. When I find out what it is, I'll let you know."

The kitchen was quiet for a few minutes before Phillis said, "To me, telling him about your love for his father benefits no one. Why not ask him what he wants to do with his life?"

"Oh. Maybe so. I've always planned everything for him. His grade report came last week. Houston Junior College is a waste of his time and my money. I'm out of ideas and out of patience."

Phillis shook her head, helpless to think of what to add. She patted Miss Maymie's arm and trudged upstairs overwhelmed by her sadness for this woman whom she had believed to be so lacking in compassion.

6/19/28. Exciting to watch Junior play ball. So mad at Stanley for his row with Teddy. Miss Banion's love story. I can't let go of any of this. Another sleepless night. Maybe a story about loyal Houston fans and Buff Stadium. It was quite a show. Baseball nicknames, my nicknames. I hate most of mine. Only one person ever called me "Scottie." A long time since I heard this nickname. Junior's nickname is perfect. Carter sure was mad. He's a sore loser.

CHAPTER TEN

May the outside world not take this lynching as symbolic of the Houston spirit. It was not men like these who died in the Alamo. It was not craven creatures like these who fought at the Battle of San Jacinto. Men of that low, vile character did not build the Texas or the Houston of today.

"They Are Ghouls" *Houston Press*
MEFO (Marcellus Foster)
June 20, 1928

Wednesday, June 20, 1928,

IT WAS ALMOST TEN-THIRTY WHEN PHILLIS went downstairs for breakfast. It was a gloomy day outside and even the kitchen was dark. No lights on. No food in sight. She shook the cold enamel pot on the stove, relieved to hear coffee swishing around inside. After lighting it up, she pulled out a box of Post Toasties from the cupboard.

"Miss Phillis, you gettin' youself some breakfast?"

"Good God, Josie," Phillis exclaimed. "Why are you sitting there in the dark? Can I turn on a light?"

As Phillis pulled the light cord, she saw Josie in her rocker and realized something was terribly wrong.

"You've been crying. What's the matter?"

Josie bowed her head and held her kerchief to her nose. "Miss Phillis, I cain't tell. Charlie said keep my mouth shut."

"What in the world's happened?"

"I'm 'fraid. Plain scared. He thinks Houston's still safe. It don't feel like a good place to me." Her moan raised the hair on Phillis's arms.

"Forget Charlie, just tell me. You're scaring me to death."

"Coffee's boiling. Git you a cup and let me settle myself down."

With her hot cup of coffee, she sat next to Josie who was rocking back and forth. "I'm not moving from here till you tell me what's wrong," she said firmly.

Josie sighed and refolded her arms across her chest. "I hope they write it up in the newspapers. Charlie and I know sometimes it never gets there."

Phillis waited, alarm bells going off in her head.

"Last night masked men swooped into Jeff Davis Hospital and stole Robert Powell right out of his bed."

"What!" Phillis exclaimed.

"They took him to that road behind Memorial Park and hanged him from the bridge. Left him hangin' there till a man found him at six-thirty this mornin'."

"That's not a hanging. That's a lynching. You're not telling me a lynching occurred this morning in Houston?" Phillis exclaimed as she reached out and grabbed Josie's arm. "Who's Robert Powell?"

Josie pulled away, "He's the colored man they say shot a police officer on Sunday. Police arrested Mr. Powell. They took him to Jeff Davis because he got shot bad in the stomach. A guard stood beside his bed every minute to keep him safe. I ask you," Josie said, rising from the rocking chair and hobbling across the room. She stood at the table across from Phillis. "I ask you, if a policeman's guarding, how'd a gang of men git hold of him?"

Josie looked back at her rocker. "I wasn't sure I could even get out of that chair. Will I ever smile again? My bones ache and my heart hurts."

Phillis's head dropped as she fell silent, remembering the horrible lynchings she wanted to forget. The casual newspaper accounts of the mob violence.

Too weak to continue standing, Josie hobbled back to the rocker and sank down on the chair. "Miss Florinda, she's a colored lady what works at the hospital. Her mama cleans for old lady Fletcher over there," pointing to the cottage next door. "She told me these men wore white robes that covered their clothes but a dark blue sleeve with a striped patch stuck out of one."

Josie began crying into a handkerchief she pulled from her apron pocket.

Pausing to take a breath, she sighed. "My people say there's no KKK in Houston. Sounds like policemen or the Klan. Sometime they're the same."

Phillis pushed away her coffee, nearly overturning the cup. She nodded and asked, "What Florinda saw sounds like these lynchers were Houston policemen? Men who wouldn't wait for Mr. Powell to go to trial?"

Josie nodded. "Miss Phillis, what's gonna happen now? Are colored folk safe in Houston? Are these white men through?" She searched Phillis's face for assurance. "Nobody told me white folks acted like this in Houston."

Nobody told me either. I thought I left this savagery when I got out of north Texas. She remembered too well, Fort Worth and Dallas voters electing Klan members to every city and county office. Only the *Dallas Morning News'* condemned these masked outlaws who were blasting into the South for the second time, nearly costing its editor George Dealy his newspaper as subscriptions dropped. At Baylor only Phillis and her friend Violet, scorning what they considered their spineless friends, joined the Anti-Lynching Crusade and the League of Women Voters when three black men were burned alive just north of Waco. Outraged by their gruesome deaths that made headlines across the nation, they watched local lawmen turn their backs on the crime.

The knot inside her stomach grew as Phillis held Josie's twitching fingers. "If it's the po-lice did this? Nothing's gonna happen."

"I hope that's not the case. I need details. I'll get downtown as fast as I can and find out. The afternoon papers will be out in a few hours."

"Mr. Richardson, he owns the *Informer.* He'll write about it for black folk. His paper comes out Saturday. Maybe everything's better by then."

Phillis's heart went out to this woman who wanted her world to right itself. "In six days, more people than you and I've ever seen at one time are coming here." The horror of this crime was now hanging over Houston while this morning paper's headline had read, "Hooray, hooray, Old Houston Welcomes you." The visiting journalists Stanley had said came early must be pounding on their typewriters in their hotel rooms, composing juicy news stories for the Associated Press to send out from coast to coast. Her only consolation was that the lynching of Robert Powell would not be buried. *What will this so-called "progressive" city do now?*

She stroked Josie's arm. "I'll find Stanley. He'll know what's going on," Phillis said softly. "Houston's shamed," Phillis said. "I know you're afraid and I'm afraid, too. You and Charlie are right to stay indoors."

"Wednesday's the day he carries Mizz Hinkle to the farmer's market."

"I don't think it's wise for him to go anywhere."

Phillis grabbed her notebook and purse and hurried out the front door. Though it was after eleven, passengers on the streetcar sat calmly reading the morning *Houston Post* whose morning deadline prevented it from covering news of the lynching.

Other than Josie's account, Phillis knew little about what had happened. She was frantic to find out the details. Her horror at the act mixed with her recognition that this could be a career breaking event. *I am right here. I can write about this.* Transferring to the Leeland trolley, she arrived at the Houston Press building as Stanley was getting out of a taxi.

"Hey, I was just going to call you," he began. Phillis cut him short.

"I already know. Josie told me. News gets around fast in the colored community."

He grabbed her arm and hustled her into the building, then bounded up the stairs ahead of her to his office. The pressroom door was wide open revealing a pandemonium unlike anything she had ever seen. Typewriters clacked. Reporters were coatless and hatless with rolled-up sleeves, yelling and cursing each other, half-smoked cigars and cigarettes hanging from the corners of their mouths. Crumpled paper littered the floor. Unanswered telephones rang incessantly as the telegraph machine spit out its monotone dots and dashes. The whole room was chaos, a bedlam more exhilarating to her than a trumpet fanfare.

"This is exactly where I want to be." Her words went unheard amidst the roomful of men sharing what they knew and what they thought they knew all at one time.

This was her career. Tragedies and troubles, frustration and criticism were what everyone in this room was feeding on and for the first time she shared their energy as they experienced the pain of this horrible crime. She wanted to know exactly what had happened, who did it and why it happened. What was in the minds of these white men who yanked this wounded man out of his hospital bed and left him hanging from a bridge at the edge of town? What hatred drove them to do this? Did these killers think people in Houston wanted them to take the law into their hands?

"Benjy tell us what's going on," Stanley said to a smart-aleck newsie who knew the scoop on the afternoon edition before it hit the streets. "You've always got your ear to the ground."

"Mefo's got a front-page editorial in today's paper."

"Well, don't just stand there. What does the boss say?

"'He calls them 'Ghouls.' That's the headline." Benjy interjected with his usual spiel, "Front page. Read all about it!" Eying the men who encircled him, the boy recited the words from memory, "These lynchers are cowards. These aren't the heroes who died at the Alamo. They're ghouls. Golly, I love that word." Benjy's whole face grinned. "Man, I bet I sell a hundred papers today."

Stanley rumpled the kid's hair and replied, "And you should. I hope to God east coast newspapers pick up Mefo's editorial. I can imagine what the visiting reporters are sending to their editors. Houston's gonna be slammed all over the world. And they deserve every bit of it."

Phillis pulled his sleeve, pointing to the door. "I'm going on the street to see what people are saying. Talk to you later." No editor would publish a woman's account of the lynching. Accounts of how people here were reacting, might land her a story. She would concentrate on Houstonian's reaction to this tragedy. Did they care? Knowing this would help her decide if she wanted to stay in this place where men take the law into their own hands.

The trolley taking her back to Main Street was nearly empty. A surprising breeze wafted in from the open windows, the result of this morning's rain shower. Houston's streets were shiny clean, but the rest of the town was dirtied from harboring men who would commit this heinous crime. The Rice Hotel was no place she wanted to go. Same for the Lamar where meeting Reggie and Brad would not be pleasant. Billy McKinnon's sign flapped in the breeze as she walked in. It was deserted. Local reporters were at their newspaper offices trying to figure out how to write today's tragic news.

She reversed her direction and walked south on Travis, approaching McKinney Street. A woman wearing a raincoat and a close-fitting hat stood there at a trolley stop reading a book. "Good morning, ma'am," Phillis said.

"Morning," she replied without looking up.

"My name's Phillis Flanagan," Phillis said. "I'm here from Fort Worth to cover the convention for the *Star-Telegram*."

The woman lifted her head and gave Phillis a curious stare. "Welcome to Houston. I don't think I've heard of that newspaper. Is it a daily?"

Phillis nodded and asked, "Do you know there was a lynching here in Houston last night."

"Can't say as I have," she murmured, turning back to her book.

"Did you hear what I said? A colored man was kidnapped from Jeff Davis Hospital and driven to the edge of town where they hanged him from the Post Oak bridge."

The woman's head jerked up and her mouth dropped open. "What are you saying? Are you crazy? That doesn't happen here. It wasn't in this morning's paper."

"Happened too late for the morning deadline. He wasn't found until six-thirty a.m."

"Really. Oh my God. Well, if it's true, it'll be in the afternoon papers. Wish I'd bought one."

"You don't recall any lynching's in Houston?"

"Absolutely not. We've never had one. Been here more than forty years. We call our city 'Heavenly Houston.' Whites and colored persons say it's a boomtown for everyone. They have their world, we have ours. We don't mix, and that's how everybody likes it. What you're claiming makes no sense."

Phillis said, "May I have your name so I can . . . ."

"Oh, here's my bus." And she was gone.

The woman's bragging about "Heavenly Houston" was garbage. No colored person thought this city or any other city in America was "heavenly," and Phillis wondered if anyone in their right mind, white or black, would think it was after today's lynching. The South's continued pride in the Antebellum history had become an incurable curse. With a vengeance, these Houston men continued the practice of lynching. What kind of men were they? Would they be brought to justice?

She needed a place to think. A cool place. The Dallas library had been her childhood haunt, especially after moving to Highland Park. The welcoming world of books, where no one was judged, had comforted her. Maybe the downtown library here offered a similar respite from the pavement that burned right through the soles of her shoes while the celebratory bunting hung limp and lifeless in the afternoon heat.

Slipping through the doorway onto the polished red tile floors, she sighed as her body sucked in the cool air. Yanking off her hat, she fingered her damp curls and reached for a hanky to wipe off her face. The reading room. A quiet place, a good place to think. Amid shelves stacked with venerable volumes, recounting man's injustices to his fellow man, she would find the solace she sought. From her purse, she took out her tablet and pencil and began to write.

The scratching sound of another pencil alerted her to the presence of man sitting at her table. A slight, mostly bald-headed man clad in a worn trench coat, was busily filling in the squares of a *New York Times* crossword puzzle. A visiting journalist. Her knee jerk curiosity overcame her desire for solitude.

"Sir, what newspaper has sent you to cover the convention?"

He looked up and gazed at her bemusedly. "What did you say?"

"Are you here as a journalist covering the Democratic National Convention?" she spoke a little louder, thinking if the gentleman had a hearing problem, the library reading room would not be a good place to interview him.

Encouraged by his nod, she asked, "Are you enjoying your stay in Houston?"

"Yes, thank you very much," he replied. "Houston is lovely. All this brilliant sunshine. Which is why I'm indoors. My eyes can't stand your blinding sunlight, much less the heat. I'm from Pennsylvania. After this morning's lynching, I'm just sitting here waiting to see what happens next. You haven't heard any new developments, have you?"

"My name is Phillis Flanagan. I write for the *Fort Worth Star-Telegram.* And you are?"

"I'm Neal Busby, *Pittsburgh Gazette*," he responded. "My train arrived from Kansas City last night and this morning the Rice Hotel is buzzing with this news. A hideous beginning to my stay here in Houston. I am sure your city would be happier had this lynching occurred a little farther from the convention hall."

"Yes," Phillis agreed. "Far better would be no lynching at all."

"This lynching puts me in mind of chefs fighting in the kitchen just as the company is about to sit down at the dinner table." Busby shook his head. "A helluva curtain raiser for this event."

He looked back at his crossword.

"I would call this lynching a lot worse than a kitchen fight, unless the cooks picked up butcher knives. Houstonians are shocked and horrified by this crime. No one can remember a lynching here."

"Really?"

She nodded.

"You know why they're upset, don't you?" Busby asked.

"Well, of course I do. It's a horrible crime and shameful whether the victim is white or black. And, of course, there is the convention."

Busby explained, "Lynching throws a shadow of shame. Terrible for a community's reputation. The possibility of a KKK factor. Kluxism is bad for business. From what I read in your Chamber of Commerce pamphlets; Houston's called the 'up-and-coming city in Texas.'"

Phillis wanted to scream, *Yes, this is exactly what I thought when I came here.*

"Do you think the lynching will affect the convention?" she asked.

"In a way, yes," Busby replied. "It's definitely a political embarrassment for Houston and the Democratic Party. It can't be ignored or dismissed with a wave of the hand. Perhaps, it will convince Democrats to put in an anti-lynching plank like the Republicans did last week in Kansas City."

Busby looked at the clock on the wall and stood.

"You're speaking for your newspaper?" Phillis asked, taking down his words and hoping they would prove true.

Busby nodded and said, "Yes. Good luck, Miss Flanagan. You gals have a tough time of it. Hope I helped you some."

She thanked him and waved goodbye. His idea about the adoption of an anti-lynching plank, something good coming from something so horrible, made her hopeful. Maybe, Democrats admitting that lynching was a terrible crime was a subject she would be permitted to write about. She could call the Powell lynching the impetus which brought this on. Excited, she made notes. The insignificance of reporting on bright-colored frocks and tea parties was never more obvious than at this moment.

A STOP AT JONES'S NEWSSTAND BEFORE catching the Heights trolley provided Phillis with copies of all the afternoon papers. With a line of people clamoring for the afternoon edition, Harry Jones gave her a brusque wave as his assistant took her nickels. Lynching headlines blazed across the front pages. She bet Stanley's newsie was selling his papers like hotcakes.

Gratefully, she climbed aboard the trolley and collapsed on a seat headed for home. Accustomed now to the clickety-clack of the trolley wheels, Phillis flipped through the newspapers in her lap, grateful that each contained lengthy front-page articles about the lynching. Scanning the accounts now written in black and white for everyone to read somehow magnified the horror of the deed, at least for Phillis. Mefo's editorial stood out for its forceful rhetoric, using damning epithets she had never seen applied to lynchers in print. What weight would his words carry in Houston? Certainly, the city seemed to be taking the right steps. She could share all of this with Josie when she got home.

Phillis was surprised that she thought of 1750 Harvard as home. After five days, the creaky house with its cool welcoming interior provided a surprising level of comfort. She spread the papers across the dining table and called to Josie who came running.

"Here's what the Press says about the lynching. Right here on the front page. Mefo calls the lynchers 'Ghouls.' He says they are not man or woman. Not Houstonians, not even human. He asks us not to hold the city to blame for this crime."

Josie nodded her agreement, "I dunno, dead is dead. Mr. Powell was just twenty-four. Charlie says he had a good job with the city working on a garbage truck."

"Mr. Foster wants Robert Powell's ghost to haunt the five cowards who killed him."

"Yes, I like that. I knew a lady haunted. She never had minute of rest till she lay down in her grave. Does the paper say who these bad men were?"

"City Council has put up $10,000 to find them. See right here across the top of the page."

Josie pulled out a pair of silver framed spectacles and peered at the headline. "Maybe so," she pursed her lips and nodded.

The back screened door slammed shut and Miss Maymie called a greeting. Soon all three of them were reading.

"We've got a terrible mess with this lynching," the landlady announced.

"I would call it a tragedy, a heinous crime" Phillis replied, waiting for Maymie to say something to console Josie. "The visiting journalists have described this so-called mess as having 'the odor of lynching,'"

"I'm sure that's true. Some of the reporters who are in Hoover's camp claim it's a visitation of 'God's ill will upon the Democrats.' Isn't that tacky?" Maymie removed her spectacles and rubbed both sides of her nose. "I almost blew my top when a visitor at the coffee shop in the Esperson Building snarled, 'For southerners, lynching is an everyday event.'"

Phillis nodded, thinking to herself, if you included the entire South, this was only a slight exaggeration. "I know what you mean. A journalist from Pittsburgh told me this act could add an anti-lynching plank to the Democratic Platform. What do you think?"

"Not sure if Southerners would support that," Maymie mumbled as she quickly changed the subject. "I'm mad clean through that a bunch of hoodlums broke into a hospital and kidnapped a wounded Negro from a hospital bed and hanged him. We've worked for five months to get everything neat and tidy, built a palace to hold the event, and knocked ourselves out planning entertainment."

Phillis shut her eyes, waiting for her to cry out against this foul crime that took a young man's life rather than ranting about the havoc this lynching had caused the city.

Through lips pursed in a straight line, Maymie spit out the words, "I'm sure Mayor Holcombe and Jesse Jones will huddle till the wee hours trying to get us out of this hole."

"Finding these 'ghouls' as Foster calls them quick as possible will be the best help I can think of," Phillis pronounced.

"Let's hope for the best." Maymie finally thought to pat Josie's shoulder as she turned to go upstairs.

"Well, I'm looking for a story," Phillis said, exasperated. "There's no chance any article on the specifics of a lynching, written by a woman, will make it into a Texas newspaper. An account of how people here were reacting, could land me a story."

"What about Mrs. Davis?" Maymie asked.

"Who's she?"

Maymie Banion exploded. "Didn't you read about the detective being shot? That's what brought on all of this. I don't understand why you don't read the newspaper more carefully. It's your livelihood, isn't it?" She pointed her finger at Phillis who reddened angrily.

"Alma Davis's the widow of the detective Robert Powell killed. The Davis family lives over on Waverly Street, less than half a mile from here. The funeral procession stretched all the way down the Boulevard."

Phillis put her hand on her mouth remembering the cortege she saw from the trolley.

'The service was at his home on Monday. The widow's a member of our Heights Sunshine Club. We already took up a donation. I'll drive you to her house or you could just walk over after supper by yourself."

"Thank you, Miss Maymie," said Phillis, excited by the prospect of an interview. "Would you come with me?" she asked as pleasantly as she knew how.

BY SIX THAT EVENING, THEY WERE ON their way to the Davis home. The small, gray-shingled cottage sat forward on the lot, pink petunias bordering its front walk.

Two barefooted boys played kickball in the front yard. When their rubber ball bounced out into the street, the older boy ran to the curb and held his hand across his brother's chest to keep him from chasing it.

"Wait here," he said, as he looked both ways, ran out, grabbed the ball, and then ran back. Eyeing the two visitors apprehensively, he sidled back to his brother and put an arm around his shoulder. Both boys wore short pants and faded cotton shirts. The younger boy looked about five, his brother, perhaps, seven. Phillis guessed they were the two who had just lost their father.

"Hey there," Maymie Banion greeted the older boy. "Good to see you."

He looked down at his feet, not acknowledging her. "I'm not afraid of spiders." Raising his head, he asked, "Who are you? My teacher's got red hair just like yours. What do you have in that sack?"

"Hush," the eldest reached for his brother's hand and continued to stare suspiciously at the two women.

"My name's Phillis. I hope your teacher likes her red hair better than I like mine. When I was in school, kids teased me about my hair and some people still do."

"Boys, who're you talking to?" a woman called from inside the house.

Maymie stepped forward and knocked on the screened door. "Alma, it's Maymie Banion. Just checking to see how you're doing. I've brought my friend Phillis Flanagan with me."

A slim, tired-looking young woman smiled wanly as she opened the door and reached for the boys who came running to her.

"Oh, Maymie, my sons look like ragamuffins. Miss Flanagan, so sorry you found them barefooted and wearing play clothes."

She smoothed the younger boy's cowlick and looked up questioningly. "You came to visit? There's been so many people in and out of the house, I can't keep track of them."

Maymie handed her a brown paper bag. "Alma, we only came to bring the boys some ginger cookies and see if there's anything you need."

"Can we have one now? Just one, mama."

She shrugged her shoulders, "I guess so," handing them two cookies from the bag. "Come on in, Maymie."

The boys remained outside as Phillis and Maymie followed Alma inside. "The house is a mess," she apologized. "I can't seem to keep things straight."

A large basket of orange gladiolas brightened the sparsely furnished front room. Alma motioned them to sit on the divan as she took a seat in the rocker.

"I got the Sunshine Society's gift box, Maymie. I'll send a thank you. My life is strange and bewildering. I keep expecting Worth to telephone or walk in the door. We were babies in Heights Hospital, born two days apart. Sweethearts from eighth grade on. Married when we were seventeen."

Phillis noticed the framed photograph on top of the radio console. A handsome, dark-haired man wearing a suit and tie and carrying his straw boater smiled broadly. Nothing about him suggested he was an armed detective on the Houston Police Department's payroll.

Twisting her wedding band, Alma Davis fought back her tears. "I thought once he was promoted to detective and didn't have to ride that motorcycle anymore, he would be safe." Laughing mirthlessly, she wrung her hands as if she thought it would help.

"You know, he got his promotion six months ago. Two days after his birthday. We both just turned thirty. He was the second-youngest detective on the force."

"Chief Mike told me," Maymie said. "Alma, everybody praised Worth for all the burglars and thieves he put behind bars."

"That doesn't help me, does it?" Alma cried.

She gave Phillis a hollow-eyed look as if her world no longer made sense. "And now, losing him is even worse because a gang lynched this colored man who they say killed my Worth. Hanged the man from the old railroad bridge. Broke his neck and left him there for anyone to see. That's not what I wanted. Revenge doesn't make things better."

She held her hands on each side of her face and cried, "They say the poor man was just twenty-four years old. Worth hated lynchings and the Klan and everything they stood for. Did the KKK do this? I hope not."

Alma's grief-stricken words filled the room.

"Worth was the kindest man I ever knew." she continued. "Now he's gone, and his killer is gone, and Houston is branded. Oh, the shame of it."

"You're right, Alma," Maymie said. "The shame of kidnapping a man already dying of his wounds, taking him to the edge of town and throwing him off that bridge with a rope tied around his neck. Houston's not like this. We don't have lynching's here like up around Dallas." She shook her head and patted the young widow's shoulder.

"How will I raise my sons, Maymie? They'll have to grow up knowing their father's killer was hanged by a bunch of hoodlums. Not convicted by a judge like he should have been. Instead hanged before he could even apologize to these fatherless boys."

Phillis thought of them, innocently playing outside, not yet comprehending what they had lost, and their fragile young mother whose life had just been upended. What would happen to them? Was there a pension plan to support the families of fallen officers?

Motioning to Phillis, Maymie stood and when Alma rose, she put her arms around her and whispered, "If you need anything, call me."

Phillis left the Davis house, puzzling for a way to reconcile her reactions to the grief-stricken young widow, the image of Robert Powell hanging from a bridge, Josie's palpable fear, and Maymie's fixation on Houston's putting this crime behind it.

6/20/28. I will never forget Alma Davis's words. This is where I will begin. I will look for more stories tomorrow. What I want to write is the story of the lynching. I know no editor will print it, but I am not sure I have the ability, the words to capture the horror, the savagery of these outlaws. Will Houston be the first city to find and punish a band of lynchers? This is fertile ground for a reporter.

CHAPTER ELEVEN

Luna Park, 2200 Block Houston Avenue, has virtually every variety of amusement device known in the world of showdom. One of its biggest features is the giant skyrocket, a roller coaster larger and higher than any other operating in the United States. It is a mile and a mile and a quarter long and at its highest point soars 110 feet in the air.

Wednesday, June 21, 1928

"WHERE'S OLIVIA?" PHILLIS ASKED as she entered the kitchen.

Bending over to pull a pan from the oven, Josie muttered, "Don't know. What you want for breakfast? Fried ham?"

"Doesn't matter. I've not much of an appetite. I'll run up and see about her. Surely, she's not sick."

Phillis climbed to the third floor and knocked. "Olivia? Are you in there?" After hearing nothing, she turned the knob, worrying she might be ill.

The room looked empty, the dresser tray filled with jars of cream and pots of rouge swept clean. No hairbrush, no hairpins, no powder box. Nothing in the closet. Phillis opened every bureau drawer, all empty. Her eyes circled the room looking for some trace of the young woman who seemed to have vanished. Walking over to the bed, she smoothed the faded pink coverlet and almost stumbled over Olivia's white lace-up oxfords which rested on the floor. A rolled up pair of white cotton stockings were stuffed into the shoes. *Yes, she would leave these behind. Why did she go? Why, no goodbyes? Was she on a train headed for New York City?*

Phillis ran to the stairwell. "Come quick. Olivia's moved out."

Josie's steps echoed through the house as she slowly climbed to the third floor. Phillis stood in the deserted room and shuddered. "I can't believe it."

Standing in the doorway, Josie wrung her hands and said, "I suspicioned something was wrong."

Phillis's soft words were barely audible. "What was it?"

Josie shook her head and fingered her apron strings.

"This makes me so sad. I just met her. Holy Moses, I'll miss her."
Phillis raced through their last conversation. During her first few days
in this strange household, Olivia's kindness had made everything better
— Miss Maymie's hurtful criticism and Della Hinkle's insults, and her
struggle for topics to write about.

Josie patted her back. "Don't be upset, baby. Miss Olivia does exactly
what she wants to. I never met a girl who was more bullheaded in my
life, unless maybe it's you."

They laughed as they walked out of the room and descended to
the kitchen.

Phillis munched her biscuit absently as her thoughts centered on
Olivia's flight. "I hope she's safe," she spoke under her breath.

Josie heard her and chimed in, "I sure do too."

SITTING DOWN TO TYPE HER STORY ABOUT Alma Davis, Phillis
knew capturing the widow's heartache was going to be a struggle. Not
only had she lost her husband and the father of her children, his death
had caused a lynching. The horror and the savagery. Hanging a mortally
wounded young man from a bridge until his neck snapped, this was the
story she wanted to write. As far as she could tell, no articles about the
lynching written by female journalists had made the newspapers.

After her waste can overflowed with wads of crumpled paper, she
felt satisfied her story was the best she could do. She was confident
her editor would publish this. Dare she hope for her first front page?

Boarding the trolley earlier than usual Phillis rode to town with the
regulars who were on their way to work. An ironically beautiful day of
sunshine here in Houston. Thunderclouds would have been a better
match for her mood.

The Rice Hotel's ceiling and majestic marble columns still soared.
The atmosphere at ten o'clock in the morning was vastly different than
Monday night when she entered on the arm of Bradley Nicholson.
Instead of soft lights and flappers clad in evening gowns, uniformed
bellmen dollied mountains of suitcases toward the elevators as visitors
with shrill Brooklyn accents checked in at the front desk.

Fortunately for Phillis, the scores of out-of-town visiting journalists
had sent their articles off and the telegraph desk thankfully had no
lines. Handing Western Union's clerk her article, she waited while he
counted the words. "Sir, please send this collect as a Night Letter to
the *Star-Telegram*, Fort Worth, Texas."

"Will do, miss. A NL, collect."

Not in time for tomorrow's paper. Orders from Amon Carter made it clear she was to send anything she wrote by the cheapest rate. The editor had held back her story on Houston women's Me-Too buttons for three days and then buried it at the bottom right side on the next-to-last page. Maybe he would like this article better.

Walking across the street to Harry Jones's newsstand, she picked up a copy of the *Post* and handed him her nickel. "What's Houston going to do, Harry?"

"Read it and see. You're in for a surprise. I'm surprised by the city's response."

Jones, whom she suspected of reading every one of the newspapers he sold, piqued her curiosity. She needed to find a place to sit and peruse the paper. Yesterday, Maymie recommended the Junior League tearoom. She would welcome a pot of tea and some biscuits right now.

A snappy navy-and-white-striped awning and a smart little sign "Junior League Lunchroom," marked the entrance. A young woman wearing a yellow dress and white pinafore told her, "Sorry, lunch isn't served until eleven thirty."

"I thought you served tea all day. Can't I get a cup?"

"No, ma'am. Kitchen's not open yet."

A second woman entered and was told the same. Though strangers, they looked at each other, realizing their common need. Phillis turned to the uniformed Junior Leaguer and asked, "Can you direct us to the nearest coffee shop, please?"

"Around the corner at the San Jacinto Hotel."

"Shall we go grab a cup of coffee or tea?" Phillis asked the other woman.

"Good idea," she replied, and they were soon ensconced in a booth at the hotel's coffee shop.

"I'm Phillis Flanagan, covering the convention for the *Fort Worth Star-Telegram*. How about you?"

"I'm Etta Henderson, here in Houston as an advance scout for my boss, Emily Newell Blair."

Taking a closer look at her, Phillis realized Etta was young, pretty, and well groomed. Her hair was neatly tucked under a black straw cloche. Dressed in a slim-cut black linen suit and gleaming black leather high heels, she cut a stylish figure. And she had an authoritative air, a determination. Who in the world was Emily Newell Blair? They both removed their notebooks and pencils and began making notes.

"Is your boss coming as a delegate to the convention?"

"Mrs. Blair is Vice-Chairman of the Democratic Party, the highest-ranking female in national politics."

Phillis drew in a breath and let it out, realizing she needed to spend time studying the list of female officials.

"In 1920, Mrs. Blair was one of the founders of the League of Women Voters. Now she rejects the organization as an ineffective use of women's time."

"For gosh sakes, why?" This made no sense to Phillis, a proud card-carrying member of the League.

"The League is nonpartisan," Etta replied. "Women can't afford to be non-partisan. We must join a political party so we can run for office. That's the only road to power."

"So your boss has done that. How?"

"Hard work. Two-hundred speeches in twenty-two states, organizing over two-thousand Woman's National Democratic Clubs across the United States, including the one here in Houston."

Phillis scribbled furiously.

"We're the most organized political women's club since suffrage."

"What's your goal? Elect a woman to be president of the United States?" Phillis asked.

"Yes. National and statewide offices."

Phillis asked, "How do women win elections on their own? I am not sure I know a man who would vote for a female dog catcher, much less a woman running for president."

"Political training schools."

"Interesting," Phillis responded.

"The Woman's National Democratic Club's school is two years old. Women all over America attend."

"What kind of courses?"

"Mainly instruction in the operation of government departments, party organization, campaign machinery, and public speaking."

"Where are the classes? What does it cost?"

Etta looked Phillis straight in the eye. "In the living room of the clubhouse in D.C., where club members pay zero to attend the school."

Phillis, at a loss for words, finally squeaked, "Who teaches?"

"A Texas woman whom you should know. If you don't, you should go straightaway to her campaign headquarters and volunteer."

"Are you talking about Minnie Fisher Cunningham?"

Etta bluntly proceeded to dress Phillis down. "Well, at least you know somebody. I am surprised you knew nothing about the school. You do now. Are you a member of our club?"

Phillis shook her head.

"That's a start after you get back from signing up to volunteer for Cunningham's campaign for U.S. Senate."

Etta, perhaps apologizing for her harshness, said, "Don't feel bad. Most women are at a loss when it comes to politics."

Still wanting to defend herself, Phillis replied stiffly, "I have voted in every election. Aren't many volunteer opportunities in Texas."

"You're a journalist, the perfect profession to make a difference. Write about our training school, investigate our congressmen and join the lobby to influence legislation."

Phillis drew back, astonished. "Excuse me, I want to report catastrophes, disasters, or personal tragedies."

"Sure, but you need to broaden your thinking. Might have a better chance of getting into print. Help create a woman's voting block by writing about our fight for equality. Persuade women to vote for women. We need a women's voting block."

Phillis nodded, "I heard her speak. When asked about farm relief or foreign allies, she gave better answers than any of the male candidates. No more than fifty or sixty came to listen to her presentation. Voters don't pay her much attention."

Etta slapped her hands on the table, rattling their coffee cups. "That's what I meant by making a difference. Stand on the corner of Main and Texas Avenue. Hand out campaign leaflets you've written. If Mrs. Minnie Fisher Cunningham can't get votes, no woman can."

She pulled a photo from her satchel. "You'd never guess she's fifty-one years old, an editor at *Good Housekeeping,* and writes a monthly column and popular novels."

Phillis was flabbergasted. Her state's successful female politicians sounded nothing like Emily Blair.

"Etta, we've got all our political leaders working here at the convention, but none of them are known outside of Texas, except for Mrs. Cunningham. Can I meet your boss? Can I interview her?"

"Guess what we call her?" Etta grinned, ignoring Phillis's request.

"I have no idea," Phillis answered.

"'Southern Comfort' — the drink that slides down your throat like velvet and about two seconds later kicks you in the chest. That's her political style, cajolery mixed with obstinacy."

Phillis asked, "Why not run for president? She's a better candidate than Albert Smith."

"Rumors are she might be nominated for vice-president. She insists a woman must win a Senate seat before we can be taken seriously."

"Yeah, wouldn't it be great if Mrs. Cunningham were the first woman senator?"

Etta nodded and both looked down at their wristwatches, realizing they needed to be other places.

"I'm glad I met you, Phillis," Etta said. "Give me your telephone number. If there's an opening in Emily's schedule, I'll call you."

Promising to talk again, they exited the hotel and Phillis boarded the almost-empty trolley headed for Houston Heights, having decided Etta Henderson was the most persuasive female political leader she had ever met. *She's a steamroller with the organizational skills of someone twice her age. If only I could interview Emily Blair.*

On the trolley ride to her home, she scanned the newspaper articles discussing Houston's response to Mr. Powell's death. Encouraged by the outrage city officials expressed, as well as their proposed action, she hoped Josie would be comforted by Houston's reaction to the dastardly act.

Phillis entered the Harvard house and saw Teddy standing in the hall talking on the telephone. "No, I can't tell you any more than I already have. Please don't call again." He slammed the receiver onto the hook and turned to face her. "Phillis, you're a reporter. What's going to happen next? You guys know it all. Will they still hold the convention? Please tell me yes. I've bought a new bowler and two new seersucker suits for my job as page."

Phillis ignored his questions and asked, "Who was on the phone? Sounds like you have a problem."

Teddy gave her an innocent look, "Who me? Have a problem? Gotta go. See you later."

Before Phillis could blink an eye, he was out of the house and down the steps. She shook her head and frowned. This strange telephone conversation needed to be relayed to Miss Maymie.

Wonderful aromas wafted through the house. "Josie, I'm home."

"Yes'um. I'm here." Standing at the stove, stirring a pot, Josie looked up and brightened at the newspaper Phillis held.

"I've brought today's *Post*, *Press*, and *Chronicle*. There are lots of plans to catch the lynchers. Come sit down. I've only glanced at them. Let's read them together."

Josie sat down beside her and held the paper so far from her eyes Phillis suspected her eyeglasses were too weak. "The city of Houston's putting up ten-thousand dollars to investigate the mob outrage. Four white citizens and two Negro citizens, all of whom are businessmen here in the community will be in charge."

Josie leaned over to look at the article Phillis pointed to. "That's mighty good. Don't see *Informer* editor Mr. Richardson's name on the list. Wonder who these men are?"

"Do you want me to find out about them?"

"No, no need." Josie sighed and rose from her seat.

"Paper says, 'Policemen are combing every inch of the city looking for the members of the mob who killed Mr. Powell.'"

"Hallelujah." Josie smiled wanly and asked, "Do they say how long to find the men?"

"Captain Hamer of the Texas Rangers already has clues. He claims arrests will be made in a day or two. They call him a bloodhound."

Josie seemed unimpressed.

"Look at this. The National Association for the Advancement of Colored People is putting up a one-thousand-dollar reward for apprehension and conviction of the killers. Governor Dan Moody says he will pay two-hundred dollars for every member of the lynching mob apprehended."

"Sounds like they mean business. What do you think?" Josie asked.

"I surely hope so."

"Charlie says he won't draw an easy breath until these killers are in jail.

Turning to go back to the stove, Josie said, "All this is good. I hope the big men runnin' this town do what's right. But, if they find 'em and put them in the jailhouse, I'm telling you, it'll be the first time I see a white man pay for doing bad things to a colored person."

PHILLIS WENT TO HER ROOM HOPING JOSIE and the rest of Houston would see justice done.

All she wanted right now was a nap. As her mother always said, "Southern ladies need to rest during the hot summer afternoons." There was no day bed here like there was in her mother's bedroom, so she pulled down the coverlet, removed her shoes, and collapsed.

The slamming of the front screened door roused her, followed by the repeated ringing of the telephone. Miss Maymie's bellowing voice carried throughout the house. "What do you mean Olivia's gone?"

Phillis slipped into her shoes and went downstairs.

"Who was on the phone?" She hoped it wasn't Teddy's earlier caller.

"Stanley Staples," Miss Maymie replied. "I told him to call back later. When did Olivia leave? Was there a note?"

Phillis shook her head, and Josie replied, "No, ma'am. We think she left yesterday."

"Well, I need to rent the room. Thank goodness, that's not going to be a problem."

As she started up the stairs, Maymie turned back and said to Josie, "Please get the room ready for a new tenant."

Phillis and Josie exchanged looks as Della Hinkle entered the hallway.

"What's wrong? You two look like you've had an upset."

"Olivia's gone. Moved out. Miss Maymie says get the room ready."

The telephone rang again. Mrs. Hinkle answered it then beckoned to Phillis who took the receiver and said, "Hello."

"Phillis, this is Stanley. You and Olivia like to go to Luna Park tonight? Hot dogs and Hires root beer or something stronger if we can find it. They're having a dance-a-thon which is always a gas to watch. What do you say?"

"Olivia has moved out, no forwarding address." Phillis paused and glanced at Della Hinkle standing there listening to her conversation. She turned away from her and answered, "Yes. When shall we meet?"

She nodded and placed the receiver on the hook.

"I assume you're not joining us for supper tonight?" Della Hinkle's stance always reminded Phillis of a prison guard at the jail's main gate.

"That's correct, Mrs. Hinkle. Mr. Staples and I are going to Luna Park."

"That place is nothing more than a den of iniquity."

"Really? You've been there?" Phillis asked.

"Of course not. Don't make a joke of this, Miss Flanagan. You obviously don't know about Luna Park's reputation."

Phillis's eyes widened as she leaned forward, "Something sensational I can write about, I hope."

"You're asking for trouble, young lady. Last month their rowdy employees roughed up a respectable lady whom I happen to know. No telling what kind of deadbeats they get to work there."

Phillis nodded and gave a salute as she started to her room.

Della Hinkle's words followed her up the stairs, "Whatever you do, don't ride that Skyrocket! Three people have already died because they fell out of that death trap."

Stanley must need a diversion, which, at this point, sounded downright idyllic. A death-defying roller coaster would be a breeze compared to today's ups and downs.

She and Stanley took the trolley to Luna Park. As they exited, Phillis said, "I didn't realize it rode on the banks of a bayou. Very nice, Mr. Staples."

"If I had thought ahead, Josie could have fixed us a picnic supper, but their dogs are decent, and they sell the best popcorn in the city."

Walking into the park, Phillis gasped as she saw the famed Skyrocket right before her and suddenly realized how believable Mrs. Hinkle's cautionary words were.

"Yep, it's a giant-sized roller coaster. Over a mile long and a hundred-feet tall with an eighty-four-foot drop. You game for a ride?"

Phillis grinned, "Only so I can brag to Della Hinkle that I rode it. I'll be terrified the whole time."

"I didn't think you were afraid of anything." Stanley cut his eyes toward her and snickered, "We'll save it for last."

He steered her toward the center of the park. "Let's see the dance pavilion first. If the contest weren't going on, we could take a spin on the floor. It's the South's largest spring-loaded dance floor. You ever danced on one?"

She shook her head and he continued. "Gives you a bounce that makes even me look good, at least smoother than usual."

They watched the fifteen couples shuffling around the floor. Stanley introduced Bubber Flake, the attendant, who described the past forty-eight hours.

"Only five couples have dropped out so far. A cute little blonde who announced she had only been married three weeks. She screamed she wanted to win the seven-hundred-and-fifty-dollar prize to make a first payment on a home. Her husband dragged her off the floor."

Phillis, astonished by the couple's stamina, asked, "Forty-eight hours? How much longer can they hold out?"

"You never know. The last dance-a-thon lasted three weeks before the girls started fainting or falling asleep."

He laughed at her raised eyebrows. "Let me tell you about the blistered, burning feet I see. One girl in Pittsburgh soaked her feet in brine and vinegar for weeks before a Madison Square Garden event. When the marathon ended, she was still feeling no pain."

Stanley whistled in admiration.

"Wow, what a woman!" Phillis exclaimed.

Bubber added, "Yep, her nickname was 'Hercules.'"

"That fits. What are the contest rules?"

"The couples shuffle for forty-five minutes. No one's really 'dancing' after the first day is over. Funniest thing, they help each other stay in the contest instead of wanting them to leave. Critics call it the craziest competition ever invented."

Stanley and Phillis agreed with him and slowly walked over to the Skyrocket structure, the focal point of the thirty-six-acre park.

"I waited on purpose to take our ride until after the sun went down. I love it when the fifty-thousand light bulbs are turned on. Feels like magic to see the park bathed in light."

Phillis stood under the swaying pine trees mesmerized by the twinkling lights that outlined the gigantic wooden structure no more than 500 feet ahead. Hurdy gurdy music floated across the park along with the smell of popcorn and cotton candy.

"You ready?" Stanley asked.

When she nodded, he went to the booth and bought their tickets. After a short wait, they climbed into a car. White knuckling the safety bar on the first hundred-foot ascent, up in the sky with a trail of stars racing by, Phillis screamed as the car hurtled to the bottom again and again. When the two-minute ride ended, Stanley helped her out of the seat and steadied her as she reached the ground.

"You okay?" he asked. "You sure screamed loud."

She looked so horrified, he burst out laughing. "But, I want to ride it again."

"Hey, the Diving Horses show begins in a few minutes. But we'll miss the last trolley. You want to stay?"

"Maybe not, but next time. Promise you'll come back with me. I've never had so much fun in my life."

His laughter ricocheted in the night air. It seemed the most natural thing in the world for Stanley and Phillis to link arms as they walked to the park's entrance and waited for the streetcar to take them back to the Boulevard. And so, their evening ended with Phillis neglecting to pick Stanley's brain as she intended, failing to pump him for insider information about the lynching and ignoring the subject of Teddy. Neither of them ever mentioned the newspaper world that controlled their lives. Instead, standing in the middle of Harvard Street, Stanley reached over and took Phillis in his arms. She could feel her heart beating, or maybe it was his she heard. When she turned her eyes up as if questioning him, he reached down and kissed her forehead and then her lips briefly as if he were testing her response. Her smile answered him, and he patted her cheek as he turned to leave.

She stood watching him walk down Eighteenth Street, whistling. His tune did not come to her for a few seconds. When it did, she smiled and went into the house humming "Together."

Phillis did not write any stories that evening, only this entry in her diary.

6/21/28. Olivia has left without a trace. Need to look through Maymie's copy of the National Democratic Convention brochure for Etta Henderson and Emily Newell Blair. Nice evening at Luna Park. Will Houston stay focused on the lynching? How much is really being done to find the killers? Wish I could learn more.

CHAPTER TWELVE

HOUSTON, Texas, June 22 (AP). Indictments charging murder were returned here today against six men accused of lynching the negro, Robert Powell, alleged slayer of A. W. Davis, a city detective.

New York Times
June 23, 1928

Friday, June 22, 1928

SETTLING IN FRONT OF HER CORONA, Phillis tried to make herself write the story on Houston baseball. Their palatial new Buffalo Stadium that put all the fields in North Texas to shame. But all she could think of was Houston's shame since the lynching. She had no appetite for glorifying Houston in print. The only memory worth keeping from that game was when Amon Carter stormed off the field as his Fort Worth Cats toppled from first place.

Her blank sheet of paper stared at her from typewriter. She thought of the Skyrocket. The exhilaration she experienced, along with thousands of others who thronged to this attraction. Could she write an article about Luna Park? The thrill of the noisy machinery carrying them straight up into the night sky before plummeting down. The crazy dance-a-thon. Soon the clickety click sounds of her keys as she filled two pages and jerked the paper from the machine. Just a filler piece the editor might print.

When she went down for breakfast, Josie exclaimed, "You sure must've liked Luna Park."

"Oh?" Phillis replied. "Well, I've got my third article for the *Star*," flashing the sheets of paper in front of her. "I'm going to run downtown to turn it in."

Josie gave her a long look as she set a plate of hot cakes on the table. "Might be more than what's on that paper happened last night."

"What's that supposed to mean?"

"I got eyes. We saw you lovebirds comin' down the street so late."

Phillis laughed and tucked into her breakfast looking up as Teddy slumped onto the kitchen chair opposite her, yawning and rubbing his eyes.

"Late night?" Phillis asked.

"Yeah, and for you as well," he said, grinning as he started in on the mountain

of pancakes Josie placed before him.

Had everyone watched as she and Stanley came home from the park?

"Where's Mrs. Hinkle? Has she had breakfast yet?" Was she going to razz her as well?

"Charlie's taking her to the farmer's market."

"Oh," Phillis said with relief. She finished her breakfast and watched Teddy wolfing down his last bite. "Don't suppose you're going my way?"

"Sure thing. Want a ride? You feel like living dangerously?" Teddy eyed her with raised eyebrows. "Just kidding. I drive like a little old lady. You ready now?"

"Yes, I'm anxious to get my article to the telegraph office."

After a couple of backfires, they were on their way toward downtown. "Stanley says put better gasoline in my car. He says my carburetor would appreciate it. No can do. Money's tight right now."

"Why so? Tell me about your bootlegging activities, Teddy? Was that what got you in trouble with Stanley?"

She watched as he cut his eyes toward her and stepped on the gas.

"See this green building beside the railroad tracks? Telge's place. He repaired my cloth top," Teddy said, pointing to a patch on his Ford's ceiling. "When his repair work is slow, he builds boats. My bootlegger friends hate him. The Feds use his boats to patrol the San Jacinto River for their stills."

Phillis said, "Oh. Are these the friends wanting your help?"

No answer.

Like talking to a stump, she thought.

Teddy dropped her at the Rice Hotel and waited for her to get out. "Thanks for the ride. I hope you're being careful." She made a dash for the telegraph counter where she handed her article to the operator. Back on the street, she heard the newsies cry, "Extra, Extra! Read all about it! Lynchers locked up in Houston's jail."

Phillis ran to Jones's Newsstand and grabbed a *Houston Press*. The shock of her life would be too strong to express her feelings as she looked at a front-page photograph of her father.

"You okay, Phillis?" Harry Jones asked. "You're white as a bedsheet."

Phillis knew she could not be sick on Main Street. The hotcakes she'd had for breakfast churned in her stomach. Weakly, she fished in her pocket for a nickel and handed it to Jones as she thrust the paper under her arm.

Where could she sit down? Knots of people buying papers, sellers hawking brass colored Al Smith ashtrays and a group of cheery women thrusting pamphlets about the danger of drinking outlawed liquor filled the street. Harry pointed to the wagon at the corner. "Some ice water might make you feel better."

The mule-driven flat-bed wagon stopped, and the driver rolled off a barrel and set it up outside the Rice Hotel. "Not there, man. Roll it down the other way," a tired looking vendor dressed in a frayed red satin suit cried, "You'll block my stand with Houston brochures. How do you expect me to sell anything?"

With a moan, he dropped his head in his hands. When he looked up, Phillis stood in front of him. "Lady, you gonna faint?" He grabbed a grimy canvas folding stool and motioned her to sit down.

Weakly, she collapsed on the seat. Opening her newspaper, she studied the grainy photos of her father and five other men plastered on the front page.

"Phillip Calloway." The phony name underneath his face did not fool her for a second. This was a mug shot of her father who, according to this account, was now behind bars in the Houston City Jail, charged with murdering Robert Powell. Yes he changed his name, but his smile was her smile, the one she saw in her mirror every day.

All around her the jubilant cries of "Got 'em," "Hope they rot in Hell," "The Texas Rangers, God Bless 'em," as people eagerly bought the newspapers announcing the amazing news. "Indictments were returned by the grand jury against six men accused of lynching the Negro, Robert Powell, alleged slayer of A. W. Davis, a city detective." Houston was collectively breathing a sigh of relief.

Six faces, but Phillis saw only the one she had sought for almost twenty years. The image that had caused her heart to skip a beat whenever she saw a man who resembled him or heard a velvety voice reminding her of the Irish tenor who sang her lullabies.

And now she had found him. How could she speak with a lyncher all of Houston was booing? Only one person she knew could get her into his cell or at least close enough to examine his face and make a positive identification — Stanley Staples, who confided the first time they met that "male reporters have to work their way out of the cellar just like you dolls." Shaking his head, he revealed, "The police beat had more swaggering police chiefs than I could keep up with as well as 'sweatboxes' to extract confessions from even the hardest boiled criminals."

Stanley would know someone who could get them in. Would he be willing to do it? Of course, he would, if she told him the truth. To confess to him or anyone that her father was now in the city jail charged with a crime, which darkened Houston's name for all time, made her want to throw up.

"Here, miss. Here's a cup of ice water." The vendor on whose stool she perched held out a small paper cup, which Phillis gratefully took, closing her eyes to his grubby, sweaty fingers as she gulped the water he offered.

With a hasty thank you, she madly dashed to the pay telephone on the corner. Slipping a nickel from her pocket, she dialed the newspaper's number.

A woman answered, "Houston Press."

She managed to spit out, "Stanley Staples?"

"Honey, he landed in here just long enough to turn in his copy and left like a scalded dog. No one knows where Stanley Staples goes off to." She made clucking noises. "Wait till noon and check the cafés. He never skips lunch."

Phillis looked at her wristwatch, realizing she had over an hour to wait. How could she keep from going crazy? It was stupid to walk around town interviewing people when the only man she wanted to question was Stanley Staples. And the only question she wanted to ask was, "Can you help me get into the jail?"

Frustrated by having time to kill when until up to now, her head swiveled as she tried not to miss a thing, she decided to walk to the hall. Three days remained until the official dedication, the moment when they would remove the cyclone fencing encircling what locals were calling, "Democracy's Cradle."

Bagby Street was a beehive of activity with workers rushing in and out of the building as they carried long wooden tables inside. Tall stacks of folding chairs waited nearby to be transported. Voices bellowed "Testing 1-2-3" into microphones as men checked out the giant public address system.

The brass band marching along Bagby playing a sour rendition of "Dixie" distracted the lone uniformed guard at the entrance just long enough for Phillis to slip into the hall unnoticed. As she pressed her tall, thin frame close to one of the supporting posts, Phillis's arms broke out in goose bumps and her mouth gaped at the sight of this enormous, empty building.

Marveling at the arched roof and the ceiling's interlocking netlike ceiling, she admired the unusual construction. Were these really short pieces of pine fitted together? Square platforms twenty feet in the air were attached to each of the poles spaced evenly around the room ready for the press photographers to take images that would be sent out all over the world. How will they get their cameras to the top?

Massive rolls of chicken wire were being laid out and nailed to the opening beneath the main floor. She knew large blocks of ice were to be rolled under the floor to cool the place. What would go underneath this wire barrier?

Her eyes circled the giant room with its open-air sides, which provided a brightness as well a surprising airiness. No other Texas city had anything like it.

Phillis was thrilled, relishing her once-in-a-lifetime chance to see the brand-new palace, echoingly empty of the twenty-thousand convention goers who would fill it on Tuesday. Shaking her head, she crept alongside the rows of box seats and strolled out the double doors.

"Hey, lady, what do you think you're doing in there?" a gruff-voiced guard asked.

Was he going to grab her by the scruff of her neck? She breezily adjusted her hat, "Would you believe I was lost?"

The uniformed guard was not amused. "Can't you read that sign? No one is allowed. Certainly not wimmen."

He waved her off as Phillis gave him a smart-alecky grin and proceeded to the sidewalk where a pitiful, dirty-faced old man grunted as he slowly pushed his ice-filled wagon. Handing him a coin, Phillis watched as the one-eyed vendor wiped the bottle off with his apron tail, popped the top and handed her a frosty Orange Crush.

"Thanks," she said. "I'll bet you'll sell a lot of these. Will you have enough for all these visitors?"

"Yes, ma'am. I'm gonna have 'em every day."

"Miss," he asked, "didn't you just go in the hall?"

Phillis laughed and took a sip of her drink. "Well, yes," she said. "You've got a sharper eye than the guard."

"Yeah, and he's got two eyes." His laugh was screechy, "Lucky you. Is it as big as they say?"

"The largest building under one roof in the whole, wide world. You'll see inside after the convention's over."

"Lady, I'll bet you I get in sooner."

His determined expression impressed Phillis who laughingly replied, "Have a good day," as she scurried back toward Main Street. Checking her wristwatch, she hoped Stanley was at McKinnon's by now.

Phillis ducked into the café, biting her lip and searching the crowded diner. He sat with his buddies, but thankfully looked up and saw her. When she remained rooted in the entry, he frowned then saw her grim face and rushed over, bending down to hear what she whispered in his ear.

Returning to his table, he took a last bite of hamburger and slammed a fifty-cent piece on the table. With a wave to his friends, he took Phillis's arm and steered her out to the sidewalk.

"Who died?"

When he saw the tears filling her eyes, he said, "Let's go somewhere we can talk."

Phillis nodded as he led her to a Chinese café three doors down. The smiling host showed them to a table, and Stanley ordered a pot of tea. While they waited, Phillis pulled out the afternoon edition of the *Houston Press* and pointed to the photograph of the man identified as Phillip Calloway.

Stanley examined it and looked at her quizzically. "'Phillip Calloway,'" he read. "Do you know him?"

"He's my father. He deserted our family almost twenty years ago."

Stanley's eyebrows rose. His horror-stricken expression conveyed his shock.

She nodded, "He's changed his name, but I look so much like him, it scares me. He's a killer. He's locked up in the city jail. What should I do?"

"Let him rot there till they execute him if he's guilty."

"What do you mean *if* he's guilty? Of course, he's guilty," Phillis wailed.

Stanley put his fingers to his lips and said softly, "Pipe down." He looked around and continued, "The police found all six of Robert Powell's killers in less than forty-eight hours and got confessions and an indictment. That's a little too speedy for me."

"What's wrong with speedy?"

He ignored her. "If I hear you correctly, I need to get you into the jail so you can talk to this man you think is your father."

He rubbed his chin. "Let me think who I still know that works at the station."

"Thank you, Stanley," Phillis said. "You're reading my mind." To herself, she knew how much more she wanted. She had waited for years to look her father in the eye and tell him he was responsible for the deaths of her sisters, as well as nearly killing her mother. Did he possess even an ounce of guilt or sympathy for his misdeeds? Yes, she was ready for these long-overdue answers.

"Doll, I need to call some people and arrange this. We can't bust into the city jail, demanding access to one of their prized prisoners. Give me the rest of the day. Maybe we can get in tonight, after they feed the prisoners. Tomorrow, I take the boat down the ship channel. It's the excursion for the visiting journalists. City officials elected me to babysit them. If not tonight, we'll have to wait until Monday."

"No," she moaned as a tear rolled down her cheek. "I will die if I have to wait that long."

"Calm down, go home, and keep your mouth shut," he said firmly. "Don't blab anything about this to anyone."

THE HEIGHTS TROLLEY BUMPED ALONG as Phillis sat lost in the few memories she had of the father she grew up not knowing — the wave he gave them as he went out the door, the twin babies' cries that smothered his final words, and her mother's prophecy, "I doubt we'll ever see your father again."

Her mother rarely spoke of Phillip Flanagan, but when Phillis was in high school, she must have thought it time for a cautionary tale. As she related the story of the red-headed Irish drummer she married and the bill of goods he sold her which was as fake as the "solid gold" Victoria chain he gave her for a wedding present, her mother pressed her lips tightly and put her hands to her flaming cheeks.

"Phillip was a cloth drummer working all over north Texas," she said. "I worked as a dressmaker in Waxahachie and had customers who loved selecting from his samples. We had a business relationship that developed into more. Our sketchy courtship took place during his stopovers from month to month. We married in my family's farmhouse. At twenty-one, dreading the thought of approaching spinsterhood, I exchanged my freedom for a wedding ring that turned my finger green three months before you were born. My father referred to Phil as 'a good egg' and Mother bragged about her handsome son-in-law who 'could sell fishing poles in the Sahara Desert.'"

"Phillip Flanagan was not cut out to be a married man, much less a father. A rolling stone. That's what I called him." She shook her head. Once a chum turned up at our rooming house and kept calling your father by different names and referring to jobs he'd held which I knew nothing about."

"'Billy Ray,' Sammy said, 'you remember when we camped in Kilgore and went up and down Main Street, calling everyone to see you peddling that unicycle and juggling those balls until the sheriff accused us of performing without a license and threatened us with jail?' After a few more shots of whiskey, Sammy asked, 'Say, Frank, whatever happened to your trombone? You played a mean horn in that vaudeville act I saw in Omaha.'"

Her mother's eyes began filling with tears, "That night when we were alone, I asked him about the stories and he said, 'Oh, come on, Lena, I was young. Sowing my oats. I did play the horn. Music's not a crime, is it?'"

She stiffened and clinched her hands. "After you were born, he spent more time on the road than at home and sent less money for our support. I eked by with my sewing until the birth of the twins. Your father wasn't overjoyed to have two more girls. Where were the tall, lusty sons he expected? Phil showed up for the last time when the twins had their first birthday, spent one night, and left us forever."

Phillis's childhood ended at age eight. That Christmas, there was little food for their family. The twins cried all the time, and she and her mother slept together with the babies between them for warmth. In February, the Spanish influenza took the twins and nearly killed her mother.

She looked forward to demanding that Phillip Flanagan account for the unforgivable misery he had caused. Just the thought of that filled her with a piercing excitement. She needed to hear her father's confession, but she dreaded it.

Glad to arrive home and find no one stirring, she realized today's discovery had walled her off from the other residents. She would follow Stanley's advice. She trusted him, and that thought was her only comfort. He would get her into the jail, and she knew he would keep her secret.

The keys of her Corona refused to move that afternoon. Frustrated, she reattached the case to slam it shut when she saw an envelope taped on the cover.

The single sheet of paper brought joy to her heart when she opened the envelope and read the note.

    Dear Phillis,

       Sorry I had to leave so soon. No time to tell you goodbye. For me, you have made all the difference. I hope this note finds you well and happy and writing. You will

*pursue your dream just like me. My money will carry me as far as Memphis. I will
get to New York somehow. We will meet again.*

   Love, Olivia

The letter brightened this ghastly day, as Phillis now knew both she
and Olivia valued their brief friendship. Her friend's disappearance at
this time did spare her strain of pretending all was well in front of the
one person who could have sensed her distress.

A knock on the door turned out to be Mrs. Hinkle, who looked like
a lady on a mission. "What can I do for you?" Phillis asked.

"You can do a lot, Miss Flanagan," Della Hinkle snapped. "We
have a chance to rent Olivia's room, only the gentleman's wife has a
bad ankle. She says she can't climb all the way up to the attic room.
I thought to myself, why don't we just move Phillis up to Olivia's
room? You're such a skinny string bean, you can easily run up and
down those extra stairs."

Mrs. Hinkle smiled as she smoothed her hair back and patted her
bun, ignoring Phillis's dismayed expression.

"This couple drove to Houston all the way from east Texas. They
are fine Lutherans; I can assure you of that. Viola and Clarence Mueller.
Lived in Diboll all their lives. Salt of the earth."

"Trouble is," Della Hinkle continued firmly, looking Phillis in the
eye. "They need to move in right now."

As Phillis started to reply, Della Hinkle cut her off.

"They're coming over before supper. Hurry up and get your things
together. You have so little anyway, I assured them you could move
yourself upstairs right quick like. Charlie offered to help. I said, 'No
need for that. She's young and strong.'"

As she turned to go back downstairs, Della Hinkle said, "Just so you
know, they are paying thirty-five dollars a week. Isn't that glorious?"

Phillis retorted angrily, "I'll be out by five o'clock, not one minute
before. I am going to take a bath before I move upstairs."

Mrs. Hinkle sniffed in disappointment as she clomped out of the
room.

It was true. Phillis had little to move. This was still an insult. Her
large airy room had been a refuge, a haven. So what. Moving was a
small thing compared with today's thunderbolt.

CHAPTER THIRTEEN

Wyatt C. Hedrick, a Fort Worth designer, developed plans for the Harris County Criminal Courts and Jail building in 1927. Located at 624 Bagby Street with stories in the Greek classic style for $750,000. Granite steps near the immense spreading oak tree (Hanging or Stanley Oak) lead to the main doorway. Prisoners were kept on the fourth floor. The eighth floor was reserved for a chapel and exercise room.

"Harris County Courthouse and Jail" prepared for
Harris County Historical Commission by
Janet K. Wagner & Thomas McWhorter

PHILLIS ENJOYED HER BATH THAT AFTERNOON, knowing she was delaying Mrs. Hinkle. She could hear her rustling around in the hall, slamming the linen closet door and closing bureau drawers, signaling her irritation with this delay.

Once she thought about it, moving to the attic room pleased Phillis. More privacy. Old Hinkle hated the steep stairs and the narrow passageway, so she figured she would be spared any further visits from her. The meager possessions took no time to gather, and she easily transferred them with still time for a catnap before dinner. Unfortunately, two Phillip Calloways appeared in her short dream. One who yelled, "Are you a crazy woman? I'll bet I'm younger than you. I ain't never had no kids, anyway. Hey, warden, get rid of this nitwit." The other disturbed her even more. "Well, look at you! All growed up and nothing to do but badger your poor old papa. Git outta here. Don't you know I never wanted a daughter?"

Phillis bolted upright and realized it was time to dress. What should I wear to visit the man I have not seen in twenty years who currently resides at the city jail? She chose the pink blouse and her simple, gray skirt. Surely, one did not dress up to visit the local prison. First, she had to get through dinner.

MAYMIE BANION SAT AT THE HEAD OF the dinner table; Judge Clay Mansfield was to her right next to Teddy and Phillis; and Mrs. Hinkle, at the foot of the table.

Miss Maymie introduced the new boarders, who were seated to her left, and it was clear Viola and Clarence Mueller had formed an instant friendship with Mrs. Hinkle. Maymie began the evening by welcoming the newcomers and calling Josie to bring in the food.

Everyone was about to take the first bite when Clarence Mueller cleared his throat rather menacingly and asked, "Who will give the blessing?"

The diners fell silent. "Guess I'm elected, say hey?"

With bowed heads, they waited for their self-anointed proselyte. After his amen, Mrs. Hinkle started in on her usual Prohibition tirade, this time directed toward the Mueller's. "The WTCU holds meetings from noon until sunset at the Rice Hotel every day to pray this fish-eating Catholic will not win the nomination."

Viola Mueller said, "Father, let's put this prayer meeting on our list of things to do here in Houston."

He nodded, grabbing another piece of steak.

Judge Mansfield asked, "You and your wife live in east Texas?"

Mr. Mueller nodded again, chewing away.

"I've heard the good people there take their politics seriously because they have nothing to do all day. Just climb pine trees and throw cones at each other."

Phillis snickered and shot a look at Miss Maymie, who stepped in, "Shame on you, Judge, for saying that. Our Diboll visitors have come all this way for Houston's event, not to hear jokes like this about their neck of the woods."

Turning to Mr. Mueller, she asked, "What business are you in?"

"I'm a chiropractor."

Maymie laughed and slapped her hand on the table, "You're one of those back crackers? We have a new spine puncher down the street. Hiram Sloop just set himself up in business on the Boulevard. He's in your Odd Fellows Club, isn't he, Judge?"

Maymie's smile widened. "Mr. Mueller, do you have an Odd Fellows chapter in east Texas? If so, then you three will have something in common. Wouldn't that be something?"

The Judge agreed drily and eyed Mr. Mueller just as Stanley Staples appeared in the doorway.

Phillis smiled, recognizing relief when she saw it. As she walked out, she heard Mrs. Hinkle say to the new guests, "I must warn you, Miss Flanagan keeps the oddest hours of anyone in this house. And some of the places she goes. Well, they aren't places I would recommend."

Phillis and Stanley laughed all the way down the front stairs, shaking their heads at how Mrs. Hinkle would view their plans for this evening.

The southbound trolley rolled up right as they reached the stop. Once they sat down, Stanley spoke softly, "Keep your wits about you this evening whatever happens. It's not going to be easy."

Phillis paused and turned to look at him. "Did I tell you how much I appreciate your help?"

Stanley blushed and said, "You look really nice. I like the pink and gray together."

Grateful for his lack of fashion sense, Phillis sarcastically replied, "I wanted to look my best since I haven't seen Phillip in so long."

"How did you recognize the photo of him in the newspaper? It was so grainy I could barely make out the faces."

"When I was home from college one Christmas, I found a photograph of him in the trash which had been torn in half by my mother. I fitted the two pieces together and knew instinctively it was my father since she always called me 'his spitting image.'"

"Tough luck, kid. I'm damn lucky I don't look anything like my dad since he was the town drunk. It's why I live in Houston instead of Corsicana. I could probably be editor of the newspaper there if I didn't mind putting up with my old man."

Never had Stanley mentioned any family members and his admission explained a lot.

"Could just as easily be my dad sitting in the county jail," he said.

While she appreciated his remarks, her heart pounded, and she felt sick at her stomach. What if she collapsed when she saw Phillip Calloway? No, absolutely not. She straightened her back, lifted her shoulders, and raised her head. Stanley must have been watching for he gave her a thumbs-up sign.

They walked down Capitol to Bagby where Stanley guided her to an imposing red granite building. "Here's the new Court Building and Jail. Just opened last year. Quite a pile of stone, isn't it."

Phillis ignored him, focusing instead on the huge oak tree near the front steps. "That's the biggest tree I've ever laid eyes on." Phillis pointed to the oak, smiling at the magnificent leafy branches that offered a cool respite from the glaring sun. "This is surely the most beautiful tree in Houston. Do you know how old it is?"

"No, I don't. It's a gorgeous tree all right, but sadly, it's called the 'hanging oak.' Legend has it, eleven criminals were hanged from this tree almost a hundred years ago. That's how come it's still known as that."

"Ye Gods and little fishes. You mean Houston would build a jail overlooking a tree where they hanged people. Were they just wanting to remind prisoners that this is what awaits them?"

"Yeah, I suppose so," Stanley guided her up the wide stairs, shaking his head at her dismayed looks. Inside she sniffed and shrugged her shoulders. "Still smells like new paint."

"It's not even a year old — give it some time. You'd be happier if it were old and dingy?"

"No, but it does seem rather fancy for a jail."

After climbing to the fourth floor, they followed what Stanley later told her was an amazingly polite warden who led them down a long hallway, stopping in front of two armed guards who sat at a rickety table playing cards. They sat in chairs beside an electric fan which blew air into the aisle. Holstered pistols hung from their belts.

The iron bars cast shadows around the cell where the solitary occupant sat on a cot facing the back wall. He stood at the sound of their footsteps and whirled around, looking straight into her eyes without even a flicker of recognition. Shifting out of the dim light, she moved nearer to give him a better view.

"Hello, Father. Remember me? Phillis?"

"Phillis? Is that you? Oh, my God. Why?"

She thought that to be the perfect opening. "Why am I here? Yes, that's a good question. Why would I want to acknowledge a father who deserted his family when I was eight years old? Especially a father who left us destitute in the middle of winter. The apartment was freezing cold. Your babies got the flu and died. But you were long gone and never looked back.

His mouth dropped open and he hung his head but did not speak.

"Why would I admit to having a father who's now hanged a man from a bridge? Did you tie the ropes or just stand and watch? You are despicable."

His head rose and he raised and lowered his right shoulder. With his old easy smile, he dispelled any of her doubts about his identity. Her mother always called it his glad-handing smile.

"You have your grandmother's red hair. Looks like you got her spunk as well. How'd you get in here?"

"Yes, I have her spunk and that's all you gave me worth anything more than a tinker's dam. Tell me why you hung Robert Powell." she commanded.

With his hand held to his forehead and his eyes shuttered half closed, he whispered, "Please don't talk so loud? I've got a terrible headache."

Phillis snorted and shook her head. Everything about him gnawed at hers.

"Why did I hang — what did you say the man's name was? Don't rightly know, Phillis. Can't figure out why I'm here."

"You don't remember tying a rope around the neck of a wounded man and pushing him off a bridge? It was probably easy for you to forget you had a wife and three daughters, how could you forget killing this man? Only a few days ago."

"I don't think I did that," he said. "Don't know what happened. Can't remember where I was."

"Really? How tragic you'll be tried for a crime you don't remember committing. Will they hang you like you hanged Powell?"

Her father sank back down on the cot, looking queasy. "I met a gal; we were at a place over by the port. We sort of tied one on . . .When I woke up, I couldn't seem to think. I was groggy, sort of stumbling along some street. Yesterday some cops came along and threw me in a wagon and hauled me here."

Turning away in disgust, she told the guards, "I'm ready to leave."

It was only after she and Stanley stood outside that she was able to draw a full breath. "Now you've met my father. If Houston finds out my father is one of the lynchers, I might as well kiss my dream of success good-bye. At least in this town. How will I get through his trial and sentencing? As big as it is, this town's not big enough to hold us both. Oh, Stanley I've never been so afraid. I thought there was nothing on earth that could frighten me. I'm no scaredy cat, but this is awful." She looked up at the hanging tree, its branches now black and menacing against the night sky. Goosebumps rose on her arms.

"You're right, it'll be rough if folks find out. You suppose he really was that drunk? Maybe the woman he was with can provide an alibi."

She bit her lip and fought to keep back the tears.

"Let's get back to Main Street," Stanley said as he took her arm.

At Texas Avenue, he said, "Gotta scram, kid. My Saturday column is due as we speak. Like I told you, tomorrow, I gotta lead an excursion down the ship channel," he said. "Are you okay taking a trolley home?"

At first, Phillis panicked at the thought of his leaving. A cool Gulf breeze ruffled her hair and whirled around her sweat soaked blouse. Shivering, cold and scared, she concentrated on the cracks in the sidewalk. Finally able to lift her head, she looked Stanley in the eye, "I appreciate what you've done for me. Don't think I don't. I'll be fine." *Phillip Flannagan now has the power to destroy me. This is my problem, not his or anyone else's.* She laughed mirthlessly, "And I thought Amon Carter was a problem."

Stanley raised his eyebrows and nodded as he studied her pale woeful face. He'd never noticed all her freckles. Must be Houston's sun. He halted and rocked back and forth. waiting for her to speak.

She stood there chagrined that he was party to this mess, but comforted by his empathy. *What must he be thinking? A ninny. A nuisance. Yet he's here for me. He understands.*

"Thanks for coming with me tonight," she spoke to the sidewalk.

"Yeah, you've already said that. You promise me you'll be all right?"

"Yes. I wish I could have gotten some answers."

"Me too," Stanley agreed. "As my grandpappy used to say, 'I don't understand all I know.'" He gave her a hug and chucked her under the chin. "We'll figure this out. Go home and get some sleep. You look whipped."

She laughed and poked him in the chest, "Be sure you wear a life jacket tomorrow on that boat ride. See you around, pal."

As Phillis rode the trolley back to the Heights, she stared out at the dark streets, ticking off the ways her father would ruin her career, oblivious to the other passengers. When someone slid onto the seat beside her, she glanced up, dismayed to see Mr. Dexter, the kindly gentleman who gave her refuge at the Episcopal church the first day she arrived in Houston.

Of all people to meet up with tonight. She took a deep breath and greeted him, hoping he was not in a chatty mood.

"I just finished choir rehearsal at Christ Church," he explained. "What about you? Pretty late for a ride downtown."

"I needed to telegraph articles to my editor in Fort Worth." Phillis lied.

"How are you liking Houston, Miss Flanagan?"

"Until the criminals took the law into their own hands, I loved Houston."

"I know what you mean. Thank God the 'ghouls,' as Mefo called them, have been caught."

Phillis thought of the ghoul she just visited and shuddered.

"Houston stands under a dark cloud right now," Mr. Dexter continued. "We should be hanging our heads in shame. Contemptible prejudice, despite the fine churches we pride ourselves on having." He shook his head and lowered his voice, "What troubles me is no one attacks the root of this evil. People claim Negroes are happy. Religion and singing keep them from being upset about Jim Crow. How stupid. Politicians in the South won't talk about the horrible laws passed to keep Negroes in their place. These must be addressed to bring about change."

"Yes, but at least, the lynchers have been indicted." *What will he answer?*

He gave her a searching look. "What they did is a symptom of the problem. I suspect their punishment will be administered by God."

"Not by a Houston jury?"

Mr. Dexter looked around the car and fiddled with his silk tie. "So, what do you like best about Houston?" he asked.

Phillis bowed her head and pressed her hands to her temples to ease the pounding. All she could think of was Phillip Calloway and his cruelty. Would Mr. Dexter's God punish him adequately? She wanted to damn him to hell.

"Are you okay, Miss Flanagan," Mr. Dexter asked kindly.

"Sorry," she replied. "I have a slight headache."

"Probably the sun. It was terribly hot today," Mr. Dexter chirped. Phillis wished it were only the city's heat that occasioned her pain.

"There's an island nearby that is cooler," he said.

She shot him a dubious look.

"Galveston Island. Have you been? My wife's a native I met her when I got off the boat from London."

"I could tell you were British," Phillis answered flatly. His chirpy voice was wearing on her nerves.

"You should plan a trip to Galveston."

She shook her head, wishing to go no place except her bedroom where she could lock the door and pull the covers over her head.

After what seemed like an eternity, she and Fred Dexter reached their stop, exited the trolley and exchanged farewells.

The night air was heavy and smelled like rain. She climbed the steps, grateful for the dark, silent house. Near the staircase, she jumped when the telephone jangled loudly and turned back to grab the receiver before the next ring. "Hello, this is Phillis Flanagan."

"Thank God I don't have to speak to that old harridan again."

Phillis almost smiled for the first time that day. "This must be Bradley Nicholson."

"Right. Trying to find the elusive Scottie Flanagan. You're coming with us to Galveston tomorrow morning," he announced. "We'll pick you up at ten o'clock sharp."

"Absolutely not. I can't possibly do that," Phillis answered crisply.

"Sure, you can, I insist. We're going down to cheer for Daisy. She's entered a beauty contest. Isn't that swell?'

Phillis thought of the long Saturday facing her as she tried to forget her father's presence in Houston and heard Fred Dexter's words, "There's an island nearby."

She needed a change of scenery. Whether it was the hanging tree standing so sassily in front of the county jail, or the shiny new facility that mocked the heinous crime committed just outside the city limits? Suddenly, bathing beauties sounded like a good idea. Maybe she could interview a bootlegger. The island was supposedly their natural habitat.

"Okay, I give in," she said with a brassy laugh.

"Are you okay, Scottie? You don't sound like yourself."

"Of course I am. See you in the morning." She slammed the phone down before he could answer and started up the stairs where Mrs. Hinkle stood glaring at her.

"I forgot to warn the Muellers about the late-night telephone calls you receive."

Phillis ignored her and continued up to the attic room. After readying herself for bed, she took out her blue notebook, and wrote the date. She ran through today's events in her mind then made an entry:

6/22/28. My childhood wish happened. I met my father who did not recognize me and did not remember hanging an innocent man from a bridge. If anyone figures out he is my father, I might as well move on. Were the guards paying any attention to my conversation? Tough luck for me.

CHAPTER FOURTEEN

Fifty miles south of Houston — accessible by train, electric tram, or over a just completed glassy highway — lies Galveston Island, once the legendary lair of Jean Lafitte, dashing Louisiana pirate.

Allen V. Peden
Houston Gargoyle
June 26, 1928

Saturday, June 23, 1928.

WHEN SHE AWOKE IN HER NEW ATTIC BEDROOM, Phillis learned the sun beamed into the dormer windows earlier than on the lower floors. Covered only by flimsy paper rollup shades, no alarm clock was necessary.

Rising, she looked around her small room and smiled as she dressed. She hadn't gotten a nosebleed from the raised altitude of her accommodations and there was something to be said for being on top of the world. "I'll bet this is the highest point for five miles."

Josie outdid herself with the breakfast offerings — platters of fried eggs and ham, bowls of grits, and a mountain of hot biscuits fresh from the oven — undoubtedly to please Miss Maymie's new, high-paying guests.

Phillis greeted the couple who now occupied her former room. Viola Mueller, slathering butter on a biscuit, looked up and smiled. "We sure enjoyed your bed, honey. I hope you slept okay up in the rafters." Shoving the biscuit in her mouth without waiting for a reply, she dug her elbow into Clarence's ribs. "Sweetie, please tell this young 'un how much we like her room."

Clarence grunted affirmatively, keeping his attention focused on a dripping egg yolk.

Devilishly, Phillis interrupted their concentration on Josie's vittles as much as possible. "What will you and your husband be doing today, Mrs. Mueller?"

After slurping her coffee, Viola called out, "Josie, can you please pour me some more?" Turning back to Phillis, she asked, "Now what were you wanting to know, miss?"

"I wondered which of Houston's sights you were taking in today?" Phillis repeated.

"We're going to see the city, you know, the downtown part. Not about to stay here in Houston Heights. This looks just like Diboll. All these wooden houses. Sam Houston Hall. That's where we'll go, then walk around. A lady back home told me, there are buildings make you think you're in a canyon."

Her husband spoke up, "I want to see this Rice Hotel I heard so much about since it's the place too full for sure 'nuff Texans. They only have rooms for New Yorkers."

"Not entirely. Five-hundred journalists from every part of America are staying there," Phillis explained.

"You're the young reporter from Fort Worth, right?" Clarence Mueller asked. "Miss Banion told us about you. She says you've actually written articles for the newspaper. Vi, wasn't there a luncheon you read about in the Diboll paper before we left? I bet you're in high cotton writing about Houston's society events. I don't read that stuff. I'm more into the sports pages and the comics. You know, the guy who writes 'The Boarding House' is coming for the convention. Now, that's who I want to meet. Gene Ahern. To heck with all these politicians. Major Hoople's gonna be in Houston all week."

"Major Hoople and even a rodeo," Phillis exclaimed. "There's a chance Will Rogers might even perform. It's being held at Rice Institute."

"Never heard of that. It's a school?" Clarence asked. "How many stories do you have to write? Don't envy you a job like that."

He took out his pocket watch and chuckled, "Speaking of jobs. Ma, you'd just be finishing the milking about now. Missing it yet?"

His wife laughed. "Missing it like I'd miss a bad cold."

With a smile, Phillis rose and took her plate to the kitchen. "Josie, thanks for the super breakfast. I'm spending the day in Galveston."

No sooner had she spoken than the repeated blare of a horn shattered the Saturday morning's peace and quiet.

Mrs. Hinkle stood at the front door, tapping her foot, and watching Phillis grab her bag and cram on her straw hat. She eyed the snazzy blue Studebaker convertible waiting at the curb and warned, "I have no notion of where you are headed. I do hope you get there in one piece."

"Off to Galveston. Back this evening," Phillis threw the words over her shoulder as she ran down the front stairs to the street.

Grateful that Brad sat at the wheel rather than the less-reliable Reggie, Phillis went to the rear of the car and climbed up into the rumble seat, barely getting positioned before he gunned the engine and sped down Harvard.

She envied the sunglasses Brad sported; a luxury too expensive for her to think about. His snazzy Panama straw hat looked new, and she figured it set him back a pretty penny as well.

"God, it's too early to be going anywhere," Reggie groaned. "What a toot last night." He blinked his eyes repeatedly as he turned to look at her. "That blinding sun's beating a drum on my head. Phillis, you, unfortunately, look fresh as a daisy, damn it. Speaking of whom, did Brad tell you she's in a bathing beauty contest today in Galveston? Has a suite at the Galvez Hotel fronting the Gulf. That's why we're hurrying down to the shore."

"Yes, Brad told me," Phillis replied, debating whether to tell him why she came today. She decided to keep it under her hat. "So, Daisy's already in Galveston?"

"Oh, yeah." Reggie replied. "I bet she's broken twenty hearts since she arrived on Friday."

"What do you care, Reggie?" Brad asked, elbowing his friend. "Or are you still madly in love with the meat packing heiress?"

"Guys let's talk about something else, please," Phillis called out from the rumble seat, preferring not to be entertained by a discussion of their love lives for the next hour and a half. Reggie's New York sophistication was wearing thin.

"Maybe we should raise the top, old pal," Reggie suggested. "We're getting too much sun."

"Isn't that why we're going?" Brad replied. "To get some of this famed Texas sunshine. Put your hat on instead of trying to use it as a fan."

Reggie slapped his straw hat on top of his face, using it as a screen. "Ah, that's better." His snoring soon competed with the engine's humming.

When they reached Harrisburg Boulevard, Brad announced, "Here it is. The paved road to Galveston everyone's bragging about. They finished it just in time for me."

He turned south and fed the gas pedal, barreling down the glassy highway.

Phillis was relieved the increased road noise discouraged any further conversation. The brown tweed seat cover was rough to the touch and she felt it through her thin rayon skirt. Never having ridden in the rear of a roadster, she better understood now why some called it the "mother-in-law seat." A concrete bench was more comfortable. Not the complaining type, she pulled a ribbon from her bag, tied her hat on, and tried to recall what the *Gargoyle* article said about this island fifty miles from Houston that called itself the "Playground of the South." A long, skinny stretch of land shaped like a tadpole where the bootlegger whiskey business operated on a larger scale than anywhere in the state. With a little luck, she would find out who ran the illegal operation that supplied alcohol to much of America. Daisy's beauty contest was the perfect distraction for Brad and Reggie, who would be too busy to notice her slipping away to do some investigating.

For those convention visitors who complained that Mayor Holcombe's promised Gulf breezes failed to cool off Houston streets, Galveston offered lower temperatures, sophisticated night clubs, and plenty of alcohol, as well the obvious beach activities.

"You asleep back there?" Brad's voice boomed out above the noise.

"No, I'm resting my eyes," Phillis yelled back. "I don't have the big dollars to shell out for sunglasses."

"Oh. Here. I'll share mine."

"No, no. You're driving. It's important for you to have eyeshade protection. I'm doing just fine back here. You do remember I can drive an automobile" After no response to her hint, she announced, "I came down to see the ocean. You've probably been to the New Jersey shore. Not me. I'm anxious to see a sky full of more water than land."

"Won't be long now."

"Have you read about the bootlegger gangs on the island?"

"Nope. Reggie told me it's called the 'Free State of Galveston.' Governs itself and ignores the Volstead Act."

"I must have read the same article."

"We're about to see for ourselves. Here's Broadway Boulevard, Galveston's own Park Avenue."

Mansions lined the spacious street, the esplanade filled with towering palm trees.

Brad poked Reggie in the ribs. "Hey, buddy. Time to wake up."

Reggie responded groggily, "Where's the water? All I see are bushes with pink flowers."

"Oleanders, Reggie," Phillis hollered. "Galveston is known as the 'Oleander City.'"

About a mile later, the boulevard ended at the Gulf of Mexico, and she got her first look at more water than she had ever seen.

A red-uniformed brass band stood on the seawall playing "Hello! Ma Baby," while oversized black letters on an enormous white canvas banner welcomed them to "The International Pageant of Pulchritude."

Daisy Leatherbury stood to one side of a popcorn wagon on Seawall Boulevard, clad in a scoop-necked, red-and-white-striped bathing suit that hugged every inch of her body. She held a matching umbrella while a group of photographers clicked photos of her scuffing sand with her red-and-white bathing shoes. Instead of a bathing cap, she wore a flattering red-jersey cloche. Phillis cringed, thinking of the contrast between Daisy's costume and the black wool-swimming suit she brought.

Brad and Reggie's jaws dropped as they took in Daisy's scantily clad figure.

Reggie whispered, "This is like Ziegfeld, only way closer. Holy smokes, her hips and legs are naked. Look at the ones over there posing on the rocks."

Phillis pasted a big smile on her face and yelled, "Hiya, Daisy."

Daisy winked at the photographers as she walked toward some girls similarly attired. "Inez, Roxie, come meet my best friend from Dallas."

After stopping to buy soda pops from a boy pushing an ice-filled cart, the two strolled over. Daisy pointed at her, and said, "Phillis."

"Tell me your names again." The girls giggled and responded, "She's Roxie and I'm Inez." They took a swig from their pop bottles and spoke in unison like wind-up toys, "Pleased to meetcha."

Despite their bizarre swim outfits, Inez and Roxie were more covered up than Daisy. As she looked more closely, Phillis figured out Roxie was the one wearing a pink-satin, skirted bathing suit swirling in the breeze above knee-high, white silk stockings and pink high heels. Inez wore a black-and-white-striped suit with a matching cape that extended to her knees. A wide chinstrap conveyed an unfortunate regimental impression but did keep her hat from sailing away.

Seeing ten or twelve similarly garbed women, Phillis asked, "Is there a prize for the best costume?"

The girls giggled again and nodded.

Daisy explained, "This is the preliminary tryout. These contestants are from all over the world. If I'm chosen, I will be here tomorrow for the finals." She batted her blue eyes and moistened her red lips as she apologized, "Sorry, Phillis. Can't keep the photographers waiting."

All the girls posed for photographs and began singing and swaying in a long line. After an hour of listening to the amateur performers, Phillis was ready to sneak out.

Although she had never seen a beauty contest, Daisy looked like a shoo-in. "You'll win, I'm sure," she yelled and walked back toward Brad and Reggie, who were seemingly tongue-tied by the scenery. Their eyes glued to the row of beauties, the two men edged nearer and nearer until the contest official, a nasal-voiced older woman screamed, "Get back, young men. You're crowding my girls." Sheepishly, they took a few steps backward.

Phillis, realizing the timing was perfect for her getaway, asked the soda vendor where she could find a cheap lunch. "You gotta get off the seawall. Try the Kewpie Sandwich Shop that away," he suggested, thumbing toward the west. "No view of the water. Food's cheaper."

She easily found the orange neon sign advertising the diner, took a stool at the counter, and ordered a fish sandwich and chocolate malt while she waited for something to happen. Hopefully, her peek at the Gulf and lunch in this greasy spoon would not be all Galveston offered her today.

Photographs of fishing boats, fishermen holding up their catches, and the Ball High School baseball team adorned the dingy walls. A brusque voice to her left asked, "Miss, could you please pass me the ketchup?"

Phillis swiveled around and saw a paunchy, ruddy-faced man wearing a Roman collar. She held out the bottle of ketchup. Grabbing it, he blobbed the contents onto his plate of fried shrimp and French fries and chewed the shrimp past the tails. "Why aren't you down on the beach wearing one of those scanty bathing suits? Are you too old to be a contestant?"

Phillis laughed heartily, "Bingo. Bathing beauty contests aren't my style. I'm here from Houston to see other sights."

"Oh," he grunted. "My name's Father Murphy. You'd better run back to the seawall and watch, or you'll miss out on what the Galveston Beach Association calls 'the island's finest money-raiser.'"

"You don't like the beauty contests, Father Murphy?"

"Aside from the contest being held tomorrow on a Sunday, my concern is the morals of Galveston's residents. We've never had half-clothed girls parading for all to see. It's a public spectacle." He lowered his head and continued filling his mouth with fries.

"The event is drawing a big crowd," Phillis agreed. "Is it held annually?"

"Third year and likely will go on forever. Ought to be something more uplifting on folks' minds than shocking costumes aimed at turning an ordinary Miss Nobody into a somebody. They claim it's clean and wholesome. Damn their hides."

"Father, I'm a reporter and this contest makes for a great story and terrific photos. But, I agree, women using their bodies and pretty faces to win a two-thousand-dollar cash prize disgusts me too."

"A female reporter?" He threw the words back at her and spread his fingers toward her neck as if he considered choking her. "That's as bad as a beauty contest."

"I beg your pardon," Phillis replied stiffly. "You don't know what you're talking about."

As she saw the man sitting at the end of the counter drop his newspaper, she realized her voice was louder than she intended. No matter, she thought to herself. It is my turn to shout.

"Reporting's not a respectable job for women?" she asked.

"Nothing's dirtier than a press room unless it's a courtroom. Neither is a place for women. Chronicle says over five-hundred women are traipsing to Houston for this political convention. They should stay home where they belong. Not be out voting on things. Women are supposed to propagate the species. Period, dot, dot."

Phillis jumped off her stool, turned her back on Father Murphy, and put a dollar on the counter. "Miss, may I please have my change?"

The waitress handed Phillis sixty-five cents. Phillis put a dime on the counter for a tip and pocketed the rest.

Throwing open the sandwich shop's door, she stormed out onto the sidewalk and collided with a tall, barrel-chested man who grabbed her tightly.

"Young lady," he laughed, "I love having you in my arms. May I ask your name?"

Looking up, Phillis tried jerking loose from the man's grip without success. With a glowering look, she shoved him away. He abruptly dropped his arms and gave her a calculating once over.

"Your skirt's not short enough for a flapper. You're too skinny to be one of the bathing beauties. So, what's your game?"

Phillis stepped back; the diamond stickpin centered on the man's purple necktie nearly blinding her. He wore a lavender linen suit with a matching pocket-handkerchief. Oh, my gosh, he was exactly the person she came here to meet.

She extended her hand, "My name's Phillis Flanagan. I write for the *Fort Worth Star-Telegram* and I'm here in Galveston for the day."

He bowed, took her hand which he brushed with his lips.

"I'd like to interview a bootlegger. Would you happen to know one?"

His boisterous laughter rang in her ears. "Little lady, it's your lucky day. Here I am, the kingpin of Galveston bootleggers, Johnny 'Jack' Nounes, at your service."

He bowed again, tipping his hat just enough to reveal his shiny bald head.

"Swell." Phillis clapped her hands, "Is there somewhere we can talk?"

Mr. Nounes put his fingers to his lips and whistled, prompting a long, maroon limousine to appear at the curb.

"May I help you in, Miss Flanagan?"

Phillis looked back devilishly to see if Father Murphy or anyone else was watching her climb into the back seat. Emily Post's rules for a single woman occupying an automobile with a stranger, amused her. What about riding with a man who instructs his chauffeur to keep driving until told to stop? It sounded like dialogue from a talkie.

Settling herself, she patted the soft mohair seat covering and admired the abundance of chrome knobs and fittings. This was certainly her lucky day for she already knew a lot about this bootlegger.

"The newspapers say you're a very generous man, Mr. Nounes, giving toys to orphans at Christmas and one-hundred-dollar bills to needy folks. Did you really throw a party in New York City and fill a bathtub with champagne for Clara Bow to swim in?"

She watched his reaction, assessing his tolerance for gossip.

"Since what you read is second-hand news, you'll never know the truth. Champagne baths are tame stuff for Gotham City. The paper correctly reported that the shindig at the Pennsylvania Hotel set me back forty-thousand dollars."

He eyed her speculatively and asked, "Want to know about my fling with Theda Bara? Nah, of course not. That's old news." He grinned and winked at Phillis as if they shared a secret.

"What else would you like to know?"

Before she could answer, he asked, "Miss Flanagan, why were you at the Kewpie? Was it because you know I own that joint? Were you looking for me?"

"No, sir," she replied. "I arrived in Galveston two hours ago. I know nothing about this town. I dashed into the Kewpie because I was starving. I had a pretty good fish sandwich before I left so angry, I failed to watch where I was going."

Phillis smiled mischievously and returned his wink. "Sorry I ran into you. Please excuse my rudeness."

He patted her on the shoulder. "What got you so upset?"

"Do you know Father Murphy?" Phillis asked.

"Honey, I am B.G.I. I was born on this island," he replied. "There's no one I don't know. Of course, I know Aloysius Murphy as well as his bishop. Is this about the pulchritude pageant?"

"Yes," Phillis said. "I agreed with him when he criticized rewarding women for their physical attributes instead of their achievements. When he moved on to condemning women's right to have a life outside their homes, I blew my stack."

Phillis rolled her eyes, hoping Nounes understood her position. When he nodded, she continued, "He infuriated me, and that's when I blew my stack. But, arguing with a man of the cloth seems indecent."

Nounes only laughed, "Okay, Miss Flanagan, what do you need for your story? I've got this island in my hip pocket."

His bushy raised eyebrows dared her to question his power. "Just ask me, baby, and it's yours."

Phillis gasped. In less than five minutes this mesmerizing man had cast a spell on her. Poof! Her qualms about being alone with him in his automobile evaporated.

"Do you mind if I take notes?"

He shook his head and she rummaged in her bag for her notebook and pencil.

"When did you become a bootlegger?"

"When I decided I didn't want to make my living butchering hogs," he answered with a grin.

"Why did you start?"

"To make money, of course," he replied. "Why does anyone work?"

"Do you sell genuine alcohol?"

"Of course not. Gordon's Gin doesn't exist anymore. Nor any other brands."

"What you sell is fake liquor?"

"Yes, ma'am. Just like every other bootlegger."

He stopped abruptly and warned, "What I tell you now is off the record. I'm trusting you to keep this out of your article, okay? If you don't, well..."

Phillis looked at him and paused. "I promise, I'm trustworthy." She stuck her pencil behind her ear.

"The alcohol I sell is different," Jack Nounes began. "My booze is very fine fake stuff. My labels are from Germany, printed in England. The liquid is bottled by hand. The white of an egg goes over the cork so it looks like salt water has seeped in from being transported."

Proudly thumbing his lapel, he dazzled her with his cockiness. She bit the inside of her cheek to refrain from laughing. "Can I write about how proud you are of the fake bottles you sell?"

"Yep, that's okay," he responded. "I've been doing this for eight years. I've gotten rich and I've brought happiness to a lot of people. If my stuff's not real, nobody gets sick. I don't sell poisonous booze like a lot of stuff on the market. If my customer finds out he's paid for phony merchandise, which he hardly ever does, only his pride is hurt."

As the driver headed west on Broadway for the second time, Nounes pointed to a glistening white church on the north side of the Boulevard.

"That's Sacred Heart, Father Murphy's church. I go to St. Patrick's over on the west side. The two churches are a world apart. Murphy's church is old Galveston money; mine's just old Galveston — the immigrants, the dockworkers, the real heart and soul of the island. Anything else you want to ask me?"

"No. Thank you very much."

"Will you please add this to your story? I never met a man who refused a drink because it's illegal and no one I know calls bootlegging a crime. I am proud of what I do and if you and I were each holding a glass of bourbon, I would say, 'Here's to Al Smith. God bless him.'"

"I don't get it," Phillis said. "When Smith's elected, the repeal of the Volstead Act will put you out of business."

"That's where you're wrong, Miss Flanagan," Nounes replied. "There are many other fish in the sea, little lady, and I'm a very fine fisherman. Speaking of fishermen, do you like boating?"

Phillis nodded cautiously, wondering what he had in mind.

"My boat is the *Cherokee*, the fastest in the Gulf. Care to go for a sunset cruise?"

She looked at her wristwatch. Was there time? A sunset cruise on an actual bootleg runner boat? A great story. What plans might he have once it was dark?

Looking up, she smiled, "I'll take a raincheck. I have to get back to Houston."

He looked out the car window at the sunshine beating down on the street and gave her another wicked smile.

"I understand completely," he said. "Thank you for your company. It's been a pleasure."

His car stopped in front of the Kewpie Sandwich Shop where it had picked her up. The driver swung open her door and handed her down to the sidewalk.

"Good luck, Miss Flanagan. I look forward to seeing you again," Nounes said as he drew back into the car that disappeared so quickly her experience seemed like a dream.

It was nearly five o'clock when Phillis reached the seawall, ready to head for home. The shiny blue convertible was nowhere in sight. Strolling west along the seawall on the lookout for Brad and Reggie, Phillis delighted in watching the swooping seagulls she only knew from pictures in books, shrieking as they plummeted reaching for kernels of popcorn and crusts of bread. Departing tourists plodded along, clutching their straw hats and satchels, sunburned by a day at the beach.

The curling waves flattened as the tide shifted the water out to sea, beckoning Phillis. Descending the wooden steps to the sand, she shucked her shoes and stockings and felt the sea air on her bare legs. Slowly, she walked to the edge of the water and dipped her toes into the Gulf. The water slapped at her calves, sloshed all around her. New sensations. Gulls screeching over her head, the sun gentler now as it began dipping down in the sky. She stood stock still, waiting for something. The sea, the sky and the sun wooing her, winning her heart.

Mr. Dexter was right. She needed this. Slowly, she dragged herself back to the shore, her feet and legs now coated by the coarse sand. Gathering her shoes and stockings, she walked across Seawall Boulevard up to the Galvez Hotel, dusting off as much sand as she could in order to squeeze her bare feet into her shoes. Stockings stuffed into her bag, she entered the hotel and asked for Daisy Leatherbury's room number.

When Phillis exited the elevator on the seventh floor, she knocked on the door which flew open immediately as Daisy screamed, "Oh, thank God you came!" She turned to Roxie and said, "Phillis is here. She'll know what to do."

"What's happened?" Phillis asked as she entered their room.

Daisy choked out the story, gulping back her tears. "Brad and Reggie and I drove the convertible down the seawall to find the country club so we could have some liquid refreshment. The boys kept drinking silver fizzes." She stopped to sip what looked like the last of a martini.

"Then they took a notion to find the 'velvet' speedway. It's past the country club way out on the open beach. They jazzed the motor and leaned on the gas to see how fast the convertible would go and smashed right into a big, old log hidden by the sand. The car made a horrible noise and stopped dead still."

"Who was driving?"

Daisy reached for her handkerchief, "Reggie," she sobbed. "He'd insisted on taking the wheel like he always does when he's been drinking. Scared me half to death."

"Brad would never have driven like that," Phillis interrupted.

Gooey black stuff oozed from under the car and one of the tires flattened like a pancake.

"So, how did you get back?" Phillis asked. "Where's the car?" When she had accepted their invitation, being stranded in Galveston had never occurred to her.

"I got a ride on a motorcycle that came barreling down the beach. The driver's name was Woody. He was so keen," Daisy said, her tears gone. "They say tourists camp out and sleep on that deserted beach all night. Not me. Besides the ride was great. Wind blowing in my face. First time today I was cool. Woody said he's a lifeguard. With his muscles, I believe him."

With a cold hard look, Daisy said, "Your boys from New York walked off looking for help. I've not seen them since."

Inez chimed in, "These Yankee high brows — they think they're so smart. Anyone knows you better be careful driving on a beach."

"True," Phillis agreed. "But, it's doubtful they've ever driven on sand."

This was not her problem. She was not going to spend the night with these zozzled want-to-be beauty queens.

"Girls," she said, "As much as I hate to leave you, I have to get back to Houston tonight. Tell Brad and Reggie, if you see them, that I took the Interurban."

"You mean you're just going to leave?"

"They're not kids, they'll manage."

Flouncing off to her bedroom, Daisy said, "I'm changing clothes and going down to the bar, I'm not gonna be stuck in this hotel suite all night."

WITH A FAREWELL SALUTE, PHILLIS WENT back down to the desk clerk. "The trains leave every hour on the hour, even on weekends, the Interurban station is just up the street. Twenty minutes later, Phillis settled into a comfy seat on the *Galveston Flyer*, a handsome electric train that transported people back and forth between Houston and Galveston. Now she understood why New York Mayor Jimmy Walker and his friends, including Mrs. Al Smith and her party, had sailed to Galveston by steamship and booked rooms at the Galvez. What a great holiday.

Phillis was pleased with the return trip, except for the $1.95 fare, which was an unexpected cost. Lucky for her she had enough cash to cover it. The Interurban's handsome arched windows set into mahogany-paneled walls provided excellent views of the doll-like communities along the way back. In an hour and forty minutes, less time than Phillis, Brad, and Reggie had spent driving to the island, she arrived at the Houston station and caught the Heights trolley.

Tomorrow, she would call the Lamar Hotel to confirm the safe return of Brad and Reggie and apologize for leaving them.

"HOW WAS YOUR TRIP?" MAYMIE CALLED out from her room on the second floor.

Her landlady had removed her hairpins and was vigorously brushing her hair.

"Now I've seen Galveston," she said with a yawn.

"What did you like best?"

"The shrieking gulls, bouncing waves, and a bootlegger whose story enchanted me."

"Who was it?" Maymie asked. "Sam or his brother Rose?"

"Neither one," Phillis replied. "Johnny 'Jack' Nounes."

"Oh, my God!" Maymie exclaimed. "The *Chronicle* reported he just got out of Leavenworth Prison. And that's the second time he's been there. I hope you didn't get too close. He is a terrible scoundrel."

"Yes, that's exactly how he struck me." Phillis smiled. She climbed the stairs to her room wondering how she could capture Johnny "Jack" Nounes on paper.

6/23/28. Galveston — a magical island full of fascinating people. This will be fun to write about. Wish I could spend a week there. Do they have cheap rentals? Maybe the island can be a place to escape if what I fear comes true. I'll bet The Free State of Galveston accepts anyone. Who knows I might get that boat ride anyway. Johnny Jack's cockiness reminds me a little of the way Dad used to talk. What is my father doing right now? Is he thinking about me?

CHAPTER FIFTEEN

Sam Houston Hall, built within 64 days at a cost of about $200,00 — will be dedicated at 4 p.m. today. Twelve special trains bringing Governor Dan Moody and other delegations are due today. Twenty thousand visitors will be in the city by tonight.

Houston Chronicle
June 24, 1928

Sunday, June 24, 1928

PHILLIS QUESTIONED LEAVING FOUR HOURS early for the dedication of Sam Houston Hall. Only a fifteen-minute streetcar ride from Houston Heights. Maymie Banion convinced her that the dedication activities would be in full swing way before the four o'clock opening.

When Phillis descended from her "roost," as she was now calling it, Maymie frowned.

"Why are you looking at me like that? Phillis asked.

"Is that all you've got to wear?"

"Considering the thousands coming today, my appearance is of no consequence." Then she looked more closely at Maymie's outfit and laughed. "You'll wow everyone there."

"That's the point. You need to look a little hotsy-totsy yourself. You dress like my typing clerk. How will you get an interview if no one even notices you?"

"I want people to tell me their stories, not obsess about what I'm wearing. I'm a reporter not a clotheshorse."

"Yeah, yeah, I hear you. But, today, you need to shine a little. Let me have that hat for a minute. I'll be right back."

Phillis turned her attention to the *Houston Post-Dispatch* that was appearing on their doorstep ever since Clarence Mueller told Miss Maymie "You expect me to eat breakfast without any morning paper to read? What kind of boarding house is this?"

"Only for a month so don't anyone who lives here get used to it," Maymie advised the rest of the residents as she wrote out a check for the subscription.

"The radio broadcast wouldn't begin at noon if nothing happens till four," Teddy announced, slipping Phillis the editorial page before handing the paper to Mr. Mueller. "Ushers have to be at their stations early. They'll let us in the back gate."

"I thought you were supposed to be a page," Phillis said.

"I've been promoted to Chief of the Ushers."

"Swell," Phillis smiled. "Congratulations."

Clarence Mueller looked at today's schedule on the newspaper's front page and laughed, "Sounds more like church than politics. Says here, every clergyman in Houston will be there. How many is that, Teddy?"

"Probably a thousand or more."

Phillis looked up to see Miss Maymie holding her transformed hat, a salmon-colored daisy pinned to the new orange ribbon circling the crown.

"Stand up and put this on so I can play with it. Okay, now let's go."

"Say, you look swell." Teddy grinned while Maymie admired her handiwork.

Phillis's eyes popped when she saw her sassy straw hat in the hall mirror. Stanley appeared at the door just as she stepped forward.

"That orange ribbon makes your hair redder. I like it, doll. It goes with your sunburn. You must have gone to Galveston." He gave her a grin, and it was such a grin.

Phillis nodded, her color deepening.

THE ROLLICKING CROWD OF RIDERS ON BOARD the downtown trolley confirmed Maymie's prediction. They wore circular Smith pins as big as saucers. Others clutched white satin flags printed with "Talk Prohibition, Dream Prohibition, and Sleep Prohibition."

At Main Street, everyone piled out and headed for Sam Houston Hall. "Phillis and I are stopping here at the Rice Hotel," Stanley told Maymie. "We'll catch up with you later."

"Corner of Prairie and Travis no later than three," Maymie ordered.

In front of the Rice Hotel, three hurdy-gurdies cranked out different tunes while a boy dressed in a faded denim shirt, homespun knickers, and worn-looking boots held a cage crawling with hundreds of horned toads. Stanley asked, "Where'd you get all those frogs, son."

"Sir, I got twelve-hundred horned toads here that I brought from West Texas. Aren't they beauts? Gonna give one to any visitor who wants it. As a souvenir. For free."

Phillis politely overlooked his large tin cup marked "Donations" and responded, "I'm from Fort Worth. You know, the 'Gateway to the West.' To me, this is the ugliest lizard in Texas."

"Don't say that, miss. The horned toad's the official Texas reptile. These are free souvenirs. I fix 'em up in one of these nice boxes with a net over it. Visitors can carry them home as a pet."

"Like a dog or kitty?" Phillis laughed.

"Well, they eat ants and lots of other insects. They don't hurt nobody. Don't you want one?"

Stanley shook his head, "Give 'em to the visitors who aren't from Texas, son."

The hotel's double front doors were wide open. Phillis laughed and asked, "Sure we can squeeze in? This place is packed."

"Bedlam, Phillis. It's a sweat box and we'll enjoy every minute. It's called celebrity watching."

"Five-hundred people must be packed in this lobby. It's like an oven."

Stanley pointed upward, "Look up at the mezzanine. I think it's closer to fifteen-hundred."

"Didn't you read what Will Rogers' wrote?"

Phillis shook her head.

"He said so many visitors jammed this place, he reached up and mopped three sweating brows before he could find his own."

Four-foot-tall lithographs of Al Smith hung down from the mezzanine's railing with red, white, and blue bunting and streamers floating in between.

Phillis edged closer to a gentleman in a wrinkled tan linen suit to hear what he was saying.

"Don't ever let anybody tell you there's no difference between the Democratic and Republican parties." The man's head swiveled as he eyed the crowd. "This circus makes the Kansas City Republican pow wow look like elderly Quakers discussing how to relocate the village cemetery."

A red-faced musician perched on a stool, was playing an accordion attached to a mouth organ that he blew on while beating a bass drum with his free foot. The thin, squeaky sounds the instrument emitted did not impress a Vermont delegate who remarked, "I knew Texas was a bad idea. This confirms it."

Phillis wondered what he thought of the little girl dressed in a spotless white organdy pinafore, wearing a tilted brown derby and carrying a banjo, who soon replaced the accordion player. No more than eight-years old, she hopped up on the banister that led to the mezzanine and began strumming "The Sidewalks of New York." The boisterous crowd sang with her, clapping loudly.

Someone yelled, "This convention proves the United States is divided into two songs — 'Sidewalks of New York' and 'Dixie.' Any band in Houston's gonna play one or the other."

And sure enough, a band marched in playing another rendition of "Dixie."

The shiny-faced musicians wore high-collared, long-sleeved blue wool jackets and three-foot-tall black fur shakos.

A man yelled, "Are they crazy? It's a hundred degrees in here."

Stanley laughed and pointed to the front door. "I'll be damned if someone didn't think to bring a jackass."

A comely young woman garbed in a brief white-satin skirt and halter-top led a live donkey right across the marble floor. The crowd laughed and cheered and pinched their noses as the smelly animal trotted past.

"Only in Texas," yelled a woman stuck behind a tall, heavy-set man who answered, "At least she's dressed right."

"See that woman over there in red?" the gentleman in the linen suit asked his lady friend, pointing to the drama queen majestically waving a red-feathered fan. "She's Gertrude Atherton, the novelist from California. Remember when her book was made into a silent movie, 'Black Opal'?"

"They ought to remake it now we have talkies," his companion commented. "Wonder what brought her to the convention? They say the Democratic Party holds the record for assembling more people than everybody's heard of before?"

"Good God!" the man exclaimed. "Here's the Beau Brummell of New York City! Proves what I just said."

The crowd parted to let the handsome young man, faultlessly dressed in a plum-colored suit, a sand-colored shirt, and a dark green tie, swagger in the front door. Cameras all over the room began clicking as photographers strained to get a photo of the person New Yorkers called "The snappy mayor of the world's snappiest city."

Mayor Jimmy Walker bowed his way up the stairs to the mezzanine, shaking hands with young and old as he posed for photographers.

An elderly lady, who looked like she would faint any minute, simpered, "Isn't he too sweet for words?"

The gentleman who seemed to be conversant on any topic commented, "His nickname is the 'Prince of Wales.'"

The mezzanine elevator doors opened, and someone cried, "Wait for the mayor."

The female operator remarked in her Texas drawl, "Aw, be yourself. That youngster ain't no mayor."

Everyone died laughing.

"Now you've seen his honor in person, let's go." Stanley motioned Phillis toward the door. "He's forty-seven, no gray hairs. Does he dye them?

Phillis nodded, "Maybe so, I've only seen photos of him before today. No wrinkles either. He's terribly good-looking."

"Yeah, well, the darling Mayor of Broadway couldn't miss the chance to support the candidate who gave him his job on a silver platter. Walker's very beholden to Smith. Both of 'em have what's called 'Tammany's Stamp' on them."

Phillis rolled her eyes, "I'm sure most politicians are beholden to someone or several someone's."

"But some are more beholden than others. Al Smith's not coming to Houston because New York is the only place he allows himself to be seen in public with Tammany Hall members."

"What do these guys think about Texas? A man told me most are here because they want to visit the state. You believe that?"

"Of course. A one-man band tooting a jazzy horn, a confused donkey, creepy horny toads, and an eight-year-old banjo player, all of whom are crowded in and around Houston's swankiest hotel packed with over a thousand guests. These visitors have never seen anything like it."

"Well, I hope they keep liking the city till Saturday," Phillis answered.

"Sure, they will. You going to the rodeo?"

"Of course. Been to a bunch but never attended one held on a college campus, especially an institute usually referred to as the 'Harvard of the South.' Rice is also renting dorm rooms to convention visitors."

A man yelled, "Noise, heat, and two songs. That's Houston."

Stanley's head jerked around to look at the speaker and asked, "You aren't, by any chance, from a newspaper in Brooklyn?"

The guy grinned, "Bud Colgate, the *Brooklyn Standard Union*," and reached to shake Stanley's hand. "Where's your home?"

"Right here at the *Houston Press*. I'm glad to call this my home despite the 'noise' and 'heat.'"

"Sorry, didn't mean to hurt your feelings. Just think it's stupid to hold a convention in Houston in the summer. It ought to be in Marquette, Michigan, or some other thriving town on the shores of Lake Superior where you can't poach eggs in what your hotel calls a 'cool bath.'"

"Well, Bud, we don't mind our heat so much. Sorry it offends you."

"That's okay. In one day, Houston has more noise, color, and sights than the week-long Kansas City Convention."

"You got the message, then. Houston's a city to talk about."

Jostled by the thickening crowds out on the street, Stanley steered Phillis to the corner where Maymie Banion was selling convention programs for fifty cents. "You two need a program, don't you?"

Stanley fished out two quarters and handed the program to Phillis. "Can we share?"

She nodded, joining Stanley and Maymie as they walked toward the crowd already gathered around rows of chairs set up for the participants. With Mrs. Woodrow Wilson, a thousand clergymen, church choirs, and fifty bands taking their turns entertaining the thousands of onlookers. 'Pomp and Circumstance'everywhere one looked.

"How was your Galveston trip?" Stanley asked.

"It provided a good story." She threw her hands up in the air as a grand gesture. "I'm in a new arena, Galveston and Houston, these are towns filled with stories that matter. Why do I feel ready to write any story?"

Stanley grabbed her hand. "Because you are," he said.

With bowed heads, the crowd listened as Bishop Hay began the invocation. Twenty-thousand people and all was quiet. After an hour of speeches, band music, and applause, Jesse Jones rose to speak. "We still say, 'Howdy, friend' down here in Texas. This convention is the biggest thing that's happened to Houston, and we're happy you came so far south. Today is sort of our coming-out party. We've put on our best clothes. No sectional lines, just solid Democrats."

Rabbi Henry Barnston concluded the ceremony and the crowd surged forward, no longer restrained by the cyclone fencing around the hall.

Phillis grabbed Maymie's hand, "I wish you hadn't given away your ticket. Here, take mine," she said, handing her ticket to the older woman.

Maymie pushed it away. "I'll get in the last day. Visitors will be leaving early, probably anxious to go see more of Texas."

Despite Phillis's sneak peek inside, the sweeping lines, the graceful, curved ceiling, and the immensity of the interior took her breath away again. She looked skyward with thousands of others whose eyes circled the curved netlike ceiling, still the most riveting sight. Gold badges flashed everywhere as delegates and dignitaries swarmed around them. A band played "The Eyes of Texas" disputing the visiting journalist's reference to Houston's limited repertoire.

Phillis turned to Stanley, "Are you bowled over? I am. Grand, isn't it?"

"Thirty percent larger than Madison Square Garden," he replied. "Look at this crowd. There's Teddy on the speaker's platform. He's arranging the chairs."

"It's an important job for him, even if it only lasts four days. Doesn't he look nice in his new suit?"

"Dressing well has never been his problem," Stanley said dryly. "It's what's between his ears that worries me."

Phillis laughed and grasped his wrist. "Hush. Let's walk around the hall and get our bearings."

"Right," Stanley agreed. "I want to see where the radio booth is. My friend Johnny Jansen who works for KPRC swears he has a better view of the stage than anyone."

A fellow journalist slapped Stanley on the back, asking, "How's my favorite newshound?" The press is over there behind the speaker's platform. You're here to cover the convention for your paper?"

"No. I might include a few tidbits in my column, but Dudley Davis is our man. I want you to meet my favorite female reporter, Phillis Flanagan." As they shook hands, Stanley added, "She's cutting her teeth on this convention."

"Good luck, Miss. If you stick with Staples, you'll do okay."

After two trips around the hall Stanley felt satisfied, he had nailed down the locations of telephones, the Western Union counter, comfort stations, and cold drink booths. But on the second trip, Phillis saw the stretch of chicken wire she had wondered about on her first look at the hall. Seated behind the fencing were about twenty-five black visitors. Pulling on Stanley's coat, she pointed to the area and asked, "What is that about?"

"That's the section for colored people."

"No, I don't understand this. They're caged like animals. How can this be?"

"Blacks in the South do not vote with the Democratic Party, so they are really not welcome at the convention."

"So what! That's no reason to cage them off from the whites."

"Welcome to the South. As a Southerner, I'm surprised by your surprise."

"What I see is no justice for the heinous killing of a black man and a caged off section of this so-called "splendid" hall. It's connected, isn't it?"

Stanley nodded and cradled her arm in his. "Fraid so. The wards, Jim Crow, Powell's death and this. It's all part of the same cloth."

"I've seen enough. Let's get out of here."

They threaded through the crowd of people still thronging to enter Houston's grand new hall, walking along the sidewalk in silence.

"Tomorrow at noon, you'll see how the brow-wiping hordes of people like this place. Don't imagine they'll think it's light and airy anymore. Then there's the evening session," he continued, pointing to the ceiling. "Once the sun sets and these spotlights are turned on, trust me, this hall's gonna be a hot box. Might be called the marvel of electrical power, but delegates will be sticking to the metal folding chairs and griping about the heat."

"Yeah, I know." Phillis poked Stanley in the ribs and looked at her wristwatch. "Have to get home and change clothes for the big do-dah this evening."

"Oh, yes, the dinner for the visiting women of the press. That should be interesting."

"Maymie and I are going, compliments of Allen Peden, owner of the *Gargoyle.*

Stanley snorted, "Not sure what I think about that publication. Some of his stuff is good and all of it leans the right way politically, but he's part of the River Oaks crowd. Probably couldn't afford to put out his magazine if he weren't. Wonder how long his rag will last?"

"Well, Maymie advertises in it, and I like reading it," Phillis countered. "Peden's slick writing makes Houston sound like Gotham City."

Stanley rolled his eyes and snapped, "As long as it keeps you from hopping on a bus headed north."

Her eyes narrowed as she tossed her head, not wanting to dwell on his intent.

On the Heights trolley everyone was hot and tired from spending the day on the city streets. Phillis and Stanley looked at each other and nodded when someone complained, "that blistering heat came right through my shoes." Entering the cool interior of the house on Harvard, Phillis saw Mamie collapsed on the parlor sofa with her face turned to an electric fan purring on a nearby table. "When do we need to leave for the Downtown Club's dinner?"

"Oh, golly," Maymie replied. "That's tonight, isn't it? I clean forgot."

Phillis was astonished Maymie could forget this momentous event. "We're still going, aren't we?"

CHAPTER SIXTEEN

CENA MEXICANA in honor of the WOMEN WRITER'S attending the NATIONAL DEMOCRATIC CONVENTION, Seven-thirty o'clock. River Oaks Country Club, Houston.

MENU:
CHILE CON QUESO
CHILE CON CARNE
TAMALES
ENCHILADAS
CHILE RELLENOS
FRIJOLES FRITOS
TORTILLAS FRITOS
CAFÉ-BUDWEISER-CIGARROS

Sunday, June 25, 1928

MAYMIE, WEARING A SUNDAY-GO-TO-MEETIN' outfit, stood in the kitchen, fingering her gloves. Della Hinkle looked at Phillis's hat and raised her eyebrows.

"Looks like you blew your money on a new summer straw. Seems like you two just got home. Where're you off to now?"

"A Mexican supper at the River Oaks Country Club for all the visiting press women," Phillis answered.

Without batting an eye, Della replied, "Charlie filled up the tank with gasoline just like you asked. Be careful driving on those shell roads, Miss Maymie. River Oaks is a long way from the Heights, in more ways than one."

"What's that supposed to mean?" Phillis wondered why everyone referred to this neighborhood as being different.

After forty-five minutes, Maymie really did turn on to a very bumpy shell road, and Phillis asked, "Are we still in Houston? Looks like the country to me."

"Well, almost. Relax, we're about to re-enter the city limits."

Sure enough, she turned onto a wide paved street complete with a large grassy esplanade.

Maymie explained, "At first, this was Tom Ball Boulevard. When Mr. Ball got into a little trouble with the law, the Hogg brothers changed it to 'River Oaks Boulevard.'"

"Where're the houses? Not much going on here."

Maymie pointed straight ahead, "It's only been four years. That's the clubhouse for the golf course up ahead." She groaned, "Look at the cars. Everyone and his dog must be here."

When they entered the two-story stucco building, dusk was shortening into evening. Welcoming electric lights blazed inside where long tables covered with white cloths were set up in the dining room. Red and yellow daisies and miniature cactus plants were on each table, along with a souvenir ashtray shaped like a donkey decorated the tables. Three women in long red dresses and black lace mantillas danced to the music of a guitarist strumming "In a Little Spanish Town."

Phillis spotted Etta Henderson. Hoping for an introduction to honoree Emily Newell Blair, she walked toward them. Henderson mouthed "later," pointing to the gentleman in conversation with her boss.

What is diehard Republican journalist William Allen White discussing with Emily Blair, Vice Chair of the National Democratic Party? When she realized he wasn't the only male in the room, she sidled up to Etta, "Why all these men?"

Etta laughed. "Political conversations with big time journalists. An opportunity to display our in-depth knowledge of national concerns."

"Good strategy. Where are we supposed to sit?"

"We had place cards, but the guest list got out of hand. We have the feminine Who's Who of America with us tonight. Just look around."

Phillis grinned and walked toward Maymie, deep in conversation with an elegantly dressed older woman.

"Come meet Mrs. Stewart."

"Phillis Flanagan, Fort Worth *Star Telegram*," she smiled and extended her hand. "So happy to meet you, Mrs. Stewart."

"Mellie erected the Niels Esperson building you've often admired."

"The building with the circular temple and dome on top?" Phillis said. "It's the most distinctive in Houston. You defined this city's skyline, Mrs. Stewart."

"Thank you, Phillis. I would love to give you a tour. The building is my pride and joy and I assure you it's as distinctive inside as out."

"Mrs. Stewart and I need to talk real estate. I'll catch up with you later."
Her dismissal tickled Phillis who planned to circle the room.

Seeking a restroom before the dinner began, Phillis walked into an underwear disaster of the first order. An attractive older woman stood in the lounge area of the ladies' restroom, holding a pair of pink silk step-ins. She looked Phillis up and down and asked, "Miss, do you have a good-sized safety pin I can borrow?"

"Of course. Just a minute." Searching through her pocketbook, Phillis located the pin in her coin purse and held it out to the woman whose waistband elastic had broken.

"Thank you." Deftly pinning the two ends together, she gracefully slipped the garment back on under her dress.

"You're amazingly limber to be able to don those so easily," Phillis remarked.

"That's kind of you. Thanks for the compliment. For twenty-five years, I've begun my day with calisthenics. Used to spend only fifteen minutes. After turning sixty, I doubled the time. Makes a huge difference for me. I keep recommending it. Most women laugh at me, act like I'm wasting my time."

"Ma'am, I cannot believe you're sixty. I would love to give your regimen a try. How do I get a description of these calisthenics?"

"Come join me at my table and I will find paper and a pencil to write down your address so I can send you a copy of my exercises. The least I can do to repay you for the safety pin. How could I have gotten through this evening without your help"

She linked arms with Phillis and walked to the front of the dining room. Sitting down at the head of the table, she motioned Phillis to the chair beside her and announced, "Ladies, this young woman was kind enough to rescue me from an embarrassing wardrobe problem. I've suggested she join us. I'm sorry. I forgot to ask your name."

"Phillis Flanagan, reporter for the *Fort Worth Star-Telegram* here for my first national convention."

"And I'm Mrs. Charles Dana Gibson. Please call me 'Irene.'"

Three others introduced themselves as Miss Elizabeth Marbury of New York, Mrs. Le Roy Springs from South Carolina, and Miss Esto Broughton from California. Phillis hoped her face did not reveal she was pinching herself under the table.

Mrs. Gibson suggested, "Let's share our stories with Miss Flanagan. She needs to know why we traveled so far from home to spend four days with twenty-five-thousand Democrats in this unspeakable heat."

"You begin, Irene?" Esto suggested, "Yours is the best story."

"Our lives are remarkable compared to our mothers," Irene pointed out. "I live in New York City, along with Bessie, but was born in the South."

Esto interrupted, "No, Irene. Begin with your fifty-nine marriage proposals."

"That's how she got to be the 'Gibson Girl,'" Miss Broughton explained to Phillis.

"Tell Miss Flanagan about your sisters," Bessie suggested.

"I'll tell the story my way," Irene said firmly. "My husband was the first man who pleased me. I turned down proposals because the men were pompous and unwilling to 'give me' the freedom I demanded. My husband's view of womanhood suited me." She pointed to Esto and Phillis. "Keep this in mind if you decide to marry."

Bessie Marbury interrupted and said, "The man her father called 'an out-of-work house painter' is now publisher of *Life* magazine."

They all laughed. "For years, my husband used me as a model for his drawings.

But today I'm no Gibson Girl. I'm a Gibson grandmother."

Phillis piped up, "You certainly don't look like a grandmother. When did you get interested in politics?"

"Same way everyone here did. The suffrage fight. The passage of the Nineteenth Amendment gave us the vote. Now we're looking for more."

Mrs. Springs smilingly announced, "Five-hundred women have come to Houston, many of them as delegates or alternates. The Republican convention drew only four hundred."

"We're helping choose the presidential candidate. The next step is a woman nominated," Irene explained. "Esto, you talk about this."

"Politics and journalism are my passions. For twenty-four years, I've served as an elected official in California. Serving with a room full of men is no picnic. They don't want us in politics, but that's not stopping us in California."

Irene nodded to Mrs. Springs who boasted, "I call myself a 'workhorse.' I deal with soft-spoken gentlemen who won't budge an inch on anything. Southern belles who hide their brains until I want to shake them. I've learned the ropes, and I love it."

"Do the men listen to you?" Esto Broughton asked. Turning to Phillis, she explained, "She's the first woman ever nominated for Vice-President of the United States."

With the Mistress of Ceremonies signal to begin the evening's program, Irene whispered, "Ladies, I've saved the best for last. Bessie, you'll tell your story after the speakers finish."

Mrs. Emily Newell Blair stood at the podium and received a standing ovation lasting almost a minute.

"Thank you for your generous applause," she began. "As my term of office ends, I share with you my reflections on the importance of women in politics. Have no fear, I will speak briefly since most of you have heard my words before and I don't believe in lengthy speeches."

Laughter rippled through the banquet room along with more than a few sighs of relief.

"American men have spent one hundred and fifty years as reporters and politicians. Women became citizens only eight years ago. I started out a housewife and mother until realizing how few rights I had. I wanted to vote, and I wanted my daughter Harriet to be able to vote. Her brother could vote. How could I explain the limitations she would face? For eighteen years I worked to change our status. When the Nineteenth Amendment was passed, we knew a joy like none other we ever experienced. But voting was just the beginning.

Tonight, I look at the capable women here, journalists, members of legislatures, National Committee Women from every state in the Union, powerful distinguished women. Ours is not a simple task. Despite the prejudice we must overcome, I am optimistic about political women's success. Thank you for your time and attention."

As the thunderous applause died down, the maître d announced, "Dinner is served. Enjoy your meal."

Irene Gibson threw up her hand and said, "Great speech! Emily's an excellent vice-chairman and we all know men who fear women entering politics."

Turning to Miss Marbury, she said, "Bessie, it's time for you to tell Miss Flanagan why you're here."

"The short answer is I follow Al Smith," Bessie Marbury began. "Where he goes, I go because I believe in the man, I support him, and I think it's high time we elected him as our president. This will be the second time we've nominated him to be our candidate. It's time for him to get the job."

Irene said, "Bessie, tell about your thirty-year career as a Broadway producer and agent which has made you the most powerful woman in American theater. Bernhardt, Barrymore, she knows everyone. Her syndicated magazine column is read all over the country. Now she makes her mark as the National Committee Woman from the State of New York."

"I sailed here on the *S.S. Algonquin* to stop 'steamroller tactics' from being used in Houston. I should be in New York where my Broadway show's ready for production. Instead, I'm in Houston, a ninety-degree sweatbox. Thank God, I'm not staying at the Rice Hotel. I took a suite at the Galvez, which is a little more civilized."

Galveston with its bootlegger empire is civilized? Phillis wondered how closely Miss Marbury had looked at the port city.

"After the last convention in '24, I realized men don't play fair. This time they're going to give us the power that should have come with the vote. My credo is 'Opportunity does not make us. We make our opportunities.'"

"Miss Marbury," Phillis asked, "when are you going to run for office?"

"Girl, use your eyes. I'm seventy-one. Too old and too fat to appeal to today's voters. The editorials call me 'the grand old lady of the Democratic party.' I leave campaigning to the younger women."

Phillis made sure she got a statement from each of the guests, lingering to ask Miss Brannaugh if she would consent to an interview. "Thank you, Mrs. Gibson, this is an evening I will never forget."

Exchanging farewells, she stood, realizing Maymie was behind her. When Maymie saw her face, she asked, "My gracious, girl, did you win a lottery?"

"Better than that, Miss Maymie. Better than that. This evening has been the best of the best."

6/24/28. What I kept feeling tonight were possibilities. I came to Houston looking for stories. These incredible women gave me better look at women's politics. It is not that different from newspapering. The men stand squarely in the way. Makes me think about Etta Henderson's suggestion. Should I use my writing skills to join this battle?

CHAPTER SEVENTEEN

We commend the police department and Sheriff Binford for the remarkable dispatch with which they cleaned up last week's atrocious lynching. It can go a long way in counteracting the unpleasant publicity received from this affair itself.

The Houston Gargoyle
June 26, 1928

Monday, June 25, 1928

STANLEY SPOTTED IT YESTERDAY. THIS morning, it was worse. For the dinner last night, she concealed it with a thick layer of face powder. This morning's sunshine revealed more problems. She smeared on some of her prized Valaze cream and examined her face in the mirror. Messy hair never mattered that much. A pink, peeling face! The awful sunburn highlighted every freckle.

The telephone's *brnng* echoed through the house as she started down. On the lower landing, she heard Clarence Mueller mumbling and Viola's shrill response, "Our telephone is in Diboll, Mr. Mueller. It's not your problem."

Smiling, Phillis took the rest of the steps two at a time and reached the telephone just as Teddy did. He plucked the receiver off the base and answered, "Maymie Banion's house. What can I help you with? Oh, just a minute. She's standing right here." Handing the phone to Phillis, he gave her a smirky grin and said, "It's Stanley Staples."

"Good morning, Stanley."

Wasting no time on amenities, Stanley relayed his news, "Your father has requested another visit. Can you be ready by eleven?"

Phillis's stomach dropped to her toes and her voice broke as she answered, "Yes. I'll meet you there."

Another visit? He certainly had shown no interest in her. Why would he want to see her again? Had he remembered what he did to land himself in jail? No doubt, he's fixed up a pretty story to get him out of this mess. She would take bets against Houston letting him loose.

She stomped angrily into the kitchen looking for a cup of coffee.

Della Hinkle winked at Josie, "My, someone got up on the wrong side of bed, didn't she?"

"Hard to do when your single bed is pushed against the wall," Phillis said, throwing her a dirty look before asking Josie for some coffee.

Whisking a white mug out of the cupboard, Josie poured the coffee and set it with the cream pitcher beside her. "Thank you, Josie," Philllis said.

Maymie entered the kitchen and raised her brows at Phillis's downcast face. Turning to greet the Muellers, she smiled warmly and said, "Let's all have a seat in the dining room."

She motioned to Phillis to follow her there.

"What would you folks like for breakfast?"

"Coffee, strong and hot with cream and sugar, for me," Viola said. "Mr. Mueller drinks his weak as a baby and adds nothing. Can we have exactly what you fixed yesterday?"

"Now, Mother, they may not have the same groceries on hand," Clarence said as he stuffed his napkin into his collar.

"No problem, I assure you." Miss Maymie twirled her finger and looked at Josie, expectantly.

Hoping to fill out the story Phillis was writing about the Mueller's, she politely asked, "When did you arrive in Houston?"

"Last Wednesday. Rolled in about noon. Found Memorial Park's campground with no trouble. The park's big as all git out. Got our tent set up alongside about a hundred other folks. Real nice workers there to help. Everything great till the sun went down and the mosquitoes arrived."

"Sorry, honey," he said, giving his wife an embarrassed look. "When I planned it, I didn't know these Gulf Coast skeeters were so big they could carry off a small kid. We never slept a wink. The Park attendants gave us oil to keep 'em away. Didn't do any good. I'd read about the facilities in the *Diboll Weekly*. Sounded perfect. A city park converted into a tent city just to accommodate convention visitors. Comfort stations, electric light bulbs strung on wires in the trees, even a big radio set everybody could listen to at night."

"It wasn't to your liking?" Phillis asked.

"Not by a long shot. Aside from the bugs, the toilets plugged up by eight o'clock that night and the electric lights flickered on and off. Viola twisted her ankle tripping over a tree root as she walked back to our tent in the dark. The radio? All it talked about was that fishmonger from New York who takes his orders from the Pope of Rome."

'I've heard Al Smith is his own man," Phillis contradicted.

"I already listened to everything he has to say on my barbershop's radio set in Diboll. His voice is so high-pitched and shrill. It's awful. Have you ever heard anyone from Brooklyn talking?"

Phillis shook her head.

"I can't imagine voting for that pipsqueak." Clarence smiled at Josie as she brought their coffee. "Miss, we're dry and always have been. Didn't take a law from Congress to make us stop drinking hooch."

Phillis nodded solemnly. "I need to excuse myself. I have to get downtown."

She left the diners and went up to her room to reread the article she had written last night about Mr. and Mrs. Mueller. This morning's breakfast provided more details. Every time the Muellers opened their mouths, she gleefully cringed. Most of her readers would regard the couple as 'reg'lar folks.' Maybe she should lead with something about "Home Folks Wisdom," Phillis thought as she ran downstairs.

As she pushed the screened door to leave, Maymie called, "Phillis, please come by my office this afternoon."

A raised eyebrow and an emphatic nod were the only explanation she received.

WHEN SHE REACHED THE JAIL, SHE spied Stanley before he saw her. His fedora was pushed back, and he sprawled on a bench reading the *Post-Dispatch*. She walked up and asked, "Who wrote the article in Saturday's *Press* about the newspapermen's amazement at Houston's reaction to the lynching?"

"A buddy of mine," Stanley replied. "He talked to a bunch of visiting reporters from all over who said they'd never seen an entire city rise in protest so rapidly."

"Are you impressed?"

"Not really. Houston's just trying to save its bacon."

He stood to escort her into the building. "Here we go again. Let me walk ahead of you."

A guard led them down the same hall to Phillip Callaway's cell. He sat on his cot, cleaning his nails with a tiny wood splinter. When they stopped in front of his cell, he looked up expectantly.

"Hello, Phillis. I hope you don't mind coming back down here."

She glared at him through the iron bars, her feet glued to the cement floor.

"Holy smokes, you don't make it easy on a fella, do you?"

Phillis shrugged her shoulders and wrinkled her nose as if smelling something terribly unpleasant.

"Don't look at me like that. You're my daughter. I need to tell you something."

She shrugged her shoulders again and kept on staring.

"Phillis, I didn't kill that colored man. Got hooked for this because I was standing in the wrong place at the wrong time. I didn't do it."

"You've said that twice. Why're you changing your story? You have an alibi?"

"I would if I could remember her name. Just believe me, I was nowhere near Jeff Davis Hospital or Post Oak Road."

"Police must not believe you since you're still here. Why should I?"

"Can't say I've made you proud of me, but I wouldn't hang nobody, no matter what they'd done." Phillip bowed his head and ran his fingers through his hair."

Phillis admitted begrudgingly, "I pity any man who is unfairly jailed. Being executed for a crime you didn't commit is a crime as well. What about the other men who were indicted? Are they innocent, too?"

"I never met these guys in my life. They've never put us together in the same room. The guard says we're all in solitary confinement."

"So, what happens next?"

"We'll go on trial. We won't be convicted."

"What makes you think that?"

"I just know it won't happen. That's all."

"Well, I hope you're right. I can't think how you'll get off."

Stanley put his hand on Phillis's shoulder, "The guard says we have to leave."

Her eyes narrowed to slits as she gave her father a hard look and turned to go. Only Stanley saw the tears rolling down her cheeks as she walked back down the hall.

Leaving the jail, he took her arm and guided her down the steps. Heading for the large Pin Oak tree shading the front sidewalk, she turned to face him.

"I believe him," she said. "He's innocent. My mother always said he was too lazy to get out of his own way. He's a loner. The only time he'd join a group is for a poker game. I'll bet he never loved or hated anybody enough to commit this kind of crime. You saw his response to finding out his twin babies died."

"It's been a long time since you've seen him."

"I'm sure he's innocent. He should not die for this crime." She grabbed his sleeve and asked, "What can I do? Go to the police? Write an article?"

"Phillis," Stanley asked slowly, "don't you think it strange he's certain he won't be convicted?"

"Yeah, that's weird. But he was always a cocky kind of guy." Phillis agreed. "Do you know why he's so sure? Has the grand jury indicted innocent men?"

"I've been waiting for this question. I've already said I don't understand all I know."

"You mean these aren't the lynchers?"

Stanley quickly put his hand over her mouth as two uniformed policemen strolled beside them, then whispered "Hush." Dropping his hand after the men had walked out of hearing, he tilted her face up and pulled her close to him.

Phillis wondered if he was protecting her or the blue-coated men. With a shake of her finger, she stepped away, lowering her voice as she asked, "No one will investigate this further, will they? It's a sham indictment, isn't it? The guilty men are police officers, aren't they?"

Overhead, a large flock of crows startled her as they flew out of the oak tree, hovering above her. Phillis watched as he fingered the brim of his fedora, then blurted out, "Well, I'll write the story and blast the Houston police and Judge King, who handed down the grand jury's indictment. Just watch me. I'll be damned if I don't."

"You won't. You can't. No one can." He studied the ground and kicked some acorns to one side. "There're always some stories you can't write."

"No, that's not true." She covered her mouth. "What a terrible thing for your city. No justice for Robert Powell?" She bowed her head and then mumbled, "Is this how your town operates? Is this the Houston I've praised in my articles?"

"I know what you want to hear. Have you forgotten Fort Worth and Dallas's version of law and order? When the KKK ruled Tarrant County? You've seen miscarriages of justice. Every reporter has. This lynching's shamed Houston at the peak of its cock-a-doodle glory. I can only hope the city will change because of this crime."

Phillis waited as a passerby hurried toward the corner. "What can I say? You've taken my words away from me." She slapped her hands together and studied his face. "Don't give me that pitying look. That's not what I want from you."

"My advice," he started to say then paused, changing his mind. "I can't offer you any advice that makes sense except, don't ever forget the lesson you've learned here. Pick yourself up and move on." With a tip of his hat, he turned and left her standing there deep in her thoughts of crime and punishment, decency and injustice, right and wrong.

His words had stunned her, sucked the life out of her. For Stanley, this was just another lesson she needed to learn. With an alarming suddenness, Houston was now providing her with a school of experience. This was her story, her scoop, her chance for a front pager, but not really. In her heart, she knew a flight to the moon would be more likely than an editor publishing her story exposing the convicted men as nothing more than innocent skid row bums.

Off Stanley sauntered, probably headed to McKinnon's for another greasy cheese sandwich, another afternoon of pounding the keys to grab his readers' attention with a new story.

Phillis, exhausted, unable to think coherently, made a bee line for the trolley stop. When she hit the house, she headed upstairs to her room knowing what would happen next.

Locking the door behind her, she threw herself on her bed and had a good cry. The worst miscarriage of justice she had ever seen, and she was helpless to write about it. *How little control I have over anything.*

Dragging herself from the bed, she poured water into the washbowl, wet a cloth she applied to her eyes, slipped off her shoes, and lay down on top of the coverlet. The dark wooden rafters of her ceiling looked too much like the iron bars in Philip's cell. A replay of the events that led her to Harris County Jail flashed through her brain as she tried to make sense of it all. How does one explain the inexplicable? Coincidence? Fate?

Both were working overtime in her life. Her father, who had been absent for most of her life, had now reappeared as a murder suspect, currently lodging in the county jail. Worst of all, even if an editor would print a front page story written by her, she would be run out of town if she exposed Phillip Flannagan's innocence and Houston's sham indictment of these five men.

She drifted off, awakened by a pounding on her bedroom door. "Who is it?"

Della Hinkle called out, "Did you forget your four-o'clock meeting downtown with Miss Maymie?"

Phillis sat up. "Oh no," she moaned. "Is she on the telephone?"

"Sure is. Asking how long it's gonna take you to get there. What'll I tell her?"

"Tell her I'm on my way. Where's Teddy? Could he run me downtown?"

"He's at Sam Houston Hall."

Why in the world did she have to be at Miss Maymie's office? With a groan, she dragged herself off the bed and wiped the cloth over her face again before lacing up her oxfords and heading out.

Leaving the trolley, Phillis entered the Scanlan Building and took the elevator to Maymie's floor. Her secretary Gloria said, "She's with someone. I wouldn't go in if I..."

Phillis breezed past her and reached for the doorknob where her hand froze as a surprisingly familiar voice stopped her in her tracks. "Has Phillis seen her father yet?"

Phillis waited for Maymie's response, "I'm not sure."

"I wish I could see her."

"Well, Mother, here I am."

Lena Belle's mouth dropped open as she reached for Phillis and burst into tears. Patting her back, Phillis murmured, "It's okay, Mother. I've visited him in jail twice. He's changed his name again. For the first time in twenty years, we know where he is." She looked at Maymie and then back to her mother and asked, "How'd you get here?"

"We drove. Mr. Wilkerson has a new touring car. A Cadillac almost as long as a train car. I wish you could see it. More chrome and color than a barbershop pole. He wanted to take it on the road and decided on Houston. Curious to see the new hall. Of course, I jumped at the chance to come along since Maymie called last week to tell me about your father's troubles."

"I would call being put in jail and indicted for the murder of a young colored man more than 'trouble.'"

"Well, anyway, I wanted to see you. We're driving to Liberty to spend the night with friends of Mr. Wilkerson's. We'll leave soon so we can arrive before dark."

"So, Maymie, this is why you insisted I come to your office. Apparently, you're the only one who thought my mother shouldn't sneak out of town without seeing her only daughter." Phillis wanted to throttle her.

"You heard me say I wished I could see you." Lena Belle wrung her hands and looked at her anxiously.

"Why weren't you going to make this happen?" Her mother's wilting face told her the answer. "Horace Wilkerson, that's why. He made you promise you would not make time to see me."

Her mother faintly demurred, "It's just that Mr. Wilkerson…"

Phillis threw up her hands and snapped, "Mother, Liberty's more than forty miles. Time for you and your husband to get on the road. I hope it's not black as pitch when you arrive."

"We have four electric headlights almost as big as watermelons. Let's talk about your father."

"There's nothing to say. Phillip Flanagan was standing, or more likely trespassing, in the wrong place at the wrong time. Got pulled in during a police raid."

"You mean he's not guilty?"

"That's what he says. He has no alibi and being new to town, no one to speak for him."

"Well, I'm sure he's guilty. Always was a liar. Nasty person and never pays for anything he does. Always gets off. I hope his luck's run out."

"Mother, you can't tell me you want an innocent man to be executed for a crime he did not commit."

"I can't believe you're defending him. He's never been a father to you. I rue the day I met him. Damn Irishman."

Horace Wilkerson stomped into the outside office, slamming the door and bellowing, "Where's my wife? She's supposed to be here with Miss Banion."

"Yes, sir, they're in her office," Gloria said. "I'll announce you."

"No need, I'll go in," he said, opening the door and pointing at his wife. "Lena Belle, my car's parked at the curb being watched by an attendant. Say your goodbyes and come on out now."

Phillis stepped behind the door when she heard his voice.

"Just give me a minute."

Her mother shooed him out, then blew Phillis a kiss and hugged Maymie Banion, slipping something into her hand. Straightening her elegant wide-brimmed straw hat, Lena Belle clutched her purse and exited to the outer office. "You're late, Horace. Are you sure we can get to Liberty before dark?"

"Now, Mother, we'll be fine. That jewel of a car can do anything. Had fun showing off my new Caddy. No automobile's this nice in Houston. Even Mr. Sakowitz was impressed. He took me to his club for lunch. Fine fellow." Phillis shook her head as she listened to Horace Wilkerson's voice trailing down the hall.

Maymie let out a heavy sigh and patted her shoulder. "Time to close up, girl. Let's go home. Your mother left this for you."

Phillis looked at the ten-dollar bill and said, "I wish I could afford to say, 'throw it in the trash.'"

Muttering "blowhard, pompous ass," she followed Maymie to the elevator and down to the street.

Little conversation ensued as they drove away from the Scanlan Building. Lena Belle's whirlwind visit had rattled them both. Though angry because she could not tell anyone about Houston's trumped-up solution to the Powell lynching, she heeded Stanley's warning to keep quiet. She would gain nothing, and it could cost her a great deal.

The telephone rang as Phillis and Maymie entered the back door. "You get it, Phillis," Maymie said. "I've got to talk to Josie about dinner."

Stanley's voice boomed in her ear. "Can't believe you picked up the phone. Where's old lady Hinkle?"

"Guess she is resting in her room, Stanley. What's up now?"

"Got a serious question for you."

Phillis hesitated. Dear Lord, what had happened now? A dozen horrors flew through her mind. It must be about their meeting at the jail this morning.

"Go ahead, ask," she said, her heart racing as she stood stock still trying to brace herself.

"Do you have any old shoes?" Stanley asked. "Shoes you don't mind getting messed up. I'll drive my car. Some of the time, we'll have to hoof it. To get up close."

Every pair of shoes Phillis owned was old and none could be spared for a nighttime lark with Stanley Staples.

"What for?" she asked. "Are we going to Luna Park?"

"No, we're going to the parts of Houston that convention visitors will not see."

"When?" She frowned, disturbed by his troubled voice.

"I'll see you at eight o'clock tonight. I've found a new topic for my column., but I need another pair of eyes."

"Of course."

As the telephone line went dead, Phillis looked down at her shoes. Whatever she put on her feet was unimportant compared with the chance to explore Houston with Stanley. What was on his mind now?

CHAPTER EIGHTEEN

Thousands of visitors coming to Houston . . . a fair city with her wide streets, grand homes, manicured boulevards, tall trees waving in gulf breezes, completely improved to the last modern dot. A city to live in, as well as to grow rich in. Yes. . . for white people!

The Houston Gargoyle
June 19, 1928

HE ARRIVED SHORTLY AFTER DARK, PARKING his jalopy in front of 1750 Harvard. She had not known he had an automobile.

Teddy yelled, "Phillis, Stanley's here."

When she rushed down, he pointed at her and then outside at the car he was driving.

"Is that his car?"

"Yeah, it's his, all right. Hope it gets you wherever you are going without losing a fender. Take a gander at that rust bucket if you don't believe me."

Stepping outside, she started to laugh. Much of the car's exterior green paint was gone, and the mudguards were bent and battered.

"It's a 1922 Chevy. God, it's been treated bad. How come he didn't put it in a garage?"

"I guess it's because he doesn't have one. Don't be so high-hat."

Teddy gave her a sheepish look. "Okay, sorry. Where in the world are you two headed?"

Phillis ignored his question as she ran down the front steps.

"You ready?" Stanley asked. Phillis's eyes sparkled as she nodded.

"Good. Here we go." Stanley started the car and rattled down the street toward what he called the Fifth Ward. Once there, he drove slower down Odin Street, dodging mud puddles and stray dogs prowling around. He pulled off to the side and killed the engine. "Our first stop. Let's walk the rest of the way."

"It's so dark I can't see my hand in front of my face."

"No streetlights," Stanley replied. "Do you see any houses lit up?"

"No. Everything is dark."

"That's 'cause there's no electricity in the colored section of Fifth Ward. Nor in Third Ward or Fourth."

He got out of the car, picking up a flashlight from the back seat. The beam from his light helped Phillis make her way through the slimy mud. Flimsy shotgun houses lined both sides of the street, jammed so close together biscuits could be passed out the windows from one to another. There were no sidewalks or trees.

"Once you get off Odin Street, the twisted alleys are more mud. Watch your step and hold your nose. Privies are behind the houses. There's no sewage connections."

Walking back to the Chevy, they picked their way through the quiet, dark alley, a flickering oil lantern and a voice shushing a barking dog providing the only signs of life. "Okay, now we're heading to Third Ward. It's just up the road a ways."

Shaken by what she had seen, Phillis nervously picked at a piece of lint on the musty seat cover, wondering what horrors their next stop would bring. *I bet I could write this story. Talk to the mothers, housecleaners, laundresses who live here. A woman's viewoint—Newspapers always ignore this.* She lacked the confidence to suggest this, even to Stanley.

"City ordinances say Houston houses have to be fifteen feet apart," Stanley announced grimly. "These shanties are built on top of each other. Building codes don't apply to the Wards." He stepped over a broken apple crate. "Shacks rent for five or six dollars a week. Landlords make almost three-hundred-percent annual return on their seventy-five-dollar investment. When a house needs repair, it's so worthless they just tear it down and build a new one."

Stanley pointed to a dark pool of standing water. Phillis remembered the hard shower that day which had thankfully cooled things off. Not always a blessing for these folks. "The street's a cesspool when it rains," he said.

They drove back to West Gray Street and turned left. As they crossed Main Street, Stanley said, "Here's Fourth Ward, home of the infamous San Felipe District."

Phillis rared back. "Why is it 'infamous'?"

"The Camp Logan race riot began here during the War, and Robert Powell, the man who was lynched, lived here."

"It's got gravel streets," she pointed out.

"Only because they're surrounded by white neighborhoods," Stanley explained. "How would you like to meet a car travelling down one of these narrow roads?"

"Maybe residents don't have cars."

You got it. So they don't need streetlights either. Hey, they got two streetlights. Not one for every block. Two for the entire fifteen or twenty blocks."

As he drove, Stanley explained. "In my article I'll give credit to current city officials for graveling more of the streets in Fourth Ward as well as for their proposed plan to install a storm sewer in the Scott Street area. Streetlights are budgeted for next year. They're needed right now. It's a disgraceful lack of electricity and sewage. If I arouse citizens' indignation maybe I can get the ball rolling."

"Who lives in these neighborhoods?" she asked.

"Most of Houston's black folks slog through these muddy, stinky-smelling streets to take the trolley or bus to the white homes where they work as cooks, maids, yardmen, and nurses. How do they pass their evenings here in the dark?

Think about the health of the residents deprived of city services?" Stanley shook his head in frustration.

"The women ruin their eyesight mending clothing by the light from an oil lamp while the men gather and play cards sitting on wooden crates on the street corners, drinking rotgut whiskey to take their minds off their lives. Next thing you know there's trouble. Arguments, fights, you name it. Much of our city's crime happens after dark in the San Felipe District."

She felt helpless and sad as she listened to his passionate words.

"I will write about this," he said. "I want citizens to find out about these city slums. I'm betting my readers will insist on improvements. I know how disgusted you are with the city fathers, but Houston has people who care about their city. Before I write my column, I needed to share this picture with someone I respect and trust."

He looked at her apprehensively. "God, I hope you understand me, Phillis."

What Phillis understood was that Stanley Staples had a lot of sides to him. Despite his column's popularity, she suspected this one would not sit well with some readers, especially the slum landlords who always rebelled at improving their property. Undoubtedly, he knew this.

"I get it. The message needs sending. You're doing this for Houston." Phillis took his hands and squeezed them as she asked, "What caused these conditions?"

"One thing is the damn White Primary Bill passed in 1923. The Texas Senate threw the Fourteenth Amendment in the trash and took away fifty-four-thousand Negro citizens' right to vote. As of now, all they can do is accept what the state decides for them. No altering that, but I intend to expose their living conditions in Houston."

"You better not write this until these visitors leave the city. Our smug leaders don't want them to see these parts of Houston. They are only showing them areas where white people live and get rich."

"Sorry. This is gonna be Thursday's column. I intend to diminish the charm of River Oaks and Southmore."

They exchanged knowing looks, and Phillis grinned at the thought of the city's white folks reading his account. She and Stanley walked back to the automobile, leaving Fourth Ward and driving back to the planned Houston Heights, where well-lit streets, electric light switches, and flush toilets were taken for granted.

6/25/28. What I learned today at the county jail will stay with me always. A story I can't write. Being ordered to conceal the innocence of my father. The city fathers protecting guilty lynchers. Walking through the Negro wards. It all makes me want to throw up. Houston's flimsy coverup and their slums are tied together. Everybody in Houston wants Powell's death to disappear. Will Stanley's column change anything? He can write his story, but I cannot write mine. Where's the sense in that?

CHAPTER NINETEEN

Tuesday, June 26, 1928

AN EARLY LUNCH AT BILLY MCKINNON'S BEFORE the first session began seemed the simplest choice and as luck would have it, Stanley Staples' colleague, Bess Scott, was sitting at a table alone. Waving her over, she motioned Phillis toward the empty chair opposite. "You look like things are going better," she said as Phillis sat down.

Phillis's thoughts skipped back to yesterday's meeting with her father and struggled to answer. "Yes and no. I just saw Step-in-Sanders."

"Isn't he barbaric? He makes great story material."

"He's leaving quite a legacy. A legislator who will go down in history for trying to force women back into petticoats. But the women parading around the Auditorium Hotel lobby screaming insults at him looked more like Macbeth's witches than progressive female delegates."

"They should have used the press to reduce him to the idiotic male that he is. Maybe a political cartoon?"

They laughed together, but she could tell, Bess's laugh rang hollow. "What's the matter?"

"Our mothers warned us, 'Pride goes before a fall'?"

"What happened?" Phillis asked.

She paused, took a bite of her ham sandwich then shook her head. "Yesterday, I stopped by the library on my way to Sam Houston Hall. Asked by a librarian if I wanted a story, I followed her to a study table where Dr. Will Durant, the man who wrote the bestseller, *The Story of Philosophy*, sat reading a book."

Phillis leaned in to hear her lowered voice over the hubbub in the café.

"I introduced myself and asked for a few minutes of his time, to which he graciously agreed. He's only forty-three, just five years older than I am. Imagine being a celebrated author so young. Dark-haired, bushy eyebrows and a neatly clipped mustache. You should have seen him. He wore a formal dark suit. I swear it looked like wool. A stiff-necked white shirt collar, and a silk tie yet he looked cool as a cucumber."

"Laying down his book, he began talking about Al Smith, saying his editorial will be in Thursday's *Press*." She fiddled with the toothpick she had removed from her sandwich. "Imagine meeting this famous author and interviewing him. I hurried to my office, wrote up my story, and turned it in. The editor wanted a photograph, so I got one from the morgue, a metal 'cut' instead of a photo, and approved it for the afternoon edition."

Bess sat back, and tears rolled down her cheeks. "This morning, Mefo slammed the newspaper down on my desk with the photo of Durant circled in red. 'This is not Will Durant!' he shouted."

"But who?" Phillis asked.

"The owner of the Durant automobile factory in New York City. My editor kindly accepted the blame, saying we were in too much of a hurry. There it is, my nice story, ruined."

"Terrible," Phillis sympathized. *Lordy, a new journalism pitfall.*

"It's the worst thing that's happened to me lately," Bess said, motioning the waitress over. "Two chocolate sodas, please," nodding she smiled weakly. "My treat."

"Thanks," said Phillis. "Tell me about the Clark Gable column Gladys Rumsfeld told me you wrote."

"That was last month," Bess said, blushing the color of a fire engine. "Another faux pas. Luckily, this one had a better ending. You know Gable lives off and on in Houston?"

"No," Phillis answered excitedly. *How would I know that?*

"He got the lead role in a production with the Arthur Casey Players. It's a great Houston stock company. His colleagues say Gable likes to play. Parties all night, cuts rehearsals, and doesn't learn his lines. Opening night, I was assigned to write the review. Gable was terrible, ad-libbed throughout, awkward love scenes. I wrote that he 'made love like a bull in a china shop.'"

Phillis laughed as they both sipped their sodas.

"Right after the edition hit the streets, in comes Mr. Gable looking for me. The *Press* employees, especially the women, were agog."

"I should think so. He's so handsome."

"Well, yes. He stomped across to my desk in the City Room's far corner and asked 'Mrs. Scott?' I nodded. He bowed from the waist and announced, 'I'm Clark Gable.' With a grin, he said, 'So I don't know how to make love. Would you like to teach me?'"

Phillis's laughter brought the waitress over to see what was happening.

Bess laughed as well. "I told him 'touché' and we went for coffee and are now sort of friends."

"Now, that's fun. A great story."

Stanley Staples' stern voice interrupted their merriment. "What are you girls doing here at three o'clock in the afternoon? You missed Clem Shaver's first gavel-pounding. Did either of you catch Damon Runyon's column today? Pretty funny!" He pulled up a chair and eyed their sodas.

"What did Runyon say?" asked Phillis.

"He claims our New York visitors are surprised to find what they call 'signs of human life' this far south. Guess that puts us in our place."

Bess shrugged her shoulders and said, "The New Yorkers aren't complimenting Houstonians. I heard a man say the streets around the hall look like a circus midway and complained our tamales are so hot they explode in your hand."

"A guy from Brooklyn said he's afraid to sit anywhere for fear some horrible contraption will go off with a bang underneath him," Phillis added.

"Are you going to the Woman's Breakfast tomorrow morning, Bess?"

"No, you have to be a hoity-toity for an invitation to that event."

"Maymie Banion's going," Phillis said. "We'll have to read about it in the newspaper." They chuckled and looking at their watches, agreed they should leave.

"No, you can't leave," Stanley protested. "You haven't finished your sodas. Besides, I have news about your boss, Phillis."

Bess waved the waitress over and slipped her a dollar. "Gotta go," she said, smiling at Stanley and giving Phillis a hug. "Thanks for listening."

"Bess had an upset with Mefo," Phillis explained.

"Yeah, I heard." Stanley shook his head and frowned.

"Will your news about Amon Carter upset me?"

"It'll answer your questions. Last night I had a drink with a *Star* reporter in the Rice Hotel's bar and asked him, 'How's it going?'"

"What's his name?" Phillis asked.

"Bubba Bakersfield. I suspect, he's the low man on Carter's totem pole."

"You're right about that," she replied.

"He's bunking at the Rice Hotel in a third-floor suite with guess who?"

Phillis shook her head.

"None other than Amon Carter and the sheriff of Tarrant County. I might add, H. L. Mencken is a frequent visitor. He says Rogers sits in his underwear at a table in the middle of their suite's living room, trying to stay cool while he types up what runners bring him from the political pow wows. All the windows are wide open."

Stanley watched Phillis's jaw drop.

"Bubba invited me to join them anytime. Says it's open house day or night." Stanley raised his eyebrows up and down. "Amon brought cases of whiskey with him from his ranch's underground cellar where he stockpiled a ton of booze before the Volstead went into effect."

"No wonder everyone comes to his parties," Phillis commented sourly.

"The bathtub's filled to the top with ice and beer. Bubba said when housekeeping came in to clean yesterday, the poor cleaning lady backed right out of the room fast as she could."

Phillis pulled out her notebook and scribbled entries. *What about the articles I am sending to Fort Worth. Is Carter reading them too before they are sent off?*

"So," she said disgustedly, "Amon's gang is having fun while filling up all the *Star's* holes for Houston convention stories."

"Maybe. At any rate, the elevators are driving Carter crazy. Even his 'toads' are calling him a firecracker about to go off. You better stay out of his sight."

"Everyone laughs about his temper," Phillis admitted. "I saw him circling the convention hall after the dedication and ducked out of sight. He's spitting mad and looks like a box of snakes. We've only met one time. I doubt he would remember me."

"Kiddo, you're hard to forget."

Phillis blushed and stood to leave as Stanley chuckled, enjoying her discomfiture.

"Remember, we have a rodeo date tonight."

Phillis waved and nodded as she left him sitting at the table looking awfully pleased with himself. Riding home, she resolved to look up Bakersfield and find out if Carter was killing her stories. Without Stanley, she would never have known the insider gossip about her boss and his activities at the Rice.

CHAPTER TWENTY

The hospitable Houstonians have galloped themselves to a lather welcoming the visitors. The New Yorkers insist on calling it 'Hous-in" the first syllable pronounced the same as a well-known street in their hometown. They feel they have undergone no little privation making the long journey to the Lone Star State, a journey perhaps fraught with great peril from wild Indians, wild cows, wild rattlesnakes, wild mule whiskey, wild wide hats, but your true New Yorker is willing to undergo any danger to do Al Smith a favor.

Damon Runyan
San Francisco Examiner
June 26, 1928

"JOSIE, I COULD SMELL YOUR PORK ROAST all the way down Eighteenth Street." Phillis entered the house and popped her head in the kitchen to give the cook a thumbs up before she realized she had no time to bathe before dinner. Now that she lived in the attic, the bathroom was not as accessible. Besides, she could hear the new boarders lumbering around in the upstairs hall. Better to only change her shirt and spritz herself with some cologne. She reread her article about Luna Park and thought about Stanley. The idea that someone cared about her was an unexpected surprise that made her smile. Generally, people did not find her oddities endearing, yet Stanley respected her, sought her advice, and went out of his way to assist her. Then there was the appearance of her father in the city jail. How in the world could she have managed without someone she could trust? Her relationship with Stanley was not something to be taken lightly. But still, she had always thought of romance as a trap, almost a curse that steered women away from their goals. Is that what was happening to her?

The jangling bell followed by the slamming screened door interrupted these musings as she slipped down the stairs to greet him.

"The more I think about it, the madder I get. After all the time I've spent waiting for this convention, I sit there with Bess drinking milkshakes and miss the opening session. I thought it didn't matter. Now I've thought about it, I'm sorry."

"Well, gal, come on down here and let me fill you in so you won't be so down-hearted."

Stanley watched her descend and led her outside to the porch swing. "It all began with the debonair silver-haired Clem Shaver, the most boring man you'll ever meet, banging his gavel on the podium and boom. That's all you missed."

"I'm sure it was more exciting than that. You're such a wet blanket." Phillis laughed and thought how she loved teasing him. "Was the hall full of people?"

"No. They'll all be there tonight to hear Claude Bower. Have you ever seen him? Go get today's *Chronicle*. The keynote speaker, known as the supreme rip-roaring, rabble-rousing, spellbinder of the whole Democratic Party. Pretty funny since he doesn't weigh more than hundred-and-thirty pounds. Probably a head shorter than you."

"Never heard of him," Phillis replied.

"He'll get 'em going tonight. Bring some life to the convention. Would you rather go hear him than rodeo out at Rice?"

"Can I do both?"

"Just like a woman." Stanley laughed, "Wants to have her cake and eat it too. Okay what if we drop by the convention on our way to the rodeo."

Phillis checked her watch. She lowered her voice, looking through the open window into the parlor. "Dinner time. I'm sure Clarence is pacing the floor."

"Clarence?"

"The new boarder. You won't believe Clarence and Viola. Tonight's a dry dinner since Teddy's working the convention."

"Phillis, I've been meaning to tell you what's going on."

"About what?"

"Remember the problem with Teddy at the ball game? When I blew my top."

"You think I'll ever forget that?"

"He fell in with bootleggers, the ones he bought Miss Maymie's booze from."

Phillis eyed the open window. "Shh, Clarence has ears like a fox."

Stanley nodded. "Local gangs need to get more booze for the convention. Teddy stupidly offered to find stills for them in northwest Harris County."

"Could he do that?"

"Of course not. He's a fool trying to make a few extra bucks. Thank God, he's learned his lesson. I know these guys. They don't bother to extract blood from turnips. But, they scared him so bad, I believe he's cured."

"Thank goodness, when Al Smith wins this election, Volstead goes away."

"Kid, you're dreaming. Have you seen all these women, not only from the South? The Midwesterners too. The protesting I've seen against Smith, I don't think his chances are so great.

Phillis squirmed and rose as if to go inside.

"Don't get in a huff," he said. "We're just having a discussion, right? That's what civilized people do. I'm just saying the only thing to overturn the Volstead is a disaster that will be worse than Prohibition, if you follow me."

She sat back down and sighed, "Let's change the subject. Obviously, you've helped Teddy. Now if you could light a fire under him. I'm sure Miss Maymie would be grateful. Did you tell her the whole story?"

"Hell, no, that information stays right here," Stanley said, tapping his head.

Josie's dinner bell brought them to the dinner table where bowls of sweet potatoes, steaming okra gumbo, and a platter of sliced pork roast swimming in gravy. Taking their seats, they watched as Clarence Mueller passed the cornbread after helping himself to the biggest piece.

"Maymie, you should have been with us inside Sam Houston Hall," Stanley said. "Phillis was bug-eyed."

"You were too, Stanley Staples," Phillis laughed.

"Not really. I appreciate the engineering of the hall. Maintenance man told me the ceiling is sixty feet from the floor. The architect, Kenneth Franzheim, liked our city so much he may move here from New York City."

"Well, somebody needs to tell him how bad his roof leaks," Miss Maymie suggested. "I've heard when this convention leaves, they'll take down the political stuff and use it as a roller rink."

Della Hinkle said, "Roller rink, my hind foot. Twenty-five people are gonna look pretty silly in that Godless temple. No skating rink ever has more people than that at one time. All that money spent for nothing. A wild, four-day drinking party that's disgracing our city."

"Mrs. Hinkle, do you spend a lot of time roller skating?" Phillis asked.

Maymie giggled and exclaimed, "Oh, Della, don't say stuff like that. Houston's on the tip of every tongue."

"The closest I'm coming to that building is the prayer meeting on the sidewalk." Mrs. Hinkle replied. "If he's elected to be president everyone says the Pope of Rome is moving into the White House to run everything."

Viola Mueller looked troubled.

Maymie asked, "Della Hinkle, who's feeding you this malarkey? You sound very foolish."

Mrs. Hinkle's face turned splotchy as she stood abruptly and stormed out of the dining room down the hall. Phillis was shocked. Leaving a plate full of food on the table was most unlike her.

The diners continued eating in silence. When they were finished, Josie entered with a coconut cake so heavy she could barely carry it in. "Where's Mizz Hinkle?"

Maymie said, "Went to her room. She's upset. Is that cake for her?"

"It's her birthday," Josie replied. "I made it special 'cause it's her favorite."

"Oh, no," the diners said almost in unison.

"Phillis, go find her," Miss Maymie said. "She has to eat her birthday cake. We can't cut it without her."

"Why me?" Phillis asked.

Miss Maymie jerked her thumb toward the bedroom at the back of the house. "This contest between the wets and the dry's is very trying," she said as Phillis left her seat and headed down the hall.

Tiptoeing to Mrs. Hinkle's door, she started to knock. Pausing, she saw it was cracked open and heard something hit a hard surface. "It's my birthday. I'm gonna sit here in my rocking chair and enjoy the rest of this bottle. Dear Lord, please send a swarm of locusts onto the head of Albert Smith."

Phillis swallowed hard, stifling her laughter. This was too good, Hinkle's love for booze confirming Stanley's description of her hypocrisy. Her awful self-righteousness, her cold glassy blue eyes heaping scorn on everything about her. Phillis had stuck in Della Hinkle's craw from the moment they met. When she successfully ousted her from her second-floor bedroom up to the attic, Phillis detected a slight softening, but so far it was too little and too late. Despite this triumph over her arch enemy, Phillis felt pity for the bitter old woman. It was like she could not back down and let herself enjoy anything. Phillis pressed her fingers to her lips and tiptoed back to the dining room. The guests looked up with expectant faces.

"Where is she?" asked Viola.

"She's indisposed. I think we should slice her cake and save her a piece for tomorrow," Phillis said, winking at Stanley.

After they all partook of Josie's celebratory confection, Phillis and Stanley excused themselves to set off for Sam Houston Hall.

Inside the streetcar, zooming to town at fifteen miles per hour, Stanley patted his stomach, "That was a good supper. Should last me till morning."

Phillis tilted her head, "You alluded to Mrs. Hinkle's drinking when I first came. When Maymie asked me to see about her tonight, she was rocking herself to sleep with a bottle of peach schnapps."

"Yes, lots of times, women dry's are all mixed up. It's even crazier for their husbands who brag, 'I vote dry especially against a wet candidate. If I did anything else, I wouldn't dare go home for fear my wife would find out.'"

Phillis laughed, "I can't see a woman telling you how to vote."

"I dunno, maybe the right woman could," nodding as his eyes circled her face.

Ignoring his remark, she replied, "Will Rogers is right. Prohibition's created a generation of hypocrites."

As they neared Main Street, Stanley stuck his head out the window to look south. "Looks like we'll get a shower before the evening is over. Dang it, I didn't bring an umbrella."

The roars of the crowd filled the air as they neared the hall. Phillis grabbed Stanley's hand and said, "Let's hurry. I don't want to miss Bower's speech."

Using their red press passes for the first time, they entered the melee, ringing with the cries of wildly excited conventioneers.

Phillis counted four bands lined up as Claude Bower invoked the gods to bring floods and rain to the evil Republicans. He no sooner said this than the threatening thunderclouds opened up and the Lamella roof failed again, sprinkling water on the frenzied Democrats who were jammed into the hall.

When Bower's speech ended, the bands started up, playing everything from "On the Banks of the Wabash" to "Sunny California" and "Iowa, My Iowa." Phillis thought the musicians were going to wait their turns. Instead, they overlapped, resulting in a brass cacophony Long lines of delegates marched around the hall holding banners and signs printed with their state's name and candidate. It was jolly, rollicking fun, and Stanley whistled between his teeth while Phillis jumped up and down and cheered, "Al Smith's the man to beat."

"Do you see the man in the yellow-and-brown checked suit and pork pie hat sitting at the press table?" Stanley asked.

"The one wearing wire spectacles?"

"Yep, that's Damon Runyon. I've been following his columns for almost twenty years. His beat is supposedly sports — baseball and boxing. His real subject is the human condition. I devour his stuff."

Phillis took a closer look at the celebrated New York columnist. He didn't appear noteworthy in the looks department, she thought as she watched him lean forward, his head moving as he looked around the hall, focusing on a demonstrator, then snapping back to Mrs. Al Smith's box or the speaker's platform. "I see what you mean," she said. "He's in action even when he's sitting still.' *He reminds me of an inquisitive turtle.*

"I'm anxious to read more about his take on Houston and what he calls this circus that's come to town."

When the hubbub slowed down, Shaver banged his gavel and named the members of the Resolution Committee. This was the group of delegates charged with writing the party platform.

Phillis pulled Stanley's sleeve, "Do you see any women on the committee?"

"Yes, I think there's one or two."

"Good." Phillis hoped the women wouldn't be "steamrolled" as Bessie Marbury feared.

Stanley said, "Thursday night the delegates will choose the presidential candidate."

Phillis nodded, wondering what his point was.

"A lot of New Yorkers are afraid the Texas delegation will nominate Jesse Jones for President."

Her mouth formed an "O" and she eyed him curiously. "Not that unusual. He's the favorite son."

"Yeah, I know, he's the white-haired fairy-godfather who brought this convention to Houston. The richest Democrat in America invited everyone to his party here; now he wants a payback." Clamping his teeth together, he scowled and said, "The New Yorkers think he wants to be something bigger than a 'favorite son.' They claim he's double-crossed them, and some of the Texas delegates are saying so, as well."

Why do I know so little about backroom politics? "Smith's supporters don't' look worried."

"Just wait awhile. This is coming back to bite Jones. You ready to leave?"

Phillis nodded and she and Stanley scrambled to get to the front door. They hit the pavement just as the rain ended. Another of Houston's short showers, Phillis thought, looking up in disbelief. Spreading across the evening sky was the most beautiful rainbow she had ever seen. She stood there in wonder. Surely this was a sign of good luck for the opening evening session of the largest Democratic National Convention in history.

Stanley spoke before she could get her words out. "Kid, I can read your thoughts. Rainbows are meteorological events, not omens."

"Rhatz, you do that every time." Though Phillis knew he was right, she preferred her own interpretation.

CHAPTER TWENTY-ONE

The convention rodeo will open at 3:30 pm at Rice Institute Athletic Field. All of the contestants were in Houston Saturday and the Rice Field resembled the range at round-up time, with pens of cattle and steers, tents, and cowboys trying out their various mounts for the various contests. Prizes for the contests will mount to $10,000.

Houston Press
June 25, 1928

AT MAIN STREET, THEY BOARDED A TROLLEY on the South End line. The cloudburst was over but cars were bogged in black gumbo on the side streets.

"What kind of Prohibition plank do you think they'll write?" Phillis asked.

"The best the South can hope for is a plank like the Republicans wrote for theirs. 'An honest effort to enforce the Eighteenth Amendment.' You have to laugh to keep from crying. We've been saddled with this amendment almost ten years."

"Yeah, I know. I was nearly sixteen when it passed."

"You that old?" Stanley teased.

"Oops, a lady's not supposed to reveal her age."

"You're just a girl," he said as he patted her arm.

"Speaking of girls," she asked, "Have you ever heard of Fox Hastings?"

"No, is he a rodeo star?" Stanley answered.

"I said 'girls.' He is a she. The first female bulldogger in history."

"I know what a bulldogger is, but I've never seen a woman wrestle a steer. Wrestle it to the ground? Whew, that's a tall order. A woman can do this? Sounds like an Amazon?"

"No, just a regular five-foot-three female who ran away from the Catholic convent her parents sent her to at sixteen. Joined up with a Wild West show and married its star performer, Mike Hastings, who says he taught her everything he knew. She took her mother's maiden name and became Fox Hastings, a name the press loves."

"I take it you've seen her bulldog?"

"I saw her perform at the Fort Worth Stock Show four years ago. She rode her horse alongside a twelve-hundred-pound steer, seized his horns, and twisted his neck until he dropped on his forelegs. Jumped down and kept twisting his horns till he cried 'uncle,' then jerked out her rope and tied all four of his legs together."

"We're gonna see her do this tonight?"

"I don't know. This rodeo will be tamer than the real McCoy. Limited space. Flimsy fences. It might not be safe."

Stanley pulled the bell and motioned her toward the trolley's exit. Once off the streetcar, they walked several blocks before they saw Rice Institute's impressive Sallyport. The fading sunlight shadowed the mammoth stone archway. "It's a handsome entrance to what I hear is a fine school," Phillis noted. Stanley nodded, leading her along a path which bordered the recently erected cyclone fencing and signs advertising the rodeo.

> **TWO PERFORMANCES DAILY**
> **3:30 & 8:30 * JUNE 24-30**
> **$15,000 IN PURSES**
> **250 COWBOYS AND COWGIRLS**
> **500 WILD HORSES AND STEERS**

Stanley's shelling out two dollars for their tickets embarrassed Phillis. There was no way she could have afforded to spend that much cash on a rodeo ticket. Thirty minutes early, they easily found bleacher seats. Across the field, Phillis spied Fox lounging near the announcer's stand. "Come with me. Let's see if I am lucky enough to swing an interview."

"Worth a try," Stanley said as he followed behind her.

Phillis pointed to the cowgirl wearing a high-crowned black Stetson, high-topped cowboy boots, and a purple-satin blouse tucked into what looked like men's trousers, who stood out from the others milling around her.

"You're right, she's short."

"She straps on a football helmet to protect her head if she's bulldogging." Phillis grinned excitedly, glad this evening she could show him something new for a change.

She walked over to Fox.

A photographer approached at the same time and started clicking pictures, unnerving Phillis as she began her pitch. "Fox Hastings, I'm

Phillis Flanagan from the *Fort Worth Star-Telegram*. Just a couple of minutes, please."

Fox nodded and Phillis ploughed on. "Four years ago, I saw you perform at the Stockyards. You're the first woman bulldogger in America, right?"

Fox nodded confidently.

"And one of the most successful?" Phillis continued.

Fox replied, "Honey, if I can get my fanny out of the saddle and my feet planted, there's no steer that can last against me. It doesn't matter whether the contest is bulldogging or just wrangling."

"At the Kansas City Roundup," Phillis said, "the spectators thought you'd been killed when your horse fell on you. Fifteen minutes after they carted you off the field, you reappeared in a big open-topped automobile and asked the judges for a re-ride. How'd you recover so fast?"

Fox looked at her slit-eyed, "I couldn't let those judges or my fans know how bad I was hurt. The only way to show 'em was to get back on a horse and ride the best I knew how."

Phillis heard the announcer warming up and knew she was out of time. Pumping Fox's hand, she thanked her for the interview.

Though red-faced and out of breath, Phillis almost strutted back to the bleachers. They'd lost their good seats and had to stand on the sidelines to watch Fox win the "trick riding" contest during the first half of the show.

During the intermission, Stanley elbowed Phillis, pointing to a man dressed in jeans and boots with a toss-haired forelock resting on his forehead who walked beside them. Speaking to no one in particular, the stranger griped, "When I can't stand looking any more delegates in the face, I come out here and look at the calves and bucking horses. It's a kind of relief to escape to the rodeo and watch some real action."

His Oklahoma twang and wide grin were instantly recognizable. Resting his hand on a nearby tree, he said, "Feel that nice cool breeze that blows all the time. Nobody in Houston goes outside."

Phillis pulled out her notebook as he turned toward her and pointed at Fox. "See that cowgirl. On Sunday night, she rode Buster, her pony, and downed a steer in eighteen seconds. The gal standing beside her is Claire Belcher. She and Fox are about to hold the first steer wrangling contest ever staged between two females. That's what I'm here for."

"Wow," Phillis hurriedly wrote down his words and grinned. *I guess that answers that question. This Rice rodeo is the real thing.* Phillis stepped closer and addressed him, "Mr. Rogers, Phillis Flanagan, *Fort Worth Star-Telegram.* Are you surprised so many women are attending this convention?"

"Not a bit. A band of the 'fairer sex' hailed me yesterday and asked me to write something to help them get 'equal rights.' I told 'em I thought they had too many rights, and I hoped they wanted to split some with the men."

Stanley burst out laughing and clapped. "You got that right."

Closing her notebook, Phillis smiled thinly and shook his hand just for the record. Surely, being able to say she shook hands with America's favorite cowboy humorist would count for something?

When the second half of the show began, they yelled, and groaned for the riders who were unseated or failed to down a calf. This article would be easy.

The hour was late when they returned to Harvard Street, and she was pooped. Stanley sensed her fatigue as easily as he did everything else. Taking her in his arms, he planted a whisper-light kiss on her forehead and said, "See you around, kid," then walked off down the street whistling, "Sleepy Time Gal." She stood on the porch watching him until he disappeared from view.

6/26/28. Too tired to write much. Cannot go to bed without reporting the first evening of the convention exceeded all my expectations. Stories from everyone's lips. There are no "plain people" at the Democratic National Convention. It's a grand jubilee. Surprised the Texas delegation never planned to vote for Smith. Stanley is so much more than a friend. I've never had this kind of support. He asks for nothing in return.

CHAPTER TWENTY-TWO

Thirty thousand perspiring Democrats are an active part of a mad scene here that makes the slaughter of the Christians in 'Ben Hur' look like a Sunday school picnic and the battle scenes in 'What Price Glory' and the 'Big Parade' resemble a peace conference.

Louella Parsons
The San Francisco Examiner
Wednesday, June 27, 1928

"IS MISS MAYMIE STILL HERE?" PHILLIS ASKED Josie just as she heard footsteps in the hallway. Maymie Banion's linen coatdress with matching shoes and cloche were quite stylish. "You are stunning and your garnet brooch is perfect," Phillis said enviously.

"No one's called me 'stunning' in a long time," Miss Maymie said. "I'm leaving right now. See you this afternoon."

"She's off to the big event," Phillis informed Josie. "The Women's Breakfast at the Rice Roof."

Josie looked puzzled. "It's a big deal, Josie. You had to buy your ticket in April."

"Too bad you're missing it, Miss Phillis. Glad to know where she's going so dressed up."

Josie put her finger to the side of her head, "Did Mrs. Hinkle tell you about your phone call?"

Phillis, instantly alert, shook her head. "Where is she? I'll ask her."

"She's over there talking to a neighbor lady," Josie said.

Phillis finished her cereal then went outside where the two ladies stood in the yard, examining a large pink rose bush planted in a monstrous, old-fashioned concrete basket.

Phillis cupped her mouth and yelled to Della Hinkle, "Who called me yesterday? They leave a name?"

Della stepped over to the sidewalk. "That New York fella you went to Galveston with."

"Dang it, I never called and to check on Brad and Reggie."

"What'd you say?" Della asked. Phillis waved and went back into the house.

She thumbed the pages of the telephone book, dialed the Lamar Hotel, and gave the operator Brad's room number.

"You didn't return my call," Brad responded coldly to her greeting.

"Sorry, I just got the message. I expected you to call when you got back. How did you get home?"

"By spending a whole lot of dough to have that breezer dug out of the hole. We had to sleep in the car. Couldn't get the ragtop to come up. No protection from the mosquitoes. Ran out of ciggies, booze, and food. We were towed back to town the next morning only because Daisy sent a truck after us."

"For crying out loud, that's awful."

"Didn't think you cared. Scat dog left on the first train out of town, according to Daisy."

"Sorry, I needed to get back. Been trying to find stories to write. I apologize, Brad. I hope everything's okay now."

"Yeah, see you around, girlfriend," he said hanging up.

Phillis hung up furious at his pathetic attempt to make her feel guilty. Glad Bradley Nicholson's slipping out of her life was leaving no smudges on her heart this time. It had been entertaining to give it another whirl, but she had no wish to cross paths with him . . . again. Or did she? New York City was always on her mind.

Phillis sat at her typewriter imagining Maymie hobnobbing with elite women visitors as she noted what each was wearing. What would Will Rogers say to these ladies in his keynote speech? Seeing him last night reminded her of his performance in Fort Worth. His broad smile so often pictured in magazines was so familiar to her and everyone in the country, it was hard not to greet him with, "Hey, Will, how's it going?" That is the way she had felt when he stood beside her under the tree at Rice college, sporting blue jeans and an old plaid shirt. Was he repeating his words from last night? She doubted it, but Maymie would tell her everything.

The rodeo story flew off the keys. Surely the editor would love it. What about the articles he killed? Alma Davis and Buff Stadium. Who was really making the decisions? She had to find out. Just as she entered the -30- she heard the telephone and Mrs. Hinkle calling her name.

Daisy's voice on the phone was a surprise, and her request maddening. "Please dress up nice and come to my suite this afternoon?"

"Sorry, Daisy, can't spend the afternoon at the Galvez. I've got a job."

"No, no. I'm in Houston, not Galveston. I told you I took a suite at the Plaza Hotel when I arrived in Houston. Even offered to share it with you."

Phillis gritted her teeth and rolled her eyes.

"It's straight-out Main Street. Don't worry about the location. I'm sending a car to pick you up at one-thirty. What's your address?"

Phillis said, "1750 Harvard."

Daisy replied, "See you later" and hung up.

"What have I agreed to now?" Phillis muttered. "What does 'dress up nice' mean to Daisy?"

"Isn't she the friend you took off to see in Galveston?" Mrs. Hinkle asked.

Startled, Phillis had not realized she stood there, listening. "I'll be going out this afternoon," Phillis said shortly.

"If you can find something to wear that's nice,'" Mrs. Hinkle said tittering as she walked back down the hall.

Phillis fled up the stairs wondering the same thing until she remembered her travel suit. Luckily, she had picked it up from the dry cleaners. *Why agree to anything that spike-heeled over-rouged flapper requests?* If this did not produce a story, she would wring that ditzy blonde's neck."

After lunch, she brushed her hair smoothing it into a chignon with the help of fifteen hairpins. Inspecting her tan cloche, she flicked off the dust and checked her image in the mirror. Her looks pleased her. The summer sun put bloom in her cheeks that made her dark brown eyes look larger. Josie's great cooking had added some pounds to her stringy figure. Most of all, she was happier. Even with her father's appearance and the horror of the lynching, she felt more alive, more excited. Like she was moving in the right direction.

Did Stanley contribute to this or was it the 'reporter' in her responding to these horrors. He probably accounted for why she felt nothing for Bradley, a man whose feet were much too small for Stanley's shoes. As she picked up her gloves and pocketbook, Mrs. Hinkle called "Miss Phillis, I think one of those Godless lemonzines is out here waiting."

She descended carefully to avoid scuffing her pumps. Adjusting her hat one more time, she was surprised to hear Mrs. Hinkle.

"Very nice. You'll do," the housekeeper said without a smile. This tepid vote of confidence satisfied Phillis, and she straightened her shoulders and sailed out the door.

The driver standing at the curb helped her into a shiny brown car that stretched halfway to forever. He started the engine, and the automobile rumbled down the Boulevard before she even got herself settled. After checking to make sure she had her notebook and pencil, Phillis leaned back on the tufted mohair seat thinking of her only other ride in a limousine.

"What kind of automobile is this?" she asked the driver.

"A Model J Duesenberg, miss," he answered.

"It's certainly comfortable. I believe I rode in one like this in Galveston."

"Yes," the driver answered, "there are several rum barons down there whose drivers I've met."

Phillis smiled, certain Johnny 'Jack' Nounes would love this label. "I've never owned a car," she said.

The driver responded, "Neither have I."

She doubted if she ever would but maybe they would become more common. Like radios. She couldn't ever imagine owning a radio. They took up so much room. How would she ever have a place large enough?

In high school, Bradley had taught her to drive his green Chevy roadster. She had forgotten that it was he who spent the hours patiently waiting for her to learn how to double clutch to change gears. Having enough funds to purchase any automobile was unimaginable. Yet, being a licensed driver filled her with pride.

Smoothing a wrinkle in her pleated skirt, Phillis remembered last Christmas when her mother handed her a large, expensive box stamped "White Hall." Inside was the suit she wore today.

"This is from your dad and me. I hope it fits." Lena Belle always persisted in referring to her second husband as Phillis's dad, but the word never passed her lips. To her, he was Mr. Wilkerson.

"Don't even think about going to the University of Texas. I don't want a flapper daughter." A ridiculous charge. If he had ever bothered to look at her, much less listen to anything she said, he would have known she was not the flapper type. He was a pompous, domineering man. Over the years, his exclusive dress shop had flourished along with his ego.

Accepting the flawlessly simple suit as graciously as possible knowing her mother had selected it, she thanked her stepfather through clenched teeth. Phillis pinched a pleat and thought of Daisy who always had money to burn. She probably had ten of these suits. "I'll send a car for you," she said, just as if she were ordering a bottle of milk. "No worries, no cares," Phillis murmured. "So why does she need me?"

"Did you say something, miss?" the driver asked.

"No, sorry, just daydreaming out loud. Are we almost there?"

He pulled the car into a circle driveway in front of a new-looking beige brick building and said, "This is the Plaza. Wait while I get the door for you."

Of course, he would say that, since he correctly guessed, she was not used to riding in limousines and would not have known to wait for him to hand her down.

Phillis sat patiently until he came around. Walking up to the hotel's brass-trimmed double doors, Phillis was greeted by the bellman, who with a grand sweep of his right hand, welcomed her into the cool interior. She picked her way down the dark patterned Turkish rug running the length of the lobby to the desk where she inquired as to Miss Leatherbury's suite. The clerk snapped his fingers and a bellhop appeared and beckoned to her, "This way, miss." The elevator carried them to the tenth floor where he walked her out into the hallway and stopped in front of a door identified by a brass plaque as "The Martha Washington Suite."

While she could think of no one with whom Daisy had less in common than the mother of their country, the fancy entrance indicated accommodations luxurious enough to suit the occupant. Indistinguishable voices came from inside the room as a uniformed attendant answered her knock and invited her in. The two women seated on the divan looked at her expectantly, and Phillis's brain raced, questioning again why she was asked to come.

"Oh, Miss Flanagan, sorry for the short notice." Daisy shook her hand formally, but the other hand encircled Phillis's waist and fingers jabbed her ribs discreetly as she turned to introduce her guest. "Miss Louella Parsons, this is Phillis Flanagan, my advisor."

Daisy raised her eyebrows, tilting her head as if checking to make sure Phillis knew who her guest was.

Hollywood's premier journalist. Wow!

Phillis nodded back to reassure Daisy and shook hands with the beautifully groomed woman who motioned her to an adjacent chair.

Daisy explained, "Miss Parsons has a full schedule. You return to Hollywood on Friday, right?"

"No," Louella Parsons said. "I go to New York on 'the Convention Special,' the private railroad car Mayor Walker and I rode to Houston, then back to California sometime in July." Turning to Phillis, she said, "Daisy tells me you're a well-known businesswoman, Miss Flanagan."

"My office is downtown," Phillis lied glibly. "I have an insurance agency with Miss Maymie Banion, along with other interests."

Daisy sighed with relief and took a sip of her martini. "Miss Flanagan, what can I offer you to drink?" she asked. "We can have room service bring something or I have a few bottles I brought back from Galveston."

"Nothing now. Thank you," Phillis replied. "Miss Parsons, how do you like Houston?

"Honey, everybody calls me Louella, even Mayor Walker. I tried to chat with him yesterday. Let me tell you, these females visiting Houston are barracudas. They mob him every time he leaves his room. It's no wonder he has a suite in Galveston where he can escape.

"His trip south was awful enough. When he got to Fort Worth, high and mighty Amon Carter boarded the car, bribed a porter to pack Walker's clothes, and ushered him from the train."

Parsons stubbed out her cigarette.

"The mayor of New York City highjacked, so he could spend the whole damn day fishing with him, H. L. Mencken and Will Rogers."

Miss Parsons lit another cigarette and continued, "Jimmy said Rogers cracked one joke after another. Everyone knows he has nothing to do anyway but fish and tell stories, but Menck was hoppin' mad."

Louella thanked Daisy who refilled her glass from the martini shaker. "Imagine, Jimmie trying to catch a fish. The only fish he likes are served on a plate, hopefully with a nice tartar sauce."

She smiled and said, "I laughed when he said he got chigger bites."

Phillis flushed and studied the rose-patterned carpet. *Amon Carter is a lunatic.*

"Has either of you eyed Mayor Walker since he arrived? Everyone's copying the way he has of turning up the brim of his Panama hat." Louella put her hand to her head imitating the tilt.

"Now, back to you, Daisy Leatherbury," Parsons said, no longer smiling. "First of all, my pet, your name. They'll axe it. The studio has special people who do that. My real name is Rose Oettinger," she confessed. "Do you have a bio? What have you won besides the Miss Pulchritude Contest? Anything in high school? Write it all down. I'll tell MGM to expect you by July 1, okay?"

Miss Parsons wrote in a notebook as she talked. "You've never been married, I assume."

Phillis spoke up. "She was married to a Spanish nobleman, but he passed away."

"A widow? Goody-goody," the publicist smiled. "That makes you a tragic figure. What else?"

"I went to Mrs. Smitherman's Select School for Girls."

"Forget that. Hollywood likes orphans or girls who rise from the cinders."

"She's definitely not an orphan," Phillis said firmly, "and she's not poverty-stricken."

"Oh, but when the Hollywood writers finish with her, who knows who she will turn out to be."

"Are you okay with that, Daisy," Phillis asked.

"Of course. I just want to be in pictures. Do you have a contract for me to sign, Miss Parsons?"

"No, that will come later. The studio head will decide. I'm the one who brings you to their attention. I give you your big break. And you'll always remember what I did for you, okay? Don't ever forget it because otherwise I'll have to remind you."

"Miss Parsons, we need to qualify her obligations to you?" Phillis spoke firmly.

"Some of this and some of that," Louella Parsons replied vaguely. "Little tokens of remembrance, passing on tips to me and what we call 'insider gossip' about film stars. Not anything much. Everyone does it for me. That's why I am the Hollywood correspondent for all Mr. Hearst's four-hundred newspapers. And I have this job in perpetuity," she finished, eying Phillis to make sure Daisy's "business advisor" understood.

"Daisy, don't you need to think about this?" Phillis asked.

"Certainly not. I'm ready to pack my bags." Daisy fidgeted with her cigarette lighter. "Phillis, I mean, Miss Flanagan, everything sounds swell, doesn't it?" Daisy asked winsomely.

"I suppose so," Phillis replied with a frown. "You'll need to have a Hollywood attorney look over the paperwork. Promise me you'll do that."

"You needn't worry, Miss Flanagan, I will be there by that time," Louella Parsons said. "Mr. Mayer has his own attorneys to check out the contracts they've drawn up. There're never any problems." Turning to Daisy, she said, "I will see you in Hollywood."

Changing the subject, she continued, "I'm trying to enjoy this convention but whoever called Houston a melting pot, nailed it. We're certainly melting from this heat. Even your Southern gentlemen are getting out of sorts. One of them shot a pistol into a hotel elevator."

She stood and tipped up her martini glass, gulping down the remaining contents. "You know, I first went to California because I had tuberculosis. They gave me six months to live. Now I'm fine. I assure you; the West Coast cures anything that ails you. But Houston? I'm not sure so much heat is good for my heart."

As she put on her gloves, Louella Parsons asked Phillis, "Are you coming to California with her?"

"No, I wish I could, but I have my business here in Houston. It's wonderful Daisy is going to be a film star in California. Doesn't get any better than that, does it?"

Phillis stood up and shook the publicist's hand. "Nice to have met you, Miss Parsons."

After Daisy returned from seeing Louella to the door, Phillis asked, "You've decided you'll be the next Mary Pickford?"

Daisy whispered, "Something like that," in a breathy voice.

"Well, good luck to you. I remember when Reggie asked if you were in films and I assured him you weren't. I didn't know you'd studied acting."

"Are you kidding? I've never taken a lesson," Daisy giggled. "Look at Marion Davies. She's an actress. Is that really a requirement?"

"When W. R. Hearst has been your patron since you were fourteen, you don't need training. Speaking of acting, I wish you'd given me forewarning before casting me as your legal advisor."

A starry-eyed Daisy looked up at her and said, "Didn't have time. I knew when she called me this would be my chance to become a star." As she poured herself another martini, Daisy chirped, "Whoopsie, this is gonna be fun."

"Can you arrange for the driver to take me home? I'm worn out and hungry for supper."

"Sure, I'm going to dinner with a new beau. There are so many single men here. At least they say they're single," Daisy finished with an impish grin.

RIDING HOME IN THE DUZZY, PHILLIS reflected on the fairyland drama she had witnessed. Daisy, never bound by ordinary rules, was packing her bags for the land of sunshine and oranges. Her blonde ringlets, her naughty eyes, her rouged knees, everything about her screamed Hollywood. Phillis's cautionary suggestions never went anywhere, and she had to admit, this flapper's new destination was exactly where she belonged. An opportunity for Phillis, as well? She would definitely keep in touch with Daisy. There would be a story after Daisy passed her screen test, not one Louella Parsons would like, but an article emphasizing young screen stars' vulnerability and their lack of brains. *But would the Star-Telegram even run it?* Only three of her articles had made it into print.

She thought of Bubba Bakersfield, whom Stanley claimed knew everything. She wanted to ask Bubba why her stories were being axed. "Please drop me off at the Rice Hotel."

"Sure thing," the driver said as he smoothly navigated the downtown traffic and pulled up to the hotel. She thanked him for the ride and tried to give him a dime, but he shook his head, smiling.

Phillis loved the bellhops' swift response to her limo and entered the Rice searching the crowd for someone she knew. A group of men milled around, and she realized how easy it was to spot reporters. "Do any of you know Bubba Bakersfield?"

"Check the bar." A guy leaning against a marble column pointed behind him.

Sure enough, he stood there drinking a glass of beer. "Should've known I would find you here, Bubba."

He stood and motioned to the adjacent stool. "Hey, Red, come join me. Best free lunch in town."

"Heck, I've already eaten lunch."

"Sit down, order a beer. Gene will bring you a glass of Southern Select."

She looked at the remains of a plate of cheese and crackers sitting on the counter. "What a deal." The bartender responded quickly to her raised hand. "Bring me the same."

"Yeah, and bring some more olives too."

Phillis sipped her beer and grinned at Bubba like a long-lost friend. "Too few of my articles have made it in the *Star*. Why?"

He dropped his head and studied the floor. "Dunno," Bubba answered too slowly as if framing his reply.

"Come on, you know everything that's going on." She gripped the frosty glass and lifted it to take a deep swallow as she waited.

"It's coming from the top, Gal. You can talk to Edwards or your editor in Fort Worth, but I don't think you'll have any luck."

"Why? I'm writing about women just like the boss requested, usually." Phillis's steely voice had no effect.

"You're whipping a dead horse. Just do what you were assigned to do. That's all I can say."

She drank another swallow of beer, carefully positioned a slice of cheddar on a saltine and took a bite. The cracker turned to sawdust.

Sliding off the stool, she said, "Thanks, I owe you" and walked out of the bar and out the double front doors. All she could think about was Bubba's veiled allusion to Carter. By the time she got off the trolley, she had convinced herself to complain to Edwards. But she changed her mind three times before she entered the house.

Maymie was reading the newspaper in the front parlor and Phillis asked, "Tell me about the Women's breakfast. I'm dying to know."

"Are you sure?" asked Maymie. Phillis nodded and grinned.

"A gosh-darn disaster," Maymie replied. "That's the only way to describe it. Horrible, just horrible."

"How so? All those stellar women in one room."

"The whole thing was miscalculated, mismanaged, and poorly planned." Maymie peevishly fussed with her collar. "You've been to the Rice enough times this week to know it's crammed full of hotel guests. Carrying a thousand guests up to the top floor took over two hours. Ladies dressed in their finest smashed into the elevator like sardines. On the roof, tables are jammed into every inch."

Maymie shuddered. "We threaded the way to our table in the annex section they must have added just for this event. I never saw the head table, or the honorees much less Will Rogers, who was the keynote speaker."

Phillis still wished she could have attended. "What about the food?"

"Terrible. No water served at all. A cup of cold coffee."

"Did Mrs. Wilson come? I heard a rumor she might."

"Oh, yes, Edith Wilson breezed in late as usual, wearing an incredible white-and-black organza dress with, of course, a matching hat."

Maymie pursed her lips and shook her head. "The microphone was lousy. I couldn't hear a word. On the way out, someone said Will Rogers called the Breakfast a 'luncheon' because it started two hours late."

Phillis was sad to hear of the Women's Democratic Club's debacle. Etta Henderson must be furious. All her planning for an event that turned out to be a morning of horrors. So many distinguished guests who deserved a ticket, and unfortunately, they had all gotten one.

"I was determined to see Will Rogers," Miss Maymie said, "so I edged around to the head table and there he sat, wearing a seersucker suit, looking sweaty and bored. Apparently, he'd decided to just sit where he was until they all left."

"For sure, the newspapers will have a field day. Never miss an opportunity to poke fun at us. I'm going upstairs to write some articles, but I'll leave this one alone."

6/27/28. What a day! Daisy is set for life. Hollywood is waiting for her. Louella Parsons is slippery. Will Bubba tell Amon Carter what I asked? Probably, so maybe I should go directly to Carter. Can I persuade him to change his mind about my stories? Fat chance of that! My job here ends in three days.

CHAPTER TWENTY-THREE

Certainly I'm a wet — The saloon ought to be brought back just as it was in the old days. It's better than blind pigs and bootleggers. The boys need the real saloon, free lunch, music and the picture of Venus behind the bar — it helps the poor man get a taste of life better than the one he gets at home. And the rich man, too — lots of rich men have bum homes.

H. L. Mencken as quoted in *Houston Chronicle*
Thursday, June 28, 1928

STANLEY'S STACCATO VOICE CAME BARKING through the wire. "Be outside in twenty minutes. We're goin' downtown."

"I'm not even awake. What's happened now?"

The phone line went dead.

She jumped into her clothes, grabbed stockings from her makeshift clothesline, and was slipping on her brown oxfords when she heard a "tap, tap" on her door.

"Are you dressed, Miss Phillis?" Teddy called softly.

"Teddy, why're you up?" she said as she opened her door.

"Don't you remember, I'm a working man, Miss Phillis? I heard you answer the phone as Josie was fixin' to make my breakfast. Do you need a ride to town?"

"Shame your roadster only seats two. Stanley and I are both on our way downtown as well. But thanks for the offer."

Phillis grabbed her hat and adjusted it in the mirror, slipping her notebook into her purse as she headed down the stairs. Stanley waited on the front sidewalk looking at his watch. "Another minute and I was leaving."

"Sorry. Teddy delayed me. He could give us a ride if his car weren't so small."

"We don't want a ride with him," Stanley snapped.

"He's not such a bad driver," Phillis said. "Would've saved us the trolley fare, plus at this hour, the streetcar will be packed. What's got your goat?"

"You'll find out soon enough. Nothing for Teddy to know about or anyone on the streetcar, I might add. You'll see when we get there."

Once they were in town, he guided her to the Rice Hotel where he headed for the bellhop stand with Phillis tagging behind. After a brief exchange of pleasantries, Stanley said, "Say, Louie, some said shots were fired here yesterday. Anybody hurt?"

The smartly uniformed young man shook his head.

"Weren't the police called?"

Louie pressed his lips together, his eyes darting from left to right. Even Phillis could tell he was hiding something.

After a few moments, he whispered, "I think one of the elevators was too slow."

"Yeah, everybody gripes about that problem. Who fired the shots?"

"Can't answer that," Louie replied.

Stanley frowned and turned away as he saw a *New York Times* reporter exiting the elevator. Accosting him, he asked, "Murphy, tell me what happened last night. Did you see anything?"

"Nothing. I sure heard gun shots. I'm wiring home for a coat of mail. After all, this is Texas."

With a chuckle, Stanley casually crossed the lobby where a policeman stood. Phillis chasing behind him, watched as he flashed his press badge and asked, "Officer Berryman, what happened here last night?"

"We're trying to keep it quiet, so no one panics. An accidental shooting. No harm done. Put away your notebook. No story here."

When a bellman called the officer outside because a touring car blocked the hotel's entrance, Stanley strode back to his close-mouthed bellhop, "Louie, let's talk some more."

He slipped a bill into the bellhop's vest pocket and asked,"Okay, Louie," Stanley said. "Give me the goods. What happened?"

Louie spilled the story so fast Phillis could barely catch what he was saying. "Amon Carter wanted to visit a friend on eleven. That sheriff, the big guy that's usually drunk, was with him."

The bellhop looked across the lobby to make sure the officer had not returned. "Three elevators passed without stopping, even though Mr. Carter kept slamming the call buzzer. When the fourth one passed him, he exploded and grabbed the sheriff's pistol out of his holster. That big holster, covered with real rubies. The one he says a Fort Worth bootlegger gave him."

Stanley hissed impatiently, "Louie, get on with the it before Berryman comes back."

"Okay. Okay. So, Mr. Carter fired the gun into the elevator."

"No, don't kid about this. You say Amon Carter shot a gun in the Rice Hotel? Must've been the sheriff. You got your story wrong."

"I'm telling you; it was Carter who shot three, maybe four, bullets into the glass door." Louie broke out in a sweat and lowered his voice. "Every guest in the hotel heard the shots. They poured out into the hall. The next elevator stopped for Carter and the sheriff, and they calmly rode to eleven as if nothing had happened."

Louie grabbed a load of suitcases from the cart and walked off just as Officer Berryman came up to Stanley. He glowered at Stanley.

"I know what you're gonna say, Officer. Don't worry, I know the rules. Have a good day." Stanley tipped his hat and pulled Phillis alongside him as he exited the hotel. "Let's get some breakfast at Billy's."

Stanley sank into a booth and motioned Phillis to do the same. "Jeez Louise. Houston has enough problems without Amon Carter playing cowboy. He's your boss, not mine, thank God."

"I'm horrified. A hotel packed with visitors, and he shoots a gun into an elevator shaft? He could have killed someone. At least jail him for disturbing the peace."

"Yeah, but policeman don't treat Amon Carter like they treat a regular Joe. No one was injured. In Texas, firing a pistol is a natural sign of discontent."

He gulped some coffee and grimaced. He'd forgotten the sugar.

"It's just another story that can't be printed. I'll write about a drunken visitor who got tired of waiting and beat on the elevator door with the butt of a gun or something. My column will mention no names."

When the waitress came over, Stanley looked up and said, "I need sugar and the breakfast special, please, with an extra egg and some grits."

"What'll you have, doll?" he asked Phillis.

"Coffee with cream and a piece of toast."

Phillis couldn't decide if she would even be able to digest the toast.

"This is what power's all about, isn't it? Being able to operate outside the law. If you're important or have enough money, you get your way, regardless of who you hurt." She spread her fingers flat on the varnished wooden table. "Tell me, Stanley, do high muckety-mucks ever pay their dues to society?

"Oh, I've seen it once or twice. Not often."

Phillis remembered Josie's words, "No white man pays when he hurts a colored man."

She asked, "What's next? Go back home, crawl into bed, and try to forget Amon Carter is my boss?"

"Sure, if you don't want to meet the man." He cocked his head and his eyes twinkled as he gave her that look, she had come to know.

"What man?"

"Time for a show, baby," he replied. "We're going — well, at least I'm goin', not sure about you — to meet the big cheese. If you keep quiet, don't ask any questions, and stand behind the tallest guy in the room, I think I can sneak you in."

"Thanks a lot," she said sarcastically. "That sounds like a barrel of fun."

"Say, if you don't appreciate being included, just vamoose."

"I wouldn't leave now if you paid me," she smiled. "Is it Al Smith?"

"Better than that," he said, smiling back. "It's H. L. You know? H.L. Mencken."

Phillis gasped and clapped her hands together. "How soon?"

"Hold your horses. We've got a few minutes. Time enough for you to tell me if you still want to spend the rest of your life as a reporter. Or are you ready to chuck it? Don't guess I would blame you. You're a sweet kid, and Houston's ups and downs kinda knocked you sideways."

"I'm not a kid.' I'm not that much younger than you and aging faster since I got to Houston."

"I've walked down the paths of much older men since I left home." His eyelids drooped and his crinkly laugh lines disappeared as he vanished into the past, a time and place way before Robert Powell's tragic death and Amon Carter's violence.

"You're letting those grits go cold," Phillis said, "may I have a bite?"

He pushed the bowl toward her and grinned. "You got me going, doll. I went back too far. You ready to go meet the colossal Mr. Menken?"

WALKING BACK TO THE RICE FELT LIKE returning to the scene of a crime. They ascended the wide stairway to the mezzanine, entering a room packed with reporters and cigar smoke. Phillis slipped behind a man who towered over her. He looked familiar. At this point everyone in Houston resembled someone familiar.

A deep-voiced man read from a sheet of paper someone handed him. "My name is Harry Cohen. I am the foreign advertising manager of the *Houston Press*. Sitting beside me is my boss, the legendary Marcellus Foster, or Mefo, as he prefers to be called. Also, on our panel is author Henry F. Pringle, who has written the fine biography of our soon-to-be-elected president, Al Smith. Our honored guest today is the esteemed journalist and author H. L. Mencken."

Mr. Pringle asked Mencken the first question. "Sir, since this convention largely hinges on the question of wet or dry, can you address Prohibition?"

"Ah, yes, the 'Noble Experiment'. That unenforceable law that's increased drunkenness, crime, disease, and poverty. America rocks with the scandal caused by the Eighteenth Amendment."

Mencken stopped and tried puffing on his oversized cigar. It was dead, so he struck a match and relit it.

"I keep thinking, surely Prohibitionists will admit they're wrong and give it up. No, they instead push for more punishment."

Pausing, he held up one finger with exultant glee. "Possibly, it's the Puritan's yearning to browbeat and terrorize any of us who show signs of being happy?"

The room full of reporters clapped and yelled their agreement.

Pringle asked, "And what are your views on politicians, Mr. Mencken?"

"Oh, you fellows are baiting me in anticipation of...what? a blackballing?

A good politician is as unthinkable as an honest burglar. For that reason, every election is a sort of advance auction of stolen goods."

The audience burst out laughing and someone whistled.

"Democracy is the art and science of running the circus from inside the monkey cage; however, in this world of sin and sorrow there is always something to be thankful for. As for me, I rejoice that I'm not a Republican."

Harry Cohen took over the floor and asked, "What about Al Smith versus Herbert Hoover?"

Mencken paused and finally said, "I'm at a loss as to how to answer. How to compare the capable, genial fishmonger who says he's never read a book with Herbert Hoover who, if he had to recite the Twenty-Third Psalm, would make it sound like a search warrant issued under the Volstead Act?"

Phillis applauded along with the whole roomful of men who loved Mencken's sledgehammer wit. She clenched her fists when the floor was opened to questions, mindful of Stanley's warning.

Sweating profusely and chewing on his cigar, Mr. Mencken took questions from the floor, none of which were as interesting as hers would have been. Having read Anita Loos' satire written to publicize Mencken's affair with the dumbest blonde of all, she would love to ask how a Ziegfeld Follies girl bewitched him.

As if sensing her pent-up questions, Stanley abruptly shepherded Phillis from the room. "I need to go to my office and write a column," he apologized. "Can I leave you here?"

"Sure," Phillis said. "I'll go over to the League of Women Voters' headquarters. Thanks for bringing me. I learned more this morning about politics than I did in four years at Baylor."

"Glad to be of help, doll. See you."

She watched him lope out of the Rice Hotel, dodging bellhops and tourist groups, then walked to where she spied the LWV's red-and-white banner.

Disappointed to find no one at the welcome table, she removed her press pass and LWV card from her pocketbook and showed them to the women sitting around chatting. Finally, one asked if Phillis needed assistance.

"I'm looking for a member who can give me a story for my newspaper. I am with the *Fort Worth Star-Telegram.*

"Local headquarters are at the Chamber of Commerce Building on Main Street. That's where the action is."

Phillis thanked her and hustled downstairs. At the curb, she asked Louie, Stanley's favorite bellhop, who pretended he had never laid eyes on her, for directions.

Four blocks sounded easy until Phillis realized a recent rain shower had increased the humidity significantly. Steam rose from the sidewalks and coupled with the merciless sun provided another typical afternoon in Houston.

Spotting the building, inside she found the LWV headquarters filled with members, all of whom seemed to be talking at once. Being in the room with this many fellow Leaguers was fun, and Phillis quickly pulled both her membership card and press pass out again.

A soft-spoken woman asked, "Where's Miss Marbury?"

"Over at the convention hall trying to look inconspicuous."

The woman beside Phillis, snickered, "Tammany Hall wants the New Yorkers to blend in, not stand out like sore thumbs."

"Bessie Marbury has never been inconspicuous a day in her life," retorted a stylish woman dressed in black with three strands of pearls and a high-pitched New York accent. "Nor have I, come to think of it. Hope it's cooler where she is."

Her eyes circled the room. "I'm in this dreadfully ugly building that is hot, hot, hot, handing out these stupid booklets. Honestly, the things I do for friends."

She fanned herself with the pamphlets. "I knew when I agreed to board that ship and sail to Galveston for a political convention in June, things would not be great for this old goil. God knows why I'm wasting my time here in this hellhole called Houston. I don't give a fig for politics."

"Say, goilie," she said, noticing Phillis, "would you go get me a glass of lemonade? I'll give you a dime."

It took a second for Phillis to realize she was the "goilie" to whom this woman referred. "Of course, madam," Phillis gave her a sunny smile. "I'm happy to do a favor for a convention visitor, especially one from New York."

Phillis scooted out the door to find lemonade. She ran to the corner vendor she had passed on her way from the Rice Hotel. He not only had lemonade, but he also had ice to cool it down. She waited for the drink knowing instinctively, despite her atrocious accent, this short, slim woman with her magnificent pearl necklace and square-cut emerald ring was someone very important.

When Phillis returned, the woman had not moved an inch. She took the drink then looked at Phillis. "Goil, whattcha want?" she asked. "Oh, yeah. Your dime."

"No, ma'am," Phillis replied politely, holding up her press pass. "I would rather have a story."

The woman's laugh was as grating as her speech, a shrill crescendo bouncing off the interior limestone walls. "You think a dime's worth of lemonade obliges me to give you an interview?"

"No, I do not," Phillis replied, "but I am interested in why you're here. It's your first time in Houston?"

"You got that right, kiddo. So, what do you wanna know?"

"Your name, the reason for your trip, and how it is you have more style than anyone else in the room."

"That's a long story. You can never imagine what a gorgeous life I've lived."

"I'm waiting, ready to take down anything you say."

"Isn't there any foiniture in here? I need to relax in a comfortable chair."

Phillis found a small-upholstered chair against the wall and beckoned the woman over.

"'Just my size,' as the baby bear said. Ugly as everything else in this place." She perched on the maroon cushion and disparagingly eyed the armrests.

"Well, Miss Flanagan, is it?" she said looking at Phillis's press pass, "You asked my name. I was born Elsie de Wolfe in New York City. Last year I became Lady Mendl when I wed Britisher Sir Charles Mendl. He's a little younger. I adjusted my birth date on the marriage certificate so as not to embarrass him. My friend, Bessie Marbury, was unhappy. Marriage was one of the few things I'd never tried."

Phillis struggled to keep a straight face.

"You complimented me on my style," Elsie continued, fingering her pearls. "In order to have style, you have to learn about taste. I described all of this in the *Delineator* when I wrote a column for them. Goilie, I *invented* interior decorating. Then I wrote a book about it. No more ugly wallpaper, bric-a-brac, stained glass, potted palms, and oriental rugs."

"You're the one who got rid of Victorian clutter?"

"Oh, yes. My secrets are white paint, plenty of optimism, and chintz. It's cheery and inexpensive — the English have used it for years. I brought it to America."

"What about the way you dress?"

"For ten years I was an actress, a terrible actress, but audiences loved my clothes. Ethel Barrymore was my understudy. *Harper's Bazaar* named me the Best-dressed Woman of the American Stage."

"Why did you stop acting?" Phillis asked, tired of standing but afraid to break the spell Elsie cast by going off to look for a chair.

"I turned forty and it was time for me to do something else, so I decorated houses. For money, of course. After I decorated Bessie's and my house at Sutton Place, all New York City was agog. Everybody wanted the 'Chintz Lady' to do their house. I wrote a column for the *Ladies' Home Journal* and then a book, *The House in Good Taste*. I gave 'em do-it-yourself tips like how to decorate with mirrors and how to paint garlands on pine dressers."

"How marvelous," Phillis said, doubting she would ever seek out this book.

"Bessie and I bought a villa in France. When the Great War came, we turned it over to the French government as a base for hospital supplies, and I volunteered as a nurse on the front lines."

She paused. "I know it sounds boastful," she continued after a few minutes, "I was awarded the *Croix de Guerre* and the Legion of Honor in 1922. I burst into tears when the French general stepped forward and tapped my shoulder with his sword."

"Lady Mendl, is there anything you haven't done?"

"No, I can't think of anything?"

"And why have you come to Houston? Is this your first political convention?"

"I wish it were. I hate politics. Now, Bessie is the National Committee Woman from New York. Back when all she did was produce plays, that's when we were the happiest. We were friends with Cole Porter and all of the fun theater crowd."

"Can you tell me how you've remained so youthful?" Phillis hoped she would be flattered by this question.

"I stand on my head every day. You should try it. You have terrible stooped shoulders."

"Thank you, Lady Mendl, I appreciate your advice," Phillis replied as she put away her notes.

No sooner had Elsie de Wolfe finished her story than she slumped in her chair and croaked, "I think I am going to faint."

Phillis called out, frantically, "Does anyone have smelling salts?"

A kind-looking gray-haired woman rushed over and introduced herself as Dr. Wright. She felt Elsie's forehead.

"If you're a real doctor, you're what I need. It's dreadfully hot in this room."

Dr. Wright suggested, "Let's get you outside, away from all these women. Why don't you see if you can stand up?"

As Elsie de Wolfe tried to rise from the chair, Dr. Wright asked, "How old are you?"

"You think I'm going to tell you that?"

"I'm sixty," Dr. Wright informed her.

"Humph, I got you beat by three years, Doc. You don't look near as good as I do."

"I couldn't agree with you more. I've spent my life treating patients in a tuberculosis hospital. No time to fuss with my appearance."

Phillis held her breath waiting for Miss de Wolfe's reply. Not the put down she expected. Instead, her face softened as she said, "A medical doctor. That's splendid. I admire your courage."

Dr. Wright smiled slightly as she passed a vial of salts under the woman's nose. "There now, isn't that better?"

"Yes, it is." Elsie turned to Phillis who was still holding one of her arms. "Call me a taxicab. I'm going to the Rice Hotel until I can get Bessie to drive me down to Galveston."

Dr. Wright and Phillis helped her into the cab. Slumped against Phillis's shoulder, when they arrived at the Rice, Elsie de Wolfe sprang out onto the sidewalk. With a jerk on the hem of her silk dress, she straightened her pearls. While Phillis attempted to thank her for her story, she swished past, grabbing the arm of a distinguished older gentleman standing nearby. "Would you escort me into the Rice, please?" she asked him. "I feel faint."

Grinning, Phillis watched the diminutive woman strut into the hotel with greater aplomb than any runway model.

After checking to make sure her notes were safely stowed in her pocket, Phillis looked up to see Louie walking quickly towards her. "Miss, tell Mr. Stanley there's been another shooting here this afternoon?"

Phillis used the call box on the corner to telephone the *Press*. Stanley was gone for the day, so she left a message, "There's been another problem at the Rice Hotel."

Three streetcars passed her packed with passengers before she boarded a trolley headed back to the Heights. It was after six when she stamped up the stairs and entered the cool, surprisingly dark, home. A note on the hall table read, "Miss Banion and the judge are out for the evening. Josie left your supper on the counter under the tea towels. I've gone downtown with the Muellers to pray. Mrs. Hinkle."

Phillis checked her wristwatch. She had scarcely an hour before the evening session began. At least two hours before the roll call for delegates to vote for presidential candidates.

She was hot and tired. She hadn't eaten since her toast that morning. Peeking under the covers in the kitchen, she found fried chicken, a boiled ear of corn, and a bowl of peach cobbler. She fixed herself a plate and sank down at the kitchen table, pulling out her notebook. Eating slowly, she knew the longer she stayed in the cool, quiet kitchen, the harder it would be to go back downtown.

The insistent ringing of the telephone brought her to her feet. Chagrinned, she realized she had dozed off sitting straight up in the kitchen chair. Dashing to the hall, she grabbed the receiver, hoping to hear Stanley's voice.

"Is Teddy there?" a sugary voice inquired.

"No, may I take a message?" Phillis asked, trying to wake up.

"Honey, please tell him Ethel called."

Phillis wrote a note to Teddy then rushed back to the kitchen faucet and ran a cold rag over her face. Grabbing her pocketbook, she headed out the door.

THE NOISE INSIDE WAS DEAFENING. Cheering delegates marched around the hall, waving their Smith banners, keeping time to the drumbeat of the uniformed Tyler Tigers whose brass section blasted "On the Banks of the Wabash." Brownwood's "Old Gray Mare" band was waiting its turn.

Franklin D. Roosevelt slowly advanced to the podium, leaning heavily on his son's arm. A hush came over the crowd as he began to speak. Though the ceiling fans muffled some of the words, Roosevelt's powerful voice projected his words even to the back of the hall where Phillis stood. With his closing line, he praised the New York Governor for whom "Victory is his habit — the happy warrior Alfred E. Smith." Echoing his 1924 nominating speech, Roosevelt again likened his candidate to the Wordsworth poem, and the convention delegates cheered. Their wild demonstration lasted for ten minutes, giving Phillis a chance to scoot over for a look at the press box where Stanley might be sitting. No luck.

At ten o'clock Tom Ball nominated Jesse Jones, and Governor Dan Moody seconded the nomination. The Texas delegation cast all forty of its votes for native son Jesse Holman Jones, and thousands of little green balloons floated down from the ceiling as six local bands played "The Eyes of Texas" in unison. Despite this carefully orchestrated display for Houston's favorite son, if Jesse Jones truly had presidential aspirations, the evening was a disappointment. Alfred E. Smith stole the wind from his sails, easily winning the nomination on the first ballot.

Searching the crowd, Phillis never saw Stanley. Did he get her message? Over twenty-four hours had passed. She was frantic to find out what new disaster had occurred at the Rice Hotel, knowing newspapers would ever carry the real story.

6/28/28. What a day! Anyone who can get away with what Amon Carter has done is scary. He can squash me like a bug. Elsie de Wolfe bowled me over. Elegant appearance, screeching voice, and tactless. Franklin D. R has made sure Alfred E. Smith will always be "the happy warrior." an epithet, sort of a nickname. Got to find Stanley tomorrow.

CHAPTER TWENTY-FOUR

Houston, Texas, June 21 — (AP)--Gate-Crashing Champ Plans to Rush Democrats. One-eyed Connally, known the country over for his unequalled ability in getting places where he ought not to be, arrived here last night from Hollywood, where he has been in the movies, as the guest of the Southern Pacific and immediately went to police headquarters and made friends with Police Chief Goodson."

Billings Weekly Gazette
Friday, June 29, 1928

"IF YOU WANT TO INTERVIEW AMERICA'S future first lady, you'd better get set to go. She's leaving town at noon."

Phillis's looked at the forest of wooden trusses supporting the steeple of her bedroom and groaned. Once they were headed downtown in the Packard, Maymie commented, "You look peaked. Are you sleeping okay in that attic room?"

"I can't imagine anyone in Houston has slept well for the last four days. How many bands did you say are playing for the visitors? They all played different tunes at the same time in my dreams last night. The girl riding the 'Old Gray Mare' kept trying to swing me up on the horse with her."

Phillis munched on the piece of toast she grabbed from the kitchen counter as they walked out the door but what she wished for was a cup of coffee and a jelly doughnut.

"You need to put your mind to it for a restful sleep. And don't be dropping any of those crumbs in my automobile."

"Yes, ma'am. No, ma'am," Phillis replied. "Miss Maymie, how did you finagle a connection with Mrs. Smith?"

"You haven't learned a thing if you still don't know how to use your sources. Haven't seen you waving any *Star-Telegrams* around. You get anything published at all?"

"Yes, a few unremarkable pieces. No byline and not the news stories I hoped for."

"Stick with me, gal. You'll find one yet."

"Thanks," Phillis replied. "I'm keeping at it."

"Here you go," Maymie said as she handed her keys to the parking attendant waiting at 513 Main Street. "Thank you, Sonny. Looks like you're handling everything beautifully," she said, ignoring his sweaty red face and wrinkled uniform.

"We're trying, Miss Banion," he replied.

Phillis asked, "This is the Chamber of Commerce Building, isn't it? I was here just yesterday."

"Actually, it's the Binz Building, but the Chamber has the first floor and that's where Mrs. Smith is holding her press conference."

Thanks to Miss Maymie's punctuality, they were able to sit in the second row amongst a group of women who were easy to tag as New Yorkers, and as she soon realized, intimate members of the Al Smith campaign.

One of them whispered, "This is a test. Let's hope she passes."

Her friend replied in a low voice, "I'm thinking it will only be on account of Bessie Marbury. She's been grooming her."

"We've kept our future first lady away from the press as long as possible. Thank God, she's leaving at noon."

Phillis could not believe they were discussing Mrs. Alfred E. Smith, but who else could it be? She leaned forward to hear more.

"I'm praying no profanity slips out. Glad you scheduled this for ten o'clock. Too early for her to tipple."

"Right, but I'm not sure this audience would even notice, especially the locals. These Texans are not like us. They're definitely not our kind of people."

Phillis bristled. A distinguished gentleman solicitously ushered Mrs. Al Smith to a damask-covered armchair where she settled herself rather fussily, tugging on the hemline of her skirt, straightening the jade pendant which hung on a long gold chain.

Despite her finery, she looked like a washerwoman. Her green satin dress and jacket were out of keeping for the summer season, much less a morning appearance, and in no way enhanced her plump figure. The large magenta feather fan she waved around was ludicrous. Miss Maymie poked Phillis in the ribs, giving her a sideways grin.

After being introduced, Mrs. Smith began bluntly, "I don't like interviews. There's nothing for me to say except that I am a tried-and-true Democrat."

"Mrs. Smith, tell us about your trip from Albany."

"It was enjoyable. I have my family with me."

"How do you like Houston?"

"Houston and the State of Texas have shown me warm, southern hospitality."

"You've sat in your box every night, but you've turned down invitations to be honored at any of the receptions or luncheons."

"I cannot accept social engagements. Mr. Smith does not think it's appropriate."

"You and your family are staying at the Galvez, aren't you? Has that been pleasant for you?"

"Yes, except for the first day when we were caught in an terrible thunderstorm driving from Galveston to Houston for the evening session." Her voice rose with excitement, "My driver had to park by the roadside and my daughter, whose seat did not have a cover, got a terrible drenching."

She straightened in her chair and boasted, "Lucky for me, I had sense enough to turn down an offer to travel back and forth on an airplane that evening. I'm sure I would not be here today to tell about it. I've never ridden in one of these contraptions, nor do I intend to."

"You and Governor Smith have been married for many years. Tell us, please, what he was like when you first met?"

"When he was courting me, he was a dandy with his fancy vests, red neckties, and tight-fitting trousers. I can't remember if he wore a brown Derby hat, but he probably did. One of those funny ones with a narrow brim and a high crown like you see when you go to a vaudeville show."

The audience laughed but the one of the New Yorkers whispered to her friend, "I thought she was instructed how to answer the questions?"

Phillis could not hear the response.

"Tell us, please, aside from his appearance, what else you remember?"

"When he was nineteen or twenty, Mr. Smith was quite pleased with himself. The life of every party, he recited poetry for the crowd and danced with all the girls. He thought he could sing, too."

"What's your most vivid memory of your week in Houston?"

"Some man put a baby donkey in my arms. Imagine that. A city girl like me? I shoved it away and told him to send it to Albany."

"Speaking of Governor Smith, I understand you talk with him by telephone every night."

"Yes, he telephones me at nine p.m. and begins every call by singing to me. Sometimes, he sings 'My Heart's in Texas' and other nights he sings 'Down on the Rio Grande.'"

The audience laughed. "When Franklin Roosevelt nominated your husband last night, he referred to Wordsworth's "Happy Warrior." Can you tell us why you think he likens Al Smith to the hero of the poem?"

"No, I do not know Mr. Wordsworth. I have no idea what he was talking about. Seems like he said this when he nominated him in 1924."

The women sitting in front of Phillis groaned as did others sitting behind her.

"Well, yes. In light of that can you comment on Governor Smith's reading habits?"

"Neither of us has ever read books. Not for amusement nor to pass away the time. Mr. Smith says, 'Life, not dead pages, furnishes our thrills.'"

Mrs. Smith turned then to the moderator and asked, "Are we done now?"

"Yes. Thank you so much for sharing your thoughts with us. We're honored to have met you."

He turned to the audience. "Let's show Mrs. Smith how happy we are she joined us today."

Loud clapping ensued but Phillis's thoughts were of the empty lives of those who never read books: Daisy Leatherbury, whose life revolved around parties and beauty pageants and the dogmatic Della Hinkle who refused to even read a newspaper. Would reading have helped Mrs. Al Smith?

After the honoree was trundled out of the room, Maymie rose and looked toward the door. "That was enlightening, wasn't it?"

"Yes, we learned a lot listening to our presidential candidate's choice of a mate."

"Seeing her up close was something else as well," Maymie added. "Well, I'm off to my office, see you about five, back at the house"

Phillis tried to reach Stanley at his office. *At this rate I'll go broke feeding my nickles to a call box.* She walked toward the hall, pausing in front of the Hospitality House. This was the busy place that received rave reviews all week. *I should check it out and add my signature to the guest book.* The *Post* noted the pen Mrs. Woodrow Wilson used to make the first entry in the book would be donated to the Houston Public Library where it would remain as a treasured exhibit.

According to Stanley, this venue was the Hogg brothers' inspiration. The open-air facility occupied an entire block with green-and-white striped awnings, providing protection from the pitiless sun. Giant loudspeakers connected to speakers in the hall enabled convention visitors to hear the proceedings. Fans and barrels of ice water provided all that was needed. Phillis gratefully sank onto a bench and gazed at the empty building across the street.

At noon, Clem Shaver had pounded his gavel for the last time and permanently adjourned the Democratic National Convention of 1928.

The crowds had thinned noticeably now that the four-day pandemonium was over. The hall seemed to be shrinking like a balloon slowly deflating.

Two women walked into the Hospitality House, their bedraggled white ribbons indicating their political position. "I've got to go back to my hotel and rest. I'm dog-tired," the older lady announced, sinking down on a bench.

Her friend nodded, attempting to wipe her own sweaty face with a wrinkled hanky before walking over to the water barrel and filling two cups from the dispenser. "That all-night prayer meeting with First Baptist Church left me limp as a wet dishrag. Thank goodness this thing's over. Don't think I could have stood another day."

"Me neither."

When a third woman arrived, the two dry's rose and exchanged looks as they rushed out of the tent. The newcomer, a heavily made-up woman with bleached hair wore a flowered dress with wilted ruffles. She collapsed on the bench where Phillis sat.

"Are you okay?" The woman beside her was gasping for breath.

"Just need a minute to get away from that God-awful sun."

Her brassy voice sounded like traffic noise.

Phillis spoke reassuringly, "You've come to the right place. It's the coolest place in town. All week, visitors said they'd rather be here than in the hall."

"You got that right, sister, though I never made it into the big top to make a comparison," she said hoarsely.

"I'm a reporter for the *Fort Worth Star-Telegram*," Phillis offered.

"And I'm the Queen of England!" Without bothering to open her eyes, the woman let out an ear-splitting laugh that echoed throughout the tent. Eying Phillis she said, "You're saying you came here from north Texas to write a story for a newspaper." She spread her legs and leaned toward Phillis. "If you're a reporter, where's your camera? You could take my picture."

Not waiting for an answer, the woman muttered, "I've had the blues this morning, that's why I put so much red on my cheeks. Rouge cheers me up."

"Oh, I quite agree. Rouge lifts my spirits every time," Phillis said knowingly.

A volunteer in charge of manning the venue walked up. "Can I get you girls anything?" Phillis shook her head but the woman beside her asked, "You got a potty? That's what I need."

Unfazed, the apron-clad attendant smiled broadly and said, "There's a lovely ladies lounge over to the right with a mirror to check your makeup and the nicest vase of black-eyed Susan's."

"But does it have a potty? Had too much giggle water last night, need to puke. I'm still zozzled."

She stood up on wobbly legs and pointed her finger at Phillis. "My name's Pearl. Pearl Watkins. W-a-t-k-i-n-s. Be sure you spell it right when you write a story about me."

Phillis laughed and nodded. Pearl turned to the bright-eyed attendant, "When I come back, I need food. Something salty. Someone told me the dry's are offering sandwiches. Oh, and ice cream. Where's the food?"

"Yes, there's a counter to your left with free postcards and a free lunch."

Pearl snapped, "There's no such thing as a 'free lunch,' lady. I learned that when I turned fourteen."

"Do you live in Houston?" the woman inquired politely.

"I did until last night. The house where I worked got raided. Imagine that happening at Hattie's house. All these visitors from out of town and the police raid us. The sheriff promised hands-off till after the convention."

The attendant looked as if she wished she were someplace else. Phillis was sure her upbringing had not prepared her for this.

"Only luck I had was being upstairs with a john when the police whistles started blowing. I just rolled under the bed, and no one found me. Missed spending the night in jail."

Pearl went off looking for the lounge as some Ohio delegates straggled in. Phillis heard their exclamations of delight with Houston — "Great city on the bayou." "Never saw anything like this in Cincinnati." "Houston will be another New York City before long."

The contrast between the self-righteous dry's, the down-on-her-luck prostitute, and these hayseed Ohioans was striking. Might work them into a story.

Since the action was over and there was nothing for him to do, who should appear headed for a bench with a plate full of food. One-Eyed Connally in the flesh.

Now that Phillis had seen his photo at least four times in the Houston newspapers, she rued her innocence at failing to recognize the world-famous gatecrasher who had posed as a soda pop vendor. His close attention to her surreptitious invasion of Sam Houston Hall now made sense.

The newspapers quoted Connally as saying the convention coliseum would be "pie" to crash and if necessary, he would come through one of the big leaks in the roof. He made it into the first two sessions, no one figured out how, before his Houston mission collapsed. Much to the convention visitors' delight, some Texas Rangers handcuffed him to a bench outside the hall for everyone to see.

The gatecrasher's unequaled success for getting into places all over the world finally failed him at the Democratic National Convention of 1928. Released, since the event ended, he was here entertaining visitors who were asking for his autograph. She was sure he expected a donation for his signature. Would it be anything more than an "X"?

"Fool me twice, shame on me." Phillis wasn't about to give this greasy, whining bum the time of day. She looked around wishing for Stanley. Surely, he was somewhere downtown, but where? It was past lunchtime. She went to the call box and telephoned the *Houston Press* again. This time she was in luck. "Stanley, tell me about the new incident. Did it involve my boss?"

"Yep, sure did."

Phillis groaned.

"Can't talk on the phone," Stanley said. "Meet you at, um, let's see. What about Dirty's? The sign outside reads 'Quick and Dirty.' It's on Prairie and Travis. See you there in twenty minutes."

PHILLIS SET OFF WISHING FOR A BIGGER HAT to shield her from the sun. Ten blocks later, her shoes felt like sweat buckets and her blouse stuck to her skin, but she found the place. Stanley had beaten her there.

"There's my girl," he said, patting her arm as he pulled out a chair for her and began to relate the details of Amon Carter's second incident.

"It didn't take a gumshoe to figure out the second shooting at the Rice was connected to the earlier one."

"Another of Carter's jokes?" Phillis asked with a sinking heart.

"Yep. This time he was entertaining Mencken, Texas style. I bet no one enjoyed Carter's idea of fun." With a dramatic pause, Stanley eyed her and shook his head. Phillis motioned him to continue.

"Yesterday at three in the afternoon, Ku Klux Klan members, staying in the hotel across the street from the Rice, told police three bullets, which they were sure had been fired by the Pope of Rome's gunslingers, flew into their open window." Phillis gasped then laughed at the ridiculous accusation.

"Wait, it gets worse. Investigating officers confirmed the shots were from H. L. Mencken's eleventh floor room. Ready to haul him off to jail, the policemen were stopped by Amon Carter who convinced them an unknown intruder had entered Mencken's room and fired the shots while Mencken was in the bathroom.

"What really happened?" Phillis asked.

"You better know, H. L. Mencken doesn't even own a gun much less know how to shoot one. A Fort Worth hotel guest staying next door to Mencken spilled the beans to one of our cub reporters who brought me the story. She saw Amon leaving Mencken's room right after the shots were fired and watched him return when the police came. After they left, he shoved a gun into the waist of his pants and ran down the hall with Mencken yelling, 'Don't ever come back.'"

As Stanley recounted the story, he fiddled with the saltshaker until Phillis wanted to scream. "It's bad luck to spill salt," she interrupted him. "Please throw some over your left shoulder."

He laughed out loud but obeyed her request before concluding his story. "Guess that's why Dallasites call him 'Amon the Terrible.'"

"Does he think all this is entertaining?"

Stanley ignored her question. "I told the reporter to write down the witness's story and I would edit out what we couldn't print." He rubbed his chin and shrugged his shoulders.

Phillis was furious. "I can't work for him any longer. He's just plain crazy."

"I don't blame you. He's a bastard all right. But it's okay because you're not going back to Fort Worth anyway, are you?"

"You knew I needed to hear that story, didn't you?"

"Well, you needed to know what he's capable of. Houston's gonna be healthier after Carter leaves town. Speaking of which, what are your plans, post-convention?"

"Don't know yet." Stanley raised his hand to indicate a refill, but she shook her head. "I need to head for home."

"Okey dokey. Let's talk tomorrow. Billy's for lunch?"

Phillis had almost reached her trolley stop when powerful hands gripped her shoulders and spun her around.

"Found you." Amon Carter stood grinning.

Phillis jerked free and glared at him.

"Did you think I was fooling?"

Phillis shrugged her shoulders. "What do you mean?"

Carter yelled in her face, "You didn't follow my orders. Did you think I wouldn't notice? You think you're so sneaky. Well, I'm not publishing your pitiful stories about grieving widows, Houston's fancy new stadium, and female rodeo stars. Got nothing against Fox Hastings, but you're supposed to be writing society news. That's what I'm paying you for."

Phillis stood there with the boiling sun beating down on her as this grown man threw a fit right there on Texas Avenue. He wore his fancy Stetson while trickles of sweat rolled down his fiery-red cheeks. Arms flailing, he stomped his cowboy boots on the concrete like a tap dancer. Passers-by glanced at them curiously but did not stop.

"Don't . . ." Phillis began. Then she remembered Mary Frances, the former *Star* reporter Carter shoved to the ground when she tried to interview a legislator's wife at a rally. Looking down, she shuddered at the thought of landing on this scorching concrete.

"You're a liar and a cheat. I bet you never went to a single luncheon." He pointed to his forehead. "I figured you out when Mayor Johnson's wife whined about The *Star* making no mention of her at Ima Hogg's reception."

"That grieving widow was part of the story about the awful lynching. How could I ignore it? How could you not print it? Everything I've written . . ."

"Who cares?"

"That's your reaction when a man is hanged from a bridge?"

"Do you see anyone around here that cares about that." He snapped his head, looking from side to side as if to prove his point.

"But that's our job, to make them care." Phillis grimaced, hating his words which she feared were all too true.

"Woman, you're crazy if you think I'll ever let you write a news story. You owe me money. I didn't get what I paid for."

She gasped at him, her fury so intense that she threw caution away and disregarded Stanley's warning, "Mr. Carter, you're the crazy one here. Shooting a loaded gun into a hotel elevator. You could have killed someone."

His face paled for a moment, then his fingers slowly curled into balls. He looked like a pot of boiling water about to overflow. "Don't you dare accuse me of anything."

"What you did was dangerous. People could have been killed."

"Lady, you may find out how dangerous I can be." His anger seemed to cool as he narrowed his eyes and smiled. "You're fired, Smarty Pants."

She laughed. "You can't fire me because I quit."

Spinning around, Carter charged back toward the hotel, leaving Phillis to wonder if he had gone to get his pistol-packing sheriff. Would she be his next target? She decided to take herself out of his sight as fast as she could.

When she arrived home, Maymie Banion looked up. "What's wrong?"

"Amon Carter just fired me."

"Who got fired?" Teddy asked, coming up from the basement.

Phillis raised her hand and looked around the room sheepishly.

"If you're smiling, you must be happy about it," Teddy joked.

Looking up from the sock she was darning, Mrs. Hinkle broke the silence. "It's high time. You're too good for the likes of him." With a flick of her fingers, she dismissed Amon Carter, oblivious to Teddy's soft whistle and Maymie's open-mouthed gasp.

"Thank you," Phillis chirped as she fought back unshed tears at hearing Della Hinkle's unexpected support.

"After all that's happened, you should be happy about it," Maymie chimed in.

"Yeah, I was gonna quit anyway, but I wish he hadn't beaten me to it."

With a glance at Maymie, Phillis rose. "I'm going upstairs to write my story on Mrs. Al Smith." She laughed, "Ouch, I have no reason to write anything. As of now, I am unemployed."

"That's okay. I have a job now." Teddy straightened his shoulders, his face wreathed in smiles. "I'm through with college and Maymie says it's okay with her."

"Who gave you a job?" Phillis asked.

"Our neighbor up the street, George Hawkins. He's got an automobile dealership, downtown. I begin tomorrow."

"Wow, Teddy, I think you're about to turn a corner."

Maymie nodded again slowly and answered, "Yes, all of this is good."

Can't wait to tell Stanley, Phillis thought as she climbed the stairs to the room, where she could spend only two more nights before the rent came due.

CHAPTER TWENTY-FIVE

Never in all my life have I gone thru the siege I just experienced. We had fifteen thousand people here, and I saw ambassadors, paperhangers, bootleggers, delegates, lobbyists, mayors, congressmen, firemen, loafers, policemen, street-hawkers, etc., all in one hectic day. I shook hands with all of them. Spent hours at the Convention Hall, and never missed a one of the eight sessions.

Letter from William A. Bernrieder,
City of Houston's Secretary to Mayor Oscar Holcombe,
written to his brother.

Saturday, June 30, 1928

BEING ALONE WAS NOTHING NEW FOR PHILLIS. She had never had a circle of friends or a large family. For almost ten years after her twin sisters died, it was just her and her mother, a small life. When Horace Wilkerson blundered into the picture bringing his son Junior, the four of them became a family, but were never even as close as the "family" here at the boarding house. Faced with leaving, Phillis realized she was tired of being alone.

But the event that filled every minute of her life was over, the visitors had left, and she was out of a job. Now, she had "nowhere to go and nothing to do." Maymie housed no non-paying guests. She needed to leave before being asked.

As she filled her bowl with milk and cereal, Maymie sat down across from her. Phillis dreaded what she suspected was coming.

"When are you returning to Fort Worth?" she inquired.

"I told you I'm not going back there."

"Just checking to see if you had a change of heart. Your mother thought you might be ready to come home. I bet her you would not return to north Texas. Any ideas about what you'll do next?"

"I've never wanted anything but journalism, but to me, being a reporter means city news. With three telephone calls, Amon Carter will blackball me from Houston's dailies."

"How about magazines? You met Allen."

"Allen?"

"Allen Peden."

"Hmmn. Is the *Gargoyle* a possibility?"

"My dear, anything's a possibility if you put your mind to it. What do you have to lose?"

Phillis waved her hands from side to side excitedly, and said, "Okay. Okay. I'll call see about making an appointment."

"Good. Your mother will be pleased and I'm glad to have you. Do you want to move back to your old room?"

"Wait a minute. You act like I already have the job."

"Well, I did put a bug in his ear."

"Oh, Maymie!" screamed Phillis. "That's called meddling."

"You know there's nothing I wouldn't do to help you."

"You've helped me enough. Now a job?" Phillis was intrigued by the idea of learning to write the slick copy that filled his magazine and greatly relieved Maymie had not suggested Phillis help her sell insurance.

"I like having you around."

"That's a happy thought," Phillis smiled. "But, just so you know, I enjoy living in the attic roost. Helps me wake up early."

Maimie nodded her approval. "I know I'm changing the subject," Miss Maymie said. "but to my mind, Houston's put on a helluva event."

"True enough. In my wildest dreams, I couldn't have imagined the past fourteen days." To Phillis, it felt was more like a tornado than a party. With high hopes for an opportunity to leave obits and women's tea parties behind, she never dreamed her chance for a frontpage story would be censored by one of the unwritten rules of journalism.

Teddy, dressed in starched white shirt and pressed slacks, entered the kitchen, clicking his heels. "How do I look? Too dressed up for washing cars but I wanted to make a good impression. First day on the job."

Maymie beamed and Phillis gave him a thumbs-up. That's what she needed, a simple job like washing cars.

IT WAS TIME TO ANSWER THE LETTER she received yesterday from Olivia. She was glad she waited. Now jobless she would reread it with different eyes. Who knows if Maymie's pitch to Peden would result in a paycheck.

Dear Phillis:

I finally got to New York City. On the envelope is my new address. Here's the thing. My mother is white, and my father is colored. There, I've said it.

Yes, my father's really a doctor. I left home with his blessing because there was nothing for me in Louisiana. My parents live on the edge of Shreveport. Neither white nor blacks accept them or me. My light skin makes it easy to pass, and my family encouraged it. Some of the time, I enjoyed being white. Eating in nice cafés. Attending films without having to sit in the balcony and a front row seat in the streetcars.

The lynching terrified me. Afraid if I said anything about it, I would give myself away. I packed my suitcases that night. Now I'm here in New York. Don't ask how I got the bus money. They call Harlem a 'Renaissance.' I had to look this up in a dictionary. Writers, musicians, dancers, singers, a whole neighborhood happening. The color of our skin does not matter. A writer I met at the Cotton Club called it 'finding a new soul' and that is how I feel. I grew up where being black meant you were nobody. Here, I can be somebody without passing anymore. It's just me, as I am, working on the stage, singing and dancing and loving every minute. Please come to New York City. There's a man here named Jean Toomer who says 'Yea! To life.' That's how I feel.

Love, Olivia

OLIVIA'S IDENTITY SHOCKED HER. Did Josie and Charlie know? Probably. Before the lynching, they acted like they felt lucky to live in Houston. Surely, they had friends who lived in the wards. Knew about the lack of electricity and indoor toilets. For certain, they must have seen through the sham indictment of innocent men to conceal the real identity of the lynchers. But, unlike Olivia, they stayed here.

Should she follow Olivia to New York City? Take her chances in the big-time world of journalism with a pitifully short resumé? She could probably borrow the bus fare to get herself there, but with no prospects for a job and no funds to carry her till she found work, the idea seemed premature. *If the Gargoyle hires me, I'll dance a jig.*

She typed her response, congratulating Olivia on her new home, commending her bravery, and soft pedaling the envy she felt as she described her own sketchy career plans. Closing the case of her bright red Corona, Phillis sighed, knowing without a job, she could never afford the monthly payments, much less paper to type on.

THE TROLLEY SWAYED, THE BELL RANG at every block, and the passengers' conversations filled the car. Phillis tuned them out as she rode downtown to meet Stanley. He deserved answers.

The macabre two weeks welded them together and she readily admitted this man had become her confidant, someone she trusted. He seemed able to change people's lives for the better, hers included.

The strings he pulled for her to meet her father and the places he took her were beyond what she could have done alone. Tying herself to a man, even if he was something of a paragon, she had known for two weeks was what teenagers did. Unlike Bradley, he did not play with people's feelings. Was she playing with his feelings? This was what he wanted to know. And it was a fair question.

Arriving downtown, she hoofed it over to Billy McKinnon's where snippets of conversations — *Holcombe's promised 'Gulf Breezes.' Lord knows we hustled. Elevators such a problem.* — mingled with the sizzling smells coming from the kitchen.

This greasy spoon cafe was now as familiar to her as the toes on her feet. Sighting Stanley's buddies at their regular table, she waved.

"He'll be here shortly," Joe responded, motioning to an empty chair.

She greeted each of them by name and sat down. Stanley walked in a few minutes later, and the whole table watched his face light up when he saw Phillis. He crossed the room to where they sat. With a glare at his pals, he whispered something in Phillis's ear, and she blushed. He looked at his friends, "Okay, what have I done now?" he asked.

"You're late, for one thing," replied Joe Eason.

Before he could respond, his friend Pete jumped in, "Tell me how you got that story about the mounted cop finding a taxi for the visitor from Florida?"

"Just a lucky break," Stanley answered.

"Yeah, you have more luck than anyone I know," said Al.

"The harder I work, the luckier I get," Stanley laughed.

"You don't work any harder than we do," Pete whined.

"Yes, he does," said Phillis, startling Stanley.

Al snorted, "A reporter's popularity can mean he could be bending his words to please someone."

Stanley laughed, holding up his hands, "You can't call me down on that," he said.

Phillis nodded, "Right, that's something you would never do."

Oblivious to the tension between Phillis and Stanley, Pete asked, "Phillis, you gonna go back to Fort Worth tomorrow?"

Before she could respond, Stanley put his hands on her shoulders. "That's what we're here to talk about, guys."

Phillis rose and allowed Stanley to steer her toward a quiet corner table, as he called over his shoulder, "So please give us some privacy."

He pulled out a chair and said, "I saw you at the Hospitality House yesterday." His easy grin, and it was a grin to warm her insides.

"Maymie and I also went to Mrs. Al Smith's press interview, "I know you weren't there. All the guests were women."

"Our first-lady-to-be is a kind-hearted person, a loving mother, and a very devoted wife." She reached for the menu and added, "The sweetheart of every man's dreams."

"Not mine." Without bothering to pick up his menu, he quipped, "Those aren't my dreams."

"Aren't you going to eat?" she asked, ignoring his comment. "What do you want?"

He looked at Phillis and asked, "What is it *you* want?"

She doubted he referred to food. "I'm trying to figure that out. I'm off Amon Carter's payroll, so I'm focused on finding a job."

"What happened?"

"I quit. Sorry to say, he fired me first."

"Was he ugly about it?"

Phillis turned red and ducked her head. "Yes, he was very ugly."

"I've been worried about that. I'm just relieved you're here and you are safe. The man's out of control."

She nodded and rolled her eyes.

"You staying in Houston for good?" he asked, examining her face as intently as if he were seeing her for the first time.

"Not sure yet. I have to be able to earn enough to feed myself while I'm deciding."

She licked her thumb and flipped through the pages of the menu. Ignoring him as she read every line, Phillis said softly, "I'm not prepared to discuss my ideas right this minute."

"After I bled my heart to you the other night in Fourth Ward?"

Her face flamed.

"You're blushing!" Stanley crowed. "Your face is as red as your hair!"

"I've told you before, my hair isn't red; it's auburn!"

His loud guffaw startled her. "Krazy Kat says red's the world's best color. Red sunset, red roses, *Red Badge of Courage,* and now red cheeks."

She propped her elbows on the table. "Be serious, please, Stanley. I have some questions for you."

"Shoot," he replied.

"Has the trial date been set for the lynchers?"

"October fifteenth."

"Will my father stand trial?"

He nodded again.

"I'll stay in Houston until then," she said, sitting back.

"That's just five months. Who's gonna give you a five-month job?"

"Maybe someone will actually read my stories."

She looked him in the eye, rubbing her finger back and forth across her chin. "Maybe Allen Peden."

"Ye gods!" Stanley exclaimed. "Don't tell me you want to write for that high hat? Anybody except him."

"He doesn't go in for yellow journalism like the *Press* does if that's your objection. His magazine's entertaining and newsworthy. I enjoy reading most of it."

"Have you contacted him?"

"No. I plan to on Monday."

"Good idea," Stanley reversed his objections. "We have a lot of time to figure all of this out."

"We?" Phillis asked. "When you asked me about my feelings...?"

"Ye-e-e-s?" he replied slowly.

"Two weeks is not enough time for me to have feelings."

"Uh oh, I think something 'woundish' is happening to my heart, "to quote my pal Krazy Kat again." After a long pause, he smiled wryly. "Sorry I'm such a chucklehead."

Looking up at the waitress who had appeared, he asked Phillis, "What about hamburgers?"

Nodding, she let out a sigh, relieved by his humorous reaction. He was not given to piques, another quality she liked about him. Tapping her steepled fingers together, she steered the subject in another direction. "Your hero Damon Runyon wrote that this convention was nothing but a joy ride for Houston. A chance to show off their money, their booster spirit, and love of parties."

Stanley smiled, and Phillis continued, "For me, it was much more. Runyon suggested handling the nomination by telephone. No reason to come all this way and waste people's time."

Her throat choked with tears as she struggled to control her emotions. "Reducing these two weeks to a telephone conversation would have been a terrible loss for me."

A large white handkerchief flew across the table.

"What I've seen, what I've learned, the good and the bad, have presented me with a new world, new ideas. Don't know where I'll go. I need time to figure that out."

"But you're glad you came to Houston?" he asked.

"Yes." She laughed. "A political cartoon sent me here. Dangled a golden opportunity to change my life."

"So has it?"

"Of course, it has. Just look at what I've seen. A lynching knocked this city sideways in front of every top journalist in the United States, who spit out AP articles as fast as they can type them. Seeing them in action helped me realize how foolish I was to think I could grab a front page. Pretty dumb wasn't I. Besides they never let women write about the really bad stuff." He said nothing, but his agreement was obvious from the expression on his face. She spoke so softly, he leaned in to hear her words, "The sham indictment. You helped me figure out my father's story, but it was another front-page story I was forbidden to write. So much for my hopes, my grandiose schemes, etcetera."

"Sad, but true for me as well. I'm looking at a pile of ashes. You were right."

"What?"

"My editor killed my column about Houston's wards."

"God, no. I thought you could write about anything you wanted to."

"I did too, and I have up until now. He said it would not be politic to print at this time. Later, maybe, after the folks from up north have left town."

"Well, at least it will be printed. Nothing like that for me."

"Hey, don't say that. The fact is you came to Houston, intending to skip about six rungs of the career ladder. You've got to pay your dues and writing obits doesn't count. Take this job at the *Gargoyle* or anywhere you can write about something. Get some solid stories behind you. Your writing is good, but it could be better."

She cringed at his words and tears caught in her throat again, but she held them back and nodded. With only a slight catch in her voice, she thanked him and rose to leave knowing she had to get out of this diner before she broke down in front of everyone.

Stanley, smiled but made no effort to rise, letting her scurry out the door and into the hot afternoon sun. He hoped he had not been too tough on her, but it was time she wised up. *What will she do next?*

ANYONE WHO WATCHED PHILLIS'S PATH during the next hour probably wondered the same. In spite of the cruel heat which had driven most Houstonians inside, she stopped to look at store windows, ducked into the Interurban station, examining the scheduled trips to Galveston posted on the wall, then plodded down Texas toward Bagby until she finally reached the deserted Hospitality House where she found a bench and looked across Bagby Street.

Vendors whose booths circled the hall were packing their gewgaws. Workers loaded folding chairs on waiting trucks and pulled down flags and bunting. Band members packed up their instruments and whipped off shakos, cowboy hats, and military caps, anything they could shed for relief from the blazing sun. The "old gray mare" chomped pieces of ice dropped on the on the sidewalk by soda-pop sellers who were dragging their wagons home.

For the past week, all roads led to Houston, the city whose name sprang to the lips of thousands. Sixty radio stations enabled millions of listeners across America to hear the familiar voice of Graham McNamee and listen to the convention's speeches. The only female star, Nellie Ross, former governor of Wyoming, received thirty-one votes for Vice-President on the first ballot and delivered a seconding speech for Al Smith's nomination.

All week, newspapers across the country carried front page headlines announcing women's rise to power — "WOMEN IN STAR ROLES AS GREAT CONCLAVE OPENS," "WOMEN DEMOCRATIC LEADERS SEE STRONG MOVE TO PUT ONE OF SEX ON TICKET," and Phillis's personal favorite, "WOMEN TO STAY IN CONGRESS FOREVER." Five-hundred women came to this convention and wanted to know when it would be their turn.

It was all history, but Phillis was convinced it would never be forgotten. She had been moving to the rhythm of this town for the last two weeks. It was time to make a choice. *My old life is gone. I will no longer look for my father's face. My mother has lost her hold on me. I'm free to make a new beginning.* And yet, there was something about Houston that was keeping her here. Was it the noise, the unfinished messiness of Houston? It would never be a neat and tidy city.

Stanley's attention was flattering and gave her a pitty-pat heart, but romance was too often a trap for women. Steered them off course. She still intended to pursue her career as a journalist. *If he really cares about me, he will still care about me tomorrow or next week or whenever it suits me better.*

A voice behind her asked, "Did you think you could get away from me that easily?" He reached for her hand and his lips brushed her cheek. When she stood and turned to him, he winked and gave her a cocky salute, then loped off down the street, headed for who knew where. With a laugh, she realized neither of them knew what would come next.

EPILOGUE

November 4, 1935

THUNDERSHOWERS DUMPED TWO INCHES on Bagby Street during the night, but a weak sun and just enough blue to cut a pair of pants for a dutchman assured Phillis the wrecking ball would swing today as planned. Her rain spattered Ford coupe was parked outside her apartment on Rosalie Street. Only a ten-minute drive to the old Sam Houston Hall.

Demolition would make room for the Fat Stock Show's bigger and better new home. A brick coliseum, designed by Jesse Jones' architect, Albert Finn, would replace the yellow pine convention hall always meant to be a temporary building. She watched the steam shovel and wrecking ball crash the structure as easily as a child smashing a sandcastle on a Galveston beach.

In less than an hour, Phillis headed for her office to pound out the story of Houston's first national claim to glory. How could she capture the majesty and the sparkle the hall displayed for everyone who attended the 1928 convention? The shiny green and gold paint, the flags and banners, and the thousands of perspiring visitors who gawped when they first saw it. Though the great arena was gone, Houston would always remember this convention, but would the city remember the lynching or ever discover the shameful cover-up that occurred those two hot weeks in June? For her, these were unforgettable events. Overhead, the dark clouds were rolling back in, a gloomy sky to match her gloomy mood. Sam Houston Hall had been her birthplace. It was hard to let it go.

ACKNOWLEDGMENTS

My deepest thanks to my husband, Peter, for believing I could complete this novel and reading the manuscript more times than I can count. His encouragement and input were invaluable. My friend Randy Pace read and reread the manuscript, sharing his valuable knowledge of Houston Heights and Houston history, as well as doing a fine job of copyediting. Betty Chapman's multiple readings were invaluable. My brother-in-law, Dr. Thomas Weil, Laura Bernal, and Henry Lynne were also readers who contributed suggestions and support for my literary treatment describing the events in Houston during June 1928. Sandra Lord's editing of the first draft brought the downtown Houston vibe to my book.

Writers need encouragement and support, and my family and friends provided an abundance of both. Johnny Zapata and Lisa Cari are two friends who supplied IT support. Members of my critique groups, including Hardy Roper, Kay Finch, Kay Kendall, Julie Herman, Bob Miller, Amy Sharp, Laura Elvebak, Dr. Joann Schulte, Susan Hairston, Rebecca Nolen, Carolyn Johnson, Marilyn Lewis, Tom Kenan, Rosemary Ford and Diane Teichman read and reread chapter after chapter. I cannot thank you enough for standing by me. Lastly, I thank my publisher, Kimberly Verhines, as well as my agent Kathleen Niendorfer.

The Julia Ideson Building's restored reading room provided the setting for convention journalist Will Durant's interview with Phillis, and Houston Metropolitan Research Center's staff welcomed my tiresome requests for the 1928 Convention's archives. Two excellent articles in the *Houston Review*, "Parley of Prominence" by Jon L. Gilliam and "In the Name of Decency and Progress: The Response of Houston's Civic Leaders to the Lynching of Robert Powell in 1928" by Dwight Watson, provided the background for my novel. The African American Library at Gregory School provided additional information about the Robert Powell lynching as did Deborah Sloan, who shared her research about the 1928 lynching, including Powell's Harris County Death Certificate. Sarah Jackson, Harris County Archivist, provided

1928 maps and valuable statistics. Railroad historian George Werner answered endless questions about train travel in the 1920s.

The bi-weekly *Houston Gargoyle* magazine contains a wealth of colorful accounts of the local scene from January to July 1928. Newspaper archives provided convention facts, anecdotes, as well as interviews with the celebrity visitors, enabling me, through my main character, to walk in their shoes down Bagby Street and Texas Avenue. *Houston Post Dispatch,* the *Houston Chronicle*, and the *Houston Press* published articles written by some of the five hundred visiting journalists, but it was my exploration of Newspaper.com that led to articles the journalists wrote for their local papers, many of which were not so polite views of Houston's weather, Jesse Jones and his convention hall, and the events occurring during their stay at the Rice Hotel. I drew upon H.L. Mencken 's papers, sealed from public view until 1994 for the second Rice Hotel shooting.

Other primary sources were *My Story*, convention visitor Mary Roberts Rineheart's autobiography; *You Meet Such Interesting People* Bess Whitehead Scott's, autobiography which details her covering the 1928 convention as well as her other experiences as a reporter for the *Houston Post Dispatch*; and the *Houston Press. These Modern Women, Autobiographical Essays from the Twenties*, edited by Elaine Showalter was helpful. Two unpublished manuscripts, "Sob Sisters: The Image of the Female Journalist in Popular Culture" by Joe Saltzman and "The Woman Journalist of the 1920s and 1930s in Fiction and in Autobiography" by Donna Born provided insight into the struggles, goals, and motivations of female reporters in the1920s. My friends Nell Stewart, Jimmy Brill and Charlie Burgess shared with me their wonderful memories of the Houston convention.

Reference books invaluable to my research included: Frederick Lewis Allen's *Only Yesterday*; Norman Brown's *Hood, Bonnet, and Little Brown Jug*; Marie Phelps McAshan's *On the Corner of Main and Texas, A Houston Legacy*; Monte Akers' *Flames after Midnight*; Allyson Hobbs' *A Chosen Exile, a History of Racial Passing in American life*; and Richard Zelade's *Austin in the Jazz Age*. Howard Beeth and Cary D. Wintz's *Black Dixie* is essential reading for an understanding of Afro-American Culture in Houston while *Room at a Time* by Jo Freeman, *Front-Page Women Journalists, 1920-1950* by Kathleen A. Cairns, and *Bobbed Hair and Bathtub Gin* by Marion Meade addressed the conflict between career women and flappers. Gary Cartwright and Ray Miller's books about Galveston vividly portray the "The Free Galveston State," as did *Galveston's Maceo Family* Empire by T. Nicole Boatman, Scott H. Belshaw, and Richard B. McCaslin.

Biographies critical to my understanding of the players at this convention include Steven Fenberg's *Unprecedented Power*; Baskin Timmons, *Jesse H. Jones*; Richard D. White's *Will Rogers: A Political Life*; Richard M. Ketchum, *Will Rogers*; Walter Johnson's *William Allen White's America*; *Ladies and Not So-Gentle Women*, by Alfred Allan Lewis; and Jimmy Breslin's *Damon Runyon*.

Author Sue Monk Kidd calls historical fiction "the art of grafting fiction onto to history." Phillis Flannagan and Stanley Staples, the main characters in *Her Choice*, are witnesses to events that occurred during the last two weeks of June when Jesse Jones brought the Democratic Convention to Houston. I created a way for Phillis to recognize the city fathers' cover up. The five men arrested for the lynching and whose mug shots appeared on the front page of several newspapers three days before the convention began were never convicted. No one was ever convicted of the crime.

Her Choice takes place during a time when women's history was being rewritten. The 1920s was a crossroads decade. Many of the newly enfranchised voters were ready to enter politics and choose new professions, while others were choosing new lifestyles. Women's optimism was palpable.

Despite our recent loss of freedom here in America, I share Elizabeth Cady Stanton's 100-year-old pronouncement that "the triumphs of women in art, literature, science, or song rouse my enthusiasm as nothing else can."

QUESTIONS FOR DISCUSSION

1.   How do you interpret the novel's title? What are the ways it echoes throughout the book?

2.   During the novel, Phillis's passion for journalism is the motivation for most of her actions. One critic has said, "The most hard-boiled newspaper man is still a knight in shining armor, self-appointed to save a lovely woman from the perils of the news assignment." How does this apply to the obstacles Phillis encounters?

3.   Understanding the male ego and its language is one approach newspaperwomen used to make their way out of the obituary/society news coverage. How does Phillis do this? Is that strategy still used? Do any examples come to mind from your own experience?

4.   Do you find Phillis appealing? Interesting? Disappointing? Does she realistically reflect the 1920s?

5.   Amon Carter is often credited for inventing the larger-than-life Texas cowboy that captured the imagination of New Yorkers, Hollywood moguls and movie stars and many who reside in Texas today. In what ways is the Texas cowboy still a national icon?

6.   In what ways did this convention serve Jesse Jones' ambitions for the City of Houston?

7.   Discuss the visitors' reactions to Houston and its residents.

8.   In what ways does the novel expand your knowledge of Houston?

9.   Women's rights, women's equality, women's struggles are themes in the novel. Were you surprised by any of the women's struggles mentioned?

10.   In 1928, women had no inkling of the political obstacles they would encounter in the next 100 years. Discuss their optimism and the ways in which their ambition was squashed. Ruth Bader Ginsburg is the first woman to lie in state in the U.S. Capitol Rotunda and Kamala Harris is the first female Vice-President. When will a woman be elected president? Will it be in your lifetime?